The Witch Is Back

Also by Brittany Geragotelis

What the Spell

Life's a Witch

The Witch Is Back

A **LIFE'S A WITCH** BOOK

BRITTANY GERAGOTELIS

SIMON & SCHUSTER BFYR

NEW YORK LONDON TORONTO SYDNEY NEW DELHI

SIMON & SCHUSTER BFYR

An imprint of Simon & Schuster Children's Publishing Division
1230 Avenue of the Americas, New York, New York 10020

For information about special discounts for bulk purchases, please contact Simon
& Schuster Special Sales at 1-866-506-1949 or business@simonandschuster.com.
The Simon & Schuster Speakers Bureau can bring authors to your live event. For
more information or to book an event, contact the Simon & Schuster Speakers
Bureau at 1-866-248-3049 or visit our website at www.simonspeakers.com.
Also available in a SIMON & SCHUSTER BFYR hardcover edition
Book design by Krista Vossen
The text for this book is set in Granjon.
Manufactured in the United States of America
SIMON & SCHUSTER BFYR paperback edition January 2015
2 4 6 8 10 9 7 5 3 1
The Library of Congress has cataloged the hardcover edition as follows:
The witch is back / Brittany Geragotelis.
pages cm.—(Life's a witch)
Summary: After leading her coven into battle against the Parrishables,
teenaged witch Hadley Bishop is looking forward to a relaxing,
love-filled summer with boyfriend Asher, until his ex-girlfriend,
Brooklyn, shows up and a power struggle ensues.
ISBN 978-1-4424-6688-3 (hc)
[1. Witches—Fiction. 2. Magic—Fiction. 3. Dating (Social customs)—Fiction.]
I. Title.
PZ7.G29348Wi 2014
[Fic]—dc23
2013028192
ISBN 978-1-4424-6691-3 (pbk)
ISBN 978-1-4424-6692-0 (eBook)

To anyone who's ever been judged, bullied, rejected, teased, ignored, or targeted . . . you are *extraordinary* and one day others will know it, too.

ACKNOWLEDGMENTS

I owe so much thanks to those who had a hand in making this book happen.

To everyone at Simon & Schuster—Justin Chanda, Bernadette Cruz, Paul Crichton, Lucy Cummins, Catherine Laudone—thank you for making my publishing dreams come true. You've been incredible. Christian Trimmer: Your enthusiasm for this book has been unmatched. Thanks for all your editorial expertise!

I couldn't have done any of this without my wonderful team: Kevan Lyon at the Marsal Lyon Agency (Lit agent extraordinaire); Taryn Fagerness at the Taryn Fagerness Agency (Rockstar of the foreign market); Brandy Rivers at Gersh (Queen of Hollywood); Deborah Wolfe at Frankfurt Kurnit Klein & Selz (My legal bodyguards); Samantha Martin (PR maven), Sandy Han and Anna Osgoodby at Media Maison. I'm so grateful to have you all on my dream team.

Of course, my besties are the ones who keep me sane and happy in this often *insane* world. You're my biggest supporters. You make me laugh. And you pick me up when I'm down. Hugs and kisses to: Tammy West, Amanda Healy, Jessica Grant, Kate Chapman, Mary Eustace, Courtney McCabe, Darcey West, Rebecca Schuman, Alicia Chouinard, Sue Chouinard, Colleen Woodsmith and Siena Koncsol. Also, I have to say a HUGE THANK YOU to everyone at A.G., Wattpad and Pips Place NYC. I love you all!

Lastly, the love and support of my family has meant the world to me. Your advice, positivity, and encouragement has kept me going over the years. Thanks so much to: Mom, Dad, Jacey, Amy, Cody, Cash, my aunts and uncles (both related and not), Andrea, Price, Ryan, Katy, Chelle, and Maya. Thank you for always believing in me. **Matt—you are the reason all my dreams have come true. Thank you for loving me. You amaze me every single day.**

June 4, 1692

The funny thing about betrayal is that by the time you know about it, the damage has already been done.

Bridget Bishop should know. Her life had been surrounded by it as of late.

And as if the betrayal itself weren't bad enough, when it came from your friends, family, and community members, it's an especially hard slap in the face. The realization that you were cared for so little that you deserved the public humiliation and heartache coming to you, was enough to send a person over the edge.

Luckily, Bridget still had the love and support of her only daughter, Christian, to keep her fighting for her life, otherwise she might have saved the executioners the trouble and done the job herself.

The others who'd been accused hadn't been blessed with this kind of loyalty from their families.

Bridget looked around her cell and then let her eyes sweep

across the dungeon to those shackled to the floors and walls. Dozens of people filled the space, one more hopeless than the next. But Bridget felt as if she couldn't complain too much, given the fact that people like Tituba, Sarah Osborne, and Sarah Good had been confined to the prison much longer than she had.

And not everyone inhabiting the jail were witches.

That's not to say that most of them weren't. The majority were members of the Cleri, while others were members of other covens or simply innocent bystanders. Well, *innocent* might not have been the right word for some of those included in the trials, considering the darkness of their past actions, but they certainly weren't practicing witchcraft.

Bridget turned to the three women closest to her own cell. The two Sarahs and Tituba had been among the first accused and therefore had experienced the brunt of the initial backlash. Osborne was in there by mistake, having been shunned by the community because she'd stopped going to church. Of course, she'd only stopped attending because an illness had taken over her body, but nobody wanted to hear that fact. Still, church or no church, a witch she was not.

Good and Tituba, however, were both members of the coven Supre, and neither had ever hurt another living soul. That wasn't the purpose of the coven after all. Bridget knew this because the Cleri had convened with the Supre at annual gatherings. The sister coven had always been kind and otherwise harmless.

Lord knows why Tituba eventually confessed to practicing dark magic, saying that Good and Osborne had convinced her to sign her soul over to the Devil. Those of us who knew the women knew it wasn't true, but nothing could be done to convince her to change her story. Bridget could only guess that the pressure of being hated by the whole town had driven the woman mad.

Sarah Good, however, seemed to be taking things the hardest. She'd always been an outcast in Salem, but had managed to find a home with her fellow Supre members. They'd been the only ones to overlook the fact that she was homeless, often looked dirty and unkempt, and wasn't above going door-to-door to ask for charity. Given Good's already stunted relationship with the townspeople, the realization that they found her capable of doing harm to others shouldn't have been all too surprising.

But apparently it was that, coupled with Tituba's treachery and the fact that her husband and even her four-year-old daughter had testified against her in court, that had worn Good down until she was practically skin and bones.

When she bothered to talk—which was rare by this point— it was only to claim her innocence. It cut through Bridget every time she heard the woman sobbing in the dark at night.

"Visitors!" one of the guards announced as he opened the heavy wooden door and ushered a handful of people into the room.

Though Bridget recognized the four women, she'd never talked to them herself. She did, however, know their husbands, as they frequented the pub she owned before she'd been dragged into this god-awful place. Bridget had heard the men complaining about their nagging wives and therefore knew them to be judgmental gossipers who looked down at most others in the town.

Bridget had a growing suspicion that the women's visit wouldn't be pleasant.

The four walked over to the cell next to Bridget's and stopped to stare stone-faced at Tituba and the two Sarahs. The woman who took up the front of the pack placed her arms behind her back as if to keep herself from reaching out and getting too close to the accused.

"Disgusting pieces of filth you are," the visitor whispered, squinting her eyes at the three women. "How dare you attempt to harm our children in your quest to do Satan's bidding."

"Witches!" another shouted.

"Thieves!"

"Dismissing the *church* . . . ," the leader said to Sarah Osborne, ". . . a lowly *slave* . . . ," to Tituba, ". . . and a dirty, murderess *beggar*," finally fixing her stare on Sarah Good. "I always knew you were the Devil's spawn, not worthy of our respect or company. Now the rest of the world knows it, too."

Silence filled the room as the free stood before the prisoners. Finally, a voice broke through, surprising all of them.

"I have not done that which you accuse me of," Sarah Good said quietly. Her eyes were swollen from so much crying, and though she was one of the youngest being held, she looked at least twenty years older than her time on Earth.

"Then why hath your own family forsaken you?" the woman spat back nastily. "God did not even find you worthy of motherhood and took your child away before you could do it harm as well."

There was an audible gasp at this and Bridget wasn't sure whether it had come from the rest of the women in the room or from Sarah herself. Either way, everyone knew the woman had gone too far.

By now, it was common knowledge that Sarah had been pregnant at the time of her arrest, and despite the stress and horrible living conditions, had managed to give birth to a baby girl she'd named Mercy. No doubt a plea to the Lord to be set free. However, her plan hadn't worked and Sarah had watched desperately as her own kin perished in the jail. It was hard enough losing a child, but to then be told it was because of your own wickedness—that is a cross no one should have to bear.

"Ladies, it would be a good idea if you were to leave now," Bridget warned, drawing the attention over to herself. The distraction worked and the group took a few steps toward her.

"Oh, Bridget . . ." The lady clucked her tongue as if she were scolding the aging woman. "I should think you are not in a position to be ordering anyone around. Besides, you are just as vile as she is."

"You do not know what you say," Bridget returned, sitting up a little straighter from her place on the floor.

"Oh, I think I do. But that does not matter, because God knows what you have done and He will punish you for your unholy atrocities," the woman said, pointing her finger at Bridget and then at the other women locked up. "He will punish each and every one of you."

Then, without a backward glance, the women turned and began to head back the way they came. Besides the sound of their shoes hitting the stone floor, the only other noise was the sobs coming from Sarah.

Bridget watched as they left, and promised herself that they would get what was coming to them.

They all would.

And then, with a hollow clanking sound loud enough to wake the dead, Bridget and the others were locked inside, their fates sealed along with the door.

Chapter One

As the door slammed on the women's fate, my eyes flew open with a start. I searched the room in a panicky attempt to figure out where I was. At the same time, I willed my hands to move, still feeling the weight of the shackles on my wrists. Relief washed over me as I was able to bring them up to my face and brush away the hair that was matted to my forehead.

It was just another dream.

Oh, who was I kidding? By now I knew enough to understand that the dreams I had were more like memories from the past—my ancestor's past to be more accurate. And as often as I'd had these little trips down memory lane, I still couldn't get used to the feeling of betrayal and fear that they left me saddled with. This, along with the fact that all the horrific things that I was seeing had actually happened—that my great-grandmother several times over, Bridget Bishop, had been the first person hanged during the Salem witch trials—and well, you can see why I couldn't count on getting acceptable beauty sleep.

Luckily, there was a spell for that.

Lately though, my dreams had branched out to include the lives of others accused during the trials. Sarah Good and

Tituba, especially, had become regulars in my flashbacks, and disturbing as it was, I was beginning to feel connected to them in a way that only someone who'd lived through that awful time period could. Most people had to search ancestry.com to discover what was on their family trees. My relatives were hung from ours.

"Had!" a voice called, breaking through my thoughts and bringing me back to reality. "Breakfast in ten and then we'll go for that run?"

A glance over at my bedside clock showed that it was just a little past 8 a.m. I sighed heavily.

So much for sleeping in during the summer.

"Okay, Dad!" I shouted back. "I'll be there in a minute!"

As much as I longed to pull the covers over my head and go back to sleep, I flung them back dramatically and shimmied my way off the bed until my feet hit the floor. I couldn't exactly back out of our morning workout, since I'd been the one to suggest it the night before.

Ever since Mom had died at the hands of the evil coven, the Parrishables, I'd been putting more of an effort into spending time with my dad whenever possible. For a while, I'd thought I'd lost both of my parents in the fire that had killed most of the adults in the Cleri. But then Dad had shown up, untouched and alive. Not that Samuel Parris hadn't tried to do away with him, too. He'd just been luckier than Mom and the others when the Parrishables had finally hunted him down.

The Parrishables.

The dark coven run by Salem native and overall bad guy, Samuel Parris, tried to destroy the Cleri several months before, hoping that it would make them the ultimate superpower when it came to the magical world. And they'd almost succeeded. Until they'd come up against the younger members of our coven. That's where they'd messed up.

Much to my shock, it turned out that the Parrishables were actually after *me*. Apparently I'm some kind of magical powerhouse. I'd always known that my casting skills were superior to those of the rest of my coven, but until I'd gone up against Samuel, I hadn't realized the extent of my abilities. Once armed with that knowledge, we became an unstoppable force.

In the end, it had taken all of the twitches (our term for teen witch) in the Cleri—including our relatives who had already passed on—to defeat an evil that had begun in Salem.

Which brought me back to my dream. Memory. Whatever.

Yawning in protest, I walked into my bathroom and looked at myself in the mirror. "Ugh," I mumbled, squeezing my eyes shut against what I saw. Then, without another peek, I said, "Renewbus freshimo perfecto."

As my mouth began to tingle and take on the taste of mint, I felt the rest of the changes happening. I didn't need to look to know makeup was being applied, hair was being smoothed, and my skin was taking on a dewy glow. When I felt the spell wind down, I opened my eyes again slowly. The transformation was amazing, but since I used this particular spell so often, the result wasn't exactly surprising anymore. While I preferred actually going through my whole beauty routine, the shortcut was a lifesaver on those days when I didn't have time to get ready. Or in this case, when I'd dreamed of Bridget Bishop the night before and had the bags on my face to prove it.

Thanks to the Renewbus spell, sparkly gold shadow now swept across my lids, making my eyes shine brightly. Dollops of pink danced on the apples of my cheeks and my full lips were perfectly glossed with just a hint of color to them. My dark hair, which had been a hot mess just a few seconds before, was now pulled back into a braid that swept across my forehead and then back into a ponytail in the middle of my head. I smiled at myself in the mirror, and caught a glimpse of my too-white-to-be-natural teeth. I was practically a walking toothpaste commercial.

A slightly more awake version of myself headed back to my room and pulled on a pair of black Soffe shorts that I retrieved from my drawer, along with a sports bra and oversize tank. I snagged my tennis shoes from the corner and laced them up in double-knotted bows.

A girl should always be prepared for any situation, and the last thing I needed was to trip over a lace and give myself a *reason* to get a nose job. I was sort of attached to the one I already had, thank-you-very-much.

"Had, breakfast is—"

My dad let the sentence trail off as I appeared at the kitchen door and then plopped down at the table.

"Impressive spread," I said as I looked at the pancakes, bacon, eggs, fruit, yogurt, and toast that was piled in the middle of the table. I scooped up some plain nonfat yogurt, topped it off with blueberries, raspberries, and strawberries, and then settled back into my chair to eat.

"That's all you're having?" he asked me. I could tell he was disappointed I wasn't eating more and instantly felt guilty.

"Sorry, Dad, but if you want me to actually be able to run after this, I can't exactly eat heavy now," I said apologetically.

"Oh, uh, right. Of course," Dad said, like the thought hadn't occurred to him until now. And it probably hadn't. I watched him scratch his head absently as he looked around at all the food that was going to go to waste. "It's just that they say breakfast is the most important meal of the day and all. . . ."

I didn't ask him who "they" were, because I already knew. He was talking about the parenting books and chat rooms.

It had been like this a lot lately. Him going overboard on his parental duties, as if he'd forgotten everything he'd ever known about being a parent. Suddenly, he was worried about me eating three meals a day, whether I was doing all of my homework, and if I was dating anyone. The week before, he'd even asked me if I had a bedtime.

But I got it.

Without Mom around, we were both sort of learning how to live together again. Just the two of us. I mean, Mom had always handled the day-to-day household stuff before. So now whenever Dad *was* home and not traveling, he tended to take things a bit too seriously. And as much as I liked the attention, it was a bit much.

At first I'd been dealing with a healthy dose of fear over the prospect of his leaving town again for work. After all, the last time he'd gone, we were all almost killed and I didn't think I'd ever see him again. So, you can understand my apprehension. But Dad had to pay the bills and we both needed to move on, so I'd taken Dad's spurts of overcompensation—like this morning's banquet-size breakfast—with a grain of salt, always reminding myself that it could be worse.

A lot worse.

I took a big bite of my breakfast and ate it like it was the best thing I'd ever tasted. "The fruit and yogurt is really good though, Dad. Totally what I wanted," I said, trying to wipe the disappointment off his face. It seemed to work and he smiled slightly.

As I went for another scoop, there was a knock at the back door and I heard the familiar turn of the metal knob. The sound brought me back to the dream I'd had and I couldn't help but shiver despite the warmth of the kitchen. Even months later, I was constantly on edge, waiting for the Parrishables to come back. But running on fear was no way to live, so I forced myself to stay glued to my seat and fought through the thought that something bad was about to happen. The only way to get over fear was to walk through it. My mom had taught me that.

"Hey, Had," Asher said, breaking the silence and kissing me on the cheek as he came up behind me. I relaxed as he took a seat at the table. "Wow, Mr. Bishop, are you feeding an army?"

"Apparently not," Dad said, frowning as he placed a few eggs and fruit onto his own plate.

"Need some help getting rid of it?" Asher asked, eyeing the food hungrily, but not yet moving to take a plate.

I could see the instant relief in my Dad's face, and my heart swelled with gratitude for my boyfriend. Since we'd arrived home from the cabin after defeating the Parrishables, he'd been the model guy: taking me out on dates, going to games to watch me cheer, and hanging around the house to get to know my dad better. All things I would've never thought possible when we'd first met. In fact, given that our whole relationship had started off as a lie, I thought we were doing pretty well.

It was hard to believe that less than a year ago Asher had been secretly batting for Team Parrishable. Back then, he was just this amazingly hot guy with jet-black hair, styled in a metro-looking faux-hawk and eyes that seemed like they could pierce my soul. And his lips?

Very kissable.

After some flirting, a few major fights with other witches, and an innocent—but awesome—sleepover, I'd found out he'd been working with the enemy. Well, kind of. Turned out, my nemesis, Samuel Parris, had been holding Asher's sister hostage and was threatening to hurt her unless he did as he was told, which included infiltrating the Cleri and relaying our secrets.

I was pretty pissed at first, but could hardly blame him for trying to save his sister. And by this time, I'd already fallen in love with him, which made everything more complicated. In the end, Asher had stepped up and helped us take down Samuel. Literally. He even jumped in front of a speeding spell to save me, risking his life in the process.

Now, back in the nonmagicking world, with Samuel gone and Asher's sister back home safe and sound, we could finally be a normal couple. Well, as normal as a couple of twitches could be, anyway.

And it was amazing.

"Help yourself," Dad said, gesturing to the food in front of us and popping a blueberry into his mouth.

Asher didn't wait for him to offer again and immediately dug in.

After our run, I freshened up and headed over to Asher's. Slipping in through the side gate, I found my boyfriend—man, I loved the sound of that—my *boyfriend*—the words were totally delicious—standing in the backyard a few feet away from a man in an oversize trench coat and striped fedora. The stranger had his back turned to us, so I couldn't make out who he was, but I was instantly suspicious.

Furrowing my brows, I took in the scene before me. Who wears a trench coat in the middle of the summer? People who are up to no good, that's who. I began to fall back into a fighting stance, but before I could do anything, Asher let loose a spell of his own.

"Flameeble ignitus!" he yelled at the ominous figure.

Almost instantly, a puff of smoke exploded at the guy's feet, creating a steady stream of white, which circled and covered the area in wisps. I had no idea what was happening, but the man in the hat wasn't moving.

"Dammit!" Asher said loudly as he walked over to the man and pulled off his hat forcefully. Then he began to fan the area until the smoke dissipated. Thoroughly confused, I made my way across the yard until I was close enough to see what was going on.

"Did you just turn him into a mannequin?!" I asked, slightly horrified and impressed at the same time. "Asher, I'm sure you had your reasons, but . . ."

"Huh?" he asked, looking over at me as I walked up. "No. I mean, I know. He already *was* a mannequin. I was trying to cast a flame, but all I ended up doing was setting off a smoke bomb. Great for stupid high school pranks, not helpful in defeating bad guys."

Waves of relief rushed over me.

Though I was embarrassed to admit it, I *had* thought for just a moment that maybe Asher was back to his old tricks. That he was using less-than-savory magic for his own purposes again. It was only for a moment though, and then I remembered that the lying, sneaky Asher wasn't the *real* him. But I couldn't help the knee-jerk reaction. Apparently I still had some trust issues that I needed to work through in that regard.

"Well, maybe Brighton will be good for us after all," I said, seeing how frustrated he was by the failed spell.

"I'm just a little rusty, that's all. I didn't use magic at all when we first met, and lately I've been too busy to practice," Asher said, placing the hat back on the dummy's head and giving me a pointed look. This was his way of letting me know—not so subtly, I might add—that this was because of me.

The truth was, spending all our time together had made it difficult for either of us to focus on magic lately. Except for the kind we were making together. But that wouldn't come in handy if we were going up against guys like the Parrishables again, which was still a possibility, considering that many of Samuel's followers had run off into the night after we'd banished their leader.

"Brighton will give us both a chance to catch up on the things that we've let slide," Asher said.

I walked over to him and threw my arms around his neck.

"I still think we could have done that here," I said, kissing him on the cheek softly. Then I moved my lips up to his temple and kissed him there, before heading over to the space below his ear and lingering for a moment. His body stiffened beneath mine. "Then we'd be able to be *alone*. I bet it'd be easier to concentrate without all those other people around."

"You're the only thing I'd concentrate on if we stayed here, and you know it," Asher said, pulling away from me but keeping his arm on my waist. "You know I love you, Had, but not all of us are magical geniuses who don't need to practice their craft. I've been letting that side of my life slide these past few months. Don't get me wrong—it's totally been worth it, but still . . . Let me put it this way: I respect you for being the kick-ass witch that you are, but I want to at least be in the same stratosphere as you. You might not need me to save you from evil, but I don't want to be a liability, either."

As a witch, I understood what he was trying to say. Magic was important to both of us, and in a way, it *should* trump our relationship. But as a girl, all I heard was that Asher would rather go to some summer magic intensive than spend time alone with me.

Ugh, is this what it's like to be in love? Blinded by rainbows and unicorns, and sappy soundtracks that played in your head whenever you were around each other, and having all logic and sense of self thrown out the window? Had I turned into the kind of girl who put a boy before her magic?

15

All of these thoughts must have been running across my face, because Asher pulled me back in for a kiss. "We'll still have plenty of time for *us* this summer," he promised. "But I *do* think we need to make magic a priority again. What happens if Samuel comes back and I can't even do a simple flame-throwing spell? With my skills as they are, I'll only be able to give him smoke inhalation."

"Hopefully we won't have to test that theory," I said, willing myself to believe my own words.

Ever since we'd been back, the Cleri had been getting together at night to perform protection spells and location spells to ensure that we wouldn't be caught off guard again. So far, it looked like Samuel and the rest of the Parrishables were gone, but none of us were naive enough to stop with the precautions.

"I agree," Asher said, looking into my eyes. "But if it's not him, you know it could be somebody else. There are a lot of bad people out there who, just like Samuel, are itching to get their hands on our power. *Your* power."

I frowned. He was probably right, but the last thing I wanted to do was worry about all the bad things that could happen. Not when things were finally starting to feel normal again. I wanted to get back to being a *normal* twitch, with a *normal*—but abnormally hot—boyfriend, whose only worry was leading her *normal* coven and heading off to the *normal* college of her choice. I didn't want to be carted off to some summer intensive I'd never been to before, where I was going to once again be forced to focus 100 percent on spells. It sounded too much like summer school, and tests and homework were *so* not my idea of a good time. I wanted to find a balance, a way to have it all.

But I couldn't ignore what Asher was saying. We had to stay on top of our magical game, and since Jackson, who'd been in charge of training us, had expired in the fire along with our parents, there was no one to run our magic classes anymore. So, after a few emergency meetings between the guardians of the remaining Cleri members, the adults had decided the best thing to do would be to send us all off for the summer, where we could learn more about our heritage in a safe and supervised environment.

Just the way I fantasized spending my first summer with Asher. *Not.*

The only catch was that the Brighton Summer Intensive was an *exclusive* program—one that twitches had to be invited to attend. Which meant that it wasn't as simple as our parents just handing us over for a month. We had to prove that we were among the best and brightest in the witching world. I'd received invitations to attend in the past, but since it fell during the same time that I was away with my squad at cheer camp, I'd always politely declined. Still, it was an honor to be invited, and this year, most of the Cleri had made the cut. This was mainly due to their ability to survive the war with Samuel, but none of them were complaining.

So me, Asher, his sister Abby, Sascha, Jasmine, Fallon, and Jinx were all welcomed to come to the witch-owned cabin in Colorado for the summer. Peter had been invited as well, but was stuck in summer school. Poor kid was totally broken up about it, worrying that he was going to lose his place in the coven if he didn't go. No matter how many times I told him this wasn't true he wouldn't believe me.

"Maybe you're right," I said, with a sigh.

Asher smiled at me, brushing my long dark hair out of my face. "Think of it this way: It'll be like our first vacation together . . . just us and sixty strangers."

Chapter Two

It was going to take us roughly two and a half hours to get to Colorado. Asher, Abby, and I were the only ones who'd ever been on a plane before, so that was an interesting experience for all involved. Jasmine, the goth-looking girl in our group with a badass attitude to match, turned out to be terrified of flying. We were all more than a little surprised to see her squeezing her eyeliner-smudged lids shut on takeoff and chanting the same thing over and over again.

"Please don't let me die in this flying tin can," Jasmine prayed as the jet took off down the runway. Her pleas didn't stop until we'd been in the air for at least a half hour. And even then, she gripped her armrests so tightly that her knuckles turned white.

I would've laughed if she weren't so clearly terrified.

Sascha saw this as her chance to bond with her polar opposite, chatting nonstop from the time she sat down next to Jasmine in their assigned seats to the time we landed. With bouncy blond hair and a look similar to Glinda from *The*

Wizard of Oz, Sascha couldn't have been more different than Jasmine. Upon first look, you'd probably think she was a bit of a dumb blonde, but underneath her bubbly exterior was a smart witch with natural talents that allowed her to juice up fellow witches who'd been depleted of their powers. Sascha had the uncanny ability to fight her enemy one minute, and then apply lipstick meticulously without a mirror the next.

We'd barely gotten through the in-flight movie when the captain announced that we were beginning our descent into Colorado. As the plane started dipping lower and lower, I felt an uncomfortable tickling in my stomach.

Nerves.

It was something I rarely felt when heading into new situations. In fact, maintaining my high level of confidence at all times had always been easy given my natural ability to charm those around me. My mom called it the gift of *persuasion*. Not that I could control people—they still had basic free will—but you know how some people can convince others of anything? Well, that was me. The joke in our family was that I could sell ice cubes to an Eskimo.

Even though I imagined that camp would be no different, here I was with butterflies. And I had no idea why.

Of course, I knew enough by now not to ignore these feelings. After having been betrayed by our former Cleri member, Emory, I'd begun to read up on honing one's intuition. I couldn't help but think if I'd just quieted my mind back then and listened to my gut, I could've somehow known that Emory wasn't our ally. Unlike psychic phenomena—man, I wish I had *that* power—intuition, according to scientists, was something each of us had within us, but didn't necessarily use. Children were so much better at utilizing this skill, because they hadn't yet been bogged down with what adults called "logic." So lately I'd been trying to look at the world with childlike faith and listen to my instincts. All of them.

And right now my instincts wanted me on guard for some reason.

Asher must've noticed that I'd grown quiet over the course of the trip, because he squeezed my hand and gave me that smile of his that always stopped my heart.

The butterflies started fluttering even harder. But in a good way this time.

"Everything okay?" he asked. I was still amazed how in tune we'd managed to become in just a few months.

"I'm fine," I said, forcing a smile onto my face. No use stressing anyone else out with my *intuition*. "I'm just itching to see what this place is like."

"I can't wait to be around other twitches," Fallon said, obviously eavesdropping from the seat in front of us. He'd just turned sixteen, but I still saw Fallon as the immature, little pain in my ass that was constantly challenging me. True, we no longer looked at each other as *enemies*, considering that we'd saved each other's butts on more than one occasion, but we weren't besties, either. Fallon might not have turned out to be evil, but it didn't mean he couldn't still push my buttons.

"And what are we?" I asked, hitting the back of his chair lightly. His brown hair, which had grown longer over the last few months, went flying around his face. When he turned to glare at me, I noticed that he was starting to grow into his features. His hair was getting lighter now that the weather was warm again and his locks fell into his blue eyes haphazardly. He still looked especially young to me, but I swore he was getting taller every day. Pretty soon he'd tower over me. "You realize you won't find a better group of twitches than us, right? Who do you want to impress, anyway?"

Fallon licked his lips nervously and his eyes darted over to his right, briefly settling on Asher's sister, Abby. She'd opened up a book right after sitting down in her seat and had barely looked up the whole trip, except to stare out the window listlessly a few times. Even now, as this exchange was going on, Abby seemed glued to her page. Not that I could see her face, since it was currently being covered by the same dark hair that Asher had, falling around her shoulders like a curtain. When you were able to see her face, though, she was surprisingly pretty.

I had to admit, her looks matched her personality. Ever since we'd brought her home after vanquishing the Parrishables, she'd pretty much kept to herself. It was like she didn't want to be noticed at all. Asher said this was how Abby had always been, but it felt like something more than that. I couldn't imagine what she'd been through while being held by Samuel Parris and his cronies, and wondered if this was why she wasn't as outgoing as the rest of us. She was still dealing with what had happened while she was gone. Per Abby's request, Asher dropped the subject and let her be. He explained to me that it was the least he could do considering he let her get taken in the first place. Of course this wasn't true, but his guilt was alive and strong.

And I wasn't so self-absorbed as to think her actions were all about me, but I did worry that it was *me* that Abby didn't like. That she just didn't approve of her brother's choice in girlfriends and that's why she never hung out with us. But there was no way that was the whole story.

Since we were rooming together at Brighton, I was hoping it would give us more of a chance to bond. Because although I wouldn't admit it to her—or even to Asher for that matter—I wanted her to like me. She was the most important girl in

Asher's life besides me, and I knew our getting along meant a lot to him.

But the look on Fallon's face just now made it clear that I wasn't the only one interested in getting to know Abby better. Fallon stole another look at Asher's sister before rolling his eyes at me.

Interesting.

"Calm down, Princess. You know I'm Team Cleri all the way," he said, his usual snarkiness back. "I just think it'll be cool to see how other twitches do things. We're not the only ones on this planet, you know. Contrary to *popular* belief, I mean."

I heard Abby snicker, but I couldn't tell if it was at Fallon's comment or at something she was reading. Apparently Fallon thought it was the former, because a satisfied smile crossed his lips before he turned back around in his seat and prepared for the plane to hit the tarmac below.

I frowned, but let the comment go as everyone got to their feet and gathered their things from the overhead bins. Asher took both of our bags in his hands and led us off the jet. Jasmine practically ran up the ramp and didn't stop until she had reached the terminal. This time, I *did* laugh, and so did the rest of the twitches.

As soon as we stepped into the baggage claim area, I knew exactly where we were going. Bouncing in the air not ten feet away from the exit was a highly decorated sign. Glitter, foam letters, painted images, and stickers were strewn across the three-foot poster board. It read WELCOME BRIGHTON CAMPERS! in all caps.

The color assault didn't stop there. Attached to the welcome sign was a woman in her mid-forties, dressed like a walking collage. Waving her arms spastically, she had dozens of pins covering every available inch of space on her vest. They clanked against each other like an off-key tambourine. My eyes drifted down to the final touches of an already unfortunate outfit: old, faded acid-wash jean shorts that stopped just above her kneecaps. The overall effect was nearly too much to bear.

"I thought witches were supposed to fly *under* the radar," Asher said, quietly.

"They are," I answered as I plastered a smile on my face and walked forward to meet our TGI Fridays tour guide.

"Hi! I'm Hadley Bishop and this is the rest of the Cleri group," I said to her.

"Oh, super-duper-iffic!" the woman said, jumping into the air as if she were making an exclamation point with her body. I winced at the sudden movement and took a slight step back. "I'm Miss Peggy, one of your counselors, and we're *so* happy to have you at Brighton this summer! Why don't we get you all packed up and into the van, and we'll be on our way! You're the last to arrive, so you have the car *all* to yourselves!"

"Goody!" I said, clapping my hands together and then making a face at the others.

Every word Miss Peggy said was delivered with major enthusiasm and I could practically feel the energy buzzing off of her. The stimulation was almost too much to handle, and besides Sascha, who seemed to have found her emotional doppelganger, the other Cleri appeared hesitant to follow such an *enthusiastic* person to an unknown cabin in the woods.

"Is she for real?" Jasmine asked quietly as Miss Peggy ran ahead to start the engine of the big rainbow-colored van.

"Do you think it's safe to get into a car with her?" Jinx asked me nervously.

Jinx wore worry on her face like it was an extra layer of makeup and I instantly felt guilty. Because I knew that if I'd been stronger and quicker and smarter, I could've prevented everything that had happened to her.

And Jinx wouldn't be the scared little girl she was now.

With light brown hair that always lay perfectly in its place and a string of delicate pearls that fell just above her clavicle, Jinx looked every bit the part of classy witch on the rise. But underneath the sophisticated clothes and naturally pretty looks, she was damaged. The wounds she'd incurred while fighting the Parrishables had almost killed her. A particularly nasty spell had blown her side wide open, charring the skin surrounding the gaping hole and leaving her in the hospital for weeks. Even though the injury had been healed for a while now, the black tint to her skin in the spot where the magic had hit her was a daily reminder that she'd come close to dying.

"I don't think we have much of a choice, Jinxy," I said. "But I'm pretty sure she's harmless." Giving her a reassuring smile and a careful pat on the arm, I gestured for the rest of the Cleri to follow Miss Peggy to the car.

Chapter Three

"Holy mother . . . ," I said, leaning forward in my seat to get a better view of where we'd be staying for the summer. I barely flinched as my forehead smacked against the window; I was too impressed with the massive structure in front of me to care.

A sprawling log-and-brick lodge sat in the middle of a lush field of green. The place was shaped like a tiara, the tallest part of the house in the middle, followed by smaller sections on either side, making up five parts in total. Windows spanned from floor to roof and decks separated the three stories. White brick stacks crept halfway up the sides of each section, like it was some kind of castle/cabin hybrid and the roofs each curved up slightly at the ends like a mischievous mustache.

I'd never seen any place like it in my life.

Then again, I wasn't sure if anyone outside of the witching community had seen anything like it, either. After leaving the airport, we'd ventured about a half hour outside of the Denver area before the van began to slowly crawl uphill and into the mountains. The last fifteen minutes of driving had been devoid of other cars and houses. With thickets of woods surrounding us on all sides, it was clear that we were alone out here.

Asher whistled out loud as he took in the grounds. "Dad used to show us pictures from his summer camps, and they didn't look *anything* like this," he said, as Miss Peggy pulled up and around the circular driveway. "His cabins were practically falling apart."

"This place looks like a freaking resort," Jasmine blurted out.

"He said they'd go hiking in the woods and have to pitch these tents—" Asher continued his trip down his father's memory lane.

"If I'd known Brighton was like this, I might've come sooner," I murmured, taking in the scenery in front of me.

"Dad said they taught him how to boil stinging nettles and eat them for dinner. Said it tasted like soggy salad."

"I have a feeling we won't be eating stinging nettles here," I said, shooting him a grin. I hadn't heard Asher talk about either of his parents much over the last few months, so it was nice to hear him bringing up his dad now. Sometimes I even forgot that he'd lost his mom and dad a few months before Samuel Parris had killed my mom. That I wasn't the only one who was hurting.

Sometimes our own personal grief had a way of blinding us from the pain that others were going through. I made a mental note to ask him more about it later. Right now I was in utter awe.

Listening to our banter, Miss Peggy turned and smiled with pride. "Sounds like your dad went to a mortal camp growing up," she said. "Brighton's a different beast entirely. Since the location and its inhabitants are hidden to the outside world by magic, there's no chance that nonwitching people will find it. Attendees can use magic with impunity here, without having to worry about being caught. And that means there are no boundaries to what you'll find on campus. If your imagination can come up with it, it can—and probably does—exist at Brighton."

As we watched from the van, kids and their parents unpacked cars around us and wandered the grounds. People used spells to transport their bags into the enormous main cabin while others showed off tricks they'd learned to their friends. All the faces were new to me and the tingling in my stomach that I'd had on the plane started to come back. Everyone looked so happy to be there. Adults welcomed kids as they entered the main cabin. Campers approached each other, exchanging hugs and talking excitedly.

It was clear they all had their cliques, those they'd hung out with in summers past. And not just within their individual covens, but it seemed like *everybody* knew each other. To them, I was no one. A stranger. But that would change . . . it always did. Even if it didn't though, I had my own clique with me, so it's not like I was on my own or anything.

"Come on, guys," I said, opening the van door and stepping outside. I sucked in a deep breath of fresh air and then let it out slowly. God, it smelled great here. Like it hadn't been totally polluted by the rest of humankind yet. It sort of reminded me of my family's cabin, the one we'd retreated to when the Parrishables had come after us. Only, this appeared to be the *MTV Cribs* version. Less rugged and cozy, more hidden luxury.

Turning back to the others, I flashed them an encouraging look and then nodded my head in the direction of our bags, which Miss Peggy was busy piling up on the curb with a wave of her hand. "Let's check out our new digs, Cleri."

Little luggage carts like they had at fancy hotels littered the pathways and we grabbed a few that weren't in use and began to stack our bags on top. Taking our cues from the other campers, we charmed the carts to follow us toward the building in front of us.

It was going to take me some time to get used to not having to censor my magic here. And a quick look at my friends showed that I wasn't the only one. Back home, even when we were inside our own houses, we were constantly looking over our shoulders to make sure no civilians saw us using our "skills." Because if we were caught, well, let's just say none of us wanted to find ourselves in a witch trials sequel.

With my luggage now balancing precariously on the cart, I carefully bent down to pick up the last of my things: my purse, a few rag mags that I'd bought for the plane ride, and my iced coffee. Unfortunately, my cheer equilibrium must have been a bit off because of the flight or the altitude, and I teetered on my feet, which forced me to reach down and steady myself.

Maybe four-inch heels weren't a smart choice for my arrival at Brighton.

Of course, I'd been thinking more about fashion than function when I'd gotten dressed that morning. And my black patent-leather pumps were the perfect complement to the apple-red leather shorts I was wearing. So, I'd just have to be okay with walking a bit slower as I moved my stuff in. Not that I hadn't performed strenuous activities in shoes like these before.

I was a firm believer that anything worth doing could be done in sky-high heels.

Recovering as quickly as I could, I snatched up my things and stood up straight. Was it possible that no one saw that?

Hi, I'm Hadley and apparently I just learned how to walk. And stand. Either way, I looked clumsy. *So* not the reputation I was planning to have here at Brighton.

Luckily, it seemed like people were too preoccupied with their own stuff to notice my faux pas. In fact, I wasn't sure anyone had noticed me arrive at all. For once, not everyone was studying my every move, waiting to see what I'd do next, say next. No one was waiting for my approval or leadership. Oddly, there was a sort of freedom in this.

The feeling lasted for about five seconds, before I realized how weird it was. When you'd been in the public eye for so long, switching back to obscurity was a bit . . . jarring. If this continued, I wasn't exactly sure what I'd do with myself.

"This is a side of you I haven't seen before," a voice said from behind me.

My head jerked around to see Fallon standing less than five feet away from me. He had his hands in the pockets of his blue plaid shorts and was sporting a white polo shirt. An amused smile cut across his face and to be honest, he was looking very un-Fallon-like. I replaced my surprise with annoyance and gave him the look I reserved specially for him.

"I lost my balance, so what?" I said, trying to play it off. "It happens to the best of us."

"Not to you," he said, cocking his head to the side and fixing his gaze on me. "You're supposed to be this perfect witch and everything. Looks like someone might be a little off her game this summer."

Fallon looked around at the other campers, who still hadn't realized that I existed. He'd noticed it, too. Well, I wasn't going to let him know it bothered me.

"My *game* is just fine," I said, but I wondered if he was right. I wasn't usually clumsy. And I certainly wasn't ignored. Something felt . . . off about being here.

"Don't worry, Had," he said, coming in close for what he said next. "Change can be a good thing."

Then he winked at me.

Gross.

"What's going on?" Asher asked, stepping into the space between us and breaking up the weirdest conversation I'd ever had.

"I have no clue," I said, giving Fallon a pointed look.

"Right," Fallon said, raising an eyebrow. Just then, a group of younger girls walked past and smiled at him before giggling and scurrying off. Fallon smirked as he watched the attractive campers disappear into the cabin and then looked directly at me with a smile I didn't want to try to decipher. "Things are definitely looking up."

And then he grabbed his stuff and headed inside after the girls.

"Have we entered the *Twilight Zone* or something?" I asked Asher, confused by what had just happened. "Seriously, is this an alternate universe where I'm invisible and Fallon's actually . . . *cool*?"

Asher laughed and watched the other male member of the Cleri disappear through the doors. "Give him a break, Had. He's almost two years younger than us, and he's just now figuring out that girls can be more than just adversaries. Took him a while, but he's growing up. And by the looks of it, the girls here are recognizing that. Let him have his fun."

"Just as long as it's not with me," I muttered. Then, I added, more loudly, "I don't know, Asher. I have a weird feeling about this place."

He walked over to me, placing his arms around my waist and pulling me to him tightly. Just being near him made me feel more at ease. "Better?"

"Much," I said, nodding before giving him a long kiss.

"You two gonna stop sucking face long enough to come inside?" Jasmine yelled from the entrance to the cabin.

Forgoing magic for the time being, Asher grabbed the rails of our luggage cart and began to push it up the ramp and into the entranceway. A blast of cool air hit me as I walked inside and I was grateful to be out of the sun for the time being. I'd always thought of Colorado as being all snow and cold, but apparently during the summer temperatures rose as high as ninety degrees in some areas. Looks like my plans to get a sun-kissed tan the natural way were still a possibility.

Losing Asher in the crowded hall, I turned my attention to the other girls. "What do you think?" I asked Jasmine, Sascha, and Jinx. We got into line behind a few guys who were waiting to be checked in. One of the boys, a cute blond around our age, glanced back to check us out. Almost instantly, Sascha began to move around like she was posing for the mental pictures he was no doubt taking.

Uh, oh. It looked like we were already losing Sascha to the boys at camp.

"I think that if I have to share a room for the next month with *this*, I might have to perform an exploding spell—on *myself*," Jasmine growled as she motioned to Sascha, who was only slightly paying attention on account of her new crush.

As the guy turned back to his friend, Sascha finally realized that Jasmine had been talking about her and folded her arms across her chest defensively.

"Oh, no. What happened?" I asked, almost scared to hear it.

"Somebody decided Sascha should be let out of her cage," Jasmine said dryly.

"Look who's talking," Sascha said, irritated. "How'd you fit your coffin in the overhead bin?"

"Whoa, seriously, what's going on here, guys?" I asked, more than a little impressed with Sascha's ability to dish it back to Jasmine. Few people dared go up against the goth girl. Not if they didn't want a target on their back, that is.

"They fought the whole car ride about whether Heidi Klum is really just a genetic experiment funded by the beauty industry to make women feel inferior and men feel inadequate," Jinx said, clearly not taking any sides in their argument.

"And who won?" I asked, glad that the two had been sitting in the far back of the van and I hadn't had to listen to their bickering.

"I did!" both girls said in unison.

"Okay . . . ," I said, thankful to be saved by the registration table that had just opened up in front of us. A man sat there and motioned for me to come to him so he wouldn't have to yell. "Hi! I'm Hadley Bishop and I'm checking in."

The man in front of me had dark brown hair that was thinning on top, leaving little spots of exposed skin that the lights above would periodically reflect off. He was dressed in a faded green T-shirt that read BRIGHTON INTENSIVE, MAKING MAGIC SINCE 1864. His '70s-style mustache made him look more like he belonged at a dude ranch than a witch cabin in the woods. As far as temperament went, his was the exact opposite of Miss Peggy's.

"Group name," he barked, without returning my greeting or smile.

Rude.

"Um, the Cleri?" I said, taken aback by his total lack of communication skills. It was sort of an important thing to have if you were in the business of being around actual *people*. But I deduced that now wasn't the time to let him in on this little fact.

"Bishop. Ah, yes, here you are. You'll be rooming with one Abby Astley and one Colette Jordan," he said.

"There's someone else in our room?" I asked, surprised to hear this, considering we'd requested it just be the two of us. "But we asked for a double."

"There are only a select amount of doubles and they typically go to returning members or those who require special treatment," he said, completely unapologetic about it.

When the counselor didn't offer to try to make alternate arrangements for the snafu, I took a deep breath and leaned down until we were almost eye level. With a smile on my face, I said, "Are you sure there aren't any double rooms left?"

I knew it was probably wrong to use my powers of persuasion on a counselor, but I couldn't help it. I'd really been hoping that just Abby and I would be rooming together, so that we'd be able to get to know each other better. Having a stranger in with us would just make it that much more difficult.

The counselor stared blankly into my eyes and then cleared his throat loudly, making me jump back to avoid flying spittle. "Asking me to check again isn't going to make it magically appear," he said, annoyed. "Here's your key. Your *triple* is on the third floor. Elevators are behind me and to your right. Be sure to send the carts back down when you're done with them."

My smile turned into a frown as I took the keys he was holding out to me. My powers hadn't worked. I'd done the same thing I usually did when trying to influence someone, so it didn't make any sense. Maybe our powers didn't work within the walls of the cabin or something? Like when you don't have cell service in a certain area. But that didn't make sense either, because people were casting all over the place. Had Fallon been right? Was I totally losing it?

I began to walk away, but Counselor Angry called me back.

"And Hadley?" he asked.

"Yes?" I turned around to look at him, noting that the girls were still fully engrossed in their own conversations behind me and hadn't witnessed anything that had just happened.

"Don't try to use your powers on me again. It won't work and I don't appreciate it."

A rush of coldness filled my body even as my cheeks began to heat up. How had he known that I'd been trying to influence him? People had never been able to sense it happening before.

"Sure. Yeah. Sorry," I mumbled, before shuffling away from the table in a slightly shocked daze.

Cursing under my breath, I moved into the main part of the cabin and busied myself with looking around while I waited for the others to finish checking in. I had no idea where Asher, Abby, and Fallon had run off to, but in a place as big as this, it was easy to see how a person could get lost.

I took a moment to take in my surroundings, and finally saw just how stunning the place was.

The focal point of the living area was a huge round fireplace mounted right in the middle of the room. Openings to the roaring fire were placed around its circumference and a bench littered with cushy pillows invited people to sit and enjoy the warmth. Although it was the middle of summer outside, the air conditioning was on so high that the fire was a welcome attraction. I wondered if they kept things this way to lend to the wintry cabin atmosphere.

I walked around the stone fireplace until I got to the area hidden by the sign-in table. This part of the room was even grander than the entryway. A fifteen-foot cherry-wood coffee table sat between two wide couches that looked more like beds than living room furniture. The burgundy color of the fabric complemented the wooden beams and panels that were exposed around us. Four oversize lounge chairs with large armrests flanked each end of the coffee table, creating a comfy place for friends to gather.

Looking up, there was a huge chandelier, hovering in the air. There were no chains to hold the structure of twisted gold-and-black metal in place. That would be the work of magic. Dozens of large white candles flickered in their holders, giving off an almost ethereal glow to everything below.

"There you are," Asher said, sneaking up behind me and kissing me gently on the cheek. "Lost you for a minute. What are you doing all the way over here?"

"Just checking things out," I said, unwilling to admit that I was avoiding the counselor who'd scolded me for using my powers on him. Turning to face my gorgeous boyfriend, I placed my arms around his neck and tried my best to distract myself from how off I felt. "So, who are *you* bunking with?"

"Hudson Contois and Dane Giles," Asher said, reading the names off a piece of paper.

"I thought just Abby and I would be rooming together, but we've got a newbie in with us, too," I said, unable to hide my disappointment.

"Come on, Had. It'll be good for us to meet some new people," he said. "Expand our magical horizons. Make new friends and all that. I bet everyone's really cool. You'll see."

"You're probably right," I said, hoping it was true. Just because I'd had a tough time getting close to those in my own coven at first didn't mean that camp would be a repeat experience. In fact, maybe we'd have so much fun this summer that we'd decide to come back as counselors next year and then, after we'd both graduated from college, Asher would propose to me in front of all our new friends and our assigned campers and we'd get married here in Colorado and live happily ever after. All because we'd come to Brighton.

I sighed as I let the daydream play itself out and then let my body melt into Asher's.

"We're not fighting a supernatural war. Everyone we love is currently safe. We're here together. I'm not going to let anything ruin this summer," I said, leaning in to give Asher another kiss.

Just before our lips could touch, a voice I didn't recognize called out from behind me.

"Asher?"

Asher stiffened and pulled away, looking over my shoulder at the girl who'd just called his name. His eyes widened as recognition set in.

"Brooklyn?"

Chapter Four

Brooklyn? Who the heck is Brooklyn?

I stared at Asher, but he was no longer focused on me. His mouth was actually hanging open; he looked slightly in shock. I'd never seen him lose his cool before. And here it was, over another girl.

Please don't let her be pretty . . . give her a hideous growth on her chin or an awkward limp or even blah brown hair. Anything that would make me feel better about the look that is currently on Asher's face.

But when I turned around, I found that my pleas had fallen on deaf ears. In fact, what I saw was worse than I ever could've imagined.

The girl staring back at my boyfriend was stunning. Like total glamazon, Victoria's Secret model *stunning.* She had this whole hot runway thing going on. We were in the same league, only on total opposite sides of the spectrum.

Where my long hair was the color of dark chocolate, this

girl's was a vibrant blonde. It hung in soft, loose waves around her face, which was equally stunning. Her skin was dewy and sun-kissed, and a perfect shade of pink streaked across her cheeks. With lips like two plump pillows completing her look, her face could've been plastered across billboards in Times Square.

And with my luck, it already was.

Before I could ask him about her, Asher stepped around me and crossed the room to where the girl was standing, frozen in place. They hesitated once they were within touching distance, but after a brief pause, they hugged.

It was like I was witnessing a private moment between a couple, and out of habit, I let my eyes drift quickly to the ground.

Wait a minute.

This was *my* boyfriend I was watching hug another girl. I didn't have to give them privacy.

My eyes shot back up and I forced myself to take in every gut-wrenching detail of their embrace. Because that's what it was like for me to see Asher touching someone else. It was painful. It didn't matter that I had no idea who the girl was or that I knew in my heart that Asher loved me. The fact was, this horrible, soul-sucking sickness had begun in my stomach, and I had no idea how to deal with it.

But, just like that, the hug was over, and they were once again standing a safe distance from each other. Of course, it still seemed too close for comfort for me.

"What are you doing here?" Asher asked incredulously.

"This is my second summer at Brighton," Brooklyn said, showing her perfect pearly whites as she smiled. "What are *you* doing here?"

"My aunt and uncle thought Abby and I should come," he said.

I noticed that he didn't mention me or the rest of the Cleri.

"So you *did* go to stay with your aunt," she said, slowly. "I'd heard that, but . . . well, I wasn't sure."

"Oh, yeah," Asher said, looking down at the ground and running his fingers through his hair. He did that when he was nervous . . . and when he was flirting. I couldn't tell which it was in this particular moment, but I didn't like it.

"Who *is* this girl?" I asked myself quietly.

"Brooklyn," a voice answered from beside me. I started slightly before turning to see Abby standing there, a book in hand, but closed down by her side. "She's Asher's ex-girlfriend."

My heart dropped and hit the bottom of my stomach with an awful thud. Nausea crept up my throat before I could realize it was happening and I scanned the room for a bathroom to no avail. So I just stood there instead, frozen in disbelief.

"His . . . ex-girlfriend?" I asked, eyes wide. Then, almost to myself, I said, "I didn't even know there was an *ex*. And she's what . . . a *supermodel?*"

"Not a model. Just a witch," Abby said as we watched Asher and Brooklyn's reunion from afar.

This was unbelievable. Sure, I guess in the back of my mind I'd known that Asher had to have had a past. I mean—look at him. He's hot. But the subject of exes had never come up, so I thought he was like me, and hadn't really had any relationships before ours that were significant enough to merit the term "ex." And even if he had, who wanted to think of her boyfriend as having a love life before theirs? Not me. I wanted to be the only one special enough to have been with Asher like that.

Unfortunately, I could no longer convince myself that I was his one and only, because the proof was currently standing in front of me, all leggy and blond. And she was impossible to ignore.

"You just *disappeared*, Asher," Brooklyn said. It was almost a whisper and I found myself straining to hear their conversation.

"Look, Brooklyn, I can explain . . ."

But before he could finish, Brooklyn's gaze swept our way and her face changed instantly.

"Abby!" she shouted and ran in our direction.

"Oh, here we go," Abby muttered under her breath, but then abruptly shut her mouth, as if she hadn't meant to say it out loud.

I barely had time to raise an eyebrow at her comment before the eight-foot-tall stunner pranced her way over to us as easily as a ballerina crossing a stage. If I hadn't already disliked her, I might've been impressed that she'd managed to do this in five-inch heels. Christian Siriano to be specific. And with a curved heel and additional panel under the toe, this was an incredible feat.

Of course, this only succeeded in annoying me further.

Despite her lack of enthusiasm, I noticed with jealousy that Abby wasn't recoiling from their embrace out of solidarity with me. In fact, she even dropped her book during the exchange, which fell with a clunk on top of the wooden coffee table. As the pages fluttered closed, I read the title: *The Inferno*, by Dante.

Talk about light summer reading.

"I've missed you so much, Ab!" Brooklyn said, squeezing the smaller girl in her slender arms. When she pulled away, she gave Abby the once-over while still holding her hands. "What have you been up to?"

"Oh, you know . . . reading," Abby answered in her signature monotone voice. She gestured to the novel that was now lying on the table below them.

"Sounds about right," Brooklyn said, laughing easily. "Anything else? It's been a while you know . . ."

"It has," Abby mumbled.

"Whatever you've been up to, I'd love to hear it!" Brooklyn said quickly. "We have so much to catch up on." Then she looked over at Asher who had wandered back over to us while the two were talking. He seemed to have recovered from his initial shock and was back to his usual self. Only, despite his laid-back demeanor, I could tell something was up. "All of us should catch up," she concluded.

That's it. Time to step in.

I cleared my throat and sidled up to Asher, placing my hand in his territorially and kissing him lightly on the cheek. "Hey, babe! Making friends already?"

Brooklyn seemed to notice me for the first time, and then I watched as she went through the same flood of emotions that I had a few minutes before. The smile remained on her lips but her eyes gave her away. They went from friendly to murderous in point two seconds, and I knew instantly that there was going to be trouble.

"Um, right. Hadley, this is Brooklyn. Brooklyn, this is my girlfriend, Hadley." At least when he said it, he didn't sound uncomfortable. And he'd remembered to actually identify me as his girlfriend and not just, "This is Hadley." In fact, he was making the introduction the same way he would to anyone else we might be meeting at camp. It made me wonder if I was making too big a deal over this whole ex thing. Maybe they were totally over each other.

Then I thought back to the moment they'd hugged and all my defenses shot back up.

"Hi!" I said, more brightly than I'd intended, but wanting to convey that I didn't think she was a threat. I still wasn't sure if this was true, but no need for her to know that I was rattled by her appearance.

I didn't put my hand out to shake hers and neither did she. We were in a mental standoff and, considering the way she was staring at Asher and my entwined hands, I decided I was in the better position.

"Brooke!" a brunette shouted from across the room.

I took my eyes off of Brooklyn to see this other girl who was flanked by three others, all of whom were standing with their hands on their hips. The girl who'd called out to Brooklyn had short hair that was cut in a sharp, artsy bob, with bangs that just grazed the tops of her eyebrows. "You coming? There won't be any good tanning light left if we don't get out there soon."

"Be there in a minute, Eve!" she yelled back, without letting her eyes drift from us. "Well, my friends are waiting for me. Let's catch up later?"

She was looking straight at Asher as she said this. Then she turned abruptly and strutted off, leaving everyone in the room staring after her as she went. Including myself.

"She's a cheery one, isn't she?" I said, unable to keep the sarcasm out of my voice. Then I turned back to Asher. "Old friends?"

True, I already knew the answer, but I wanted to hear it from him. Would he admit how he knew her? Try to down-play their involvement? Given his track record of lying to me in the past, I couldn't help but wonder how easy it would be for him to fall back into it. Guys held back on telling the truth all the time, mostly to avoid an uncomfortable conversation with the girls questioning them. Asher wasn't like other guys, but it was still possible this was just a part of his male DNA, and he wouldn't be able to help himself.

"We used to date," Asher said simply.

I stared at him, unable to decide if I was happy that he'd told me the truth or upset that he didn't feel guiltier over having obviously just shared a moment with his ex. With me standing right there. So, I didn't say anything.

Abby looked from me to Asher and then back to me. "Well, that wasn't awkward at all," she said, breaking up the moment. Bending down to retrieve her book, she began to back away slowly. "I'm just going to . . . go find our room."

She'd only made it a few steps before I told her to wait up. Then I gave Asher the only smile I could muster before turning and walking away.

"Hello?" I called into the room with a big 3C on the door. It was the number we'd been assigned, but when we'd arrived in front of it, the door was cracked open about an inch and I could hear shuffling inside. And I didn't want to just barge in if our new roommate was changing or something so I made our presence known.

"It's open!" a voice called out from behind the door.

I looked at Abby, who simply shrugged before leading the way inside.

Nothing could've prepared me for what I saw on the other side of the door. As soon as my eyes settled on the scene in front of me, I gasped and dropped my iced coffee onto the ground, the liquid splashing all over my legs and shoes.

Chapter Five

"I know, right?" a high-pitched girl's voice said.

It was like walking into another universe.

First off, the room itself had to have been at least four times the size of my bedroom, way bigger than what should've fit into the cabin I'd seen from the outside. Not that the cabin was small by any means—it was definitely resort-big—but there was no way that the room we were standing in could fit into *that* house. Especially not when you multiplied it by about twenty, which was the amount of rooms the place had in order to house everybody at camp.

No, the cabin had definitely been magically manipulated to appear smaller than it actually was. From the outside, at least. As I looked around, I remembered what Miss Peggy had said about Brighton being a total magic zone and realized it was true. A person's imagination can run wild when not constrained by human boundaries. Brighton reflected this for sure.

"This is all *ours*?" I asked, stepping over the mess I'd made on the floor and walking farther into the room.

"It certainly appears that way," the girl said from across the room. Then she gestured to me. "My face looked like that when I first got here, too. The rooms change every year, so I was just as surprised as you were to see what we'd ended up with. Hi, I'm Colette."

She skipped over to where Abby and I were now standing and held out her hand. I took it and returned her smile. Colette was really cute—in a geek chic sort of way. Her light brown hair was tied up in loose braids and her black-rimmed, angularly square glasses were a size too big for her face. But on her it wasn't too much. Her lips were the color of strawberries, which made the freckles that decorated her cheeks stand out even more.

Colette's outfit was just as quirky as she was. Her white shirt displayed a brightly drawn cat that was wearing a pink bow near its ear and glasses similar to Colette's own. The shirt read LOVE MY STYLE. She topped the look off with mid-thigh black shorts and a pair of pink and black Mary Janes.

She looked like a walking, talking anime character—and I had to admit, she was totally owning it. I respected a girl's right to choose her look as long as she wore it with pride and it was a true reflection of her. None of that, "I'm creating this freaky public persona, when in reality I have no idea who I am" BS. When a person was being one hundred percent authentic it oozed out of every pore. And from what I could tell, Colette was the real deal.

"I'm Hadley, and this is Abby," I said in response. "And I guess we're your new roomies. Speaking of, can we get back to how *insane* this room is?"

I continued my own personal tour around our new digs and

kept finding one incredible thing after another. The area was split into four main parts. Each of the three walls across from the front door held a sleeping area, complete with dressers and lamps and freestanding closets. All usual staples for a living space. But in the middle of the room, there was a grand circular couch that held no openings except for the hole in its center, which was almost completely filled with a round coffee table. The only way to the couch's seats was to go up and over the side.

I ran my hand over the surface of the couch and felt the softness of the velvet brush against my skin. It was delectable and totally unusual.

"Watch this," Colette said and climbed over, landing awkwardly on the fluffy cushions. Leaning forward, she placed her hands on the top of the round, glass-covered table. "Show me Grumpy Cat," she commanded the table.

We watched in awe as the previously clear surface grew murky and an image began to appear across the glass. Seconds later, we were all staring at a pop-up version of a mad-looking fluffy cat.

"What the heck?" Abby said, leaning over the back of the couch to get a closer look.

"What is it?" I asked, curiously.

"It's this cat that's always grumpy. He's a meme that's become like, one of the most famous cats on the Internet," Colette said, grinning back at us.

"I meant the table," I said, chuckling at her enthusiasm over a cat. "How does it work?"

"Oh, sure. Right," she said, suddenly embarrassed. "Well, it acts sort of like a computer. Like if you want to find something—pictures, videos, sites, information on things—you can just ask for it and it appears. Only, in 3D and without glasses."

"Can you see people around the world?" Abby asked, as if she were reading my mind. The tool could come in handy if I wanted to check up on the Parrishables.

Or on Asher.

Not like I was planning on eavesdropping or anything . . . well, okay, who am I kidding? I wanted to eavesdrop. And apparently Abby had the same idea. Only, I wondered who it was she planned to spy on.

"Already tried it," Colette said, adjusting her glasses smartly. "And no. There's no live feed. At least as far as I can tell."

"Oh," Abby said, and grew quiet again.

"I hope you guys don't mind, but I took the bed on the right, because, well—I have to wake up on the right side of the bed," Colette said as if this was a logical explanation.

"Fine with me," I said. Tilting my head toward the area that our new roommate had claimed, I checked out what she'd done with the place.

As much as I liked the girl, it was like a rainbow had thrown up on her side. The wall was covered with dozens of bright-yellow and lime-green circles in all different sizes. Her bedspread was hot pink, with a sort of glittery topcoat that glistened as you moved around the room. The pillows were a vibrant blue. Her dressers were deep purple and trimmed with gold. Oversize framed pictures of bright flowers decorated the wall and seemed to disappear behind her bed.

The two areas for Abby and me were completely white.

White walls, white sheets and comforter, white dresser and closet. It almost looked sterile with the total lack of color. Definitely not my idea of an inviting place to stay day in and day out.

"I didn't realize we were supposed to bring our own stuff to decorate," I said, pulling my bags over to the bed that was opposite the front door. It held a big rectangular window and looked like it had the best natural light.

Good lighting, after all, was a girl's best friend.

"Oh, you weren't," Colette said. "That's the other cool part."

Colette pranced over to my bed and waved her hand over the top of it while closing her eyes lightly. As her hand moved over the comforter, the bed cover began to change colors, shifting until it showed four Andy Warhol–looking photos of Marilyn Monroe.

Opening her eyes again, Colette clapped her hands together excitedly. "See? You just think about what design you want and it appears. The whole room's enchanted so we can personalize our living space. You can change your walls"—she walked over to the space behind my bed and it became textured and orange—"and the pictures"—a touch of one of the frames and the picture inside changed to abstract art—"and even the furniture."

"That's sick!" I said stepping forward and surveying my now-colorful area. "Although this isn't exactly my style. No offense."

"None taken," Colette answered.

I waved my hand over the different parts of my room and within seconds, the bed had turned candy-apple red, the walls changed to black and white stripes, and my furniture turned black with feathers and crystals as accents.

"Wicked," Colette said, nodding her head in approval.

I turned around to see Abby pimping out her side too, having chosen an interesting jungle-theme for her wallpaper and a baby-blue bedspread. Not at all what I'd have expected from her, though it pretty much proved how desperately we needed to spend more time together. Clearly I still didn't know Asher's little sister at all.

"There's more. Sit down on your beds," Colette commanded, sitting down on hers and motioning for us to do the same. With a glance at Abby, who was following along without argument, we both lowered ourselves onto the squishy mattresses. As I pulled my legs up from the floor to sit cross-legged, I began to feel something weird.

It was like the bed was vibrating.

No, not vibrating. *Moving*.

Then, as I watched, all three of our beds began to rise off the floor. They continued to float into the air until we were just a foot away from hitting our heads on the ceiling.

"Whoa," I said, already wondering how we were going to get down.

"It's like a magic carpet ride," Abby said, leaning forward and clinging to the blankets tightly.

"Yeah, pretty sweet, huh?" Colette said. "I could just hang out up here all day, passing the time away."

The three of us lay back on our respective beds and took everything in. I placed my arms behind my head and stared at the ceiling in silence for a few moments.

"I can't believe this is our room," I said quietly, feeling truly content for the first time since we'd arrived. But then my mind drifted back to Asher and what I'd witnessed between him and *Brooklyn* in the lobby earlier and felt myself getting worked up again.

I had to try to get more information on her. It seemed like Asher had been genuinely surprised to see her, which meant that they obviously hadn't kept in touch. This was a plus at least, but there was still that hug between them. It was oddly intimate and I wondered if it would've gone on longer had dozens of people not been around to witness it.

I admit, it was slightly irrational to be upset with either of them for just saying hello. Neither of them was crossing any lines, after all. But I also felt strangely justified in my anger and frustration.

What had happened between them?

I wanted to grill Abby about it, but didn't feel comfortable doing it in front of Colette. And if I was being honest, I was hesitant to bring the topic up to Asher's sister at all. The last thing I wanted her to think was that I was actually jealous of some Barbie-looking girl and was capable of snooping for information on her brother.

Even if it was true. About the snooping, I mean. Not the jealousy. Because Hadley Bishop did not do jealous.

At least I didn't *think* I did. Was that what this was? Jealousy? I wouldn't have known from experience, because this situation with Asher was a first for me.

See, there'd only ever really been one other guy that I'd cared about—and in the end, ours was less of a relationship and more of a mistake. One that I'd learned from at the expense of my heart.

Before Asher, there was Kent.

I met Kent my freshman year and fell for him right away. Hard. He was this upperclassman, soccer stud, and the biggest draw of all: he was human. So when he noticed me cheering on the sidelines at one of his games, I just about died from excitement. It didn't take long for him to ask me out, and we spent several weeks going to movies, hanging out in coffee shops, and walking around town.

He was my first crush. My first date. My first kiss.

He was my first . . . everything.

The problem was, I wasn't his only.

After a while, Kent began to pull away, claiming he was too busy to hang out. I finally confronted him one day at school and that's when he'd dropped the bombshell.

"I sort of have a girlfriend now," Kent said, not at all ashamed to tell me this.

Boom.

"We had some fun, but we never said we were exclusive."

Boom.

"When Mindy found out I was seeing other people, she decided she was ready to commit. She said she couldn't stand the thought of me being with all those other girls."

Girls? As in, more than just me?

Boom.

"Look, I love her. You understand, right?"

Kaboom.

I didn't understand though. I didn't understand how he could date several girls at once, make me think he liked me and only me, and then ditch me for someone else. My heart felt like it had been obliterated, and being the witch I am, I'd instantly searched for a spell that would make him choose me instead. Because as douchey as Kent had been to me, I still liked him.

Unfortunately, love is about the only thing that witches can't mess with. I might have the power to persuade people to do what I want and create fire out of thin air, but I can't make a boy like me. It was infuriating and made me feel completely helpless for the first time in my life.

When I'd confessed to my girlfriends what had happened, they hadn't seemed all that surprised. In fact, they told me that it was a typical boy thing to do. That guys often did this as they searched for the "right" girl. After I finally stopped crying, I came to a decision that changed everything.

I would never again date a high-school boy.

The experience had made me too vulnerable and I didn't like feeling out of control. It was much safer to concentrate on other things, like my magic, cheerleading, school, and friends, than risk having my heart broken.

And then Asher had come along and my world changed once again.

Only, choosing to date Asher was more like two magnets being pulled together by an invisible force. We were a perfect match. And while I tried to stick to my old no-dating rules, I eventually gave in, telling myself it would be different because he was a witch, and not a typical high-school guy. He was special.

So, although I hadn't exactly *enjoyed* hearing that Kent had found another girl whom he wanted to date more than me, I never felt that sense of jealousy toward her. Probably because she went to a different school and I never actually met her in person. Besides, Kent and I had lasted a whopping three weeks—a lifetime at fifteen, but chump change compared to my relationship with Asher.

Given all of that, this whole jealousy thing was new to me. And I had no idea how to handle it. I so didn't want to be *that* girl. The one who screamed at her beau because he said Jessica Alba was hot. I had more self-esteem than that. And more faith in our relationship. But it was like something was taking over my brain and making me feel crazy and emotional and . . . insecure.

It was like *Invasion of the Body Snatchers*, only the monster was in the form of a tall blonde who'd probably once had her legs wrapped around my boyfriend. . . .

And suddenly I was back to hating her.

Colette lifted her arm up to her face and checked her funky plastic watch, pulling me out of my thoughts. "First class starts in fifteen," she announced, sitting up abruptly and then swinging her legs over the side of her bed. I watched as it drifted back down toward the floor.

Looking over at Abby, I could see that she'd pulled another book out of thin air and was already reading.

The girl sure likes her books, doesn't she?

"You coming?" I asked her.

"Gonna read for a few more minutes, but I'll be down for class," she answered, her attention fully on the story she was reading.

"Okay," I said, wondering if I'd be able to pry her away from her books long enough to get to know her.

I copied Colette and swung my legs over the side of the bed and let them hang in the air. As if I'd pulled on a lever, the bed began to lower to the floor until my feet were touching the ground.

"So cool," I said, shaking my head in disbelief before getting ready for our session.

Chapter Six

I'd never much minded walking into situations where I didn't know anyone. Not just because I was a natural influencer, but because I wasn't exactly shy.

Call me crazy, but I feel like powerful people have a duty to use their positions in the public eye for good, not evil. Like the saying goes, you catch more bees with honey.

Besides, history had pretty much proven that what you put out there comes back to you, tenfold. Take a look at Marie Antoinette for instance. Great dresser, but she was selfish and focused on spending money frivolously rather than helping the hungry or lessening the rising deficit in France. In the end, it didn't matter how great she looked or that she was royalty— her subjects were unhappy with the way she treated them and she paid the price for it.

With her head.

And I wasn't about to lose mine because I treated people badly. I recognized that I'd been blessed. With numerous talents like my ability to throw multiple back handsprings in a row or argue just about any topic. I'd also hit the genealogical jackpot. Being a direct descendent of one of the most powerful witches of all time had left me with magical gifts most others didn't have.

It was with this mindset that I walked into our first session at Brighton, pumped to learn and ready to rock every challenge they threw my way. I was even looking forward to making new friends. Since graduating from Astor High in May, my relationships with my old friends had grown strained. I'd heard that this often happened to people after they graduated and moved on to separate colleges, but I hadn't expected it to happen so soon.

Plans to spend our last summer together had disintegrated as I learned about Brighton. And then Sofia headed off to cheer camp, while Bethany and Trish flitted to Europe for the quintessential post-high-school backpacking trip. So, I found myself without my trendy trio for the first summer in forever.

I was friendless.

And apparently overly dramatic. But what was a girl without her friends? Nothing. The Cleri sort of filled the hole left by my old social circle, but even with them it was an odd relationship. I'd been their leader. Still was, if you considered the meetings I regularly held to make sure the Parrishables stayed gone. They still looked to me to guide them and that made for an unequal balance of power between us. We were friendly, but I wasn't sure we were "friends."

Expanding my friendship circle was exactly what I needed. Especially since I felt like there was no one I could really talk to about this ex-girlfriend thing. And I was in serious need of a sounding board. Luckily, Colette had turned out to be much cooler than I'd expected and I felt like I was already making progress with her.

"Hey guys!" I said, walking across the grass behind the cabin to meet up with the Cleri members who had already sat down within the mini amphitheater.

So far only Jasmine, Jinx, and Sascha had shown up. Like a weird Three Musketeers. Sascha was chatting excitedly as Jinx attempted to get a word in here and there, and Jasmine rested back against the edge of a stage, looking bored. Or angry. Or annoyed. I still couldn't tell any of them apart.

"This is Colette," I said, gesturing for her to come closer. She joined me, twisting the bottom of her shirt absently. But instead of looking down at the ground, intimidated by the group in front of her, she locked eyes with each of the girls and gave them genuine smiles. "She's rooming with Abby and me."

"Nice to meet you," Sascha said, sliding her butt off the edge of the stage and coming forward to shake Colette's hand. Jinx followed suit, but when I looked at Jasmine hoping she'd at least try to be friendly, she just nodded her head and said, "What's up?"

"So good to meet you guys!" Colette said.

Jasmine took in Colette's outfit and stared at her blankly. "What's your deal?" she asked finally.

If Colette was offended, she didn't let on. Instead she just stood there, and answered as if she were asked the question all the time.

"Well, what do you want to know?" she asked genially.

"What's with the outfit?" Jasmine asked back.

This was the sort of thing I'd been afraid of. The rest of us were used to Jasmine's blunt nature, but to strangers, her attitude could be misconstrued as hostility.

"Jasmine!" I scolded and then turned to Colette apologetically.

But she didn't bat an eye. "My aunt Betsey gave it to me. She always sends me her latest creations," she said. Jasmine's comment hadn't bothered her one bit.

"Is this your first time at Brighton?" Sascha asked, changing the conversation to safer subjects. "We're all newbies."

"Nah," Colette said. "I've been coming here since I was, like, eight, I guess? So, like, nine years give or take a summer?"

"Is the rest of your coven here, too?" I asked, looking around for any sign of them.

"I was the only one invited this year," she answered with a shrug. "There've been others from my group in the past, but they've all graduated. Or are too young and inexperienced to make the cut. So, it's just me for now."

Even though Colette seemed perfectly fine to be here by herself, I had to imagine it was incredibly lonely. I made a vow to include her as much as possible.

"What's it like here?" Sascha asked, like she wanted Colette to spill Brighton's biggest secrets. I, myself, was curious to hear what she thought of the witches' intensive, too. So far, it hadn't been what I'd expected. On several different levels.

"Brighton is *unreal*. The teachers are all really smart and always come up with the best lessons each year. They're some of the most influential witches alive, you know? And they take time out of each of their summers to come here and teach *us*. It's pretty wild when you think about it. I mean, these are the witches that are changing the face of the magicking world. We couldn't be taught by more talented people."

Well at least I was going to be in good company. I'd never really paid much attention to what was going on in terms of current events in the witching world, since I figured it had little to do with my life personally. So I probably wouldn't recognize any of the elders for the strides they'd made in the paranormal world. But still, it was cool to find out that our teachers were so celebrated.

If you wanted to be the best, you had to learn from the best.

Other kids began to show up then and the area we were in started to get more crowded. I heard a loud-pitched laugh and turned to see Brooklyn and her posse sauntering our way. Still looking perfectly put together, the blond bombshell once again commanded everyone's attention. I forced myself to turn back to Colette and the others.

"How about the other twitches?" I asked her, hoping it sounded nonchalant despite the timing. "Everyone else cool?"

Colette followed my gaze over to Brooklyn and a shadow crossed over her naturally happy face. "Most of them," she said, fighting to keep her pep up. "Every group has its rulers."

"And Brighton's are?"

"Isn't it obvious? Brooklyn and her bestie, Eve," Colette said matter-of-factly.

"Eve's the brunette with her nose in the air, right?" Jasmine asked, unimpressed.

"How'd you know that?" I asked her when Colette nodded.

"Their room is right next to ours," Jinx said. "It's just the two of them."

Brooklyn and Eve had gotten a double room. It figured. The fact deepened my dislike for them both.

"We ran into them earlier. They walk around like there are cameras following them. The Brooklyn girl introduced herself, but Eve acted like we didn't exist," Jasmine said. "Can't say I'm a fan."

"Brooklyn seemed okay, though," Sascha said, practically salivating. She was the only one of our group who gave any importance to popularity and pop culture. She'd been a supporter of mine from the beginning, the only one who acknowledged my place in the social hierarchy. Now that I'd taken on more responsibility in the Cleri, the novelty of my life had sort of worn off for her, I think.

Sascha couldn't resist a chance to glom on to the glamorous, so I wasn't totally surprised she was impressed with Brooklyn and Eve. But would she side with me if she knew that Brooklyn had dated Asher? Or was popularity by association more important to her?

"She's fine," Colette admitted. "But Eve . . . she's like, Mormo."

"She's Mormon?" Jasmine asked. "Well, that explains a lot."

"No, *Mormo*. The demon witch who devours hearts so she can retain her youth," Colette said. When the rest of us still had no clue what she was talking about, she giggled in response. "*You* know . . . she was the Queen of the Ghouls and chief consort of Hecate, the Greek goddess of the underworld and witchcraft. Mormo."

"Read some pretty freaky fairy tales growing up, did you?" Jasmine asked and went back to scrutinizing the incoming beauty barrage.

"There are demons now, too?" Jinx whispered to me. I took a look at her and shook my head, noting that she'd gone white at the mention of the otherworldly beings. Poor girl didn't need another thing keeping her up at night. She had real-life darkness doing that already.

"I can't believe Asher's here at Brighton, too!" I heard Eve say, much more loudly than was needed considering Brooklyn and the other girls were walking right next to each other. "Was there still a spark when you saw each other?"

My blood began to boil as the small brunette talked about my boyfriend. The conversation they were having very publicly meant that Brooklyn already was talking about her encounter with Asher. She obviously wasn't worrying about anyone hearing her, that was for sure. I wondered what she was planning next.

"Well, we *do* have a history, you know," Brooklyn responded, just slightly quieter than Eve had been. "We were each other's first *loves*. It takes a long time to get over something like that. Much longer than it's been at least."

The rest of the Cleri listened to the conversation as the girls talked, and each of their eyes was growing wide with shock. My hands clenched into fists and I prayed for the strength to keep from drop-kicking Brooklyn and Eve onto the stage.

"Do you think you'll work things out?" Eve asked.

They were right behind us now, and I turned my head to show them that I could hear every word they were saying. They already knew that, of course, and were unperturbed. It was the whole reason for this show, anyway. Brooklyn was trying to get a rise out of me, but I wasn't about to stoop to her level. She wasn't worth it. Asher was, however.

"We're supposed to talk things over later," Brooklyn said. She passed by us then, staring me down like she was challenging me. "When we can be alone."

I started to move toward her, either to confront her or claw her eyes out, when a hand clamped down on my arm, holding me back. I expected it to be Jasmine, possibly Colette, but when I looked back, I saw that it was Fallon.

"Down girl," he said quietly. "You're giving her the daggers that you used to reserve just for me."

"Guess the torch for World's Most Annoying Person on Earth has finally changed hands," I said between clenched teeth, but not dropping my gaze at Brooklyn as she walked away.

When she was at a safe distance, Fallon let go of my arm and clutched at his chest dramatically. "You're killing me, Bishop."

I could tell he was trying to diffuse the situation, and for the most part, it had worked. The fire that had been brewing inside me started to burn out.

"What are you doing over here, anyway?" Jasmine asked. "Aren't you supposed to be on the boys' side of camp?"

"Boys' side?" I asked, confused. "What are you guys talking about?"

Jasmine looked at me for a moment before a huge smile appeared on her face. "Ooh, can I tell her? Let me tell her," she said. Then, not waiting for anyone else's okay, she continued. "Brighton's motto is: boys with the boys, girls with the girls."

"As in, segregation?" I asked incredulously.

"As in, less PDA opportunities with your man," Jasmine said, happily.

"You've gotta be kidding me," I said, a little more angrily than the news called for. But it was like I was seeing the time I thought I'd have with Asher this summer disintegrating right before my eyes. And given Brooklyn's surprise appearance, I felt like we needed couple time now more than ever.

But it looked like that wasn't going to go my way, either.

"It's always been that way," Colette chimed in. "Ever since Brighton opened up in 1864. They say it helps everyone to concentrate more if they're not ogling each other's goodies."

"But that's why I came to camp," Sascha said, play-pouting.

"Gag me," Jasmine said and made a face. "Better yet, gag her."

"So, we don't share any classes?" I asked, disappointed to hear there would be whole parts of my day that would be Asher-free.

"We have meals and free time together, but typically, no," Colette answered, brightly. "Guess it's just us girls for now!"

I frowned in response.

"So what *are* you doing over here then, Fallon?" I grumbled.

Fallon took a step back, like he was afraid to become the first victim of my less-than-stellar mood.

"I walked over with Abby since she was by herself." And then I noticed that Abby had entered our circle at some point and was standing there silently. I wondered how much of my run-in with Brooklyn she'd witnessed.

"That's actually . . . really nice of you, Fallon," I said, surprising even myself with the compliment.

"You act like I'm usually a jerk or something," Fallon said, glancing over at Abby and then again to me.

Gee. I wonder where I got that impression.

But I held my tongue. "Did Asher come with you?" I asked, leaning around him to see if he was in the area.

"Nope. Haven't seen him since we checked in," he said. "He's probably already over with the guys."

"Oh," I said, unable to hide my disappointment. Well, at least if I couldn't see Asher, that meant that Brooklyn wouldn't be seeing him either.

Silver linings.

"As much as I'd love to be a fly on this wall, I must get going," Fallon said, tipping an imaginary hat and then taking off around the far wall to where the boys' side of camp must have been. Once he was out of earshot, Colette turned back to me excitedly.

"Um, how cute is he?" she said.

I blinked in disbelief. "You're kidding, right?" I said. Obviously Colette didn't know Fallon well enough. If she had, she'd be washing her mouth out with a soapy concoction right about now.

"No," she said seriously. "He's a little on the young side, but totally crushable. Am I right?"

She looked around at the rest of our group, waiting for someone to agree. Abby shrugged noncommittally, but there was a hint of a smile on her face when she did it, which threw me for a loop.

Unbelievable. Was there something in the water here that made everything backward?

"Hello, Brighton campers!" an obnoxiously bubbly voice suddenly called out from the stage behind Jasmine. We all looked up to see Miss Peggy standing there, in the same Brighton T-shirt that the angry check-in guy had been wearing, only most of hers was covered by her vest. "Let's get started!"

Chapter Seven

"What was that all about?" Jasmine asked, nodding in the direction of Brooklyn and her cronies. Despite the fact that our session had officially started, the others were still focused on me.

I glanced over at Brooklyn with annoyance. "It's nothing," I said, wanting to move on.

"That *wasn't* nothing," Sascha said. "Were they talking about our Asher?"

"Because the name is so common that it could be another guy?" Jasmine said sarcastically.

"I'm confused," Colette said, looking at me, and then over at the others, as if she were waiting for someone to clue her in.

"What are we talking about?" Abby asked, for once more intrigued by our conversation than by a story from one of her books.

Ugh. I *so* didn't want to talk about this in front of Abby in case she told Asher about it. He'd either think I was overreacting or

THE WITCH IS BACK

would confront Brooklyn about her taunts. And the last thing I needed was for a guy to try to fight my battles for me.

I think I'd proven I could take care of myself. Especially against jilted ex-girlfriends who were the size of a toothpick.

When I didn't answer Abby right away, Jasmine jumped in. "That Brooklyn girl was just spouting off about how she used to date your brother, and made it sound like she was planning to do some shady stuff to try to get him back," she said.

"Wait—*your* boyfriend is the guy who broke her heart last summer?" Colette said, wide-eyed.

Last summer? That meant he'd broken up with her right around the time we'd met.

And suddenly another thought popped into my mind: Had Asher been forced by the Parrishables to break up with Brooklyn like he was forced to get close to me? If that was the case, then the breakup hadn't necessarily been voluntary. Which meant that I had bigger problems than I'd thought.

"Wait, what are you talking about, Colette?" I asked, interested in knowing more about the breakup.

"Brooklyn was all depressed, for like, half the summer last year," Colette explained. "Then, she suddenly seemed to get over it, and drowned her sorrows in the other guys at camp. I mean, I never saw anything myself, but that was the rumor at least. Once she'd recovered from the breakup, it was like a switch was flipped and she turned from Suzy Sad-Pants to, well—the girl she is now." Colette gestured in Brooklyn's direction.

"Nothing sad about *that*," Jasmine muttered as we watched Brooklyn pose like she was at a photo shoot.

"Look, can we talk about this later?" I said, trying to change the subject. The fact that Asher had a girlfriend before me wasn't exactly something I wanted to have a coven-wide conversation about. "Or like, never again?"

65

I could tell the others didn't want to let it die there, but Miss Peggy was calling for our attention again, and I was relieved to have something else to distract us. Even if it was an overly enthused camp counselor romping around onstage.

"How are you all doing?!" Miss Peggy screamed out to the thirty or so of us gathered under the shaded section of the amphitheater. I briefly wondered if she was living out her dreams of commanding an audience while onstage. At least she had the costume part down.

So sad.

We all assured her we were doing fine, some of us with less enthusiasm than others. Jasmine responded with a growl that made us all turn around and give her a look. She just motioned for us to turn around and pay attention to Miss Peggy, who was in the middle of doing her own little happy dance.

How is this one of today's finest witches?

"For those of you returning this summer, it's good to have you back! And for those who are brand new, I'd like to give you all a huge Brighton welcome!" Miss Peggy snapped her fingers and a huge scroll appeared behind her, rolling down from where it hovered fifteen feet in the air. We watched as it revealed a painted welcome sign, nearly matching the earlier one she'd held up for us at the airport. No doubt this little deco was her idea, too.

As the banner fully expanded, glitter and confetti exploded above us, raining down like it was New Year's. Jinx yelped and dropped down to the ground, not realizing that it was a surprise meant for our enjoyment. Others around us "oohed" and "ahhed" at the display.

"Well, that was . . . unexpected," I said, reaching out to catch some of the reflective bits in my hand. It was a little cheesy, but it was also kind of fun. It made me feel like a kid again, like anything was possible. A look over at the others showed that they were all smiling, too. Except for Jinx of course, who climbed back into her seat shakily.

"We anticipate that this will be one of the best summer sessions yet!" Miss Peggy said. "But before we start the lessons, we need to see where you each stand. Although you're all superior in your magicking skills—otherwise you wouldn't be here—everyone excels differently. We at Brighton want to make sure we challenge each and every one of you during your tenure here.

"So, we're going to start by breaking up into groups, and a counselor will be by to observe you cast your top three spells. We'll be examining the difficulty of the spell, accuracy, and follow-through, and then will place each of you in a level appropriate to your skills. This isn't to embarrass you, but instead, to guarantee that you get as much out of camp as possible. Okay, find your roommates and stand in your groups. We'll be along shortly!"

Everyone began to get up from their seats and we all played a quick game of musical chairs until we were divided by rooms. With Abby and Colette on one side of me, and Sascha, Jasmine, and Jinx on the other, I started to brainstorm which three spells I was going to showcase. Once I'd figured that out, I helped the others choose theirs, and then waited for our counselor to show up.

A woman with fire-red hair walked up to our group, seemingly out of nowhere, and I nearly did a double take as it dawned on me who she was. The matriarch of the world's most famous family on TV was standing right in front of us dressed in a sparkly black sequined suit. I knew from watching every episode of her reality show that she looked *really* good for her age. And I noted with admiration that she looked even better in person.

I opened my mouth to say something, but couldn't get anything out. I'd had no idea that Rose Bradshaw was actually a witch. Of course, this part of her life had never been explored on her show, which pretty much proved that reality TV wasn't totally based on reality at all. Oddly, this didn't make me like her or the show any less. In fact, it was rather impressive to know she'd been able to create balance in her personal and professional lives. And now, here she was, teaching at our camp.

This was a woman I'd admired for years. Her ability to create an empire out of almost nothing, securing deal after deal for her kids as well as herself—it was a feat unmatched. As far as I was concerned, she was one of the most powerful business-witches in the world.

And there was so much I could learn from her.

"Hi girls, I'm Mrs. B!" she said, enthusiastically. She was even more of a presence in real life, and I found myself standing a little straighter to emulate her. "Lets see what you've got. How about we start with you."

She pointed at Jasmine and then led the group out into the sun and away from the clutter of the seats.

"Okay, dolls, what are you going to show me first?" Mrs. B asked, placing her hands on her curvy hips.

"I thought I'd do a twister spell," Jasmine said. When Mrs. B nodded in approval, Jasmine widened her stance and relaxed her body to prep for the spell. Experience had shown us that the more open our hearts and minds were, the better the spell went.

When she was ready, she yelled out, "Aeromus une cyclenae!"

Almost immediately, all the pinecones that had fallen underneath a nearby tree began to lift off the ground and circle around in the air. After a few moments of this, Mrs. B told her she could stop.

"Great job," the counselor said and marked something down in the notebook she held in her hands.

Two spells later and we'd moved on to Sascha, who performed the clothes-changing spell that I'd created years before
(as a way to have the latest runway creations before they were
out in stores). I'm sure Sascha was hoping to appeal to Mrs. B's
fashion sense, but when she put the older woman in a bright
blue jumpsuit, she wrinkled her nose in distaste.

"Great spell, but no one my age should wear spandex," Mrs.
B said. "Even if I *do* sort of make it look good."

She winked at me before motioning for Jinx to begin. Jinx kept
her spells on the safe side, but once she'd started casting, it was
too late for me to encourage her to step things up a bit. I knew
Jinx was capable of more complex spells, but had a feeling she
wouldn't respond to being pushed right now. In the end, she
received a polite nod from Mrs. B and a pat on the back from me.

As Abby began to take her turn, my attention drifted over
to the other side of camp, where Brooklyn and Eve were waiting to display their skills. Here was my chance to see what the
two could do. I watched as Eve went first, performing a few
spells that I had perfected when I was just thirteen.

Looks like Mormo is all bark and no bite.

Eve stepped back to join Brooklyn in line, looking prouder
than she should have felt about her casting abilities. Then,
with a nod of her head, Brooklyn gave the counselor a smile
and took her place front and center.

"Last up!" Mrs. B said to me, redirecting my attention. I'd
completely missed Colette going and was surprised to find it
was already my turn. "And what's your name, gorgeous?"

"Hadley Bishop," I said confidently. Then, I did something I
would never suggest doing in front of your idol. I totally geeked
out. "Can I just say that I'm a huge, huge fan? I've read all of your
books and seen every episode of your show, and I think you're
amazing. It's such an inspiration and an honor to have you here."

"Well, aren't you a *doll*," Mrs. B said, beaming from my compliment. "And from what I've heard, you're a bit of a legend yourself."

Was she serious? Had my biggest idol really heard about *me*? Immediately, I began to blush and looked down at the ground suddenly shy. When I glanced back up, I saw Jasmine staring at me, jaw dropped open in shock. I knew what she was thinking, because I was thinking it, too. I hadn't destroyed Samuel Parris on my own, yet mine was the name everyone seemed to remember.

"Well then, Miss Bishop—dazzle me," Mrs. B said, kindly.

I closed my eyes and let my mind quiet the best I could while being surrounded by dozens of loud teenage girls and one celebrity. I imagined the spell I was about to do and felt the power begin to build from the tips of my toes.

When I opened my eyes again, my gaze immediately met Brooklyn's on the other side of camp. Even though I was too far away to actually see her clearly, I swear she was staring straight at me. Taunting me. Without saying anything to each other, it was as if the gauntlet had been thrown.

Bring it on, witch.

Brooklyn went first, calling out an exploding spell that made contact with a tree just a few feet away from her. Splinters flew through the air, but she didn't move away, just calmly picked chips of wood out of her perfect hair.

Then, subtly, she looked over at me to see what I was going to do.

So that's how you want to play.

Abandoning the original spells I'd been planning to do, I followed her lead. Aiming at another tree, I quickly squared up and called out, "Exbiliby totalitum!" As soon as the words had left my mouth, the spell hit the middle of the trunk and exploded loudly. The force was so strong that the whole thing shook, causing more pinecones to join their fallen brothers on the ground.

"Whoa! Nicely done, Bishop," Mrs. B said.

I smiled at her and then quickly looked back at Brooklyn to show that it was her turn. She frowned, straightened up, and prepared for her next spell.

She shifted her weight from one foot to the other and then smoothed down her flirty teal skirt, which matched the flowery halter she was wearing. Brooklyn put her focus on an overturned log in front of her, which had been left as rustic seating. With a few choice words, the wood began to levitate and then hovered ten feet in the air. Severing her connection with the spell, she allowed the object to fall back down to the ground and land with a thump just inches from her feet.

Looking around for my own log, I finally found the one I wanted, and pointed at it determinedly.

"Hermia Leffner!" I said. Someone gasped behind me as I proceeded to raise an overturned log along with the girl who'd been sitting on it moments before. I lifted them both into the air as easily as if it was a feather. My unknowing participant appeared nervous at first, but the stream of magic was so steady that she quickly recognized that she was no more in danger of falling than she had been when the wood was firmly on the ground. With a grin that I hoped would annoy Brooklyn, I gently lowered the log along with the girl on it. When her feet were back on the ground, the girl jumped up and began chatting excitedly to her friends about her brief flight.

"Good use of your surroundings," Mrs. B commented. "But a witch should never test her magic on others. Not until it's been perfected at least. By the looks of it though, this wasn't your first time performing this particular spell. Am I correct?"

"No, ma'am, it wasn't," I said.

"Ew. Please don't call me ma'am," Mrs. B said, making a face. "It sounds so . . . *old*."

"Right," I said, embarrassed.

Brooklyn was already beginning to cast her next spell. I'd one-upped her each time, but now I had to bring my A game. Show everyone who was the superior witch at this camp. The crown *would* be mine.

I couldn't make out what she was saying since she was so far away, but I knew something was already beginning to happen around us. The hairs on my arms began to stand straight up and I could feel my limbs start to buzz unnaturally. I looked down at my body, trying to figure out what was going on, when the lights in the amphitheater began to dim. Then they all went completely black before flickering a few times, then beginning to pulse.

Then, as if we were watching a light show at Christmas, the bulbs began to go crazy, dancing around to their own unheard beat. Everyone stopped what they were doing to watch. To my dismay, even Mrs. B paused to take a look.

"Well, that was festive," Mrs. B said once Brooklyn was finished.

Show-off.

"Okay, last spell!" Mrs. B announced to me.

I had to make it count, so I thought about the most difficult spell that I could do without endangering those around me. The counselors wouldn't be impressed if I ended up sending someone to the hospital on the first day.

With a final glance at Brooklyn, I cast the spell that would end it all.

"Immobius totarium!"

Nearly everyone in the area stopped what they were doing

once the words had been spoken. Some were mid-step. Others were finishing up spells. But now they were all frozen. Except for the counselors. Based on Counselor Crazy's reaction to my trying to influence him earlier, I'd decided casting on the adults might not impress them after all. Besides, it was better for me if they could actually *see* what I was capable of.

"Holy smokes—" Mrs. B said, as she noticed that everyone had ceased moving.

"Keep watching," I said, grinning at her conspiratorially. Saying another spell, I sent pinecones floating through the air and into the hands of the other twitches. And for the ones whose hands weren't open, I balanced pinecones on shoulders, feet, and various other places on their bodies. Mrs. B smiled as she realized what I was doing and waited patiently as I finished. When everything was in place, I severed the energy I'd been putting into the spell and watched people resume what they were doing.

To the others, it was as if the pinecones had just magically appeared in their hands. But Mrs. B and the other counselors knew what had really happened.

And they were impressed.

You know who wasn't? Brooklyn.

As soon as time went back to normal, the pinecone that I'd balanced perfectly on the top of her head began to fall and dropped onto the ground in front of her, narrowly missing the tip of her nose as it did so. She jumped back in surprise and then, realizing that I must have been behind it, she glared at me, unhappy about being the butt of any joke. Especially mine.

"Very impressive," Mrs. B said, closing up her notebook with a snap. "I can see that this is going to be a summer *full* of surprises."

"You have no idea," I answered, returning Brooklyn's stare.

Chapter Eight

I had to admit, I was feeling pretty good after our first twitch session. It was clear that I'd won whatever magical battle had been going on between Brooklyn and me. And logically, I'd won the guy, too. Because regardless of what she was spouting off to everyone else, Asher was *mine*.

So why was I letting her get to me like this?

Truth was, I'd felt off in general since arriving at Brighton. I don't know if it was the new surroundings or not being totally in charge, but something wasn't right. And whenever my life felt out of my control, I turned to the only thing that seemed to help clear my cluttered mind.

Fashion.

We had fifteen minutes to kill before dinner, and I used it to sneak back to the room and play dress-up. It was one of my favorite things to do, and after the day I'd had, I needed it.

I fully believed that a great outfit could change any mood. A fabulous frock, a badass biker jacket—each look had the power to transform its wearer. Right now I was craving comfort. And that's what fashion was for me. I loved it with a passion that was difficult to describe to others. I prided myself in knowing designers, paid attention to trends, and loved choosing looks for friends that would compliment their figures. A traffic-stopping outfit was like a breath of fresh air for me.

I pushed my key into the lock and let myself into our room, noting with relief that I was alone. It wasn't like I was doing anything wrong or embarrassing, but it would be a heck of a lot easier to zone out if I didn't have to talk or be sociable.

I wanted to be alone with my clothes.

Crossing the room, I vaulted easily over the circular couch and rubbed my hands together before placing them on the coffee table. I'd been itching to try the thing out since Colette had shown us what it did. The surface was cool and I could feel the vibrations from its magic penetrate my palms almost immediately. It was faint, like the buzz of a snack dispenser or fridge, but it was there.

"Fab Sugar," I said out loud.

Immediately, the surface of the table began to grow hazy and then showed one of my favorite fashion websites. I began to use the table like a touch-screen phone and navigated my way through stories and galleries, looking for things to try on.

Once I'd found a few, I stood up and concentrated on the first outfit I'd pulled. It was a gold couture gown that a bigtime actress had worn to a recent charity ball. Then, raising my hand above my head and moving it down my body like a scanner, I said the magic words.

"Alluvé magniosa."

My shorts and top elongated into a floor-length gown. Elaborate and intricate designs covered the bodice, accentuating my upper half in all the right places. The bottom flared out, giving a little bit of room for my legs to move in.

It was stunning—and according to the site, it retailed for about fifteen thousand. Not exactly appropriate camp wear, but that wasn't what this session was for anyway. This was more like window-shopping therapy.

And just because an outfit wasn't right for today didn't mean I couldn't find somewhere to wear it in the future.

Next!

I bit my lip with glee as I tried on the next outfit. This one was even more outrageous than the last and as I admired the cuts and angles of the design, I felt myself begin to calm down. After about five minutes, I was fully relaxed and prepared to take on whatever came next.

But I'd need a fierce outfit to do it in.

With a surge of excitement that I hadn't had all day, I chose my final outfit carefully. There was a lot to consider. I didn't want to wear anything too fancy to dinner; we were in the middle of nowhere, after all. But just because we were surrounded by woods, it didn't mean I had to rough it.

So I chose a sheer flowery dress that was short in the front and long in the back. As I walked, the fabric billowed behind me like a cape flapping in the wind. Conjuring a thin braided brown belt, I cinched the dress at the waist to break up the design. Another simple spell left my dark hair falling around my face in beachy waves. A swipe of a pale gloss across my lips and a pair of brown gladiator sandals later and I was heading out the door to meet the others.

The dining hall wasn't actually attached to the main house. It was located in what appeared from the outside to be a small cottage about a hundred feet from the amphitheater. With rows of flowers adorning each side of the path leading up to the building, it looked more like someone's grandmother's house than a cafeteria. In fact, it was hard to believe that we'd all be able to fit into such a small space.

Of course, when I stepped through the doors, it quickly made sense. They'd obviously used the same perception spell they'd used on the main house, because inside, the place was huge. Round tables were set up around the room, each with plenty of space between the next so people could spread out. The lights were dimmed just enough to soften things.

As I continued to check out the space, Jasmine walked right past me without a backward glance, and headed straight to the food line. Shaking my head, I followed suit, picking up my own tray and stepping in line behind her, not realizing how hungry I was until I saw what they were serving.

"Mac and cheese!" I exclaimed, suddenly feeling like the day was looking up. Individual bowls of ooey-gooey pasta covered the counter and I scanned the group looking for the biggest one. "It's a Brighton *miracle*."

"Craving comfort food, are we?" Jasmine asked, raising an eyebrow at me. "Don't skinny girls like you hate carbs or something?"

"Everything in moderation," I answered, not even bothering to be offended by her question. Happily, I'd never had to worry about my weight before. I was lucky to have great genes, and I'd always been active, both in self-defense and cheerleading. Throw in the occasional morning jogs with Dad and you had a body that could burn off just about anything.

"Lucky you," Jasmine muttered. I couldn't tell if she was joking or just being her usual "cheery" self. The truth was, our little black widow had nothing to worry about either. She had nice, muscular legs and a small waist. In fact, her boobs were the biggest things on her and nobody was going to complain about that.

I watched as Jasmine opted for the eggplant parmigiana and then picked up some kind of chocolaty volcano-looking contraption. Curious over what it was, I took one too, and then filled a glass with seltzer before heading out into the seating area.

"There are the others," she said, nodding to a table in the back. Colette, Abby, Fallon, Sascha, and Jinx were already sitting down and eating.

As we walked, I scanned the room to see if Brooklyn was there. I felt like I needed to know where she was at all times so I could be better prepared for her next attack. So far, that's what my interactions with her had felt like. Attacks.

When I didn't see her or her posse, I sat down next to Abby and picked up my fork. It wasn't lost on me that Asher hadn't shown up yet either. I hoped it was just a coincidence.

I stabbed at my mac and cheese, forcing myself to tune in to what the others were talking about around the table.

"Did they make you guys show them your toughest spells too?" Sascha asked Fallon.

"Yeah," he said between bites. "And I kicked serious magic butt."

"I'm sure you did," I said, trying to engage myself in the conversation.

"For real. I knew so much more than the other guys my age," he said.

"Thanks to our boot camp last fall," I said, bringing up the sessions we'd held leading up to our fight with the Parrishables.

"Thanks to me being *awesome*," he answered with a smile. Colette giggled next to him and Abby tried to hide a smile before placing a forkful of food into her mouth. This made him grin even wider.

I ignored him. "How did Asher do?" I asked instead.

"Fine, I guess," he said, sounding bored now that he wasn't talking about himself. "I wasn't in his group, though. He has these two other guys as roommates. I was with the guys I'm rooming with. Blew them out of the water, too."

"Okay, we get, we get it. You're the baddest witch here," I said.

"You said it, I didn't," Fallon said, getting another laugh out of Colette.

"Had," Jinx said suddenly. She'd been quiet up until then, sort of blending into the background and occasionally taking tiny bites of her food. A look at her plate showed that she'd barely eaten anything. I'd already devoured more than half of my plate and she'd been sitting there longer than I had. Either I was a human vacuum cleaner or Jinx had lost her appetite.

Jinx's expression remained stony as she discreetly pointed in the direction to our right. My head swung around and focused on the front of the dining area, where Asher was now walking, his tray heaped full of food.

Keeping in step beside him was Brooklyn.

The two stared at each other intently as they spoke in hushed tones. Brooklyn pushed a piece of hair out of her face and behind her ear as Asher leaned in to say something to her. He placed his hand on her back as they weaved through a group of kids who were heading back for seconds. My eyes narrowed as I watched them, and I let out a silent scream inside my head.

So much for my Zen attitude.

He said something else to Brooklyn and she smiled. I imagined them sharing a private moment. Asher's eyes found mine then, and his hand dropped to his side limply. Rage slowly filled me as he broke off from her then and headed straight over to where we were sitting. Following behind him were two guys, carrying their own full trays.

I set my eyes on my food and concentrated on taking another bite, when in reality I'd lost my appetite. I couldn't even enjoy the mac and cheese anymore. A shadow fell over me a few seconds later and then a seat scraped across the floor as Asher pulled it out next to me.

"Got room for three more?" he asked, his voice light and friendly. Like I hadn't seen what had just happened. "Guys, these are my roommates, Hudson and Dane."

"Hey," we all said in response.

"Sher here says this is your first time at Brighton," the guy that had been introduced as Hudson said, before digging into the feast in front of him.

Sher? Then it clicked. They were talking about Asher. We'd been at Brighton for like, a hot minute. How had they found time between classes and ex-girlfriend ogling to come up with nicknames for each other?

"*Sher*'s right," Jasmine said sarcastically. Asher gave her a look that told her to play nice.

"This is my fourth year at Brighton," Hudson said, like it was a badge of honor. "I practically grew up here."

Grew was the operative word in Hudson's case. The guy was about six feet tall and had a stocky athletic build to him. The chino shorts and polo shirt he was sporting made him look like your typical country-club jock. His dark hair was cut short—probably so it wouldn't get in the way when he played sports—and showed off his caramel-colored eyes perfectly.

All in all, he was good-looking and seemed friendly enough.

"And what about *you*?" Sascha asked, turning her full attention to the other guy, Dane. She'd abandoned her food as soon as the boys sat down, and was now leaning forward and resting her chin in her hands.

Uh-oh. Someone's looking boy-crazy again.

"Just two," Dane answered. "My pad is far from here, so my folks wouldn't let me come for years."

Dane's long, wavy blond hair fell into his face as he bent forward to take a bite, but he shook it away just before it landed in his food. Asher's other roommate was similarly attractive, with wide blue-green eyes and strong cheekbones. Thinner than Hudson and dressed in khaki cargo shorts and a printed tee, he gave off a lazy surfer vibe. His looks, combined with a super-cute accent, would make him a hot commodity among the female campers.

If Sascha had her way, though, he'd be off the market soon.

"Wait, where are you from?" Sascha asked, mesmerized.

"Australia," he responded.

"Told you chicks dig the accent," Hudson said, shaking his head. "It's not fair that the rest of us have to try so hard and all you have to do is *talk*."

"Australia? That's so *exotic*," Sascha said. Dane looked at her funny, but then smiled again easily. "Do you have a pet kangaroo?"

"No one keeps those vermin as pets," he said seriously. "'Roos are particularly vicious creatures. They can easily flatten a child with a single back-heel if you're not careful."

"No way," Sascha said, her eyes growing wide. "But they're so cute." As she said it, she looked sad, like her dreams of one day owning a pet kangaroo had been dashed.

"Hey, Had," Asher said quietly as Sascha continued to pepper Dane with questions about his life down under. "You okay?"

"Uh-huh," I said curtly. My brain was still burning with the image of Asher and Brooklyn walking into the dining hall together and I didn't trust myself to say much more without blowing up.

So I looked around the room like I was really interested in all the decorations, when I was really just trying to avoid him. I could feel him staring at me though, and willed myself not to give in and face him.

"You sure?" he asked me again.

"It's just . . . been a long day," I said passive-aggressively. It was true. It felt like the longest day in my life and I was totally over it.

I suddenly felt the need to flee. If I stuck around, I was going to explode and I didn't want to do it in front of the whole cafeteria. Standing up, I grabbed my now-empty tray and looked for the closest garbage. "I'm tired. I'm gonna head back to my room."

I waved to the others and then walked as confidently, and quickly, as I could away from Asher. But after a few steps, I felt him come up on my right.

"Had, we agreed no more lies. What's really wrong?" he said softly. I slowed down as I reached the garbage can and tossed out the remnants of my dinner. After taking a deep breath, I turned to face him.

"Okay, fine," I said, feeling the anger rushing out of me in waves. "How's your ex doing? It looked like you guys were having a pretty deep conversation."

A look of surprise crossed Asher's face before turning into a smile.

"Ahhh, so *that's* what's got you so worked up!" he said like he'd just cracked the Da Vinci Code.

"What are you talking about?" I said, annoyed by his smile.

Then he took my hand in his and kissed it softly. "You are so adorable when you're jealous," he said finally.

I narrowed my eyes at him before pulling my hand away and stalking off. He quickly caught up with me again, this time cutting in front of me and walking backward to keep me from getting away.

"Let me make something completely clear," I said through clenched teeth. "I am *not* jealous. I don't *do* jealous. In fact, I don't have anything to be jealous *of*."

As the words reached my ears, I realized they weren't true, despite the fact I desperately wished they were. I'd always thought that girls with jealousy issues just had low self-esteem. But now I was seeing that it was more than that.

Jealousy is like PMS. It makes us crazy and there is no cure.

And apparently I wasn't immune.

Asher nodded in concession, but didn't look the least bit convinced. "You're right. You have nothing to be jealous of," he agreed, bending forward to try to kiss me.

But I wasn't ready to let him kiss this away. I took a step back and his lips met air.

"I don't like the way she acts around you. Or the fact that you guys are having secret conversations," I said, turning and stalking back to the main house. "And I'm pretty sure she wants you back."

I didn't tell him that she'd said as much earlier.

"We aren't having *secret* conversations, Hadley. And she doesn't want me back. But we *do* have some things to clear up, and to do that, I'm gonna have to talk to her."

My mouth dropped open as he admitted that he was planning to talk to Brooklyn again.

He saw the look on my face and started to explain. "Look, there's some unfinished business between Brooklyn and me, and we both need closure. But that's all it is: *closure*," he said, grabbing onto my arm and forcing me to slow down.

"I thought that door was already *closed*," I said, upset.

"It is," he said, growing frustrated himself, and running a hand through his hair.

I hated that Brooklyn had once been privy to recognizing

mannerisms like this. It made me sick to my stomach.

Asher put his hands on both of my shoulders and looked at me seriously. "I was wrong back then, and I have to make things right. I think it's time you heard the truth about Brooklyn and me."

Then he told me the whole story.

Chapter Nine

Leading me out of the dry Colorado heat and into the chilly air conditioning of the lodge, Asher sat me down on the padded benches at the base of the enormous stone fireplace. A few people shuffled around us, heading back to their rooms for the night. I watched a girl just a few years younger than us walk along the second-floor walkway that hugged the four walls of the room before disappearing into one of the suites. Looking all the way up to the third floor and the ceiling beyond it, I was reminded of how deceptively large this place was.

It made me feel small.

"I'm not sure where to begin," Asher said, finally.

Well, I'm not sure I'm ready to hear this, so I guess we're even. Out loud I said nothing.

Looking down at his hands for a moment, Asher seemed to be collecting his thoughts. Then, he raised his eyes to mine and began to talk.

"Brooklyn and I went to school together before I moved in

with my aunt. I was interested in her back when she was just this quiet sort of clumsy girl with no friends, who blended into her surroundings."

"Um, how is that possible?" I cut in. "The girl is practically a *supermodel*. No way she was ever a wallflower."

Asher sighed. "That was *before*. Before she used magic to change herself," he said. "See, Brooklyn's parents were sort of weird about using magic—they were always worried that people would find out they were witches and persecute them—so they bound her powers until she turned sixteen."

"I've heard of low-magic households, but I thought they were just an urban legend. Like a well-adjusted former child star—you know they must exist but you've never seen one yourself," I said.

"Right. And if you deny a witch the right to cast for most of her life, she's likely to go a little crazy when she finally does get to use her powers. Which is exactly what she did. Brooklyn changed her hair, her height, her eye color—everything about herself to ensure that she would make a name for herself at our school. Only, she sort of became obsessed with becoming popular and was willing to do anything to achieve that. Even lie and cheat."

I knew something *about her was fake.*

"Wait, so, I don't understand why you think that you need to make things right with *her* if she was really that awful," I said, confused. "Sounds like she owes *you* an apology. Not the other way around."

"I'll get to that in a minute, but first, I have to tell you what broke us up. I want to be honest with you: I liked Brooklyn. A *lot*." I couldn't help but wince when he said this. Even though I knew that their relationship was in the past, it still hurt to think of him with *her*. "I liked her when nobody else knew who she was. Not only was she my first girlfriend, but she was one of the first witches I ever got close to. I trusted her, even when I began to catch her in lies. But then she started making decisions that hurt other people—innocent people—all so she could fit in with the group of popular kids at our school. We finally broke up when she kissed another guy."

I could tell the memory hurt him and I wondered how a person could be so messed up that she could cheat on *Asher*. He was practically perfect. Well, as perfect as a teenage boy could be. Still, I could understand Asher's decision to end things immediately. I would've done the same thing. No hesitation.

"While all of this was going on with Brooklyn though, things had started to get weird around my house," he continued. More people were coming back from dinner now, and Asher and I had to scoot closer together in order for me to hear him without his having to talk too loudly. I reached out hesitantly and took his hand, letting it rest on his leg. "My parents had begun to fight and were having whispered conversations whenever Abby and I were around. They got really overprotective and wanted us home all the time. At first I thought they were having problems in their marriage, even though that didn't make any sense because they never fought.

"The day that Brooklyn and I broke up, I decided to find out what was going on with my parents once and for all. My plan was to confront them both and try to make them work things out—go to therapy or something. But when I got there, my parents were gone, and Samuel Parris was waiting for me. And well, you know the rest."

I did, and the memory brought back pangs of sadness for every life that was lost at the hands of Samuel Parris and his clan. During the weeks after my mom was killed I'd had dreams and visions, which had made me feel like my mom and I were still connected. But now, there was nothing except the occasional feeling that she was with me. And even that had been diminishing lately.

At least the memory dreams I often had of my relatives' deaths hadn't extended to her yet. It wasn't exactly the way I wanted to remember her. In her last moments, screaming as the flames bit at her skin . . .

I shook my head to try to clear it of the grotesque image I'd just conjured.

"So, I left for my aunt's right after that. I had no idea that Brooklyn tried to meet me that day. I just left. No explanation, no note, no forwarding address. I disappeared and never looked back. Of course, there was a lot going on and I had some pretty rough stuff to deal with, but I still should've at least *e-mailed* her to let her know I was alive. Even though our relationship was over, it didn't mean I didn't still care about her."

My heart swelled with love for this guy who was so *good* that he worried about an ex's feelings despite everything she'd done. Not many guys his age would care, let alone try to atone for their own misdeeds.

"And then I moved and met you, and my life changed forever. It was *torture* lying to you. Not just because I fell in love with you, but because I know how lies can ruin a relationship. And I know how it feels to be betrayed. That's why I'm grateful every day that you gave me a second chance. You're a more forgiving person than I was, and I feel like I need to learn something from you. Let Brooklyn know that I'm not mad anymore. I can understand why people do things they wouldn't ordinarily, when something they care about is threatened. We all make mistakes."

Guilt swirled around inside my head as I realized that

Brooklyn might not be the evil villainess that I'd made her out to be. She was hurt over losing Asher, something I could totally understand. It must've been awful to have him just disappear like that, with no clue where he'd gone or why he'd left. Or whether he was okay. She'd probably beaten herself up ever since. Not that she wasn't *also* at fault. There were no excuses for what she'd done to him.

"Maybe I could be nicer to Brooklyn from here on out. It sounds like she's gone through a rough time," I said, forcing myself to try to see things from her perspective.

"She has in her own way," Asher said, looking around the room as if he were just noticing the other kids for the first time. "And truthfully, she's not as strong as you are, Had. That's one of the things that attracted me to you right off the bat. I knew you weren't the kind of person who'd let anyone influence her into doing something she didn't want to do. You're a leader, not a follower."

"Aw, shucks," I said, trying to lighten the mood. "If I'd have known our fights would end with you telling me how awesome I am, then I would've gotten mad at you a long time ago."

"As cute as you are when you're mad, I really hate fighting with you," he said.

"Me too," I said. "Let's try to avoid that in the future, okay?"

"Deal. I love you, Had," Asher said, placing his hand on my cheek and then brushing his fingers back until they were resting on the back of my neck. Pulling me toward him, he planted a soft, sweet kiss on my lips. "Nothing's ever going to change that."

"I know," I said quietly. Then I sighed and looked straight into his eyes. "Okay, I guess it makes sense for you to talk things through with her. You know, just to clear the air and everything. And I'll *try* not to kill her the next time I see her . . . which is

going to be, like, every second of every day for the next month."
Ugh.

Asher just laughed. "Thanks, babe," he said. "You don't
have to worry about Brooklyn, though. Promise."

The conversation with Asher helped to put my mind at ease.
Knowing the details of their relationship turned out to be oddly
comforting. What I'd been imagining had gone on between
them was so much worse than what had actually happened.

These were the times when having an active imagination
did *not* come in handy.

By the time we'd finished talking, the sun had already set,
and we were both exhausted, so Asher and I said our good
nights and went to our rooms. When I finally got to mine and
stepped inside, I saw that both Abby and Colette were already
there. Pajamas on and makeup off, the girls sat on their beds,
suspended several feet into the air.

"Hey," I said, locking the door behind me, and crossing to my
side of the room. I began to change out of my outfit, and then
slipped into a pair of boy shorts and a matching tank. Plopping
onto my bed, I lifted my feet onto the bedspread and waited as
the mattress lifted off the ground and joined the others.

"Everything okay?" Abby asked. She closed the book and
rested it in her lap. Her initiation of the conversation was yet
another in a long list of surprises that the day had brought.
When my brain finally caught up with my mouth, I smiled at
her gratefully.

"Yeah, Abby. Everything's fine," I said.

"You guys left so fast after dinner and we weren't sure
where you'd gone," Colette said. She was in the middle of
painting her toenails a lime green color. Well, technically, she
was using magic to apply the shade to her feet. I looked down

at my own naked nails and decided to join her. She tossed me a coral-colored bottle—the "it" shade of the summer—and I began to paint.

"We just . . . had some things to talk over," I said, cryptically.

"Like Brooklyn?" Colette asked, looking up from what she was doing.

"Among other things," I said, sneaking a peek over at Abby, who'd gone back to her book.

"Can I ask you something personal?"

Uh-oh.

"Sure," I said, reluctantly.

Colette let the brush fall back into the top of the polish and twisted the cap closed before tossing it to the end of her bed.

"I couldn't help but notice that your last name is Bishop," she started, slowly. "Well, either it's a coincidence and you have a *really* famous name—or you're *her*. If you don't want to talk about it, I totally understand, but just . . . wow."

I didn't usually mind talking about my lineage and I was happy to get off the subject of Brooklyn. The Bishop name still held weight in the witch world. And even though it was a lot to live up to, I welcomed the challenge. I was proud of Bridget—she was a strong, confident woman who was more powerful than any one man. But right now, I felt too distracted to deal with a Bishop fan.

But it was Colette, and so far she'd been pretty cool to me. So I humored her.

"I'm *her*," I said, forcing a smile onto my face though I wasn't really feeling it. "My great-great-great-great-great-grandmother was Bridget Bishop."

"That means *you* were the one who finally got rid of Samuel Parris!" she gushed, touching the corner of her glasses as she adjusted them.

"How do you know about that?" I asked, curious to find out how everyone seemed to know about what happened that night. It's not like we'd taken an ad out in the *Witchy Times* or anything.

"In case you hadn't noticed, I'm sort of a magic nerd? I keep my ears open to what's going on in the witching world and know all about the most influential witches. People have been talking about what you did for months now. It's really quite incredible, Hadley. It must've been so *scary*."

That was putting it mildly.

I looked over at Abby, wishing she'd take some of the attention away from me. After all, the story involved her just as much as it did the rest of us. I cleared my throat and went back to painting my nails.

"There were scary moments," I said carefully. "A lot of people were hurt—even killed—and we were left to fight them on our own. But we all really believed in each other, and the coven, and we came together in the end. It was really hard, but we did it."

"I can't believe you killed Samuel Parris and got rid of the Parrishables," she said in awe.

There was something about the way she said it that didn't sound quite right. For one, I still wasn't entirely sure they were gone. Many of Samuel's followers had gotten away that night, and were probably pretty pissed that a group of twitches had thwarted their evil plan for total witch-world domination. Not to mention that if horror movies had taught us anything, it's that the bad guy *always* came back. But what was I supposed to do? Burst her safe little bubble and tell her I didn't think he was gone for good? Some people deserved the chance to live joyously free of worry.

Besides, I would worry enough for all of us.

"It wasn't just *me* that night, you know," I said instead. "Every single Cleri member helped to stop the Parrishables. We couldn't have done it without each other."

I knew that this was true, even if Samuel had been under the impression that I was stronger than the rest of my coven members. Trying to fight Samuel alone had almost gotten me killed, and it hadn't been until all of us had banded together that we'd become a force to be reckoned with.

I hoped that Abby was listening now. She may not have been by our side during the actual showdown, but it didn't mean she hadn't been just as brave. Or that she hadn't been an integral part in taking Samuel down. But most importantly, I wanted everyone to know that the success hadn't only been mine.

"I can't believe my roommate is *the* Hadley Bishop," Colette squealed. Then she turned to me. "How lucky am I?"

I didn't want to tell her it depended on whom she was asking.

Chapter Ten

I awoke to the sound of chirping birds. Only, the noises weren't coming from outside. I could hear them as clearly as if the bird was perching right on the pillow next to my head. It made it practically impossible to remain asleep. The alarm turned out to be just another magical touch of our room—something we learned when the chirping finally stopped as the last of our beds was once again resting firmly on the floor.

"I suppose there are worse ways to be woken up," I said, yawning as we walked to the dining hall together.

It was only eight in the morning, but the sun was already high in the sky and heating things up fast. We were in for another scorcher and luckily I was dressed for the weather *and* whatever we had planned for the day. The counselors had warned us that mornings would be spent on practical spell-work, while the afternoons would be focused primarily on magical history.

So I'd dressed in clothes that I could cast in. For me, that meant bright purple spandex shorts and a matching black-and-purple halter workout top. My hair was pulled back into a high ponytail with a strand of braided hair wrapped around the rubber band. The look reminded me of my cheerleading days and I grew nostalgic just thinking about it. Cheering had been one of the highlights of my high school experience. I'd felt absolutely free as I flew through the air and pumped up the crowd and sports teams.

The relationships I'd had with my teammates had been incredible, too. I think the bond between cheerleaders is unlike any other. The fact that someone else lifted you high up into the air and then actually *caught* you when you fell . . . it took a lot of trust to believe they had your back. Literally.

In a way, the Cleri had become my new squad. Although it was taking longer to get to the "total trust" phase in our relationship—having one of your former members switch sides and betray you makes you think that *anyone* could be an enemy—I think we were on our way. Defeating the Parrishables had bonded us all in a way that was difficult to describe. We'd been in the trenches together. Had been through unimaginable loss, and near life-and-death situations side-by-side. Though I wouldn't describe us all as BFFs, we were closer than any group of misfits could be. And I knew that if the magic hit the fan, I could trust them to be there for me.

I looked back at Abby, who was dragging ass behind us. She hadn't said much as we'd gotten ready that morning. Since it was my first time staying with her overnight, I didn't know if she was just a grumpy morning person. Colette, on the other hand, was like a walking, talking Disney character after waking up. She'd danced around the room to music while piecing together another elaborately colorful outfit. This time, a poufy teal tulle skirt with thin black stretch capris, a tank top with the face of a heavily made-up woman on the front, and black lace gloves. When I'd asked her about it, she answered, "Another original from Aunt Betsey!" Watching her pass by was like spotting a rainbow on steroids.

We walked inside the hall and filled our trays with a variety of breakfast items and then headed to the same table we'd sat at the night before. Only about a third of the camp was up this early, most opting for more sleep in lieu of food.

As I picked at a bowl of fruit, Abby let out a big yawn and then rested her chin on her hand, her eyes drooping to tiny slits.

"Didn't sleep well last night?" I asked.

She shook her head. "I barely slept at *all*. Weird dreams," she said.

"What about?" Sascha asked as she appeared from behind us and sat down next to me. I looked up as Jinx and Jasmine sat down too. "I'm excellent at deciphering dreams. Like, once I dreamed that a steamroller kept going over and over this pile of money. It was absolutely terrifying. Anyway, I'm pretty sure it was all about financial fear. I'd totally been wanting this designer handbag at the time and my dad wouldn't give me an advance on my allowance—"

"I don't remember my dreams," Abby cut in before taking a sip of coffee.

"Ever?" I asked, surprised. Considering the vividness of my Bridget dreams, it was difficult to imagine that others could forget what went on while they were asleep.

"Not really," Abby confirmed.

"I wish I had the same problem," Jinx said, looking just as tired as Abby.

"You couldn't sleep either?" I asked, surveying the circles under her eyes. "Guess it's something in the air."

Jinx just shrugged in response.

"Speaking of air, I fly in my dreams," Jasmine said, cutting into a thick waffle hungrily.

"You know, flying in dreams is actually rare. I think it means you have extreme intelligence or something," Sascha said. "Or is it extreme creativity? I always forget which it is."

"Either way, I rock," Jasmine said, with a smile. Her lips were painted deep purple, which perfectly matched her outfit and eye makeup. "As a kid, I used to fly out of nightmares and go to my happy place."

"And where is Jasmine's happy place?" Asher asked as he kissed me on the cheek before sitting down. Hudson and Dane followed behind him, saying a quick hello before digging into their piles of food. I watched with amusement as Sascha instantly sat up straighter, and began to twirl her hair around her finger.

"Somewhere Asher Astley doesn't exist," Jasmine said sarcastically. "In fact, none of you are there. It's only the people I can stand."

"So, just you?" I answered with a laugh.

"Exactly."

Asher and I looked at each other across the table and for a moment I felt like everything was back to normal. It was us against the world. I sighed and began to daydream about going on long walks through the forest with Asher and holding hands while studying the starlit skies. It all seemed incredibly romantic.

I hadn't realized I'd zoned out until the clanking of plates hitting trays pulled me out of my thoughts. Everyone was packing up around me and heading to the exits. I took a few more bites of my fruit and then followed right behind Asher. I slipped my hand into his, and the group of us took our time walking to the back-to-back amphitheaters. When we reached the girls' side, Asher gave me a flirty wink, which left a tingle in my stomach, and then disappeared with the other guys.

As I turned around, I noticed that Brooklyn was already there and watching us. There was a frown on her face and at first I was tempted to return the look.

Except, I'd promised Asher that I'd try to be nice to her.

I took a deep breath and told myself that I *could* be the bigger person. That it wouldn't *actually* kill me to hand Brooklyn an olive branch and try to call a truce. I mean, if Asher had dated her, she couldn't be *all* that bad, right? Who knows . . . maybe we'd even become friends.

Stranger things had happened.

Telling the others I'd be right back, I started to walk over to where Brooklyn and her friends were standing. When it became clear that I was headed for her, she stood up a little straighter and whispered something to Eve, who was standing to her left.

"Exes are people too," I muttered to myself when I was just a few feet away from her.

"Hi, Brooklyn," I said as nicely as I could muster. "Can I talk to you a minute?"

I didn't want to do this in front of Eve and the others, especially considering the fact that the tinier, dark-haired girl was already giving me the stink-eye. This was between Brooklyn and me—nobody else needed to be involved.

Brooklyn shot Eve a look that I couldn't quite discern and then began to walk away from her friends. She didn't go far though, stopping after only a few steps, and I knew that the others would hear everything we said.

"Look, I think we got off on the wrong foot," I started, looking her in the eye. She wasn't exactly avoiding my gaze, but she did seem slightly bored. Then again, maybe it was just her thinking face. "Asher told me what happened between you two and he hopes you can still be friends. And well, I was hoping we could be friends, too."

Or at least *friendly.*

But Brooklyn seemed unmoved by my speech. It took her so long to respond, in fact, that I wondered if she'd been listening at all. Finally, her eyes narrowed and she took a step toward me. I immediately felt like she was invading my personal space and stepped back reflexively.

"Wow. Thank you *so* much Hadley for giving me *permission* to be friends with Asher," she started nastily. "And forgive me if I don't fall all over myself at your invitation of friendship."

"Huh?" I asked, not quite sure where all her hostility was coming from.

"And I find it hard to believe that he told you *everything* about us, because if he had, you'd know that Asher and I aren't capable of being *just* friends," she said.

Then she took another step toward me, but this time I stood my ground. She was taller than me by a few inches, but I was stronger than her. If she was actually stupid enough to start something, I was pretty sure I could take her.

"Asher told me enough. He said you were *no one* before you guys started dating," I fired back, my irritation growing. "He said you gave yourself some sort of 'extreme makeover' after you came into your powers, and that you were *obsessed* with becoming popular."

This time it was Brooklyn who needed a second to recover. But I hadn't disarmed her completely.

"News flash, Hadley: Asher was the one who sought *me* out. He brought me into his circle, taught me most of my early spells, and watched after me. He said that he *loved* me," she said. "You can't just turn those feelings off."

"No, I think you did that job yourself by cheating on him," I said, angrily. "Dumbest decision you ever made, by the way. Because when he left you, he came straight to *me*."

Brooklyn sucked in a breath and for a second I wondered if I'd gone too far. I had no idea how she was going to react or just how far she would go. I prepared myself for the worst.

"You have no clue what happened between us or *what* my life is like," she hissed. "And you certainly aren't going to dictate whether Asher and I will be friends. In fact, I think I'll be talking to him as much—and as often—as I want in the future. Because you may rule over your coven, but *I'm* the ruler of this camp. And *nobody* tells me what to do."

I fought to keep my composure. I'd dealt with plenty of people in school who'd attempted at one point or another to overthrow me. But none of them had been a match. Whoever Brooklyn had been back when Asher had dated her, she wasn't that girl now. No way he'd knowingly date someone so downright vile.

I forced myself to keep my breathing even, despite the fact that my whole body felt like it was on fire. I shook slightly and knew I needed to get out of there before I exploded. Instead, I took a step toward Brooklyn, and then another, until we were practically nose-to-nose. I saw a flash of fear in her eyes, but she didn't move.

"Clearly you have no idea who *I* am, otherwise you'd be careful not to threaten me or the people I care about. Samuel Parris did that and now he's *gone*. Let me be perfectly clear, Brooklyn: Asher. Is. Mine. You can try to get him back all you want, but he will *never* love you again. So, a word of advice? Don't embarrass yourself," I said, not even knowing what I was saying until it was already out of my mouth. It was like an out-of-body experience. When I was finally able to force my legs to move again, I started to walk backward, my eyes trained on her. She was still standing there, slack-jawed and silent. "And Brooklyn? Take it from someone who defined the word popular—you can't make yourself into something you're not."

My ponytail nearly whipped me in the face as I turned and walked back to the rest of the Cleri. They were all standing stock-still, in the same places they'd been when I'd left them. Jasmine was giving me a Cheshire Cat grin, Jinx was looking around at the other campers nervously, and Sascha seemed genuinely surprised by the confrontation. I avoided looking at Abby, because I was still pissed about what had happened and wasn't ready to admit that I may have gone a bit overboard.

I'd been harsh—mean, even. My stomach felt queasy and my hands were still shaking. But I'd tried to be nice to her. I'd given her the benefit of the doubt, but she'd come out swinging. I'd simply defended myself and my relationship. Brooklyn had been the one to start this thing. Not me.

"Nice show," Jasmine said, holding out her fist to bump mine. I ignored her, and instead, began to stretch for the session we were about to start.

"What was *that* about?" Sascha asked carefully.

"It was about a witch not knowing her place," I said.

"It looked like it was almost a catfight," Colette said.

"Please let there be a catfight," Jasmine answered, too happily.

I rolled my eyes. "I'm not resorting to violence," I said. Then I paused to think about what I'd just stated. "Unless I have to."

"Whoop!" Jasmine yelled out suddenly. "We haven't seen Hardass Hadley since we were training for war! It's nice to have her back. She has all the best lines."

"Well, war is what Brooklyn's gonna get if she keeps it up,"

I said. "I thought if I talked to her, maybe we could find a way to coexist at this camp. But it looks like she wants to do things the difficult way."

"I *love* the difficult way," Jasmine said, clapping her hands together.

"Can we, just for once, *not* be the ones fighting a whole slew of angry witches? Please?" Jinx asked in a meek voice.

"I hope she backs off, Jinx," I answered. "But if she doesn't, don't expect me to be Mrs. Nice Witch."

Chapter Eleven

Brooklyn and I kept our distance during the rest of the session, choosing to stay as far away from each other as possible. This was difficult considering the camp wasn't all that big to begin with. At first, I was still buzzing from the confrontation, but once the counselors started class, I was able to get lost in the lessons. Magic can be an incredible distraction, and considering what the elders had us doing, we needed all our concentration just to keep up.

"Yesterday we got to see where you're all at in terms of your magical abilities and today we're going to start honing those skills," said Miss Peggy, who'd exchanged her vest for a T-shirt today, but had somehow transferred all her pins and buttons to its surface. Because of this, she made noise every time she took a step, like a cat with a bell around its neck. At least we always knew when she was coming. "It's important to know the basics before you move on. Even the simplest of spells can be an asset to a witch, but if you don't know how to use them properly, then they'll be practically useless."

"You're all familiar with explosion spells," a woman said, stepping forward onstage. I recognized her from the day before as one of the other counselors. Her name was Mrs. Jeanette and she had long blond hair that was pulled back into a braid, which lay down her back. She was pretty in a natural way, choosing to walk around without a stitch of makeup on. Colette had explained that she was an independent contractor for the US Department of Defense. Nobody knew exactly what it was she did for them but there were plenty of guesses. I had a feeling that the fact that she was talking to us about explosion spells wasn't a coincidence. "We're going to begin today by working on your accuracy, speed, and strength at one of the most basic of spells."

"We'll be heading into the woods, where we'll commence our first lesson. Please gather your things and follow us," Miss Peggy said and walked off the stage.

"At least it should be a bit cooler under the trees," Sascha said, wiping the sweat from her brow.

"Not by much," Jinx said, looking even worse now than she had that morning.

"Diminuous gustovo," I said, waving my hand around Jinx's head. Almost immediately, her hair was being blown off her face by a tiny blast of air as if she had her own personal fan with her.

She sighed with relief and looked at me gratefully. "Thanks, Had," Jinx said. "That's a lot better." I performed the same spell on the rest of the girls, and then finished up on myself. It was a welcome treat in the extreme heat and within minutes we all felt cooler.

Stepping over logs and through fallen brush, I silently thanked the fact that I'd had the foresight to wear tennis shoes and workout clothes rather than my usual getups. Navigating the woods in heels would've been hell.

The woods were beautiful. Strands of light slipped through branches and hit the ground around us as we walked into the canopied area. We tried to stay on the dirt paths that looked to have been carved into the earth. We stopped about twenty feet inside, and the counselors turned to face us.

We were told to spread out into a straight line across the woods, facing away from the campgrounds. Not close enough to touch the person next to us, but also not so far that we felt alone. I wondered what we were about to do and my palms began to itch with excitement.

"Wooden disks such as this will soon appear in front of each of you," Miss Peggy said, holding up a round slice of wood colored with a red-and-white bull's-eye in the middle. It was about three feet around and no more than two inches thick—an easy target for even the most undeveloped witch. "We'd like you to attempt to hit all your targets, and we will increase the difficulty accordingly. When we are finished, you will all be ranked based on your accuracy. This session will begin *now*."

Miss Peggy, Mrs. B, and Mrs. Jeanette each took their places behind us, where they wouldn't be in danger of any stray spells. The rest of us took our preferred casting stances and geared up for what seemed like magical target practice. Seconds later, dozens of wooden rounds lifted up into the air about fifteen feet in front of us.

"Are they serious with this?" Jasmine asked, as we saw how close the objects were to us.

I shrugged and raised my arm. "Looks like it."

I called out the spell and watched the disk explode easily. Jasmine did the same, and then I watched with pride as the rest of the Cleri hit their targets too.

"Well done," Miss Peggy said and then called up the next round. This time they were pulled back to twenty-five feet.

"There we go," I said as I prepared to cast again. Still hitting the bull's-eye easily, I looked around and waited for the other twitches to finish their rounds.

Each time, the targets were sent back ten more feet and we were all given a chance to reach them. As people missed their pieces of wood, they were forced to stay at that distance until they were able to successfully hit them. Within ten minutes, some of us had pulled ahead of the pack. Jasmine, Colette, and I were in the lead, and annoyingly, Brooklyn and Eve were progressing as well.

When the targets finally became so small that we could barely discern them from the rest of the woods, we were told to relax as the counselors set the stage for the next phase in our class.

"This next section will test your ability to multitask and work under pressure," Mrs. Jeanette said. "A good witch should be able to cast one spell, while focusing on her surroundings. Not only for defensive purposes, but also to become more successful in her casting life. Quick thinking and multi-casting will come in handy more often than you think."

"For this, we will break you up into groups of ten and ask you to take turns practicing," Miss Peggy said. "Please don't be discouraged if you don't hit every target. Very few witches your age can. This is a skill that you'll develop over time."

Though I knew this was likely true, I still planned to hit every target they threw my way. And from the looks on some of the other twitches' faces, I could tell they had the same idea.

We lined up in our groups and watched as the first person in each line stepped forward to hit the moving targets that were now being controlled by the counselors. The first few people in our section each hit the first and second targets that flew into the air, but as more and more began to appear and fly by, they got flustered and sent spells randomly into the woods.

When it was finally my turn, I stepped forward and rolled my shoulders before planting my legs firmly on the ground. I took a deep breath and let my mind grow quiet, focusing on the sound of the air moving in and out of my lungs. Letting my eyes rest on the space in front of me without focusing on anything in particular, I tried to prepare myself for the disks that would be flying from any direction.

"You've got this, Hadley!" I heard someone say from behind me, but by this point it was just background noise.

Before I even saw it, I heard the whooshing sound of the first wooden round slice through the space in front of me. I hit it before it had barely been cast into the air. The second came around the same time the first target exploded and my head shot to the right and zeroed in on it. It quickly became one piece of wood after another until they were all a blur. I missed a few targets, but I was still confident that I'd hit more than anyone else so far.

"Very impressive, Hadley," Mrs. J said with an encouraging nod. "You hit twenty-five out of the thirty targets."

I beamed at the compliment, but inside I was slightly annoyed that the number hadn't been higher. Now that I knew that others were aware of what had happened with the Parrishables, I was feeling a bit of pressure to live up to whatever expectations that created.

"Next up!"

Colette took my place and I moved toward the back, and then stopped to watch her. There was still plenty I didn't know about my new roommate, including her casting abilities. She seemed to be pretty knowledgeable when it came to history and current affairs, but intelligence and practical application were two totally different things.

"Ready," she said, after tweaking her oversize glasses until they were secure on her face.

The first disk appeared and Colette's head turned quickly in its direction. Whipping her hand around her head like an imaginary lasso, she shot her hand out in front of her and the wooden round shattered. It was as if she was using her arm as a magical whip and the cracking sound it made when it hit home echoed through the woods.

Suddenly she had the attention of everyone at camp.

We all watched in awe as Colette continued to hit target after target with her wild arm motions and moves. When the final piece was split in half, she stood back, breathing hard and looking like she was still expecting more. The rest of us remained where we were, completely silent as we processed what the quirky oddball had just done.

Mrs. B cleared her throat loudly. "I can honestly say I've never seen anything quite like that, Miss Jordan," she said. "And I've never seen numbers like this from a student. You hit twenty-seven out of thirty of your targets."

Colette smiled and nodded at her, and then skipped her way to the back of the line. I followed behind her, amazed by what she'd done. A part of me was jealous she'd done better than me, but I was mostly just impressed.

I shook my head at her, incredulously.

"What?" she asked, looking at me sideways. I wasn't sure whether she was joking or really that humble, but I decided it didn't matter. I had to find out how she'd done it.

"Um, nice shooting there, Indiana," I said.

"But I'm from Texas," she said, looking confused.

"I think she was implying that you're like Indiana Jones," said Abby, who'd joined us silently.

"How did you do that?" I asked.

"I used to rope cattle," she answered.

I blinked at her, trying to picture the colorful girl in front of me, kicking up dust and taking down fully-grown cows. It was hard to imagine and even harder to understand how that had translated to exploding spells.

"So, more rope and less whips," I said finally.

"Right," she said.

"Wow, okay, well, you're just chock-full of surprises aren't ya?" I said, clapping her on the back.

She just smiled.

"Speaking of surprises," Jasmine said, cutting in. "Blondie's up next. Wonder what she has up her sleeve."

I turned to find Brooklyn walking to the front of the line and taking her place confidently. As the wood was let loose, she began to cast, chips flying into the air around her. After I saw the ease of her accuracy, my stomach started to drop.

Please don't let her get a higher number than me.

After what had happened between us earlier, I couldn't afford to be shown up by Brooklyn or her friends. I knew that from here on out, everything would be a competition between us. Who was the better girlfriend? Who was more powerful? Who had the fiercest outfit—it would all be tallied up in private and held against us in this battle we'd begun.

I strained to hear Mrs. Jeanette as she counted up Brooklyn's stats, holding my breath as I waited.

"Nice, Miss Sparks," she said finally. "You got twenty-five out of thirty. Looks like you've improved since last summer."

"Thank you," she answered politely. "But I know I can do better."

When she said this last line, she glanced my way as if it were directed right at me. And that was fine, because so could I.

"Well, you'll have all summer to do so," Mrs. Jeanette said. "For now, this is a solid start."

"Okay everyone, really great job today," said Miss Peggy. "I think we've all learned that simply knowing how to cast a spell isn't enough. If your target is moving or stands at a far distance, you'll need more focus, more power, and more practice to hit it. These things don't come naturally. It takes practice and time, just like honing any other skill.

"We will be going over these kinds of drills throughout the summer and encourage you to practice on your own time. The woods are available to all of you for this specific reason, but we implore you to be smart while casting. That means: be aware of those who might be in the area around you. We don't want anyone ending up in the infirmary because of a stray spell. Stay within the area we had you in today and don't wander too far into the woods. It's easy to get turned around if you're not familiar with the land. And lastly, the woods are absolutely *off-limits* at night. This is nonnegotiable and for your own personal safety. Please don't test us on this, because you *will* be sent home."

I glanced over at the rest of the Cleri and gave them a curious look.

"With that said, we look forward to helping you grow into your magicking skills, and become useful and productive young witches," Miss Peggy said, much too enthusiastically. "You are all released for lunch now."

Once dismissed, we all began to walk back toward the dining hall. Even with our magic fans and the cover of the trees, I was sweating, and longed for the iciness of the Brighton buildings.

"What was with the ominous warning?" I asked Colette as we followed the path back.

"It's because of the Witch in the Woods," she answered.

"The Witch in the Woods?" Jasmine asked. "Who else would be out there? We're at freaking witch camp."

"It's just one witch in particular they're worried about," Colette said. "There've been rumors about her for years, wandering the grounds."

"Why are they concerned about it if it's just an urban legend?" I asked.

Colette looked over at me as we emerged from the last of the trees and stepped out into the sun. But she was no longer her chipper self. Her face was deadly serious.

"Because she's real."

Chapter Twelve

"Come again?" Jasmine asked, raising her eyebrow skeptically.

"The Witch in the Woods isn't just some folktale," Colette repeated. "She's real."

"What *is* the story of the Witch in the Woods, Colette?" I asked her gently.

By now, we were in line at the cafeteria and loading up our plates with chicken fingers and fries. Momentarily distracted by our food, Colette waited until we were seated again to ply us with the details.

"Moll Brenner was seventeen when Brighton first opened its doors in 1864. Of course, back then things weren't as extravagant as they are now. Like I said the other day, the grounds themselves change every year to reflect advances in technology, pop culture, and, of course, magic. But in 1864, it was just a simple structure that met the needs of the witches who stayed here that first summer.

"Still, the bare necessities didn't stop witches from wanting to come. The owners, Mr. and Mrs. Klenderston, were selective about attendees, even back then. That first year, there were only thirteen boys and thirteen girls found worthy enough to get an invitation. Each was picked based on their lineage, magical abilities, and natural talents. Moll Brenner was one of those lucky enough to be picked."

Colette paused as if she were remembering what it must have been like for Moll to be asked to attend the exclusive camp in its inaugural year. She was probably just as excited as Colette was the first time she'd been invited. Only, from the look on her face, this story didn't end as happily.

"At first she was excited about going, but when she got there, she didn't really fit in with the other kids. She had wild hair and was sorta awkward and sometimes talked to herself. Kids thought she was dirty, even though she bathed regularly. Moll didn't care about the other campers though, and preferred to spend her time walking through the woods alone to making friends. This, and the fact that she was an incredibly talented witch, made her an easy target for bullying. It didn't take the others long to start harassing her.

"The campers would cast spells to trip her when she walked by. They claimed she was into black magic and even started rumors that she had funky diseases, so that people would stay far away from her. She became a pariah, and pretty soon, even the counselors stopped being friendly to her. Moll tried not to let any of it bother her, but this only seemed to make the others more aggressive in their taunting."

Colette's face scrunched up in anger. I couldn't help but sympathize with Moll, too. Only, I wasn't sure what this had to do with the present situation.

"One night, about halfway through the camp session, a group of kids who really seemed to have it in for Moll woke her up in the middle of the night and convinced her to go with them to a secret place where they would initiate her into their group. They explained that they'd been hard on her because they needed to know if she was strong enough to be one of them. Nobody knows why she agreed to go. Moll was a smart girl; she had to have known they were up to something. But whatever the reason, she went along.

"They blindfolded her and took her out into the woods. After a half hour they stopped walking and instructed her to keep her blindfold on as they set up the site for the initiation ceremony. They sat her down on a big rock nearby and left her to wait by herself.

"Of course the campers had no intention of letting her be one of them. Once they sat Moll down, they all crept away and then raced back to the lodge. By the time Moll realized that they'd lied, she was totally lost. Because of the blindfold, she had no idea which direction to go in and despite all the times she'd wandered in the woods before, nothing looked familiar to her anymore."

Colette stopped talking then, picking up a french fry and dipping it into the bright red ketchup before placing it in her mouth. The rest of us were sitting around her, waiting for her to continue, completely caught up in the hell that Moll had experienced.

"Well? What happened to Moll?" Sascha asked, finally.

"They never saw her again," Colette said sadly. "When she didn't show up for classes the next day, the counselors started asking questions. And when she was still gone at dinnertime, the kids who'd led her into the woods finally admitted what they'd done. The counselors called a search to try to find her, but it was as if she'd just *disappeared*. They eventually found the large rock that Moll had been sitting on when the others had left her, but she was no longer there. There *was* something left behind though, something that proved Moll had indeed been there. Two distinct handprints in the rock, like they'd been burned into the solid surface.

"They nearly closed Brighton for good after that, but the owners decided that with a slew of new counselors and magical safety precautions in place, there shouldn't be another tragedy like they'd had with Moll," Colette said. "And there hasn't been."

We sat there quietly, wondering what it would be like to be left all alone like that. For a while, none of us spoke. We had no idea what to say.

"If Moll was at camp in 1864, then she'd be around 115 today if she even survived that night," I asked gently. "So why do people still think it's her that's doing this?"

"Weird stuff has happened around here since then. Flickering lights, whispers, shadows appearing out of nowhere. Things have been stolen from rooms, odd messages have been left in unusual places. The adults all explain it away, but it's pretty clear that it's Moll. I mean, the same things wouldn't still be happening now if it were just campers pulling pranks."

"So, you think she's *haunting* the woods, trying to get back at those who did that to her? Like . . . as a ghost?" I asked, trying to put the pieces together.

"Well, yeah. But not getting back at them per se. After all, she never really *hurts* anyone," Colette said, appearing to be working through her thoughts as she talked. "Maybe she's just making sure nobody forgets about her."

"Moll's a ghost," I said, rolling the words over my tongue to see how they felt. It would make sense as to why the adults wouldn't want us wandering into the woods alone. And the

Cleri *had* seen the ghosts of our ancestors during our fight against Samuel, so the idea wasn't entirely impossible. Only, this situation was slightly different. No one was calling on Moll, she was sort of just stuck here.

As crazy as it sounded, I could tell we all believed what Colette was saying. We knew what it was like to have what others figured was an "urban legend" suddenly prove to be real. The most dangerous thing we could do now would be to ignore the possibility completely.

"With weak-ass pranks like that, girl's never gonna get the recognition she wants," Jasmine said, finally, breaking through our thoughts. We all gave her a look, which elicited her signature eye-roll. "All I'm saying is if you don't like the way you're being treated, do something about it. If Moll wants us to know she's still out there, ghost girl needs to step it up a bit. Go big or go home."

I turned this all over in my head. If I were in Moll's shoes, would I want to stick around a world that had betrayed me? Punish those who were responsible for my unhappiness? Or fight fate instead of moving on peacefully?

In the end, there was no good answer. I just hoped I wouldn't have to find out for myself.

Asher didn't come to lunch.

Neither did Brooklyn.

I didn't want to assume they were somewhere together, but I knew it was possible. After all, I'd given him the green light to clear things up with her in the first place, so I couldn't really be surprised when he followed through.

Even if I'd agreed on it before Brooklyn had made it clear that we were not going to be friends.

Like, ever.

Although Colette's story of the Witch in the Woods had kept me sufficiently distracted for the first part of lunch, it hadn't taken me long before I'd gone back to silently seething over the situation between Asher and his ex.

Just wait it out. Once Asher makes things right between him and Brooklyn, he won't have any reason to spend time with her anymore, and things will go back to normal.

Trudging back to our afternoon session with far less enthusiasm than I'd had that morning, I tried to direct my attention to anything other than Asher and Brooklyn. The other Cleri members chatted among themselves, which gave me something to focus on until Miss Peggy began to talk.

Witch history had always been my least favorite part of our coven classes back home. For a while, I'd been convinced that learning about the past was a waste of time. I mean, it was just so *boring*. And where was the practical application of this knowledge? Sure, we didn't want to repeat the mistakes of our past, but some of witching history was so behind us that it didn't necessarily have any validity in our lives today.

Or so I'd thought.

History had somewhat repeated itself when Samuel Parris came back to try to wipe out our coven, much like he'd done to members of the Cleri during the Salem witch trials. It was only through learning more about our familial past that we were able to finally defeat him.

But I think the real origin of my disdain for history stemmed from the fact that I couldn't seem to get away from the dreams of my ancestor during her darkest days. Reliving a person's death and betrayal over and over again had a way of taking a toll on your soul. In a way, it was a morbid way to live.

So you could see why I wasn't exactly psyched to spend more time analyzing the actions of witches past. Yet here I was.

"There are many witches in our history who have made significant contributions to us as a society," Mrs. B said. "We will be spending the next month getting to know these famous witches as well as a few lesser-known ones. But don't be confused, each witch you will learn about can teach you a valuable lesson about our heritage."

"We'd like to invite you all to come up now to choose your research project topics," Miss Peggy said, holding up a purple velvet bag. "Once you have the name of your witch, it will be up to you to learn as much as you can about them. How you report what you find to us is up to you. During our last week here, you'll all be required to deliver your findings."

"We recommend that you take this project seriously," said Mrs. Jeanette. "Because if you don't, you will not be asked back next summer. Learning from those who've come before you is incredibly important. It's both a sign of respect and appreciation for the sacrifices these great witches have made."

"I thought school was out for the summer," Jasmine said under her breath as we all stood up and filed into a single line to retrieve our topics.

"Oh, but this part is *so* much fun, Jasmine!" Colette said, clapping her hands together. "Last year I drew Evelyn Rogers, the first witch to explore other planets in our solar system. It was so intriguing to learn that she landed on the moon before Neil Armstrong, and was instrumental in encouraging the US to send our astronauts up into space. She paved the way for all atmospheric exploration."

"Apparently she wasn't the only space cadet," Jasmine said.

"Jasmine!" I said, horrified by her comment.

"It's all right, Hadley," Colette answered, her smile never leaving her face. "Some of the most important people in history were labeled as weirdoes by their peers. My Aunt Betsey says you can't be afraid to live outside the box, because that's the only place you're not boxed in."

I admired Colette's ability to stand up for herself, but shot Jasmine a warning look anyway. We didn't need the other campers labeling our coven as troublemakers.

The line was moving quickly now, as each person pulled a piece of paper out of the bag and then wandered off to huddle in smaller groups and share their assignments with their friends. When it was my turn, I stepped forward and shoved my manicured hand into the hole. My fingers brushed dozens of folded-up pieces of paper until it reached one that just felt *right*. And being that I was trying to trust my instincts more, I pulled it out and stepped back.

When I was far enough away, I opened up the paper and read the name of whom I'd be learning about.

YOUR WITCH IN HISTORY IS: Sarah Good

BRIEF DESCRIPTION: One of the first people accused during the Salem witch trials, Sarah Good was found guilty of witchcraft and sentenced to death by hanging on July 19, 1692. She was survived by her daughter, Dorothy Good.

I just can't get away from it, can I?

I laughed out loud at the irony of my assignment. I suppose I shouldn't have been surprised. For some reason, this awful incident kept inserting itself back into my life. Why would camp be any different?

"You got Sarah Good?!" Colette asked, looking over my shoulder at the paper that I still held open.

"Yep," I said, folding it back up and handing it out to her. "Wanna trade?"

"You don't want her?" she asked, her eyebrows wrinkling in confusion.

"She kind of hits a little close to home for me," I said with a sigh.

As if on cue, Miss Peggy called out, "Please don't trade topics with fellow campers." A look around showed that I wasn't the only one less than enthused about my research topic. Plenty of people in other groups were complaining and trying to get rid of their subjects. "The papers were enchanted to find the perfect person for each of you. Whether you understand why yet, you were *meant* to learn about the person you've selected. Please respect the process."

Well, there you go. Fate obviously wanted me to delve into the life of Sarah Good. And who was I to question fate?

I pulled back my paper with a sigh, and then stuffed it in the tiny zippered pocket of my spandex shorts.

"Guess I'm stuck with her," I said as Colette watched me put it away.

"She really *does* have an interesting story, you know," Colette said. "And I'd think, given your lineage, you'd be empathetic to what she went through."

"Oh, I am," I said, hearing the disappointment in my new friend's voice. "Don't get me wrong, I fully think that all those accused back then were dealt a sucky hand. They didn't deserve anything that happened to them. It's just sort of . . . depressing, you know?"

"Even more reason to keep the memories of those who were mistreated alive," she answered.

"You're right," I said. "At the very least, it'll be easier than reporting on a topic that's brand new to me. I already know so much about the trials that it shouldn't take me too long to fill in Sarah's blanks."

"I bet there's more to her history than you know," Colette said, solemnly. "Remember, there are always two sides to every story."

I nodded in agreement, looking to change the subject. "So, who'd you get then?" I asked.

Colette glanced down at her paper before folding it back up and placing it in her own pocket. "I think I'm going to keep mine a secret for now. It'll be more exciting for you to learn about them when I do my presentation."

I smiled at her enthusiasm. I'd never met anyone so excited about doing research before. I thought about what her aunt had said and agreed. Colette was definitely unique, and I think that's why I liked her so much. She kept us wondering what she'd say or do next. She was a wild card, and one I was happy to have on my side.

Chapter Thirteen

Dinner came and went and before I knew it, we were all headed to our rooms. Asher had shown up to eat this time, but I couldn't get myself to ask him about where he'd been at lunch. Namely, whether he'd been with Brooklyn, reminiscing about old times. It took everything in me to keep from peppering him with questions. Because as much as I wanted to know if they'd been together, there was a part of me that wanted to live in denial. Besides, if I brought up Brooklyn now, I'd most likely have to admit that I'd already failed in trying to bury the hatchet with her.

Besides, what was going on between Brooklyn and me now actually had little to do with Asher anymore. It was between her and me.

Other than that, Asher had seemed like his usual self. Cracking jokes and holding my hand under the table. The thing that *was* different was the fact that he had guy friends now. In just a few days, Dane and Hudson had become regulars at our table, a fact that made Sascha especially happy. She'd developed this intense crush on Dane and wouldn't stop asking him questions about Australia. Poor Dane had no idea what was going on, but he tried to answer all of them politely until, finally, he decided he could save himself the interrogation if he just asked Sascha questions about herself. This was both good and bad, because it meant that he could sit there and actually eat his meal, but once you got Sascha talking—and about her favorite topic: herself—it was hard to shut her up.

By the time we'd finished eating, Asher had decided to save Dane from Hurricane Sascha by insisting that they get started on their research projects.

"You're going already?" I asked, disappointed as we all got up to bus our trays.

"I think Dane's had enough," Asher said with a chuckle and looked over at his roommate, who was nodding like a bobble-head doll at something Sascha was saying. "Besides, we sort of have a guys' night planned. Is that okay?"

He asked the question, but I could tell it was more of a statement. One that Asher was clearly hoping I wouldn't push. But I couldn't help it. Nothing about this day had gone as expected and I could use some boyfriend time.

"It's just that, I barely got to see you all day," I said, slipping my hand into his and leaning my head against his shoulder as we followed the others outside and walked back toward the dorms. "And you said we'd spend time together this summer."

"And we will. Promise," Asher said. "But I also don't want to be rude to my new roommates. We might as well make friends while we're here, right? Colette seems pretty cool. Why don't you have a girls' night and get to know each other better? Then you and I can reconvene tomorrow. You know what they say: absence makes the heart grow fonder."

As he said this, he pulled me into the shadows and kissed me hard. My lips automatically parted and we went from zero to sixty in about point five seconds. He tasted like cherry cola. I pushed my body up against his and his hands found the bare skin of my stomach under my shirt. When he teased the area lightly with his fingertips, I began to get lightheaded and had to pull away before I passed out or things went too far.

"Get a room!" someone called out as they walked by.

"Maybe we should," I said, smiling up at him.

"Tempting," Asher said, his breathing still labored. He looked like he was wavering now.

"Sher!" Hudson yelled from a place about ten feet ahead of us. "You coming?"

Asher looked in his new friend's direction and then back down at me, before touching his forehead to mine. "Will you still love me tomorrow?"

It was a silly question, because of course I'd still love him. I might be more annoyed at him, but I'd still love him. But there was an excitement in his eyes I hadn't seen before. One that was totally different than the way he looked at me. And rightfully so.

Asher was in full-on bromance mode.

And that made me change my mind just a little.

Because Asher seemed happy. He was actually making friends, which was new for him. He'd always been sort of a loner. He hadn't really bonded with the other kids at his school; actually, a lot of witches didn't feel a connection with nonwitching folks. That only left other twitches, and there hadn't been many around for him to bond with.

But now, for the first time, he had a bunch of guys he seemed to enjoy being around. And I wanted him to have that. I'd always had girlfriends I could confide in. I depended on my nonwitchy friends for my public life at school, hanging out with them at parties, cheering with them at games and doing girly stuff like throwing slumber parties and shopping together. I even had the girls in the Cleri to satisfy the magical side of me. We talked magic and casted together. We were bonded by the coven.

It must be lonely for Asher not to have any of that.

So, despite the fact that I wished we were spending more time together, I understood how important it was for him to cultivate relationships with his roommates. And I wasn't too psyched about the clingy girl I was becoming. I'd never needed a guy around to have a good time before, so why would I need to now?

Maybe Asher was right: if I let him have his guy time, it would make our couple time even more special.

"Go hang out with your friends," I said finally, swatting him on the butt like I was one of his buddies.

"You sure?" he asked, scanning my face to see if this was a trick.

"I'm sure. I'll just head back with Colette and your sister," I said reassuringly. "We can stay up and talk about boys or something."

"Oh, man. That sounds like trouble," Asher said, although he seemed relieved.

When we reached the lobby, we went our separate ways. I could hear the guys hooting and joking around until I closed the door behind us.

"I'm going to take a shower," I announced, gathering up my things.

Despite what I'd said to Asher, I had no intention of staying up late with the girls. It had been a long day—our first full one at Brighton—and the combination of hours spent casting and the heat of Colorado had left me aching to crawl into bed early.

But no matter how tired I was, I never went to sleep without going through my nightly beauty routine. So, I dragged myself to the community bathroom at the end of the hallway and stepped into one of the shower stalls, cranking up the heat on the water until the steam made it difficult to see my own hand in front of my face. I let my mind go blank as I lathered up, spending a particularly long time conditioning my locks, which had already begun to dry out under the hot sun.

I closed my eyes after a while and allowed the methodical beating of the water to lull me into a sort of a meditative trance as it worked out the knots in my muscles. I could feel the stress begin to wash away, and a feeling of calmness enveloped me.

Maybe an evening to myself was just what I needed after all.

Part of me wanted to stay in the shower indefinitely. Okay, so not *indefinitely*, but there was a kind of freedom here. No bad guys to fight. No exes to worry about. Just silence. Unfortunately, my fingers were beginning to prune and I worried about falling asleep right there on the floor of the stall. And let's be honest, there was a reason people wore shower shoes: bathroom tiles were a hotbed for disgusting diseases that are *so* not sexy.

I shuddered at the thought and then turned the knob to cut off the flow of water. Only, instead of trickling to a stop, the pressure grew, until the spray began to feel more like a fire hose than a soothing rainforest.

That's odd.

I tried again, this time turning it in the opposite direction, but the flow refused to let up even a little bit. The water was coming out too fast and hard now for it to drain properly, and it started to pool at my feet, covering up my toes within seconds.

"What's wrong with this thing?" I muttered as I tried again

to turn the water off to no avail. Finally, with a sigh, I held my hands over the faucet and said, "Igmum rushee!"

The spell was meant to stop the flow of water, but it just kept spewing out, as if I'd never said it in the first place.

That is not *a good sign.*

The knob must have been broken.

So much for a drama-free evening.

No longer relaxed, I wondered if one of the counselors would be able to cut off the water supply at the source before it flooded the whole bathroom. Pushing on the glass door, I thought about how long it might be before I could escape to my bed. But instead of the door swinging open easily, it didn't budge. I placed my shoulder against the glass, and gave it another hard shove, hoping it was just stuck.

Nothing.

Okay, *now* I was worried. Something wasn't right here. The water had already risen up past my ankles and it wasn't stopping. I moved into the spot directly underneath the shower-head to get out of the harsh spray, and then glanced up to see how big the space was above the door. If worse came to worse, I could always climb up and over.

Except, there was none.

Part of me was relieved by this fact, because it would've been humiliating to be caught in a compromising position by my fellow campers. Especially if one of those people was Brooklyn.

Brooklyn.

Maybe *she* did this. Set the whole thing up, so I'd look stupid for getting stuck inside a shower stall.

And I *was* stuck. In fact, I hadn't noticed when I'd first stepped inside, but the shower was a little like a glass box.

There was no space open to the outside, which meant I was basically trapped.

And the water was still rising.

I went to bang on the door, hoping to attract the attention of someone still in the bathroom, but as I went to touch the glass, something began to appear through the haze of the steam. Written clearly on the glass of the shower door was a message: **Get out.**

Trust me, I want to.

I blinked the water out of my eyes to make certain that what I was seeing was really there. When it didn't disappear, I knew I wasn't seeing things.

Leaning forward, I took a closer look. Strands of condensation ran down the glass, making it clear that the words were written from the inside of the shower and not the outside.

The question was, how?

"Is somebody out there?!" I yelled.

There was no response.

The water was already up to my hips and I started to panic. *Think, think, think.* I looked around frantically like I was suddenly going to find something that would help break me out of the mess I was in. But all I'd brought in with me was a razor, a loofah, and some shampoo and conditioner. Nobody had told me I'd need heavier artillery to survive my nightly shower.

Luckily, I was always prepared with my own personal emergency witch kit. Me.

My solution was a bit destructive, I admit, but by now I was convinced I had no other choice. I had to get out of this water coffin before I drowned in it. Flattening myself against the shower wall, I closed my eyes and braced myself for what I was about to do.

"Exbiliby totalitum!"

I felt the exploding spell as it left my body and waited for the sound of shattering glass. My heart sank when it never came.

My mind raced. There was no reason those spells shouldn't have worked. Even in the middle of a freak-out, *something* should have happened. A crack in the glass, a poof of smoke from the residual magic. It was as if my powers were useless. Only, I'd felt it. The magic had been cast, something had just prevented it from working.

Was this a magic shortage? I'd heard of them happening to new witches or ones going through puberty, but I'd never experienced it myself. And I'd certainly never shot blanks before. It was embarrassing, but more than that, it made me feel something even worse.

Helpless.

Without magic, what did I have? I looked down at my hands, searching for an answer, and reluctantly found it.

I began to beat my fists on the door again, screaming for somebody, anybody, to help me. I knew at some point someone would come in. This was a given. There were thirty girls at camp and only one bathroom. You didn't have to be a genius to do the math. I just hoped it wasn't too late when they finally did.

The water was lapping at my shoulders, making it more and more difficult to move.

"Please! Somebody help me!" I yelled, frantically.

"Hello?" a voice finally called out. It was hard to hear at first, over the sound of water hitting water. But then it got closer and I could see the shadow of a body on the other side of the glass.

"I'm stuck inside the shower," I called out. "And the water won't turn off. It's filling up. I need you to get me out!"

"Er, Hadley?" the voice said. "Is that you?"

Then I recognized her.

"Abby? Please, you've got to do something!"

"Okay. Stupid question, but did you try magic?" she asked.

"It didn't work," I said, too panicked to say "duh."

"Hmmm. Let me just try . . . ," she said and I could see her shuffle around outside the stall. A few seconds later, the door sprung open and water rushed out like a broken dam, soaking Abby in the process. I stumbled out of the shower, reaching for my towel as I fell to the ground. My breath came in short spurts and I felt like I'd just run a marathon. Water was still hitting my face and I realized with surprise that I'd started crying.

"Are you okay, Had?" Abby asked, concerned. She bent down and placed her hand on my shoulder, waiting for me to calm down.

"Someone just tried to drown me," I choked out. "So, no. I'm *not* okay."

Abby's face didn't change as I snapped at her. Instead, she stood back up and looked down at me confused as she tried to ring the water from her pajama pants. I took another few deeps breaths and tried to gather myself.

"I'm sorry, Abby, I didn't mean to take it out on you," I said, looking up at her gratefully. Then it dawned on me. "How did you get me out, anyway?"

Abby bit her lip and then glanced at the shower door and then back at me. It was as if she didn't know how to respond and it felt like an eternity before she did.

"It just opened," she said softly.

"What?" I asked.

"I pulled on it and it opened."

"That's not possible," I said, feeling the hysteria begin to creep into my voice. "I tried everything to get out. Nothing worked."

"Maybe it was locked from the inside?" Abby offered, but I could tell she didn't believe it.

Other girls began to wander into the shower area then and looked at us with curiosity. A few commented on the water on the floor, but none of them asked what happened. They'd probably just gossip about it later.

"Somebody locked me in and blocked my powers," I said, my teeth beginning to chatter as the chilly air hit my still-wet skin. When everyone continued to look at me blankly, I took one more look at the shower before rushing through the group of girls toward the exit. "And I'm going to find out who."

Chapter Fourteen

Call it intuition, a hunch, or an educated guess, but somehow I *knew* deep down in my bones that it was Brooklyn who was behind the stunt in the bathroom. She was one of the only people at Brighton who had a problem with me, and had all but told me to watch my back. Beyond that, outside of the other Cleri members, there were only a handful of girls who had the skills needed to pull off something like that.

The only problem was: I had no way of proving it.

As I stomped down the hallway, I contemplated going to Brooklyn's room and confronting her. Right then and there. But with my only evidence gone with the steam, it was likely I'd just come off looking like a bully. Or crazy. Possibly both.

I remembered the way Abby had stared down at me as I lay on the tile floor, clutching the soaked towel to my body. When I'd insisted that I'd been locked in the shower, she hadn't believed me. And there was something else in her eyes, too. Pity. Maybe even a hint of worry.

It made me want to scream.

I thought about going to Asher and telling him what had happened. That his psycho ex had just tried to maim me in an effort to succeed in her evil plan to get back together with him. The idea was only entertained briefly before I came back down to reality and decided to take care of everything myself. I could handle one power-hungry, jealous witch. I'd done it before and I could do it again.

But to do so, I needed to gather more information on Brooklyn. Knowledge is power and all that. True, Asher had told me a lot about their relationship, but I had a feeling there was more to the story. Like, in an effort to create less drama, maybe he'd left some details out. And to get them, I needed to talk to someone who was close to the situation but was a little less partial.

Someone like Abby.

True, she wasn't my ideal choice, considering what had just happened in the bathroom. But she was the only other person who knew Brooklyn as well as Asher did. And I desperately needed inside information.

I shoved open the door to our empty room and slammed it behind me. Still clutching the towel around my body, I stalked over to my dresser and pulled out some shorts and a tank top, and then got dressed as quickly as I could. I felt chilled all the way to the bone and slipped on an oversize hoodie to warm up, but it didn't seem to help. Stepping into a pair of fluffy turquoise slippers, I tied my hair up on top of my head messily, and then started to move toward the door to go find Abby.

Just as I was reaching the other side of the room, the door opened up revealing exactly the person I'd been hoping to find.

"You okay?" she asked, crossing over to her bed. Sitting down carefully, Abby picked up a leather-bound notebook that I hadn't noticed was lying there and pushed it between her pillows in one motion.

I mirrored Abby and sat down on my own mattress.

"I need you to tell me everything about Brooklyn. And I get that you guys were friends—are still friends maybe—and you probably don't want to betray her confidence, but she's out to get me. This thing tonight with the shower? It wasn't an accident. It was *her*. But to prove it, I need more on her."

"And if it's not her?" Abby asked, evenly.

"Then getting to the truth will prove that and I'll let everything go," I said.

"What do you want to know?" Abby asked.

I closed my mouth abruptly as I processed what she'd said. I'd been sure it would take more convincing than that to get her to talk to me about Brooklyn and Asher. Either Abby wasn't as good of friends with Brooklyn as I'd thought or she was sure that my learning the truth would exonerate her. I almost abandoned my line of questioning to ask Abby which it was, but I sort of had a one-track focus.

"Well, okay, um . . . Asher told me a little about her already. That Brooklyn came into her powers, gave herself a makeover and tried to become popular . . . yada, yada, yada. The two of them obviously dated, but then she lied to him about a bunch of stuff and kissed someone else, so Asher broke up with her."

"All true," Abby confirmed with a nod.

"I need to know if she's a match for me," I said. Then, hesitating, I amended my question to be more specific. "Magically, I mean."

"Well, Brooklyn only gained the ability to cast a little over a year and a half ago. We had to teach her the most rudimentary spells. Ones the rest of us learned as children. So, from the beginning, she was behind all of us in skill," Abby said. "But she *was* a quick study and was really into honing her craft. Since I haven't been around her since . . . we moved, I can't be sure how much she's improved. However, from what I've seen so far, I'd say she's been busy."

I nodded, thinking back to when Brooklyn had shown off her best magicking skills in front of the counselors. She wasn't up to my level yet, but she'd been able to hold her own. In fact, she was better than average.

I frowned as I thought about this.

"Is there anything else I need to know about her?" I asked. "Anything that could give her an edge, magic-wise? Something I haven't seen yet?"

Abby bit her lip as she thought about how to answer. I was putting her in a difficult position, but I had to at least ask. I needed to understand what I was up against. She had to respect that.

"I'm not asking for all her secrets, Abby," I explained when she hesitated. "Just a level playing field. Apparently everyone is aware of what happened with the Parrishables. I think they've even figured out that I'm naturally talented in the art of persuasion. All I know is that Brooklyn used to date my boyfriend, was at one time pretty boring, and just tried to drown me in the shower. I must be missing something here, because none of that adds up."

She still seemed to be considering things, and I was feeling desperate, so I pulled out the only thing I had left. "I didn't start all of this, Ab. Brooklyn did. And I'm not going to let her hurt *any* of us again."

This was the pièce de résistance. Even if Abby didn't care about me, she cared about Asher. And she'd do whatever she could to see that he didn't get his heart broken again. She started to talk.

"Brooklyn has her own 'unique' talents, too. Ones that are confined to her lineage, like yours with persuasion and the ability to telecommunicate with the members of your family."

I felt the pang of sadness that still came anytime someone brought up my mom. It had been a little annoying back then, but when Mom had been alive she used to be able to read my mind. And if her life had been more exciting, I might've utilized this particular skill on her, too. Instead, I mostly focused on shutting her out. Communicating telepathically had been something Bridget Bishop and her daughter had been able to do, too. Our powers only seemed to extend to family, though. Trust me, I'd tried for years to read others' minds to no avail. This particular gift would've come in handy in this situation, come to think of it.

"Okay. What are these unique talents then?"

From the look on Abby's face, I was sort of afraid to ask.

"Brooklyn has the power to . . . match people. Sort of like Cupid. She can spark an interest in any two people she chooses."

"She can perform love spells?" I asked, incredibly. "I didn't think anyone had that kind of power. Just like the power to bring people back to life . . . love is off-limits."

"But infatuation, crushes, lust, instant attraction—apparently those are all gray areas. And that's what she does. When she matches two people, it gives them the initial push they need to see if the sparks will turn into something stronger. Of course, the connection eventually wears off and the couple is left with their true feelings. So, if there's no love there, the pairing won't last. But if it is, then what started with a spark eventually becomes a burning fire."

I swallowed hard. "Did she use her powers on Asher?" I asked.

Abby hesitated before answering, but it was enough for me

to know what she was going to say. "Yes. It was one of the reasons they initially fought. Asher didn't like being manipulated like that. He made her swear she'd never use it on him again."

"So, he may *not* have loved her," I said almost to myself.

"I didn't say that," Abby cut in. "The truth is, Asher was interested in her *before* they ever met. My guess is that the spell just hurried things along."

"Abby, this is really important," I said, feeling sick. "Do you think she'd use her powers on him again? On others here at camp? Is she *that* evil?"

She looked at me, a frown spreading across her face. I could tell she didn't want to answer, but I found myself silently imploring her to anyway. Finally, she said what I'd been fearing most since we began our conversation.

"The Brooklyn I knew before would've done *anything* to get what she wanted. And at the time, that included dating Asher," she said. "And now she's had a year to think about the fact that she doesn't have him anymore. The question is, did she learn from the mistakes she made in the past or did the last year just give her time to think about how she could get away with it next time?"

Chapter Fifteen

I wanted to tell all the others about Brooklyn right away. About her attack on me and about her special powers. But Abby made it pretty clear that this might not go over as well as I hoped it would.

"I get that you were totally freaked out back there, but Had—nobody locked you in that shower," she said gently after I brought up filling the Cleri in. "I barely had to pull on it for it to open. And if you accuse Brooklyn when she wasn't even in the vicinity, you're just going to look jealous."

"I'm *not* jealous," I said between clenched teeth, trying to sound convincing.

"I'm not saying you are. But that's what it will *look* like," Abby said. "And I told you about Brooklyn in confidence. We may not be all that close anymore, but I don't usually go around telling other people's business."

As much as I didn't want it to be true, she was right. On

both accounts. I would need proof to show the others if I wanted their support in taking her down.

So I kept my mouth shut. For now.

The rest of the week went by in a blur. We filled our days with magic and casting, and our nights with research. But my mind just wasn't in it. Instead, I spent every waking moment obsessing over what I'd learned about Brooklyn. Discovering that she could cast "lust" spells on top of the fact that she was gorgeous, manipulative, and interested in getting Asher back did nothing to ease my mind. In fact, it sort of drove me even crazier.

I found myself studying Brooklyn during magic sessions. I craned to overhear her conversations in case she was talking about breaking Asher and me up. There wasn't a time I felt I could let down my guard, which meant that I was constantly on edge. It was wreaking havoc on both my personal life and my body, since stress was the leading cause of binge eating among teens. And girls. And especially teen girls.

It was also about to get worse.

"Omigod, I would *die* for that purse!"

Excited chatter broke through my thoughts, snapping me back to the present. Colette and I were lounging around in the sun during an unexpected break in our day; I was working on my tan and she was working on her witch history assignment. It had been relatively quiet for the past ten minutes, which had allowed me a few minutes of peace. But as things grew rowdy nearby, I found my eyes opening and zeroing in on a group of girls headed our way from the main cabin.

Then I did a double-take as my brain tried to process what it was seeing.

"Did I fall asleep?" I asked out loud. Because there, coming toward us, were Sascha, Jasmine, Jinx, Abby . . . and Brooklyn and Eve. "Seriously. Please tell me this is a nightmare and that it's not really happening. Wake up, wake up, wake up."

I squeezed my eyes shut again, hoping that what I was seeing would disappear by the time I opened them. Unfortunately, all that happened was that the group was suddenly closer to us. And louder. I could fully hear everything they were saying now.

"One of my mom's friends works at Dooney & Bourke and calls me whenever a new bag comes in," Brooklyn said, gesturing to the hot dog-shaped purse. "I could probably get you one if you wanted."

Sascha was practically salivating at this. I used to think her enthusiasm for pop culture and popularity was cute—when it was me she was following around. But now that she was applying to be Brooklyn's personal shadow, it just seemed unattractive. The others didn't seem nearly as impressed, but when Brooklyn handed them her bag to try on for themselves, their smiles didn't lie. They were enjoying themselves. Even Jasmine, our resident goth-girl-who-hated-everything-and-everyone-that-wasn't-her, didn't seem all that put off by Supermodel Barbie.

"Nothing says fabulous like D&B." Eve nodded. "If we all had matching ones, it could be like the official bag for twitches."

"Well, the *fabulous* twitches, anyway."

Brooklyn's eyes met mine briefly as she said this, but it was so subtle that I was the only one who seemed to see it. I had to hand it to the girl: she was good. Making friends with my friends so it would piss me off? Smart plan. Too bad it wasn't going to work.

It wasn't going to work, was it?

They were nearing where Colette and I were sitting now, still chatting about the stupid bag.

I scowled. Then my scowl turned into a narrow-eyed death stare. As if on cue, they all seemed to see me at the same time and guilt immediately crept over their faces. Well, everyone's but Jasmine's, but she never felt bad about anything.

"Okay, well, let me know what colors you guys want and I'll go ahead and order them. I bet we could get them here before the end of the session," Brooklyn said, ignoring the fact that they'd stopped right in front of us. Then, with a wave that would put Miss America to shame, she turned and sashayed away, Eve right beside her.

Sascha, Jinx, Jasmine, and Abby all took their places on the grass beside me. Sascha lay back dramatically on the grass, closing her eyes to the sun. I knew that she was really just avoiding eye contact with me. Hello, it was obvious.

I observed each of them individually, waiting for some kind of explanation that would make sense of what I'd just seen.

"What's with all the staring?" Jasmine asked abruptly.

"What's with the new friends?" I responded.

Jasmine snorted and then leaned back so she was resting on her elbows. "Dude, you have *got* to put an end to the crazy," she answered.

"What's crazy is that it seems like you guys are making nice with her," I said. "And she's not a nice girl, trust me. You've seen how she acts toward me."

"Yeah, how she acts toward *you*," Jasmine pointed out.

"She's always nice to me," Sascha added, still refusing to open her eyes. "Maybe you're wrong about her, Hadley."

"I'm not. I've been watching her and everything she does is sneaky. . . . ," I started.

"You might want to watch it, Had," Jasmine warned,

cutting me off. "You're officially entering stalker territory."

"You're totally exaggerating," I said, although I *was* spending an inordinate amount of time studying Brooklyn when she didn't think I was watching her. "Tell her, guys."

I turned to the others, expecting them to back me up. But Jinx and Abby were looking anywhere but at me, while Sascha pursed her lips like she was physically trying to keep them closed. My face dropped as I realized they all agreed with her.

"You're losing your edge, Had," Jasmine said, pulling the sunglasses that had been up on top of her head down and over her eyes. "You didn't even let Parris rattle you like this when he was around. And this is just the witch next door."

"That's not true," I said forcefully. "Brooklyn's *much* more dangerous than any of you know. I didn't want to have to tell you this, but she attacked me earlier this week. And she's got some special . . . skills that could put all of us at risk."

I didn't tell them that she was actually a scary cupid. I was aware of how silly it sounded and I needed them to listen to me right now.

"She attacked you?" Jinx asked, worried.

Finally! Thank you.

"Yeah," I answered. I hadn't wanted to go there, but if they wanted the truth, I'd give it to them. We'd learned through the fight with the Parrishables that when one person was threatened it affected all of us. They deserved to know who Brooklyn really was.

"Well, what'd she do?" Jasmine asked, her eyebrow arched up above her dark glasses.

"She nearly drowned me in the bathroom." I proceeded to tell them about the incident in the shower, including the message that had appeared on the inside of the door and the fact that my magic had been blocked.

"I don't know, Hadley," Sascha said slowly. "Sort of sounds like one big bathroom failure. How would she know you were even in there in the first place?"

"My towel was hanging over the door in clear view . . . and the glass is basically see-through," I said, arguing my case. "Or she could have followed me in."

"Not everyone follows you around everywhere," Jasmine said sarcastically.

"What kind of superpowers does she have?" Sascha asked, suddenly interested in the topic.

"She's like a modern-day Cupid. Abby said she can make people fall for each other. She can match *anyone*," I said.

"I thought love spells didn't exist," Colette said thoughtfully, speaking up for the first time since we'd all started arguing. So far she was the only one who wasn't giving me a hard time about everything.

"So *that's* what this is really about," Jasmine said, like it was all becoming clear to her.

"What?" I asked.

"You're worried about Brooklyn using her powers to go after Asher."

My mouth dropped open at what she was implying. "Not just Asher. She could do it to any of you. Do you really want her playing with your lives like that?"

Sascha closed her eyes again dreamily. "I wouldn't mind if she put the love whammy on me and Dane," she said. "In fact, I might just have to talk to her about that. . . ."

"It's not right, Sascha," I growled, annoyed that she wasn't taking this seriously.

"Ugh. I take it back. You're not losing your edge at all," Jasmine said dramatically. "You're still just as bossy as ever."

I sighed, feeling like the conversation had completely gotten away from me. I needed to get them to work with me on this, be on my side. And I wasn't going to instill this sort of loyalty by fighting with them.

No. A good leader knew how to get things done.

"Fine," I said, conceding. "I'm hearing you. And you want the old Hadley back? Well, I'm all yours. In fact, it's been a while since we went over the protection and location spells for Samuel and the Parrishables. Why don't we scrounge the others up and make sure everything's still quiet?"

Jasmine looked like she hadn't exactly gotten what she'd wanted in the deal, but she kept her mouth shut for the time being.

"When do you want to meet?" Jinx asked.

"Tonight," I said. "You wanted me back, so let's get to work."

Chapter Sixteen

That night's meeting was smaller than usual. And not just because the rest of the Cleri was back at home enjoying their summers off. Tonight, we were minus two people: Asher and Jinx. To my disappointment, Asher had already made plans with Dane and Hudson, which he apparently couldn't get out of. Jinx, on the other hand, had gotten too much sun while we sat around during our break that afternoon and seemed to have a mild case of sun poisoning. I'd visited her before we left for the meeting, and despite the redness of her cheeks, I could tell she wasn't herself. I promised to look in on her when we got back.

So Jinx was off the hook, but I couldn't help but be annoyed that Asher was blowing off a Cleri meeting to hang out with his buddies. Of course, if I was being honest with myself, my first thought had been that he was actually going out to meet Brooklyn. But since these thoughts would block me from having a strong casting session—a witch needed total concentration while doing magic to achieve optimum results—I pushed my feelings to the back of my mind and focused on why we needed to be constantly improving our magicking skills: threats like the Parrishables.

And maybe even love spells or other charms by certain blond enemies.

But first, my focus had to be on Samuel and his deranged followers. They were leagues more dangerous than Brooklyn and whatever games she might be trying to play with me. Although both set off alarms in my head, it was more important to make sure Samuel wasn't coming back anytime soon.

And the only way to know whether this was true was to continue to cast protection spells on our coven, our relatives, and our loved ones. The Cleri also performed location spells to see if there was any of Samuel's residual energy left in this world, as well as incantations intended to keep our eyes open to the truth in all situations. True, we'd been doing this periodically since we'd come home from the cabin, but this wasn't a one-and-done deal. I'd probably always be looking over my shoulder for the next big bad. Whether it was a not-so-dead Samuel Parris, the Parrishables, or someone—or something—we hadn't even conceived of yet. We'd have to just wait and see.

At midnight, Abby and I quietly left our room and scooted down the hallway to the back stairwell, taking care not to make any noise as we locked things up behind us. When we got down to the ground floor, there were two doors to choose from: one that led into the cabin lobby, and the other that led outside. We enchanted the knob on the outside door to make sure it remained unlocked so we'd be able to get back in when we were done, and then performed a spell to shroud us in darkness as we ran across the grounds. We didn't want anyone who just "happened" to be looking outside their windows to spot us and tell the elders.

When we were sure it was clear, we snuck out the door and rushed down the walkway, not stopping until we'd made it around the corner of the amphitheater. We'd decided that the boys' outdoor class space would be the best option for a meeting spot, since it was completely blocked off from the view of the cabin, and was far enough away that we wouldn't have to worry about anyone hearing us. Just to make sure, though, I cast a noise-bubble spell that would make it so our voices wouldn't carry past where we were standing. The bubble was only about ten feet wide, but it would completely envelop our group of five.

"How can it be so cold at night when it's so hot during the day?" Sascha complained as she appeared out of the darkness, followed by Jasmine and Fallon.

I tried not to stare as Fallon walked right over to Abby and sat down beside her. They started to chat quietly and the change in Abby's attitude was obvious.

Is it possible she really likes him?

"You guys have any trouble getting away?" I asked the others.

"Nah. It was easy-peasy," Jasmine said, plopping down in one of the dozens of empty seats around us. "It's not like this place is Fort Knox or anything."

"Still, getting caught isn't an option," I said. "And unfortunately, it'd be too much of a risk to do this indoors, with everyone around and all. So that leaves us out here in the woods."

"We're not in the woods. We're in the *amphitheater*," Sascha said and looked at her phone. "Can we hurry this up? I was sort of hoping to 'accidentally' run into Dane tonight."

"In his room?" I asked. "Because that's where Asher and the guys are."

"I figured if I waited outside of it long enough, one of them would come out and invite me in," she said, as if she had it all planned out. "Then, maybe we'd watch a movie—a romantic comedy or something—and he'd realize I was the witch of his dreams. . . ."

"Sounds like *you're* the one who's dreaming," Fallon said under his breath. Sascha made a face at him and then went back to her fantasy.

"I wonder how I could get the other guys to leave for a few hours so we could be alone?" Sascha said thoughtfully. "Had, you think you could invite Asher over for a slumber party? Maybe Hudson can come, too? I'm sure Colette wouldn't mind. . . ."

"Sascha, focus," I said, trying to get us back on task. The last thing I had time for was planning a hookup party. "Look, it's been a few weeks since we've run through these protection spells—the longest we've ever gone before. And even though we've all been distracted lately, myself included, it doesn't mean we can let up on everything. We need to be prepared for *anything*."

Sascha looked like she wasn't ready to give up on a romantic rendezvous with Dane just yet, but was smart enough to stay quiet for now. The others just waited for me to continue.

"Good. Let's get started," I said, sitting down between Sascha and Jasmine, and leaving Abby and Fallon on their own across from us.

It took us a little more time than usual to cast the spells, proving that we were slightly out of practice. We'd had the sessions down to a science before, each knowing what we had to do and which order the spells were to be cast. But being down several people and with the threat of being caught by the counselors hanging over us, we were admittedly off our game. Still, we pushed forward.

We started with protection spells, using objects that belonged to each of us as the vessels in which the power of defense was stored. The spells were intended to give us a layer of protection, sort of like magical armor. It wouldn't make us immune to evildoers, but it was better than nothing.

Each object was charmed individually as the five of us repeated the protection incantation in unison. My ring was up first. The red jewel glistened under the glow of the tiny ball of light that I'd created earlier. The magical flashlight wasn't bright enough to alert anyone to the fact that we were out there, but it was enough to see what we were doing.

For about the hundredth time since I'd found it, I admired the craftsmanship of the ring that had once belonged to Bridget Bishop before it was passed down to her daughter, Christian. The heirloom had been hidden under the floorboards of our family's summer home, where I eventually retrieved it after having one of my flashback dreams. It had been on my finger ever since, not just because it was probably worth a small fortune and vintage jewelry was making a comeback, but mostly because of the buzz I got from wearing it. There was something there, a sort of power that was worked into the metal that made me feel connected to the universe. It had become a sort of lucky charm of mine and I rarely went anywhere without it. In fact, I only took it off when we were casting these protection spells. Otherwise it was always on my finger.

Focused on the spell now, we said the chosen words and I watched the ring shine even brighter, proof that the spell was working.

Innocence and light, may you be guarded,
Wrap caring hand round those not yet departed.
Let no ill be cast against the wearer,

May danger return to that of the bearer.
If good meets evil and things look bleak,
Then protect pure of heart and leave
the other one weak.

I waited a few seconds after finishing the spell before picking the ring back up. It was still warm to the touch and felt at home as I slid it on my pointer finger. Then, we went on to perform the same spell on Jasmine's black spider necklace, as well as on Sascha's grandmother's earrings, Fallon's medallion, and Abby's locket. Lastly, we finished up by charming Asher's black leather cuff and the Claddagh ring that Jinx had worn since she was a kid.

Once each had been enchanted, we moved on to the location spell. To do this, we placed a small jar of the soil where Samuel had last stood before we'd vanquished him in the middle of our circle. While saying the designated words, I placed a snakeskin agate—a very powerful and unusual stone that helps to find lost things—on top of the jar. Slowly pulling my hand away from the gem, I watched it balance on its tip without falling.

The way the spell was supposed to work was that the stone would remain in place if the person who'd crossed the soil no longer walked the ground. If he *was* in fact in this universe—and not in heaven or hell or whatever happens to people after they die—the stone would fall in the direction that the offender stood. For months, the gem had stayed still as soon as I'd let it go. But even so, I found that I always held my breath for a bit until I knew it wasn't going to move.

Luckily, this time wasn't any different and I let out a sigh of relief when the bluish-yellow rock remained vertical. I began to get up, pulling my hair behind my shoulders and brushing off my pants.

"Okay, well, guess that's it. In the future, we should make sure to—" I began.

"Whoa! What's that?" Jasmine asked, interrupting me.

"What?" My attention drifted back to where she was now staring, wide-eyed. Then, I sat back down with a thud.

"Is the stone . . . *moving?*" Sascha asked no one in particular. It was.

At least I thought it was. The stone that had been motionless on top of the jar just a few seconds before now appeared to be vibrating. It wasn't a lot of movement, but there was something going on.

But then it just stopped.

If Jasmine hadn't been looking at it, we probably would've missed it altogether. My heart was racing now, as I told myself that we didn't need to worry since it hadn't actually fallen over.

"That was weird," I said, though it was the understatement of the century. "I'm sure it was nothing, though. Maybe a glitch because the others aren't here?"

"You sure?" Fallon asked, looking over at Abby with a worried expression on his face.

I thought about it for a few seconds and answered the only way I could.

"I hope so."

Chapter Seventeen

It was difficult getting up the next morning. Not only had we been up late casting the protection and location spells, but I'd also had a hard time falling asleep. I kept picturing the gemstone shaking and couldn't stop thinking about what it could mean.

But it hadn't fallen over.

That would be the *real* sign that Samuel was back.

After all, the movement could've been a response to just about anything. Distraction while casting. Not having the full thirteen of us in the circle. Interference from the dozens of other witches inhabiting the camp. There were a ton of excuses why the spell might've gone the way it had—yet the only thing I could focus on was the possibility that Samuel was still alive. And if that was the case, then we were all in major trouble.

"It's too early to be this hot," Jasmine whined as we walked out the front door of the cabin, dressed in clothes we could cast in. "I don't know why you guys wouldn't just let me stay in bed this morning."

The rest of us walked beside her, most of us dragging our feet the whole way. Only Jinx and Colette looked ready to tackle the day, which we knew wasn't a coincidence considering both had actually gotten sleep the night before. Sascha, Jasmine, Abby, and I, however, had no business being out among people. The dark circles around our eyes and the fact that we couldn't stop yawning were dead giveaways that we'd been up late.

"You're going to have to rally, Jazz," I said, silently willing myself to do the same. "This isn't like missing a day of school. We can actually *use* the stuff we're learning here."

"I feel so bad that I had to stay behind last night," Jinx whispered to me as Colette walked up ahead of us.

"You needed the sleep," I said. "Speaking of: you look a little better today."

It was true. The redness had faded to a light pink and for the first time since we'd gotten to camp, she didn't look like she was seconds away from passing out. She seemed happier, somehow. Even if she wasn't smiling.

I had chosen to withhold the information on Samuel and the stone, which had definitely been the right decision.

"I feel like every time you need me, I'm not there," she said, sounding guilty.

"You know that's not true, Jinxy," I said.

Without her having to say it, I knew that something was going on. Something was taking a toll on her. I'd been planning to log some alone time to ask her about it, but she'd already been asleep by the time we'd gotten back to our rooms the night before. That had probably been for the best though, since I'd been too shaken up to be helpful anyway.

"Well, I promise I'll be there next time," Jinx vowed, looking me in the eye.

I just nodded.

We were about to enter the dining hall for breakfast when Fallon ran up to us from the direction of the amphitheaters. He was out of breath and seemed oddly excited.

"You guys *have* to come see this," he said, barely stopping before turning back around. "Something's happened."

I'd been wrong. It wasn't excitement I'd seen in his eyes; it was fear. My stomach lurched.

"What?" It was all I could get out before we all started to jog toward the area where our classes were held. As we got closer, I could see that a group had started to form.

We ran around the corner that led to the boys' side and then skidded to a stop, causing several people to run into us in the process. There was a gasp somewhere behind me, and I felt a little light-headed as I tried to make sense of what we were seeing.

"Where did it all go?" Sasha asked.

In front of us, there was now a cleared-out space where the seats had been. Everything was gone, down to the bolts that had held the rows of chairs in place. Only cement steps remained. Hanging from the rafters above the stage was a ratty, old banner, with the words I'M WATCHING written in a dark red liquid.

"Is that blood?" Jinx asked, her voice shaking. "Please tell me that's not blood."

I was too busy gaping at what the message said to answer. It was eerily similar to the one that was left for me in the shower.

"Where did the chairs go?" Jasmine asked. "I mean, it's not like someone could just get up and walk away with them."

"Uh, guys?" Fallon said, causing all of us to look in his direction. When he pointed up into the air, our eyes followed his finger.

"No way," Colette said, adjusting her glasses before tilting her head back.

Up on top of the curved roof of the amphitheater were the rows of missing chairs. Each one pointed in our direction below, as if an invisible crowd were watching us. The effect was beyond creepy.

Miss Peggy walked along the roof, checking out the chairs and shaking them every few feet. Finally she stepped off the ledge, and with a few words, floated down until her feet touched the ground again safely. The move was very Mary Poppins, except for the fact that Miss Peggy's accessories jangled the whole way, sounding a bit like Santa's sleigh. At least it gave those below her a chance to move out of the way before she landed.

Hurrying over to the other counselors, Miss Peggy began to confer with Mrs. Jeanette and Mrs. B. Her tone was hushed, but I was standing close enough that I could hear everything she was saying.

"They're bolted to the roof," Miss Peggy said, shaking her head. "I tried to move them, but they won't budge."

"I don't understand how they got up there in the first place," Mrs. Jeanette said, looking back up at the chairs. "Or more importantly, why?"

"You really want to know *why*? Well, that's the easy part," Mrs. B answered, crossing her arms over her chest, smugly.

"Do you know something we don't?" Miss Peggy asked.

"I have six kids and they pull stuff like this all the time. One time, the girls took all the furniture in our bedroom and charmed it to the ceiling, so we'd think we were actually upside down," she said. "It took us nearly an entire day to put it back into place and even then, the dog was so confused that he wouldn't come into our room anymore. A fact my husband actually appreciated, I might add."

"So, you're saying this is just a prank?" Miss Peggy asked.

"Seems like a lot of work just for a gag," Mrs. Jeanette said, unconvinced. "And what about the sign? When I first saw it, I thought it was actually written in *blood*. How is *that* funny?"

"Oh, Jeanette, didn't you ever raise hell as a kid?" Mrs. B asked, lifting her eyebrows at the other woman mischievously.

The buttoned-up counselor hesitated before letting out a small smile. It was the first expression I'd seen her give that didn't scream "scientist."

"Well . . . once I rigged my father's glass to keep refilling with water, so it would look like he hadn't drunk anything. He just kept chugging it and it never went down," Mrs. Jeanette said, a sparkle in her eyes. "It took him an hour to figure out I was behind it. My mom and I laughed for *hours*."

"Wait, so you tricked your dad into *hydrating*?" Mrs. B asked. "That was your prank? Making someone drink more water? I've got news for you, Jeanette, pranks have changed since you were a kid."

"I thought it was funny," Mrs. Jeanette said, quieter than before.

"Back to the matter at hand," Miss Peggy said, blinking away the conversation. "We know that the message was left in paint, not blood, so that should be a load off our minds. If it was a prank, then what was the point?"

"At the risk of being burned at the stake . . . could it have been the Witch in the Woods?" Mrs. B asked.

My ears perked up as Mrs. B mentioned the urban legend. Until she'd said it, I hadn't even considered it.

"You aren't *actually* suggesting that the Witch in the Woods is *real*," a man asked as he walked up to the others. I recognized him as the grumpy counselor who'd refused my request for a double room. By the looks on the counselors' faces, they weren't fans of his either. "Please don't tell me you're *that* gullible."

Mrs. B placed her hands on her hips and gave the handlebar-mustached guy a look that would've been intimidating to anyone else. To someone as ego-driven as him, though, the gesture flew right past.

"Of course I'm not saying that, *David*," she said, sounding like she'd already lost her patience. "What I'm *saying* is that it might be possible that whoever did this wanted people to think it was the Witch in the Woods."

Miss Peggy nodded her head thoughtfully. "There's a chance you're right," she said. "Every summer *someone* tries to resurrect the ghost of Moll Brenner. It's a good story to tell around the campfire. And a way to place blame on someone else."

"We don't have a campfire," Counselor David said, sneering.

"You know what she means," Mrs. B answered.

"But they've never done anything this *big* before," Mrs. Jeanette said, waving her hand at the chaos around us.

"Well, we *do* have some new heavy hitters at camp this year," Counselor David said, turning to look in our direction. Luckily, I'd turned away before they could catch me eavesdropping. "Maybe it's a juvenile attempt to mark their territory, prove that they're superior? I say we look at them first."

I glanced around at the others to see if they were listening to the exchange too, but most were either talking to each other or still studying the rooftop seating. They had no idea that we were currently being implicated for something we hadn't done.

So much for being innocent until proven guilty.

"This could've been done by anyone, David," Mrs. B said, defending us.

"Well, not *really*," Miss Peggy chimed in slowly. "You haven't been up there, Rose. Those things are bolted down tight and each row has to weigh at least a thousand pounds. It would've taken a really strong witch—or several witches—to pull this off."

"Okay, but I still say we need to look at *everyone*," she said.

"And we should try to put the kibosh on the whole 'Witch in the Woods' thing before it gets out of control," Mrs. Jeanette said. "Agreed?"

"Agreed," David said.

"Agreed," both Mrs. B and Miss Peggy answered.

The four counselors dispersed then and walked in the direction of the stage to try to take down the banner, which was still dripping paint onto the floor below. Just as they were pulling it down, I felt someone come up behind me.

"Whoa, dude, what happened here?" a voice I recognized as Hudson's said. I turned to see Asher, Hudson, and Dane walk up to where the rest of us were already standing.

"Bugger, that's some epic shit!" Dane said, his accent making Sascha swoon. "Is this the type of warped activity you Yanks do for fun in the States?"

Asher, who was now standing by my side, spoke up. "I don't think this was done in good fun," he said, frowning. "Anyone know what's going on?"

The others shook their heads, but Asher had his gaze set on me.

"I might have an idea," I said, causing the others to flash me surprised looks.

"Well?" Jasmine asked when I didn't respond right away.

"Let's go somewhere we can talk . . . freely," I said, looking around at the crowd, which almost included the whole camp by this point.

We began to retreat from the scene of the crime and walked toward the dining hall. Our casting sessions were supposed to begin in less than five minutes, but from the looks of it, things weren't going to be starting on time. If at all. Might as well get something to eat and maybe a little caffeine fix in the meantime.

Asher placed his hand in mine and we pulled up ahead of the others who were already chatting behind us.

"Wasn't that where you guys met last night?" he asked, keeping his voice low so no one else could hear.

I nodded. "Yep."

"You guys didn't do it, did you?"

I gave him a look that told him he was being ridiculous. "You're seriously asking me that?" He raised his hands up in surrender as a response. "Maybe if you'd been there with us, you wouldn't have to ask."

And maybe he should've been looking at his ex instead of his current girlfriend. . . .

"You're right. I'm sorry, Had," he said, leaning over and kissing me lightly on the cheek, a feat considering we were mid-stride. "But if there was anyone powerful enough to pull that off, it'd be you."

"Don't try to butter me up, Asher," I said, but I appreciated the compliment.

"So, who's *really* behind this?" he asked. "And should I be worried?"

I took a deep breath and looked over at him. "I think we're way past worried."

Chapter Eighteen

"So, this might actually be the Witch in the Woods, then?" Hudson asked, almost gleefully, as we set down our trays of food.

"The counselors said that it *wasn't* the Witch in the Woods," I corrected. "That most likely it was someone at camp. And I kind of agree with them."

"They also said it would take a superpowerful witch in order to move those seats," Fallon said. "Now, if it wasn't *that* witch, then which witch was it?"

Nobody said anything at first, but one by one, everyone began to look over at me. I tried to ignore them at first, but even when I looked away, I could feel them staring.

"Why are we all staring at Hadley?" Dane asked, confused.

"Hadley was the one who got rid of Samuel Parris and the Parrishables," Colette said, filling him in.

"It wasn't just me," I said, exasperated. "It was all of us. We defeated him *together*."

"Dude, you didn't tell me she was *that* Hadley," Hudson said, punching Asher in the shoulder.

"No kidding?" Dane asked, looking at me with wonder.

"Your girlfriend is *famous*," Hudson said, shaking his head.

"You've *all* heard of what happened with Samuel?" I asked, surprised.

"Just because I come from the land down under doesn't mean I live under Uluru," Dane said, leaning back in his chair lazily. "I wouldn't be surprised if even the koalas in Oz knew about what you guys got up to."

"I'm not totally sure what you just said, Dane, but we didn't do this," I said bluntly.

"Is that our official story?" Jasmine asked, her eye fixed on me.

"That's the *truth*," I said slowly, confused by what she was implying.

"It's just that you were the last one to leave last night. . . ." Sascha said.

"I cleaned up like I told you I would and then went back to my room," I said. "I was like, ten minutes behind you. Ask Abby."

Abby looked up, surprised by the mention of her name. I watched as her and Fallon's hands fell apart and fought the urge to call them out on it. We both knew she'd been caught red-handed.

"Uh, I went to sleep as soon as we got back," Abby said. "Sorry, but I don't remember you coming in."

Way to have my back.

"You guys went out last night?" Colette asked, surprised. "I thought we all went to bed at the same time."

Uh-oh.

"Sorry, Colette, but it was sort of a Cleri thing." I said, not wanting her feelings to be hurt. I hated to exclude her, but it was the truth.

Colette gave me a weak smile and then looked around the table at the rest of the crew. She adjusted her glasses and then shrugged. "I understand," she said, sounding disappointed. "But I hope you know that I wouldn't mind. Being dragged into things, I mean. I get that what you guys went through was dangerous and all, but there are some things in this world that are worth the danger, you know? If I can be helpful to you and the rest of the Cleri in any way, I'm in. We may belong to different covens, but it doesn't mean we can't be there for each other."

What she said made me love her even more. I leaned over and gave her a quick side hug.

"Hate to break up this lovefest, but we still don't know who messed with the guys' side of camp," Jasmine said.

"Are we sure there's even anything to be worried about?" Fallon asked.

"It *was* sort of a funny prank," Sascha said with a giggle.

"Except for the message, 'I'm watching.' The paint was *bloodred*, Sascha," Jinx said, visibly shaken. "I doubt that was a coincidence."

"So what are we looking at here?" Asher asked, trying to keep us on task. "Possible suspects are this Witch in the Woods, who we're not even sure exists. . . ."

"She does," Colette said. "Or did."

"Okay," Asher said, looking at Colette briefly before turning his attention back to the group. "It could also be someone here at camp."

"Someone that's not me," I added.

"So, who—besides Hadley—could've done this?" Asher asked, flashing me a supportive smile.

"Well, on the guys' side, you're looking at all the top contenders right here," Hudson said, gesturing around the table. "Not to brag, but you, Dane, and I are the most powerful dudes at this camp."

"Uh, hello? Forgetting someone?" Fallon asked.

"Ah, right. Of course. That included you too, mate," said Dane. "No need to get your knickers in a knot."

"Maybe *your* knickers are in a knot," Fallon said under his breath. Out of the corner of my eye, I saw Abby place her hand on his back and rub it comfortingly. Almost immediately, Fallon relaxed. I shook my head.

"And there's no one else out of the guys who could've pulled off something like this?" I asked.

Asher shook his head. "It's pretty clear that most of the guys here are more focused on chasing girls than learning magic."

Sascha giggled and looked at Dane hopefully.

"How about the girls?" Asher asked me.

"Well, there's us," I said.

"Colette's got some mad witch action going, too," Jasmine said, giving her a rare compliment. "You should see what she can do with an exploding spell."

"Thanks!" Colette said, perking up. This was possibly the nicest thing Jasmine had said to practically anyone and we all knew it.

"I tell it like it is," Jasmine said, not acknowledging that she'd been kind in any way. "Case in point: Why do we even care about this whole amphitheater debacle?"

"Do I need to remind you what happened the last time we didn't take a threat seriously?" I said.

"But is this really a threat?" Sascha said. "Someone's watching, but they didn't say they were watching us. Who says this is even something to worry about?"

"I'm not willing to take the chance that we're wrong," I said, thinking about my mom and the other parents who'd died at the hands of Samuel.

"So, is there anyone else who could have pulled this off?" Asher asked, after a brief pause.

The others didn't answer. I'm not sure whether they were waiting for me to take the lead or if they honestly had no clue. Either way, I hated that I would be the one to have to say it.

"Brooklyn," I said finally. I didn't want to make eye contact with Asher, because I was afraid he'd see the contempt I had for her and then not take her seriously as a possible suspect. "Next to me and Colette, Brooklyn's probably the most powerful girl here."

It killed my ego to admit this, but they needed to know that Brooklyn had the potential to be a serious threat. Not just to me and my relationship, but to everyone at camp.

Asher shook his head. "It can't be Brooklyn," he said. "She could barely cast a year ago. No way she's gotten that powerful in such a short amount of time."

"She's been practicing, Asher," Abby spoke up in a rare attempt to contribute. "She's already reached *our* level . . . might've passed us, actually."

"She's not as good as me, but she can cast," I added. "And she's made it pretty clear that she doesn't appreciate some of us being here."

"You think that message was for *you*?" Asher asked.

Of course it was intended for me. Brooklyn wanted to let me know that she was watching me. That she'd been behind the bathroom thing and that she could do it again if she wanted. She was watching, waiting, and when she was ready, she'd attack.

"She wouldn't do this, Hadley," Asher said. "You don't know her like I do."

"Like you *did*," I corrected. "You knew her over a year ago. People change, Asher. You did."

"I've talked to her, Hadley. She wouldn't have done this," he insisted.

My chest constricted when he mentioned this. He'd told me he was going to clear things up with her, but since he hadn't confirmed that he'd done it yet, I'd been able to tell myself that maybe it wouldn't actually happen. But now I *knew* it had. They'd been alone together, walking down memory lane, discussing a time in their lives when they'd been in love. The thought made me sick.

"Wait, Brooklyn is your *ex*?" Hudson asked, with a laugh. "Are you kidding me, bro? How did we not know this?"

"Because it's in the *past*," Asher said, staring at me as he said it. It did nothing to make me feel better about the situation.

"We talking 'bout the blond babe?" Dane asked. As soon as the description was out of his mouth, Sascha frowned. She didn't want competition.

"Can we change the subject?" Asher warned.

"Well, if Brooklyn *didn't* do it—though I still think she's a viable suspect—then who else could it have been?" I asked. I wasn't ready to give up on my theory that Brooklyn was bad news, but I also didn't think right now was the time and place to air our dirty laundry.

"Well, there *is* one other possibility," Jasmine said. "But it's a long shot." She looked over at me and raised her eyebrow questioningly.

"What?" Asher asked.

When I didn't answer, he asked me again. With a quick glance over at Jinx, I silently prayed that Jasmine would just let it go for now. But then Jinx must have realized she was out of the loop, too.

"What aren't you telling us?" she asked, sounding both scared and angry at the same time.

Dane, Hudson, and Colette watched our exchange like it was a tennis match. Finally, Colette stood up from her chair and motioned to the guys. "I guess that's our cue to leave," she said.

"It's not like that," I said to Colette, reaching out to her apologetically.

In fact, if she and the boys stuck around, then I definitely wouldn't have to talk about our meeting the night before. And that was fine with me. I wasn't exactly looking forward to having this conversation. But the bottom line was that we'd been burned by people in the past—and had the scars to prove it. It still pained me every time I thought about how Emory had nearly destroyed the Cleri from the inside out. As much as I wanted to believe that our new friends were allies, I just couldn't yet. And if Samuel or the Parrishables were back, we didn't need them knowing we were privy to the fact. The less they knew, the better.

"Seriously, Hadley, it's okay," Colette said. "I have some stuff that I have to take care of anyway. I'm sure these guys do, too. We'll just see you in class." Dane and Hudson didn't argue with her. They just picked up their trays and followed her out the dining hall.

"Subtle," Jasmine said to me, sarcastically.

"You're the one who brought it up," I said.

"Excuse me for stating the obvious," she answered back. "We can't just ignore what happened."

"What are you guys talking about?!" Asher asked.

Taking a deep breath, I looked around the room to make sure no one was listening in on our conversation. After all, the message had said, "I'm watching." Luckily, most of the camp was gathered at the amphitheater.

"Last night, when we did the location spell on Samuel, the response was . . . unclear," I said, choosing my words carefully.

Jinx's face changed from fear to absolute terror. I'd never actually seen the color drain from someone's skin before, and the effect was haunting.

"What do you mean, 'unclear'?" Asher asked.

"I mean, we did the spell and instead of staying still like it always has in the past, the gem moved."

"It fell over?" Asher asked, eyes growing wide.

"Samuel Parris is back," Jinx whispered, staring blankly at the wall.

"It *didn't* fall over," I said quickly. "More like it . . . wobbled."

"What does that mean?" Asher asked me.

"Your guess is as good as mine," I said. "All I know is that if the gem falls, that means he's back. It didn't fall, so . . ."

"But it didn't stay still," Jinx said.

"No, but . . ."

"Should we ask one of the elders about it?" Sascha asked. "What about your dad, Had? I bet he'd know."

"He doesn't even know we're *doing* any of this," I said. "And I have a feeling he wouldn't be all that happy to learn we've been messing with anything Samuel-related. I think he's like the rest of the witch world, in that he really thinks Samuel is gone for good."

"Then shouldn't we do the same?" Sascha asked, growing exasperated.

"Do you feel that way, though?" I asked. "Deep down, do you *really* think he's gone for good? That the Parrishables will never come after us again?"

Everyone remained silent for a beat. I'd proven my point.

"The gem didn't stay still like it was supposed to," Jasmine said quietly, but forcefully.

"It could've just been an error in the spell," Sascha said, sounding more like she was trying to convince herself than us.

"So we're back to the original question. Was this the work of another camper or the Parrishables?" Jasmine posed to all of us.

I was tempted to blame Brooklyn for what had been going on around here rather than Samuel. But was I letting my emotions cloud my thinking? Or was I just following my gut, which at the moment was telling me that Brooklyn was out to destroy me and the others?

"I don't know," I said finally. "I guess I don't want to count anything out yet."

Jinx slowly stood from her chair, and without saying anything, began to walk away from the table. We all looked after her, surprised. I looked over at Asher and then rose, too.

"I've got this, guys," I said, racing after Jinx. She was hurrying away now, picking up speed with every step. I caught up with her just outside the dining hall and linked my arm with hers. She jumped when I touched her, but then relaxed slightly when she saw that it was me.

"Whoa, slow down, Jinxy," I said, like I was talking to a jittery horse. "What's going on?"

She wouldn't slow down and the shoes I was wearing weren't made for running. So, I pulled on her arm lightly, forcing her to stop and face me.

Tears streaked down her cheeks. Her eyes were wild, pupils so dilated that I could barely see any white area. But it was a different kind of blackness than the one that usually signified an evil witch. This was what happened when a person was in full-on panic mode. Jinx was trying to decide between fight and flight. And from the way her head was darting around, it was easy to see which she was planning to do.

"Calm down, Jinx," I said, worried. "Take a few deep breaths. It's just you and me. Right now, everything's okay. I promise. Just breathe."

I pulled her down to the ground beside me, so we were facing each other and holding hands. I put all my energy into making her believe that what I was saying was true. It was times like these that my powers of influence really came in handy.

"Breathe, Jinx. In and out. We're okay. *You're* okay. Breathe. Nothing is going to hurt you."

Her eyes slipped closed and her breathing slowed until she was nearly calm. When I felt like she was over the fit, I spoke to her while still using my influence so that I could keep her below panic level.

"What's going on, Jinx?" I asked. "You haven't seemed like yourself lately and I'm getting really worried."

Another tear fell down her cheek. I reached forward and wiped it away gently.

"I'm worried, too," Jinx said, quietly.

"About what?" I asked.

"The Parrishables coming back," she said.

"But the spell weirdness was probably just a fluke," I said.

"This isn't just about last night, although it sure doesn't help," Jinx said. "Hadley, I've been terrified *every single day* since I woke up in that hospital. Samuel didn't just hurt me that day when his thug gutted me. It's like he took a part of me. I'm scared of *everything*. Going outside, being alone, casting spells, hanging out in big groups . . . I feel like a prisoner in my own life. It's like I could die any minute and I'm just waiting for it to happen. I can't sleep, I'm nauseous, and nothing matters anymore. My life's a mess, Hadley. And everyone else seems to be fine. The only person who even remotely understands is Abby, and even *she's* handling things better than I am."

Jinx looked down at her hands, helplessly. My heart broke for her. I'd had no idea that things were this bad. That she'd held all of this in for so many months.

"Why didn't you say anything?" I asked. "You know you can talk to any of us. We could help you."

"How?" she asked, quietly. "Besides, I wasn't even there during the big fight . . . I don't deserve your help."

"Just because you weren't there the whole time, doesn't mean it didn't affect you," I said. "Everyone deals with things in their own way. And what happened to you was a *big* deal. You should probably talk to someone about what happened. And that's okay.

"In the meantime, I think there's something I can do to help," I said, the wheels in my head spinning. "Meet me after our last class and we'll get started."

Jinx nodded and began to stand up. She gave me a small smile, one that I thought might've even been real.

"I promise, it'll get better," I said. "I'll make sure of it."

Chapter Nineteen

The day's classes were cancelled due to the incident that teachers were now calling "a misguided and unfortunate attempt at a prank." We were instructed to use our free time to start researching our witch history projects, but most of us looked at it as a day off. Counselors also told us we were to make ourselves available to help find whoever had messed with the amphitheater. Apparently the adults were more than annoyed by whoever had rearranged the seating area and planned to punish the culprits if caught.

After my talk with Jinx, though, I decided to use the time to work a little magic of my own.

It was clear that Jinx was beyond stressed and needed a little help coping with the aftermath of our run-in with the Parrishables. And if there was something I could do to ease her mind, I would do it. My influence over her mood earlier had been effective in calming her down, but it wasn't possible for me to be around her 24/7 to make sure it lasted.

I had to find a more permanent solution. At least, until Jinx could move on and heal.

Giving the situation some thought, it finally dawned on me what to do. And once again, my mom was going to come to my rescue. Well, her wisdom was, anyway. Back when she'd been alive, Mom had owned a shop called Scents and Sensibility, where she'd created custom perfumes for clients. Each concoction focused on the person's individual needs. Mom would infuse perfumes with herbs, roots, and other elements that would bring out certain qualities in the wearer. Then she'd seal the mixture with a spell—a fact that the customers weren't privy to. All they knew was, whenever they wore it, they felt good. And they smelled great, too.

I'd learned a lot about potion-making while working at the store after school, but my mom was a master at mixing. Watching her zoom around, picking out ingredients that would be perfect for each person who came in, was like watching an artist at work.

By the time I was a teenager, I recognized each of the ingredients my mom used and the powers they invoked. Every once in a while, Mom would give me refill orders to work on. That way, I'd learn how to infuse while still keeping her customers safe. She'd just begun to let me create perfumes on my own before Samuel Parris had killed her.

That had been the last time I'd meddled with potions.

Until now.

Now I wanted to create something for Jinx. Something to take the edge off until we found a more permanent solution for her nerves.

I changed into some woods-appropriate clothes—a long-sleeve, sheer white shirt, which hung off one shoulder and covered a bandeau bathing-suit top, paired with acid-wash shorts that made my legs look extra long. Completing the look with midcalf brown slouchy boots, I took off on my new mission.

Placing headphone buds into my ears, I pressed the button on my digital music player and let my favorite tunes fill my head. The woods were too quiet for me to think. I know it sounded weird, but I'd always studied better with music on. So, as I left the safety of our cabin, I turned the volume up on Taylor Swift's latest album and began to hike.

I walked deep into the woods, looking for the ingredients I needed. It would take a lot of concentration to try to identify each of the items I'd need to make Jinx's potion. True, I'd been around the elements my whole life, but I was out of practice. And I was used to looking at plants and gems while they were organized in my mom's store, not growing out in the wild.

If I was even the least bit distracted, I would miss something. And I didn't want to do that to Jinx.

Sun streamed in through the tops of the trees and cast lines of light in the air like rays through blinds. Everything around me was green and lush. Plants were growing everywhere, making it look as if I'd wandered into a wonderland of sorts.

It was calming to be surrounded by so much beauty and I felt myself begin to relax as I studied the plants and herbs along the way. I had my list of items needed for Jinx's perfume, but depending on what was growing in the area, I understood that I might have to improvise and switch a few things up.

My mom taught me a long time ago that every living thing found in nature has a purpose and power assigned to it. Flowers, roots, and even gems and rocks can be used to help invoke a feeling or reaction within the human body or psyche. Most people were completely unaware of the kind of resources they had growing in their own backyards. If they understood, then they'd be able to save themselves dozens of unnecessary trips to the doctors.

Luckily, I knew the kind of power these woods held.

I saw the single delight first. A single flower protruded from a stemful of dark green leaves, thus the reason for its name. It was white and dipped forward as if it were looking down toward the ground. I plucked the flower and slid it carefully into a canvas bag I'd brought, and silently thanked Mother Nature for the gift it was giving to my friend.

The single delight helped to get rid of feelings of isolation and allowed for a better connection with those we're spiritually linked to. Perfect for Jinx.

Next, I searched for the osha. This herb also grew in rich, moist soil and was a part of the same family as parsley and dill, so it had a sweet and strong celery-like fragrance. The root was often called "bear medicine," because animals would use it to clean out their systems. And bears were notorious for intuitively using herbs for their own healing processes. Native Americans believed the osha root to have healing powers and often burned it as incense to ward off illness, as well as negative influences and thoughts. I snagged a few of the plants at the roots, so I could use all parts of the flower.

Then, there was the river beauty. This flower stayed true to its name and was as beautiful as it was powerful. The river beauty helped to aide in emotional recovery and encouraged those who were around it to start over after devastating experiences. It promoted cleansing and growth in people overwhelmed by grief, sadness or shock. Just right for what Jinx was going through.

Forget-me-nots were some of my favorite flowers, not just because of their magical properties, but because of their ability to brighten my day. The flowers were tiny and cute, usually bright blue, pink, or white with yellow centers, and grew in big patches. They were pretty common, which meant they'd been a go-to plant for my mom's old shop. This small but lively flower helped to release fear, guilt, and pain from a person's subconscious. And from my talk with Jinx, I knew that fear was practically holding her hostage.

I had to walk quite a ways into the forest to find foxglove and fireweed. Both plants thrived in areas of land that had been cleared or burned over. Almost as soon as I'd found the open space in the middle of the canopy of trees, I spied the two plants.

Fireweed is a willow herb that has purple flowers growing in abundance up the stalk of a single stem, and opens up to flattened flowers. It's widely used to heal shock and trauma by initiating cycles of renewal and revitalization.

Foxglove flowers are shaped sort of like long, slender bells. I used to get in so much trouble as a kid, because I'd walk around Mom's store with them covering my digits like fancy fingernails. The foxglove releases fear and emotional tension from the heart, and allows us to connect with the truth of a situation.

After leaving the clearing where I'd found the foxglove and the fireweed, I wandered back in the direction of the cabin, and before long, found a patch of carline thistle, a plant that looks slightly intimidating. Careful to grip the nonspiky section of the stem only, I snapped off a piece and added it to my bag. The carline thistle drew strength from those around the wearer, and was used for protection from harm.

I peered at the treasure trove of flowers, roots, and herbs I'd gathered and decided they were more than enough to create Jinx's perfume. If I performed the spell and made the potion correctly, then Jinx would be left with a concoction that would help to get rid of her fear, anxiety, and pain, hopefully allowing her to finally begin to heal. I smiled as I realized I was sort of following in my mom's footsteps, creating perfumes to help those in need.

Especially since Jinx was in her current predicament because of me. Because *I'd* been the target of some psycho evil witch and his crazy coven. I owed it to her to help her heal.

I looked at my cell phone and saw that I'd been gone now for over two hours. I'd missed lunch, but I wasn't terribly starved and I'd seen some berries growing along the path that I knew were safe to eat if I got hungry on my way back. Turning in the direction of camp, I started to head back, considering the afternoon a success.

I'd only made it a few strides, before my whole world was turned upside down. Literally. I felt something pull tightly around my ankles and then I was falling toward the ground face-first. Before I made impact, I was lifted up into the air, upside down, and then hung there like a trapped animal.

"What the hell!" I yelled out, looking down at the ground where my bag now lay, overturned in the flight. A few of the flowers had escaped and were scattered nearby.

Before I could take stock of what had just happened, I felt something slither its way down my leg and toward my face. My first thought was that it was a snake, which was horrifying in itself, but as I brought my chin to my chest, I could see it wasn't a reptile at all. What was coming toward me was brownish-green and plant-based.

And totally alive.

I started to cry out, but the vine wrapped around my neck and began to tighten. Almost as suddenly, I was being flipped right-side up again and pulled farther into the air. Frantically clawing at the vine around my neck, I tried to free myself from its dangerous grip. But I was only able to force my fingers underneath long enough to give myself a single breath, before it cut off my oxygen completely.

I was being hanged.

As many times as I'd experienced the feeling in my dreams of Bridget, nothing had prepared me for the real thing.

Knowing you're about to die is the worst part about dying. I felt it firsthand through my dreams of Bridget Bishop's murder. The fear of what's coming is both paralyzing and terrifying, and no matter how imminent it is, you still wish there was something you could do about it.

And of course, that desire for survival often makes things even worse. Because it forces you to fight, which often makes death come sooner.

All of this popped into my head as I tried desperately to free myself.

My breath came out in gurgles and I could feel my eyes begin to bug out of my head. The thought came that I should try to use a spell to get myself down, but I needed one of my hands to be free to do it, and if I let go now, I might pass out before I could even think the words.

All I could do was jerk around as I waited to pass out.

Just before I gave in and closed my eyes, I heard a few branches snap nearby.

"Looks like we've caught ourselves a bitch—I mean, a witch," a voice said behind me nastily.

Chapter Twenty

My eyes flew open as I continued to struggle against the vines that were attached to the tree. *Someone was here to help!* Hope flooded my body as I realized I might not die out here after all.

And then I saw who my saviors were.

Eve placed a hand on her hip and looked at me with disdain. Brooklyn stood stiffly next to her, a perma-frown on her face. I should have known they would be behind something like this.

"Fitting, don't you think, Brooklyn?" Eve said. "That she'd end up just like her ancestors?"

"It's definitely an interesting position to be in," Brooklyn said, analyzing the situation.

She was going to let me hang. Because she wanted my boyfriend. Or didn't like me threatening the kingdom she'd created. Either way, she wanted me dead.

My vision was going in and out now, giving the illusion that I was in some psychedelic dream. Brooklyn and Eve appeared to be swaying to an unheard beat, even though they were most likely standing still.

Brooklyn sighed and took a step toward me. Before I could process what was happening, she was yelling. "Exbiliby totalitum!" Brooklyn said, barely looking at the vine she was sending the spell to.

Only, nothing happened.

When Brooklyn saw that I wasn't falling toward the forest floor like she'd intended, she squinted her eyes suspiciously. "That's weird," she said.

"My turn!" Eve said gleefully, stepping in front of Brooklyn without waiting for an answer. "My aim's not awesome, Hadley, so sorry if I miss the mark."

I wanted to yell, but I had no energy or breath left to use.

The magic hit the area of vine just above my head and I felt the shock of it reverberate inside my body. It didn't hurt exactly, but it did cause me to spin a few times, which made the vines tighten just a bit more.

"Missed. Darn," she said, not sounding upset about it at all.

Brooklyn was moving now. She picked up a stick from the ground and wordlessly began to walk toward me. She closed the distance in four steps and then stood there staring at me blankly, gripping the stick so tightly that her knuckles were turning white. Visions of Brooklyn treating me like a human piñata danced in my head and I started to wonder if there was a fate worse than death.

Brooklyn said a few words under her breath and suddenly the stick turned into a knife. A sharp, shiny, long knife. One that was perfect for cutting.

Well that's not good.

A wave of blackness swam across my eyes and I thought I was going to pass out. But then it cleared again and I could see

Brooklyn moving closer to me. Finally, when she was just a few inches away from my helpless body, she stretched up and began to saw at the ropes. If I'd been strung any higher than a few inches off the ground, it would have proved even more difficult. Luckily, Brooklyn was so freaking tall that she could reach the area right above my head.

Though it felt like a lifetime since I'd taken my last breath, it had only been about thirty seconds in actuality. Still, it was a half a minute too long.

I faded out again. This time I wasn't sure for how long. But then the final threads were giving away and I was plummeting toward the ground. I didn't even have time to try to soften the fall and my left shoulder made a smacking sound as I hit the dirt. I tried to scream out in pain but nothing came. Rolling over onto my side, I lay there for a few minutes just forcing air into my lungs.

Breathe. Breathe. It was all I could focus on.

Once I could talk again, I looked up at the two girls who were standing just a few feet away, silently hating me.

"You couldn't have softened my fall with a little spell?" I asked them, angrily.

Eve shrugged. "I could have," the dark-haired girl answered. "I just didn't want to."

I would have lunged at her if my legs weren't still tied together. Instead I forced myself into a sitting position and glared at them.

"You almost *killed* me," I said angrily.

"You've *got* to be kidding me." Brooklyn snorted and then looked over at Eve, who started to laugh. "You think *we* did this?"

"Didn't you?" I asked, growing hysterical. My hands shook as I fumbled with the noose that was still around my neck and then reached down to free my ankles.

"Hardly," Brooklyn said. "This is a little . . . *cliché* for me." She motioned in my direction like she was bored.

"Besides, death is too quick. It's much more fun to piss you off," Eve said.

When I was finally free from my bindings, I stalked over to Brooklyn, pushing her hard until she stumbled backward. "If I find out you had *anything* to do with this, you're going to wish you'd killed me."

"Back off, Bishop," Eve said, stepping between her friend and me. "She just saved your butt. You should be *thanking* her."

It was true. None of what had happened here was adding up. Why *would* Brooklyn help me down if she'd orchestrated the whole thing? Well, other than to throw me off her scent, and look like the hero to Asher. Eve was right: there were better ways to torture me.

Like taking everything I loved and making me watch while she did it.

I was about to confront her about this, but Brooklyn was already walking away, dragging Eve along with her.

Reaching for my bag, I quickly gathered the flowers that had spilled out. Inspecting one of the bright purple flowers closely, I was relieved to find that they were still intact. I was still angry and rattled over what had just happened, but at least the whole afternoon hadn't been a complete bust.

"Oh, and Hadley?" Brooklyn said as I got up from the ground slowly. She didn't even look back as she addressed me. "You owe me now. And I *will* collect."

"I know they were the ones that set the trap," I said adamantly.

As soon as I'd gotten back to camp, I'd called an emergency meeting of the Cleri. We met in our room, so we wouldn't have to worry about eavesdroppers or running into Brooklyn and Eve again. This time I let Colette stay. She needed to know how dangerous the girls were, too, and if there was going to be a battle, I wanted her on my side.

Once everyone was gathered around the room, I launched into a retelling of my near-death experience, complete with the unveiling of the growing bruises around my neck. Everyone listened with rapt attention, seemingly in disbelief over the fact that there were clearly enemies at camp with us. When I was finished, they all remained silent for a few minutes as they tried to digest what I'd just unloaded on them.

"I don't know, Had," Sascha said, finally. "Why would they tie you up, only to cut you down later?"

"Hanged. They *hanged* me, Sash. And I don't know why crazy people do crazy things. Maybe they thought that by helping me escape, I'd be indebted to them," I said, not getting why she wasn't automatically on my side over this. "Which is basically what Brooklyn said before she left me out there in the woods by myself, I might add."

"Well, isn't that how it works?" Jasmine asked. "Someone bails your butt out and you do them a solid later?"

"Not if they were the ones that put you in the situation in the first place," I argued.

"No offense, but why do you even *care* about them, Hadley?" Fallon cut in. He was sitting next to Abby on her bed, looking more than comfortable with his surroundings. "I mean . . . you're *Hadley Bishop*. A centuries-old evil coven went after you last year and you beat them. Why would you let a few bitchy girls get to you? And if they're really evil, then why not take them out? Next to you they're nothing."

Had Fallon just given me a *compliment*? I glanced over at him awkwardly, not quite sure how to respond to this kinder, less annoying version of him. The even weirder thing was that he was starting to seem more like an actual human being and not just the kid twerp I grew up with. What were they putting in the water up here, anyway?

"Um, *thanks?*" I said.

"This is ridiculous. Hadley can't *destroy* a bunch of teenage girls just because they don't like her, or want to steal her boyfriend," Abby said, annoyed. The fact that she was speaking up at all caught me off-guard. Apparently Fallon was too, because he sat back, suddenly silent, clearly torn between his allegiance to me and to his girlfriend.

"Brooklyn's not trying to *steal* me," Asher said.

"She's made it pretty clear she's not thrilled about the fact that we're together," I said, looking at Asher, whose expression was pained. I turned back to Abby and gave her a pointed look. "Besides, *you* were the one who said that Brooklyn would do whatever it takes to get what she wants. Hello? How much more proof do you need?"

"The kind that shows she actually did it," Jasmine said. Of all the people to come to Brooklyn's defense, I never expected it to be her. "Look, nobody likes a good throw-down more than me, but even I think this is bull."

"Yeah, Brooklyn's not as bad as you're making her out to be," Sascha said as she played with a bracelet that hung around her wrist. It was small and gold and delicate—and completely unfamiliar to me. I glanced over at Abby and then at Jasmine and Jinx. They were all wearing replicas of the jewelry Sascha had.

If they were friendship bracelets, where was mine?

"That's because she's trying to turn you against me," I said finally.

"It seems like you're doing a pretty good job of that yourself," Jinx said quietly.

This was especially painful to hear, since I'd been out in the woods looking for a solution to *Jinx's* anxiety. It was like taking a slug to my gut.

"That's enough, guys!" Asher said forcefully. He got up and walked over to where I was sitting on the couch and placed his hands on my shoulders reassuringly. "Hadley didn't attack herself out there. Something's going on—that much we know."

"Thanks, Asher," I said, looking up at him gratefully. Suddenly all those nights we hadn't spent with each other since we'd arrived didn't seem like they'd had much of an impact on our relationship. He was still there for me when I needed him, and that's what really mattered.

"That said, I agree with the others that it couldn't have been Brooklyn who did this," he concluded.

What the eff.

"You guys *really* don't see Brooklyn as a threat?" I asked, unwilling to let it go. Not when I was so sure I was right. When they didn't answer, I frowned and looked away, disappointed.

"Sorry, Had," Asher said, touching the rope burns on my neck gingerly. The contact made me shiver. "It's not that we don't believe you, but I think you're accusing the wrong person here. It just *can't* be her."

"I know you used to date her, Asher, but she's not the same girl you used to know," I said.

"It's not that," he said, sighing as he ran his hands through his jet-black hair. The others were sitting around now, just watching us.

"Then *what* Asher?" I asked, pulling out from underneath him as I grew more frustrated with the conversation. "Someone tried to drown me in the shower and left that message in the amphitheater. Brooklyn's the only one who makes sense! What proof could you *possibly* have that she's not the one pulling the strings here?"

He remained silent for a few beats and stared down at his feet, suddenly looking guilty.

"Brooklyn couldn't have done the stuff at the amphitheater," he said. "Because she was with me last night."

Chapter Twenty-One

I must have gone momentarily deaf, because I could've sworn that Asher just said that Brooklyn was with *him* the night before.

"Huh?" I asked blankly.

"Had, don't freak out, okay?" Asher said, placing his hand in mine. I let him do it, but I didn't return his reassuring squeeze. In fact, I barely felt him touching me as the truth of what he said sunk in.

"I won't freak out, because it can't be true," I said finally, my voice not sounding like my own. "You couldn't have been with her, Asher, because you already had plans with Hudson and Dane. Wasn't that the reason you couldn't meet the rest of your coven last night?"

"Mmmm, Dane," Sascha cooed dreamily. "Crikey! Where *is* my cute Aussie tonight, anyway?"

"You realize they don't actually say that over in Australia, right?" Jasmine said.

I ignored both of them, staring at Asher as I waited for him to answer me. But he didn't. It was like we were in some sort of standoff, both waiting for the other to draw their gun first.

"Yes they do," Sascha insisted. "The Crocodile Dundee said it all the time."

Jasmine looked up at the ceiling and sighed loudly. "Well, if you saw it on TV then it *must* be true," she said. "In fact, you should *definitely* ask Dane about it the next time you see him. I'm sure he'd *love* to hear you speak his native language."

"You think?" Sascha asked, smiling like she was already considering it.

"Look, I *did* have plans with the guys last night—" Asher finally said to me.

"Glad we cleared that up," I said.

"—but when we were done, Brooklyn and Eve came by," he said.

"Why would they think it was okay to drop by your room so late at night? Or at all?" I asked, growing angrier as I pictured them prancing around in their pajamas.

"It wasn't a big deal, Had. Honest," he said. "Brooklyn said it was Eve's idea—I think she likes one of the guys or something—"

"It better not be Dane," Sascha chimed in, her eyes narrowing into slits.

"—so, I figured it was as good a time as any to clear things up with her. You know, make things right after what happened?" Asher's eyes pleaded with me not to make him go into details in front of the other Cleri members.

"And you just *had* to do it in your *bedroom*?" I asked.

He looked around the table for help, but no one was going to save him from my wrath. Especially since he was currently surrounded by girls. Looking deflated, he turned back to me again.

"Clearly, talking to Brooklyn in my room—even though it's not like we were alone or anything—was a bad idea. I can see that now," he said carefully, trying to lighten the mood. I didn't think it was funny. "Next time I'll make sure we hang out in neutral territory."

"Yeah. Somewhere there isn't a bed, genius," Jasmine said, snickering.

"Oh, no," I said, shaking my head. "No. There isn't going to be a next time, Asher. That was it. You explained things to her, you guys had your closure, there's no reason the two of you need to *hang out* ever again."

Asher wasn't a dumb guy. So why was he saying such stupid things? Beyond that, why did he even *want* to spend time with Brooklyn at all? It was clear that Asher and I connected on a deeper level; and I had no doubt that Asher loved me. That was a truth that I felt in my heart.

Still, Brooklyn had powers that I didn't. Here was a girl who could make people *fall* for her. Whether they wanted to or not.

"Had, you know that I love you. And I'd do anything to make you happy. But I can't promise you I'll never talk to her again," he said to me gently.

It was like a shot through my heart and for a few seconds I didn't know what to say. I stood up to leave—forgetting that it was my own room—but Asher gripped my hand harder to keep me from escaping.

"I have roommates," he explained. "If they want to invite Brooklyn over, I can't do anything about it. And with Eve on the scene . . . well, she'll probably be back. Which means Brooklyn might tag along. Besides, we're all sort of stuck here, babe. It's not exactly a big campus and I can't just start ignoring her. Especially since I'm trying to do the right thing this time around."

His explanation made sense, but I still didn't like knowing that there wasn't a whole lot I could do to keep the two of them apart. I wanted Asher to offer to leave the room if Brooklyn came to "hang out" again, but the gesture never came.

"Fine," I said, feeling totally over the conversation.

I freed my hand from his and scooted over the back of the couch, escaping to my bed. Pulling my legs up onto the bedspread, I looked out the window as it raised up into the air and away from Asher and the others.

The rest of the Cleri realized this was their hint to leave and I didn't have to watch them to know they were heading toward the door. A few seconds later, I heard it open and feet shuffling out.

"I guess I'll see you tomorrow then?" Asher said quietly. There was a sadness in his voice, but I felt too betrayed to care. So I just mumbled something incoherent and lay down until the last of them were gone.

I stayed there like that, even after Abby and Colette had left for dinner, just staring out the window. When I finally snapped out of it, I came up with a new game plan. One that redirected my focus from Brooklyn and back onto the people I actually cared about.

Even if they didn't seem to care about me at the moment.

I immediately got to work on creating the perfume for Jinx. Her emotional health was more important than any squabble—no matter how big. Besides, I'd nearly died getting all the ingredients and I was damned if I was going to let them go to waste now.

So, with a new fire ignited inside me, I started on the potion, first conjuring up an empty glass bottle that would work perfectly as a perfume dispenser. It was pretty. Big and round with cuts in the glass like a mini-disco-ball. In the light it even shone a little like one. I was sure Jinx would love it. Any girl would. Well, maybe not Jasmine, but she was sort of in a (dark) league of her own.

I ran my fingers over the pages of the book that now rested on my comforter in front of me. Following the strokes of the pen on the page I was currently turned to, I couldn't help but smile.

My family magic book always had that effect on me.

At first I'd wondered if it was stupid for me to take such a priceless family heirloom to a camp where the potential for someone to get their hands on it was higher than at home. But the truth was: I felt safer with it on me. Even if I had to hide it whenever I was away from it.

And by hide, I mean morph it into something else entirely, so that no one would be tempted to steal it or read the private spells located within its pages. A day of research and a simple spell later, I had successfully glamoured the giant hardback book into a distressed copy of *The Catcher in the Rye*. I figured it was a safe alternative, considering it was highly unlikely that anyone our age would pick up the classic for a light read. Even Abby thought it was a little too much emo-whining for her.

So, after switching Salinger back into my beloved Book o' Spells, I spread out all the flowers and herbs that I'd collected from the woods. Whites, purples, yellows, greens, blues—the petals were all so vibrant and beautiful, it was almost a shame I'd have to crush most of what was in front of me.

Earlier, I'd snagged some food and borrowed a small container of olive oil from the dining hall. The kitchen staff hadn't asked me why I'd wanted it, just handed the bottle over. And true, regular old olive oil had a stronger base smell to it than grapeseed oil, but ultimately it wouldn't interfere with the other scents I'd be infusing the oil with. And in a pinch, beggars can't be choosers.

I began pulling the petals from each of the flowers, placing them along with some of the roots into a bowl like the ones people used to make guacamole in restaurants. Luckily, this had been another item we'd had on campus—both in the dining hall and in the magic-supply closet, which was kept downstairs. The mortar and pestle were actually items typically found in any magicking household, so they were pretty easy to come by.

Civilians registered for plates and Crock-Pots. We witches asked for equipment to make our potions in. What are you going to do?

When I was done plucking the flowers, I took the pestle and began to crush the petals inside the bowl. Immediately all sorts of sweet smells filled the room. It was like being in a flower shop, only better, since I was squeezing out all the oils that were inside the flowers and letting their essences permeate the air. It was only through destroying the flowers that the power inside them would truly be unleashed. The outer smell of a flower faded fast, but the essence . . . the essence lasted much longer.

When I was done, the mulch in front of me wasn't anything to look at, but the smell was delicious and once added to the oil it became more than just a fragrance. It was the answer to Jinx's problems.

Or it would be soon, I hoped.

I carefully pushed the crushed-up mush through the opening of the bottle and watched as it hit the oil below and then floated in chunks near the surface. When I'd placed enough in there to fill the entire container, I closed up the top and looked at it objectively. It didn't look as pretty or professional as one of my mom's but it would do the trick.

"Now, for the icing on the cake," I said to myself, placing the bottle on the right page of my book, while reading the one on the left.

Shortly after taking my family's spell book home from our cabin, I'd begun to add other spells to it. Ones that my mom had used on a regular basis—including her perfuming spell—as well as others I'd created and ones Dad favored. I'd even gone as far as to rack my brain for spells that Grammy casted when I visited her as a child.

So now, along with Bridget Bishop's original spells and those of her daughter Christian, there were whole generations of our family's magic written between the covers of the book. It was really cool to see that much history—and power—in one place.

Reading the spell once more to myself, I picked up the bottle and took a few deep, cleansing breaths to prepare myself for the casting. My heartbeat began to slow and my brain quieted.

Clear mind, clear cast.

Recalling my mom's favorite saying, I finally felt ready to say the words to her perfuming spell for the first time since she'd died. I cupped the bottle like a precious jewel. My voice came out strong and purposeful.

> *Gifts from stone, herb, root, and flower,*
> *Infuse the wearer with thy power.*
> *Take her desires and make them true,*
> *From you to her, let her start anew.*

As I finished the spell, the contents began to swirl around, and the light tingling sensation in my hands told me that it was working. Smiling, I snapped the family book shut and peered through the glass at my first unassisted perfuming. It looked like it should and it certainly smelled good. A bit strong, but better that than weak.

I thought about rubbing some of the oil onto myself to see if it worked but was reminded of the fact that I'd been concentrating on Jinx when I'd said the spell, making her the focus of its energies. It wouldn't have the same effect on anyone else.

I'd just have to wait to see if it worked once Jinx was wearing it.

As I finished up, Colette walked through the door, followed by Abby and Jinx. Colette looked lost in her own thoughts, but bounced a bit with every step, and the other two spoke softly to each other as they crossed the room and sat down on the circular couch. Saying the words to the spell that would switch my family's book back to *The Catcher in the Rye*, I eyeballed the flowery mess on my comforter and decided to clean up later. Right now I was more interested in hearing what Abby and Jinx were talking about.

I had to settle for catching bits and pieces of their conversation, since their voices were so low. Of course, doing so was more like playing a messed-up game of Mad Libs. One where *I* was required to fill in the bulk of the story.

". . . impossible to sleep," Abby said.

". . . talked to Fallon—" This part was from Jinx.

Abby shook her head and then waited patiently as Jinx continued whatever she was saying.

"Nothing's working," Abby said, just loudly enough for me to actually hear her.

"Try doing a spell, maybe?" Jinx said, biting her lower lip as she thought about it. "On second thought—that hasn't really worked for me lately, either. . . ." Her sentence trailed off.

Which was my cue.

I threw my legs over the side of my bed and waited patiently as the mattress lowered and my heels touched the floor again. Once I was vertical, I walked over to the girls and handed Jinx the bottle.

"What's this?" she asked, warily.

"It's a present," I said softly. "Look, I know I've sort of been crazy lately and things haven't been easy for you . . . so, I made you this perfume with the flowers I got out in the woods today. I thought it might cheer you up."

I could tell she was genuinely surprised by the gesture and looked over at Abby quickly before taking the bottle from me. Abby's face remained stony, but she didn't tell her not to accept it.

"Er, thanks Hadley," Jinx said, perplexed. "That was really nice of you."

"It's no problem, really," I said, trying to make it sound like that was true. "I just hope you like it."

Removing the stopper, Jinx touched her finger gingerly to the oil and then hesitated slightly before spreading it onto her neck and wrist. It didn't take long for the smells to fill the room. And even before she'd closed the bottle back up, I could have sworn she seemed different.

Chapter Twenty-Two

"All right girls! Everyone gather around!" Miss Peggy called out from the stage in the amphitheater. On either side of her were Mrs. B and Mrs. Jeanette. Seeing them standing there together, it was clear how different they were. Miss Peggy was wearing her usual uniform of shorts and blinged-out vest, while Mrs. B chose a shiny black form-fitting dress. Mrs. Jeanette had on a pair of jeans and a light yellow cardigan. Despite their differences, the mismatched trio looked at home up there together.

"I trust you all enjoyed the time off from your typical magicking sessions, as the counselors and I attempted to put things back in their rightful places," Miss Peggy said.

It had taken two more days for the elders to unbolt the stadium seats from the roof of the boys' amphitheater. According to the rumor mill, whoever had been behind the little "prank" had done a serious whammy on the chairs. Whereas, it should've only taken one person, two people tops, to return everything to its original spot, it ended up requiring all of the elders to work together to do so. All due to a particularly peculiar enchantment, which had been cast on the bolts, making it nearly impossible for anyone to penetrate.

No one knew how the adults had finally pulled it off, but the announcement had come late last night that sessions would resume as normal this morning. Something that elicited a groan from the bulk of my peers. Most of the campers had treated these days off like it was the perfect time for typical summer fare: working on their tan, sneaking off with the opposite (or same) sex, and otherwise relaxing.

I, however, had used it to start doing some reconnaissance on Brooklyn. One thing had been made clear during my little Cleri intervention: If I wanted the others to believe me, I needed hard proof that she and Eve were plotting against me. Unfortunately, the only things I'd managed to find out about the two was that they never stopped talking about themselves and they both flirted with *everyone*.

"Since we're a few days behind schedule on our lessons, we're going to try to amp things up a bit so we can get back on track," Mrs. B said, placing a perfectly manicured hand on her side. "But we've seen you girls in action and I'd say you're all up for the challenge, right?"

"First thing we'll be learning today is how to cast as a chameleon," Mrs. Jeanette said, getting right down to business. "The chameleon is an interesting species of lizard with many distinguishing abilities. The most widely known is its ability to change color. Can anyone name something else that sets the chameleon apart from other lizards?"

Colette raised her hand immediately, and although she didn't cry out, "Oooh, ooh, me! I know it!" it was clear she wanted to answer. So they let her.

"Chameleons are capable of arboreal locomotion. Which

basically means that they can climb trees *really* well," she said, with an unusual amount of excitement.

"That's right, er . . . Colette," Mrs. Jeanette said, looking down at her clipboard. "Very good—"

"That's not all," Colette continued, not even waiting for Mrs. Jeanette to finish her sentence. "They also have crazy-awesome eyes; the most distinctive of any reptiles, actually. The eyelids are round in shape, with the opening only big enough to let their pupils show. They have the ability to check out two objects at once, with an eye looking one way and the other in a completely different direction. Their eye rotation is so great that they can see three hundred sixty degrees around themselves. So, in this case, they really *do* have eyes in the back of their heads!"

Colette started to giggle like she'd just told her best joke. I couldn't help but laugh, too. I'd never known anyone as dorkily endearing as her. You just couldn't dislike the girl.

"It looks like someone's giving you a run for your money, Jeanette," Mrs. B chimed in, implying that there might be another budding scientist among them.

But the buttoned-up scientist didn't see the humor in her words. Instead, she attempted to regain control over her lesson by continuing.

"As Colette pointed out, chameleons have many assets at their disposal and the reason that their species has survived for as long as they have is because they know how to use them," she said. "They don't let them go to waste and when they find themselves in danger, they utilize each of their gifts to ensure their safety."

"This is something that we, as witches, must become adept at doing," Miss Peggy said. "So, today you're going to learn the secret weapons of the chameleon so that you can defend yourself against anyone or anything that might harm you. I hope that none of you will need to use what we're teaching you, but it's better to be trained than left without a safety net."

Miss Peggy had no idea how right she was. There was so much that the Cleri hadn't known about magic—or even their own abilities—when the Parrishables had waged war on us. We'd had to put ourselves into spell boot camp, and even then we hadn't been prepared. If we hadn't gotten lucky with a few spells from my super-great-grandmother Bishop, none of us would be alive now.

And the more spells I knew, the more power I had over my enemies, be it evil covens or evil ex-girlfriends. Maybe these classes wouldn't be a bust after all.

Finishing with their speech, the counselors broke us up into three groups and instructed us to spread out across the grounds. The day was cooler than usual, but it was still well into the seventies and it was only midmorning. None of us were psyched to be leaving the shade of the theater, but we followed the counselors out into the sun, anyway.

"The first thing we'll be teaching you is a camouflaging incantation," Mrs. Jeanette said. "This is a higher-level spell and usually takes practice to perfect. So, don't be discouraged if you don't get it right away. Mrs. B will now demonstrate."

We all turned our attention to the red-haired woman who'd taken her place beside a nearby tree. As we watched, Mrs. B leaned against it, until her back was flat against the bark. She placed her legs as close to the trunk as possible and pressed her hands into the wood. Wiggling her eyes at us goofily, she said the words to the spell.

"Conselus disguisen camocon!"

Suddenly, she was gone. The space where Mrs. B had just been standing was empty. One minute she'd been there and the next she'd just . . . disappeared.

"Go on, take a look! You can all get closer," Miss Peggy said, gesturing for us to move forward. "It's important for you to see what this spell can really do."

Nobody moved at first, so I took a step toward where Mrs. B had just been lounging. As I went, I tried to search for the telltale signs that I was still looking at a person, but I still only saw the tree. I continued walking forward until I was so close that I could've reached out and touched the bark. And I was tempted to do it, too, only in the back of my mind I knew that Mrs. B was supposedly still there. And she probably wouldn't take kindly to being felt up. At least not by me.

"That's amazing," I said, feeling others coming up behind me and join in the staring. "I can't see her *at all*. Are we sure she's really there?"

As soon as I said this, a pair of eyes appeared . . . and blinked at me.

"Jesus!" I screamed and jumped backward, running smack into Jasmine.

People started to snicker at my reaction, but all I cared about at the moment was learning how to do the spell, too.

Mrs. B finally stepped away from the cover of the tree, and at first, the design of the bark stayed on her skin like a temporary tattoo. But as she got farther away from it, the colors on her skin and dress faded until she was back to her original self again. With the flourish of a Broadway performer, Mrs. B put her hands up in the air and said, "Ta-dah!"

"Yes, very good," Mrs. Jeanette said, although she didn't sound all that impressed. Clearing her throat, she stepped right in front of Mrs. B. "Okay, the trick to this spell is contact with the object or thing that you're trying to mimic. As you noticed, Mrs. B was leaning against the tree trunk, as well as touching it with her hands. This is imperative to creating a perfect duplication of the environment you're trying to blend in with. It will help you to draw from the essence of the object, making it easier to change."

Miss Peggy clapped her hands then, causing most of us to jump in surprise. "Why don't you say we give it a go, huh? Team up with a buddy and find an area to try to camouflage yourself into. It can be anything, but remember: the simpler the design, the easier the spell. And this one's a doozy!"

Abby and Jasmine paired off almost immediately, while Sascha and Colette decided to work together. That left me with Jinx. This was actually fine, since I hadn't been able to talk to her one-on-one since I'd given her the perfume. I was curious to find out how it was working, or if it was even working at all.

"Wanna try the floor of the stage?" I asked when we'd broken away from the others. "It's pretty bland pattern-wise and there's a roof, which means we won't be out here baking in the sun."

"Sure," Jinx said, staring down at the group. "Apparently I could use a little color. When I got out of the shower this morning, Jasmine called me Casper."

"Well, isn't *she* a morning person," I said sarcastically. "I think you're actually starting to get some pink back in your cheeks, Jinxy." It was true. Before, she'd been an oatmeally-gray color, which had made her look sort of sickly. Now, there was a hint of life back in her skin.

"I think so, too," Jinx responded. She still wouldn't look at me as we walked into the shade and toward the charcoal stage. Considering what she'd said the other day in my room, I was surprised she'd agreed to team up with me at all. "I'm feeling a little better. Like I'm getting control over my life again. I mean, I still have moments of anxiety, and I'm struggling in the sleep department, but my appetite's coming back. And I don't feel so . . . hopeless."

"That's incredible, Jinx!" I said, practically tackling her into a hug. It was the best news I'd gotten all week and I hadn't realized just how much I'd needed to hear it. But Jinx wasn't totally healed yet, and as I hopped up onto the stage and then popped back to my feet again, she chose to take the stairs.

We both sat down in the middle of the stage. No one else had had the foresight to seek refuge from the sun, so we had the whole place to ourselves. When I began to lie down on the floor so we could start casting, Jinx placed her hand on mine.

"Thanks, Hadley," she said finally.

"For what?" I asked, playing dumb. I'd never actually come out and told her what I'd put in the perfume and neither of us had acknowledged that there was magic at work here. It wasn't that I didn't want her to know, I just didn't feel like I needed the attention for doing the right thing.

She cocked her head to the side and looked at me curiously, before taking her hand back and placing it onto her lap demurely. Now that Jinx was getting back to her old self, I imagined that a manicure would be in her near future. "Nothing," she said with a smile. "Just, thanks. You know . . . for always being there and everything."

I grinned from ear to ear. "Of course. We're family. And family takes care of family, even when they can't take care of themselves," I said. Then I gestured to her and winked. "Besides, this . . . this is all you. It's your will and spirit that's getting you through this. You're much stronger than you think."

She nodded.

Lying back down on the stage, I tried to ignore the fact that I was getting my outfit dirty. At least it was a repeat outfit—a purple skirt and a black top with reflective circles all over it.

"Let's get our Chamele-*on*," I said and then started to cast.

Chapter Twenty-Three

Hours had passed. I was still outside, but had no idea what I was doing there. The sun had long since gone down, and despite the warmth of the day, it was so cold that I couldn't help but shiver. When I looked down I could see that I was only wearing my cute cotton black-and-white romper that read SMART GIRLS FINISH *FIRST*. It was my favorite pair of pajamas, but also my lightest, and wouldn't keep me warm in the breezy night air.

Why was I out of bed? How had I gotten here?

I caught a flurry of movement off to my right, and took in a quick breath as I saw a figure move out from behind a tree and then take one slow step after another into the woods beyond the amphitheater. I couldn't see who the person was, because, one, they were too far away, and two, whoever it was had on a cloak of some sort. It was dark and completely covered the figure from head to toe. There wasn't even a hint as to whether the person was male or female.

I went to shout at the late-night walker, but then stopped myself at the last minute and looked back at the cabin looming behind me. There wasn't a single light on in any of the bedrooms and I didn't want to wake the whole place up. The consequences of being in the woods at night had been made clear to all of us, and the secret plans of the mystery person had piqued my interest. I wanted to find out what the person was doing running around campus at night.

With one last glance over my shoulder at safety, I ran after the person. My bare feet grew dirty with every step and I cringed as dust and rocks hit the backs of my legs.

If only I'd remembered to put on shoes before going for a walk in the middle of the night . . .

The campus was eerily silent. Even the sound of my feet pitter-pattering across the forest floor came out like a distant whisper. I kept the dark figure within eyesight, but left enough distance between us that I wouldn't be caught. The farther we disappeared into the woods, the more concerned I grew over what might be at the end of this game of follow the leader.

Not only that, but this scenario was beginning to look an awful lot like a plot out of a horror movie. Cute girl runs through the woods alone with only her thin pajamas on. Then she trips on a root that just happens to be sticking out of the ground. . . .

At that precise moment, my steps faltered, but I was able to stay on my feet.

Seriously?

Still, I followed the hooded figure deeper and deeper into the forest. We'd long since passed the area dedicated to our casting sessions and were fully in the part that the counselors had warned us not to venture to. Breaking the rules didn't bother me. Being forced to leave my boyfriend with Brooklyn for the summer, because I broke camp rules, well, that was enough to make me think twice about what I was doing.

I realized a little too late that the person ahead of me had begun to slow, and I had to stop abruptly to keep from slamming right into them. The hood of the figure moved slowly from side to side as it tried to decide which way to go, before stepping into a clearing.

Creeping forward, I tried my best not to make any noise. Other sounds filled the night now. Whispers that I hadn't heard before, which seemed to have only started when we were far enough away from the cabin that we couldn't call out for help, echoed through the trees. At first I couldn't figure out exactly where they were coming from or how many voices there even were. They filled my head from every direction, leaving me turning in circles as I attempted to find their source. Then, as if all the other sounds had been sucked out of the forest at once, I could hear the voices coming distinctly from the direction of the clearing in front of me.

So, I followed them.

Slipping behind a large tree, I waited as long as I could before making a move. One . . . two . . . three . . . four. It felt like an eternity had gone by when I finally peeked out from behind the tree. When I did, I fought the urge to hide again. Because there stood three cloaked figures, gathered around a ball of light.

They were chanting something over and over again. Words to a spell that I didn't recognize. After a few repetitions, I was finally able to understand what they were saying.

"Discubus susperion violane spurniface," they chanted in unison. "Discubus susperion violane spurniface. Discubus susperion violane spurniface."

What does that even mean?

Two of the three had their backs turned to me, but the third was directly in my sight. Only, the hood was so large that it covered most of the person's face and I was still too far away to see any details. I could tell that the person was holding something in their hand, though. It shimmered in the limited lighting, but I couldn't figure out what it was. If I knew that, then maybe I'd be able to figure out what they were casting.

I had to get closer.

I dashed from tree to tree in a zigzagging pattern until I was less than ten feet away. While they were still in the middle of their chanting, I dared a look around the tree again.

Red stone shone like fresh blood against caramel-colored skin. The metal twined its way around the ruby, like it was hugging its child protectively. I sucked in my breath involuntarily, looking down at the empty space on my finger where a ring used to sit.

Why did these people have Bridget's ring? *My* ring?

My ears began to echo with the sounds of my own heart beating. If the chanting stopped, I was sure the strangers would hear it, too. I searched my mind to figure out what to do next.

First things first: I had to get my ring back.

Popping my head back out, I studied all three of the figures and realized frustratingly that there was nothing on them to give me any clue as to who they were. And without knowing that, it wouldn't be a smart idea for me to rush them. Not until I had one of my most prized possessions back on my finger where it belonged at least.

I was in the middle of trying to formulate another plan when I got the break I'd been waiting for. Slowly, the hood of one of the figures facing me began to move. The person began to lift their head and I was moments away from seeing their face. I held my breath as more and more skin was revealed to me, first showing a naked neck and then an angular chin, a set of full lips and then a perfectly shaped nose.

My head was screaming for the person to look up all the way. And finally she did.

My eyes flew open and suddenly I was back in my room. The sun had just begun to come up over the horizon, and the growing light was forcing shadows out of every corner of our shared space. This did nothing to calm my nerves, though.

Abby.

The dream had been so vivid.

Remembering the way she'd looked while peering out from under the hood of her dark cloak, I quickly turned over to her side of the room. I expected to find her asleep in bed, tucked in and dreaming peacefully.

Instead, the bed was empty.

Was it possible it *wasn't* a dream after all? That I really *had* been out wandering the woods and just happened upon a group of witches chanting while holding the ring that had once been Bridget's?

My ring!

I pulled my hand out from underneath the warmth of the covers and sighed with relief to see that it was still on my finger, beautiful as ever. Even in the semidarkness it shined.

This wasn't enough to convince me that what I'd dreamed hadn't really happened. I'd been part of enough crazy stuff to know that just about anything was possible, especially when it came to other witches. And Abby wasn't in her bed now, which was suspect in itself.

I threw back my covers and pulled my legs toward my body until my feet were exposed. Reaching down hesitantly, I grabbed ahold of one of my heels and brought it right up to my face.

It was clean.

Well, relatively clean, anyway. No dirt decorated my legs like it would have if the dream were real, and the pads of my feet were a rosy pinky color. My toenails were as flawless as the night I'd painted them a glittery red. Everything was as it should be. Not a thing out of place. Nothing missing.

Except for Abby.

Just as I thought it, she crept back into the room. I watched her from my bed as she quietly snuck in and took extra care not to let the lock click too loudly when she closed the door behind her. When we were once again locked in, Abby turned around and proceeded toward her section of the room.

"Where were you?" I whispered to her in the dark.

She jumped as she heard my voice and whipped around to face me.

"Geez, you scared the crap out of me!" she said out loud.

I placed my finger to my lips and motioned over to Colette who promptly turned over onto her stomach but remained asleep. Abby looked at our roommate and put her hand over her mouth guiltily. I let my legs drop down over the side of the bed and felt it begin to lower. As soon as I was close enough to the ground, I hopped off and walked over to where Abby was still standing.

"Where are you coming from?" I asked. I didn't want her to think I was interrogating her, especially since there was no proof that she'd done anything other than show up in one of my dreams. But still, coming in at 6:30 a.m. was kind of a sketchball move. Before we'd gone to camp, I'd promised Asher I'd look out for her, and this was definitely worth checking into.

I expected her to avoid the question or come up with some elaborate story, but she just held up her hand. "Brushing my teeth," she answered. She popped the toothbrush back into her mouth and wrapped one arm across her stomach, letting the other rest lazily on top of it.

"Oh, er, I mean, what are you doing up so early?" I said, trying to save face and switch up my tactics at the same time.

"Couldn't sleep," she said, and then walked over to her dresser and laid the toothbrush on its surface. "Why are you awake?" She said it easily, but it felt like she was turning the tables on me now.

I blinked. "Bizarro dreams," I answered, watching the reaction on her face for any clues.

"More Bridget dreams?" Abby asked with interest, sitting down on her bed.

I was surprised to hear her bring up Bridget, but also knew that Asher had filled her in on all the dreams I'd had about my dead relatives in the past. I hadn't told *anyone* yet about the ones involving the other prisoners who had been jailed along with Bridget—the two Sarahs and Tituba. Mostly because I wasn't sure whether it was important. But also because the last time I'd had regular dreams concerning the witch trials, we'd been attacked by the Parrishables. Given people's reaction to our last Cleri midnight meet-up and the botched tracking spell, I thought it best to keep these things to myself until I was sure there was something to worry about.

"This dream was different," I said, honestly. "You were in it."

Abby looked genuinely surprised to hear this. "Me? What was I doing?"

How much should I tell her? I didn't want to divulge everything, just in case I was supposed to be taking some sort of meaning from it. After all, in the dream, Abby *had* been performing some kind of secret spell on me. Then again, I *did* want to see if anything I described would jog her memory.

Maybe if she'd had the same dream, the two of us could piece together what was going on.

I decided to pull out some of the highlights instead.

"Well, you were outside. It was the middle of the night and you started to walk through the woods," I said. I looked for any sign that she recognized what I was describing. Her face didn't change at all as she listened. I continued with the story. "So, you were walking through the woods and I was following you. You know, to see where you were going. And you were wearing this hooded cloak. Anyway, then you stopped and you were doing a spell."

"What spell was I doing?" she asked when I paused.

"That's the thing . . . I didn't recognize it," I said carefully.

"Do you remember the words? Maybe I can help figure them out," Abby said.

Discubus susperion violane spurniface.

Abby's sudden interest in knowing the spell made me admittedly suspicious. But what I couldn't decide was whether she was curious because it was a dream about her or if it was because she had *other* motives? It was hard for me to say at this point.

Discubus susperion violane spurniface.

I placed my hand over my face and rubbed at it like I was frustrated, before reaching up to scratch my head. "I can't remember," I lied, deciding to keep that little fact to myself. "What do you think it means?"

Abby looked at me blankly and waited a beat or two before she answered.

"No clue. I'm not really good at deciphering dreams," she said, walking over to her bed and grabbing a book.

"Oh," I answered, watching her head back toward our bedroom door. "Well, I guess I'll see you at breakfast then?"

"Yep. See you."

I stood there in the darkness for a few minutes, running the conversation over and over again in my head. I wanted answers, but I didn't know whom I could trust. The Cleri were being weird about almost everything, and no way was I going to the counselors because, well, just because they were adults didn't mean they weren't capable of being evil. When I found no more answers than I'd had before, I quietly left our room and headed down the hallway to the girls' bathroom to get ready for the day.

But before I got there, someone stepped out of the stairway and nearly ran right into me.

"Asher!" I said, surprised to see him on our floor.

His reaction mirrored mine, but then it changed to a slick grin.

"Well, doesn't this bring back memories?" he said sexily, before leaning down and planting a kiss on my lips. I worried for about two seconds about whether I had killer morning breath, but then I let it go. Asher had kissed me in the morning before—plenty of times, actually—and besides, we'd been together now for over six months. An isolated case of bad breath wasn't going to be a deal breaker.

I smiled and then kissed him back, wrapping my arms around his waist. He was wearing a pair of gym shorts and a white tank top and his hair was mussed as usual. The air between us grew electric and I began to wish that we didn't have roommates. Forgetting for the moment that he'd recently pissed me off, I let myself fantasize about all the things I wanted to do to him and would let him to do me if we'd only been alone. Maybe there was an empty room, or closet, somewhere nearby that we could sneak off to.

"You *do* have the annoying habit of running into me at the worst times possible, Asher," I said, trailing my finger down his chest slowly as I remembered the first time we'd "accidentally" run into each other. We'd been at the mall and Sascha, Jinx, Jasmine, and I had gone looking for Fallon who'd taken off after having a hissy fit. Asher had claimed the meeting had been an innocent coincidence, but later on, I'd found out that he'd planned the meeting. Still, it was the first time we'd really interacted and even with the horrible timing, I couldn't ignore the heat between us.

"Annoying?" he asked, kissing me again, this time slipping his tongue against mine. "And how could there be a better time than right now?"

"Is there someplace we could go to be alone?" I asked.

As if on cue, a door opened up just a few feet away, and Brooklyn and Eve stepped out, chatting much too animatedly for such an early time of the morning. When they saw us, they abruptly shut up and walked the rest of the way in silence. As they neared the bathroom, they both turned their attention to us.

"Hey, Asher," Brooklyn said sweetly.

"Nice to see you again," Eve said, looking him up and down.

Hello, obvious?

"I'm *right here*," I said, annoyed that the dirty duo were once again getting in the way of Asher and my relationship.

Eve narrowed her eyes at me behind Asher's back. "Why, yes. I suppose you are. I barely recognized you . . . standing on your own two feet and all," she said, as insincerely as possible.

"Speaking of, how's your neck doing?" Brooklyn asked, her voice sounding concerned, but her face completely blank.

"I'm alive," I said between clenched teeth.

Asher looked at the other two girls before pulling me closer to him so our bodies were touching. "Did you two happen to see who did it?" he asked them suddenly.

Eve and Brooklyn looked at each other and then shrugged.

"Nope. We were just glad we could be there to help," Brooklyn said.

"Yeah. It's horrible to think of what might have happened if we hadn't come along," Eve added.

Then the two disappeared into the bathroom, but not before Brooklyn glanced back at the door to her room and said, "It was nice seeing you, Asher." I looked in the direction she'd been staring and then back at Asher who was still in his bed clothes and up at an unusually early hour for him.

Why was he up so early? And on this floor, too.

"Now where were we?" Asher asked, leaning down for another kiss.

"What are you doing up so early?" I asked instead, pulling myself out of his embrace completely and taking a step back so I could search his face for clues.

Asher closed his eyes and took a deep breath. When he opened them again, he'd changed. The moment we'd been having before Brooklyn and Eve had shown up was over. And we were back to being on separate sides.

"I couldn't sleep," he said, less than psyched at the temperature change between us.

"There seems to be a lot of that going around," I muttered.

"What's that supposed to mean?" he asked.

"Just that everyone's acting totally weird right now," I said.

"Well, sorry to disappoint you," Asher said, crossing his arms angrily. "Again."

Then, without saying good-bye, he turned and began to walk away from me.

"Why were you on our floor, Asher?" I asked.

I knew it was going too far and that I should've been trying to convince him to come back, talk this thing through instead. But I *had* to know the truth.

Finally, he spun around, his face twisted up in frustration. "You want to know why I was down here?" he asked me. "I was coming to see if you wanted to get breakfast. Maybe spend the morning together, just the two of us. You know, like you've been *asking* me to."

I'd officially screwed up. Brooklyn and Eve had appeared, and once again I'd let them get to me. Now Asher was mad and I wasn't sure how to make things right. Or if he'd even let me try.

"Asher," I started, but I didn't know how to finish the sentence, so I let it trail off.

"Don't worry about it," he said, sounding tired now. "I have stuff to do, anyway. I'll just see you later, okay?"

But he didn't wait for a response before taking off down the hallway, and before I could call his name again, he'd slipped around the corner and out of sight.

Chapter Twenty-Four

It was raining. And for the first time since we'd arrived at camp, it didn't feel like a thousand degrees outside. I was so grateful I could've done flip-flops around the grounds. Only, there were puddles everywhere and I would've gotten all muddy doing it.

So instead, I showed my excitement by dressing for the occasion, summoning up a beautiful red-and-black-lined cape/ poncho-style jacket. It was an amazing find straight from the runways of Milan. Large folds of fabric draped over my arms, and additional material wrapped its way around my neck, securing itself with snaps just above my breasts protectively. A belt cinched the coat at my waist, giving the garment the shape of a butterfly when I placed my hands on my hips.

Below that, I wore black stretchy pants decorated with a strip of black pleather darting straight down the sides of my legs. Nearly reaching my knees were my favorite pair of water-resistant cheetah-print boots, which zipped up the back. They'd keep my feet dry while making me look good on a rainy day.

I pulled the oversize hood up on my head before leaving the safety of the cabin and noted with glee that I looked like a couture Little Red Riding Hood. Considering everything that had been happening lately, I could use a little fashion pick-me-up right about now.

Just because my coven thought I was some crazy-jealous girlfriend monster, and Asher was barely talking to me, and it's entirely possible that someone wanted me dead, it didn't mean I had to dress that way. This was one of those "fake it 'til you make it" situations. One of the only times being fake was acceptable.

Making a mad dash for the amphitheater—which had seemed a lot closer until I was trying to avoid getting my hair wet—I listened for the silence that always came along with weather like this. It's as if the whole universe stopped whatever it was doing and took a moment to listen to the methodical plinking sounds of the rain falling to earth.

Rain equaled rebirth, renewal, and growth. In other words: despite the frizzy hair, it was a good omen. One that I was willing to take.

"Hey guys," I said, slightly out of breath by the time I got over to where Jasmine, Abby, and Sascha were sitting. They'd all been slightly frosty to me since our last meeting, but I'd decided to bury the past and try to get things back to where they'd been before we'd come to camp. Meaning, less Extreme Hadley Who Thinks Everyone's Out to Get Her and more of Laid-Back Hadley Who Has a Passion for Fashion. At least when I was around them.

"Isn't it *amazing* out?" I asked them, gesturing to the air around us and twirling around happily.

"Are you kidding?" Sascha asked, sounding more like

Jasmine than herself. She tried to flatten her hair, but it just bounced back. Humidity had found its first victim. "It's disgusting out."

"Noooo, it's not," I said, not allowing her comment to spoil my day. "This weather's *magical*! And I get to wear my new jacket. You like?" I posed to give them the full effect. "I can zap one for you too, Sascha, if you want."

But Sascha seemed too annoyed to answer, so I looked over toward Jasmine and Abby to see if they knew what was wrong with our usually perky friend. There, I was met with more frowns and scowls.

"Do you think that anyone *actually* cares what you're wearing on a daily basis?" Jasmine asked, her attitude harsher than usual. "You act like you're some kind of celebrity and that cameras follow you around 24/7 or something. This isn't a fashion show, Hadley."

Now I frowned. *Well, this isn't going the way I'd hoped.*

"I *know* it's not a fashion show, Jasmine," I said. "But what can I say? Great clothes make me happy. I wake up every day and ask myself, 'What should I wear on the runway of life?' And today I'm wearing power and fabulosity."

"What you're wearing is ridiculous," Jasmine said. Abby snorted beside her but kept her mouth zipped.

What crawled up her butt?

True, it wasn't unusual for Jasmine to be irritable. Hell, a guy had once asked her if she suffered from PMS year-round and she'd hit him. But this new attitude was something else entirely. Jasmine was being downright ornery, and it couldn't have just been because of what had happened the other day with Brooklyn.

"Whoa, harsh," I said, staring at them. "What's up with you guys today?"

But before they could answer, a few loud claps rang out behind us, commanding our attention. Reluctantly, I turned to see the three counselors standing underneath the bright lights in the middle of the stage. They waited for us to quiet down, and when we finally did, Miss Peggy clapped again just in case we hadn't gotten her point the first few times.

"All right, to start our day off . . ."

She'd barely gotten the words out when a huge boom cut through the air and we all watched in horror as more than a dozen large crates, barrels, and props that had been piled up in one of the corners of the platform flew across the area and landed on top of them.

"Omigod!" I shouted and was out of my seat before I knew what I was doing.

Sprinting over to the edge of the stage, I placed my hands on the black surface and propelled myself up into a handstand before rolling out of it and ending up just a foot or two away from the pile of rubble. I could hear the others shouting behind me as they raced to join me.

"Miss Peggy! Mrs. B! Are you guys okay?" I yelled out, trying to get a feel for where they might be trapped underneath the debris.

"Get us out!" a voice called back. I wasn't sure who'd said it, but it was all the encouragement I needed to get moving.

I turned to see Jasmine, Sascha, and Colette coming up on the right side of the stage and Brooklyn rushing over to me on the left. About ten feet behind her, Eve and the other Barbie clones followed.

Not thrilled about my choices in cohorts—between Jasmine's 'tude and Brooklyn's general suckage, I was tempted to tell them all to back off—I tried to focus on how we could do what the adults had asked of us. Get them out.

So, in this case, beggars couldn't be choosers.

"We have to get this stuff off of them!" I screamed at the others as I attempted to pick up the first crate.

"No shit, Sherlock," Jasmine muttered, but ran up next to me and began to do the same. Neither of us were having any luck though. I was a pretty strong girl, but the crates weighed a ton—too much for me to lift on my own, or even with the help of another twitch.

"What the heck are in these things? Boulders?" I asked, feeling my back strain under the pressure. A few other campers joined me in trying to move the crates, but after a couple of minutes, we hadn't even made a dent in the mess.

"Stand back and let me blast them off," Jasmine said, eventually getting fed up. She motioned for me to move out of the way.

I stepped right into her path. "No way! Jasmine, you can't just blow this stuff up. What if you miss and hit one of them? Or debris flies and hurts one of us?" I said, pointing at the other twitches who were huddled down below the stage. Their eyes were wide and a few seemed on the verge of tears. It was obvious that it was their first time dealing with a crisis.

Fortunately for those who were trapped, it wasn't mine. This was like old times.

As my eyes continued to sweep around the crowd, I saw Jinx standing all the way in the back of the amphitheater, just inside the covered area. Complete terror registered on her face and she appeared frozen in place. I wanted to go to her, make sure she was okay, but I couldn't leave the others.

"Who made you boss again, Hadley?" Jasmine asked, taking a step toward me threateningly.

"We don't have time for this," I told her, losing my patience. Turning my back on her, I walked to the edge of the debris.

"Anyone else want to step up and be the leader here?"

Nobody answered and I nodded before glancing back at Jasmine. We both knew I'd made my point.

"Okay then. Are there any other ideas about how we can get them out of this?" I gestured to the crisis at hand.

"Did anyone check out the other side? Maybe we could pull them out from there?" Sascha said.

I shook my head. "We'd have to climb over them to get there and risk crushing them even more."

"Should we go get the other counselors?" someone asked from the crowd. I ignored this. We needed to get them out *now*.

"We could do a spell to get rid of all this stuff," Brooklyn suggested. "Like, a floating spell or maybe we could make them disappear?"

I hated that so far Brooklyn had come up with the only useful idea, but it was true. Swallowing my ego, I nodded at her and motioned for everyone to take their casting stance.

As we got into place, the crates and props began to shake. The movement was small at first, but as we stood there, it became more noticeable. Then objects actually began to rise from where they'd landed, and I began to look around at the other twitches in confusion.

"Who's doing this?" I asked, looking around frantically. The other campers looked just as clueless as I was. A few even began to move away. It quickly became clear that none of us had a hand in what was happening.

But if not us, then who?

One by one, each object floated into the air and moved back to its place in the corner. It was as if someone were stacking them there, all orderly and where they belonged. The whole thing was so bizarre, that all we could do was stand there, slack jawed, and watch.

After what felt like forever, we finally saw Miss Peggy and then the other two teachers. Well, parts of them, anyway. First it was just a leg, then a head, and then, Miss Peggy's shiny vest. When the counselor's whole body was fully revealed, I noticed that her hand was outstretched as if midcast. She motioned for the last of the boxes, which had been covering the other women, to be deposited onto the top of the heap in the corner.

"What just happened?" I asked them as they brushed the dust and dirt from their clothes.

Mrs. B took out a handheld mirror and reached up to run a hand through her vibrant hair, making sure every strand was perfectly in place. For someone who'd just nearly been killed, she seemed oddly okay with it. Something wasn't right.

"Was that all a joke? Some kind of prank?" I asked, growing mad at the thought. They had no idea that for some of us, this sort of thing happened all too often. I glanced toward the back of the amphitheater to find Jinx, but she was gone. Case in point.

"If it was, it wasn't funny," Brooklyn echoed, sounding just as upset as I was at the prospect.

"No, not a joke," Miss Peggy said. Then she started to fiddle with one of the pins on her jacket. "Oh, dear. That last barrel ruined my 'Life's a Witch' button." After a few words, the button went back to looking good as new. "There we go. Now where were we?"

"We were about to tell them about the challenge," Mrs. B said, attempting to keep the kooky counselor on point.

"Ah, yes!" Miss Peggy said. A stopwatch appeared in her hand and she pressed one of the buttons on top. "Six minutes and forty-eight seconds. It took you almost seven minutes to figure out how to get us out and put your plan into action. Not horrendous, but also not very impressive. It's like the last week and a half hasn't happened at all."

"Is it possible they have brain damage?" Sascha whispered to Abby, though it was loud enough for everyone to hear.

I'd actually been wondering the same thing myself.

"Have a seat, have a seat," Miss Peggy said then. "More will be revealed."

Locking eyes with Brooklyn, I realized we both had the same look on our face. We were skeptical about what was going on and neither of us liked being the brunt of any joke. In any case, we walked off the stage and sat down in the stadium seats.

My heart was still racing over what had just happened, there was dirt on my new cape-jacket, and Jasmine, Abby, Sascha, and Jinx had chosen to sit a few rows behind where I was. The day was quickly going downhill for me.

"What's going on?" Colette asked, her eyes wide with concern as she finally showed up to class and sat down next to me. She hurriedly explained that she'd been running late and then had run into Jinx, who'd been rushing back to the cabin. It had taken Colette more than five minutes to calm Jinx down and convince her to come back. Sitting on the other side of Sascha, Jinx still appeared shaken, but she was there.

"Settle down!" Miss Peggy said loudly. Slowly, the whispered conversations petered off until the place was silent again.

"We'd like to thank you for bearing with us during our little demonstration," Mrs. B said. "And please accept our apologies for those of you who were distressed over the situation we created. Soothing spells will be provided directly after this class for those still afflicted."

"As Mrs. B mentioned, this *was* a demonstration," Mrs. Jeanette said, all business as usual. Nothing about her suggested she'd just been trapped under a bunch of heavy crates. Her hair was pulled out of her face and lay in a braid down her back—a style more for function than fashion—and she stood at attention, practicing perfect posture while peering out at us critically. "Or rather, it was a *test*."

"A test?"

"Seriously?"

"Are you kidding me?"

Everyone began to whisper to each other, which forced Miss Peggy to quiet us again.

"We wanted to see how well you'd act under pressure," she explained. "Since you arrived, we've been teaching you how to use your powers effectively. It should become second nature to cast when you're put into a situation that's potentially dangerous. Yet, when it appeared that we were in trouble up here, you all froze."

"No disrespect, Miss Peggy, but that's not true," I said. I knew the adults were trying to make a point, but what she was saying wasn't right. "We may not have freed you, but some of us were there right away, *trying* at least."

"You're right, Hadley," Mrs. B said, giving me a smile. "You *did* act immediately. In fact, some of you were quite valiant in your efforts. What Miss Peggy means, is that in all the drama, most of you forgot to use your best assets."

"You fell back solely on your human instincts, instead of utilizing your powers in tandem," Mrs. Jeanette said.

"Not that your human instincts should be ignored either . . . ," Mrs. B added, shooting a quick look over at the scientist.

"Because a combination of both is what makes us most powerful," I finished, understanding what she was trying to get at.

Mrs. B nodded at me encouragingly.

"The reason that we put this whole show together today is because we have a challenge to propose," Miss Peggy said.

"The Brighton Battlefield!" Mrs. B shouted and thrust her arms into the air spectacularly.

The other two women looked over at her disapprovingly. "I thought we'd decided we weren't calling it that, Rose, on account of it sounding too . . . violent," Miss Peggy warned.

"Oh, come on! It has a great ring to it. It's supersexy, right guys?" Mrs. B asked us, raising an eyebrow. None of us answered, considering we were still completely clueless as to what they were talking about. In this case, though, I had to agree with Miss Peggy. Describing something as a "battlefield" wasn't exactly making me psyched to participate.

"The Brighton *Challenge*," Miss Peggy continued, as Mrs. B crossed her arms over her chest and began to pout, "is something new this year and you will all be asked to participate."

"Each person will compete in a series of obstacle courses, designed to test your casting ability, reaction time, intelligence, creativity, power levels, execution of skills, accuracy, and strength of character," said Mrs. Jeanette. "You're encouraged to utilize any of the spells we've taught you here at camp as well as those you may have brought with you from home."

"You will be judged individually upon completion of each task and a point system will be put in place to keep track of who's in the lead," Miss Peggy said.

"Are you going to spring these challenges on us like you did today?" Brooklyn asked, sitting back in her chair about fifteen feet away. Her foot rested on the seatback in front of her, like she wasn't fazed by what had happened earlier. Yet, she'd been the first to ask the question we were each wondering.

"Oh, dear, no," Miss Peggy said, lifting her hand to her chest like *that* would've been crazy. "The challenge will happen three days from now. We ask that you come ready for anything. Wear clothes that you can move in, preferably nothing loose, as they could get in the way."

"The person with the most points after each challenge has

been completed will be our top witch," Mrs. B said. "The boys will be doing a similar challenge over on their side of camp."

"What's in it for us?" Jasmine asked.

The adults blinked at the bluntness of her question. I cringed as I worried about the impression Jasmine was leaving for the rest of the Cleri.

"Yeah, what do we win?" Sascha asked, her eyes lighting up at the thought of being awarded something.

"That's the best part!" Miss Peggy said, clapping excitedly. "The top girl and boy twitches will win an exclusive four-week apprenticeship with the elder of their choice. Including counselors of the past."

"Meaning—you could work with a fabulous mogul like *moi*," Mrs. B said, gesturing to herself.

"Or with a famous scientist," Mrs. Jeanette said with far less flair.

"Or any of the other dozens of powerful and groundbreaking witches we've had the pleasure of working with here at Brighton," finished Miss Peggy.

My head was spinning with thoughts of heading to Hollywood to learn from the most clever businesswoman in the world. Mrs. B would be able to teach me how to create an empire that I could use to accomplish every goal I'd ever had. Imagine what I could learn in just four weeks . . . My future would be *golden* after that.

I looked around at my fellow campers and could tell they were all thinking the same thing. Maybe their apprenticeships would be with other witches, but everyone knew that this was an opportunity that would change our lives.

I needed to win this challenge.

Chapter Twenty-Five

I'd been lying on my bed for the past hour and a half, trying to piece together the notes I had on Sarah Good. With everything that had been going on at camp since we'd arrived, coupled with the fact that I wasn't a huge fan of history in the first place, I'd been avoiding getting started on our "Famous Witches in History" projects. It wasn't like I had anything *against* Sarah Good or other historical figures, but diving into research wasn't really my scene. I sort of preferred to live in the now. Even if my "now" was less than fun.

Looking up as I heard the door open and close, I watched Colette make her way across the floor and toward her bed. She did a little turn as she went, forcing her bright purple tutu-inspired skirt to come dangerously close to showing off her underthings. I'd never seen anyone our age wear a tutu outside of dance class before, and on anyone else I would've thought it looked crazy. But Colette made it work. And paired with the black-and-white striped shirt she was wearing, it was kind of fabulous.

"You missed the craziest meal ever!" Colette exclaimed, plopping down onto her bed and turning onto her side to face me. The bed began to rise until I was finally able to look straight across at her.

"I'm afraid to ask . . . ," I said, but abandoned my iPad anyway.

"The guys did some sort of spell on their food and it launched itself around the dining hall," she said, shaking her head and laughing. "It was like a full-on food fight and nobody was safe. It was totally *spellacious*!"

I could see the tiny stains decorating her clothes now. They were all different shapes, sizes, and colors. Yet, Colette seemed fine with it. Like she'd enjoyed it even. Food all over my beautiful clothes? No thank you.

"Sounds like . . . a mess," I said, giving her a smile.

She nodded emphatically before laying her head down on her arm. "Where were you anyway? We missed you."

"I highly doubt you *all* missed me," I said, raising an eyebrow at her.

The rest of the Cleri girls were full-on giving me the cold shoulder now. At first I thought they were just annoyed, but then, at some point, it seemed to have turned into something more than that. Whenever I was around, Jasmine was especially combative with me. And Abby had begun to spend more and more time away from our room. Colette had suggested she was just spending time with Fallon, but I had a feeling that wasn't totally it. Sascha had officially joined the ranks as one of Brooklyn's Barbies and I worried that we'd lost her to the enemy forever. Jinx wasn't exactly mean to me, but it was clear she was avoiding me, too. This was especially frustrating because as far as I could tell, the perfume I'd made her was working. She no longer looked Skeletorishly thin and the smile had come back to her lips. I wanted to ask her about it but things were just so uncomfortable that I figured I'd let her come to me when she was ready.

"I still don't get what's going on between y'all," Colette said, scrunching up her face. "It's like your coven was close and then things got . . . weird. Are there typically a lot of mood swings in your group? I mean, it makes sense considering you're mostly females, but still. Seems a little excessive. Why can't we all, as women, just celebrate each other? There are enough men trying to keep us down: Why would we help to destroy our fellow female-kind?"

"Amen," I said, raising my hands up to the ceiling.

Colette and I locked eyes and then laughed. Thank God for Colette. If she weren't around, I'd be completely alone.

"So why *weren't* you at dinner then?" she asked, changing the subject, but not to a better one.

I lifted up my iPad in response. "Working on my Brighton Witch Project."

"I'm almost finished with mine," Colette said, grinning like a fiend. "How far have you gotten?"

"Research."

Silence.

"That's it?" Colette finally asked.

I nodded, but given her response, I felt embarrassed admitting it. "I've had . . . other stuff going on. Besides, we don't have to present for another week or so. I've done reports for school in less time. This can't be much different, right?" I asked.

Colette looked concerned. "Except for the fact that most of witch history isn't available on the Internet like your other school subjects," she said. "And how you do on your project can be a deciding factor on whether you're asked back next summer. The elders take witch history sort of seriously."

"I think I'll be okay," I said, even though I knew she was right. I wasn't sure whether I'd even want to come back next year, but I certainly didn't want the decision to be made for me. Better to do what they wanted.

"So, now I'm curious," Colette said, sitting up and facing me, her legs crossing underneath her. "What *do* you have so far?"

I sighed. I'd already spent a few hours on the project and had no desire to dive back into it. Colette seemed so eager though, and I didn't want to alienate the only friend who was still talking to me, so I relented.

Gripping my iPad, I placed my finger on the screen and pulled up my list. "These are just notes—it's not final or anything," I warned. "So don't judge."

"I wouldn't dare," Colette said, crossing her finger over her heart.

"Okay, well, Sarah Good was born on July 11, 1653, and her early life was relatively unremarkable. Her mother died when she was young and when her father remarried, she and her new stepmother never quite got along. When she was just seventeen years old, her father committed suicide, leaving Sarah alone with his widow and her two sons. Soon after her father's death, her stepmother remarried and her new husband took the money that had been left to Sarah and forced her out of the house.

"Sarah ended up having to take care of herself from that time on, which wasn't easy considering she was practically penniless. She survived by living on the streets and depended on the occasional kindness of others to supply her with a roof over her head and food to keep her alive."

I looked up to see that Colette seemed riveted to the story. *Man, she really* is *into witch history.* I continued.

"As a teenager, Sarah had been skittish yet curious. For this reason, most of the townspeople shunned her. It was very clear to Sarah that she was different than anyone else her age, but as the 'changes' came and things began to happen that she couldn't explain, Sarah felt even more alone and isolated. Until the day a woman, Rebecca Nurse, took her into her home. Sarah quickly took to Rebecca, who was a well-respected townsperson, and she ended up helping Sarah discover the life-changing fact that she was actually a witch and had powers that the rest of the world didn't.

"Over the next twenty-five years Sarah worked on growing her powers as well as building a family of her own. Rebecca eventually welcomed Sarah into her coven, called the Supre. Sarah then married a former indentured servant, who ended up dying just ten years after her father, thus prompting her to marry *another* man by the name of William Good. Due to substantial debt the two piled up over the years, the Goods ended up selling their land to pay off creditors, resulting in the couple having to live on the streets. William began to blame Sarah for their predicament and as his resentment toward her grew, he became quite mentally abusive.

"Even so, Sarah remained with William, and before long, became pregnant with their first child. When little Dorothy Good was born, things actually got better between the two for some time. But it didn't last, and within three years, William and Sarah were back to being in a loveless marriage. So, she turned to another man for solace. The affair lasted for just under a year, and Sarah was sure that she'd done a good job at hiding the infidelity from her husband. But he knew."

Didn't they always, though?

"Instead of confronting her and either demanding a divorce or moving his family away from his wife's new lover, William had more dastardly things in mind. He began to hold back any earnings and food he was able to procure from jobs around the town, forcing Sarah to wander door-to-door asking for handouts. This annoyed and even angered the people in her village, especially when Good would mutter under her breath as she left empty-handed.

"It's common knowledge now that the witch trials were ultimately orchestrated by Reverend Samuel Parris. But few realize that the idea for the trials was actually sparked by a single sentence spoken by William Good one night outside of a local tavern. William began to spill his guts to his friend, confiding in him that his wife was sneaking off to do unholy things, and that she had come home with mysterious bite marks on her shoulder. 'The mark of the devil,' his friend had replied. William responded, 'I want the witch to get what is coming to her' or something to that respect."

If I'd ever needed proof of Parris's wickedry, this seemed to be its beginning. He single-handedly ruined everything he touched.

"Parris felt the same way about Bridget Bishop—the woman who happened to own the bar they were currently standing in—and while overhearing this conversation, he finally knew how to take her down. As the most powerful witch in the Cleri, and likely the world, Bridget had consistently shot down every idea Samuel had ever had to advance their coven's status across their area.

"Anyways, Samuel had been looking to overthrow Bridget for some time, and being the sketchy douchebag he was, Samuel approached William and his friend, and began to lay the foundation for what would become the basis for the witch trials. After many hours, and more beers than they could count, Samuel had devised a plan to have his daughter and niece accuse Sarah and two other townspeople the men disliked of practicing witchcraft.

"On February 25, 1692, with a magical nudge from Parris, Abigail Williams and Betty Parris accused Sarah Good, Tituba, and Sarah Osborne of witchcraft. They all ended up in jail and were completely abandoned by their families and friends. But that was just the beginning. There were many more after Sarah, including Bridget Bishop, and even Rebecca Nurse."

I shook my head, finding it hard to understand what it must've been like to be wrongfully accused of performing harmful acts on innocent people. True, I'd practically lived through it in my dreams, but still. It was unimaginable.

"During the trial, the kids and their friends testified that Sarah had bitten, pinched, and abused them. Other residents claimed that Sarah would curse them when they refused to give her food. Sarah explained that she was just saying the Ten Commandments and blessed each household even though they had turned her away. But when her accusers asked her to repeat the Commandments while on the stand, she couldn't remember a single one. This was, of course, the work of Samuel, who'd placed a forgetful spell on her so she'd come across as a liar.

"Shortly after Sarah was arrested, it became clear to everyone that she was pregnant with her second child. So certain was William that the unborn child wasn't his, he ended up testifying against her during the trial, saying that he had seen 'the devil's mark' below her shoulder. William also said he believed her to be a witch or that she was close to becoming one.

"Even worse, he forced their four-year-old daughter, Dorothy, to speak out against her, claiming that she herself was a witch and that she'd seen her mom consorting with the devil. But then two of the younger accusers insisted that Dorothy had bitten them, too. Just after turning five, Sarah's daughter became the youngest person accused in the trials and was sent to jail. Ironically, Dorothy came into her own powers once the trial was over, though she'd never actually witnessed Sarah practicing magic like she'd claimed.

"Sarah ended up giving birth to her second daughter, Mercy, while chained in her Ipswich jail cell. Sadly, Mercy died shortly after birth, most likely because of the horrible conditions of the prison. Dorothy was eventually released, but evidently suffered major psychological issues for the rest of her life as a result of the whole situation. Not that *that's* a surprise. Who *wouldn't* go psycho after having a family like that?"

I didn't wait for Colette to respond before continuing.

"Anyways, on July nineteenth, a little over a week after Bridget Bishop was killed, Sarah, Rebecca Nurse, and three others were executed. While waiting for the noose to be fitted around her neck, Good proclaimed her innocence over any evil doing. At one point she even yelled out to Judge Nicholas Noyes, 'I'm no more an evil witch than you are a wizard! Take my life and God will give you blood to drink.' Looks like the jerk got what was coming to him, because he ended up dying twenty-five years later with blood in his mouth and throat. Maybe he was a vampire. . . ."

I looked up from my iPad for the first time since I'd begun to spout out Sarah Good's life story. I'd scoured the witchboards and Witchipedia and then added in what I knew to be true from my dreams. Every once in a while, it was nice having a direct line to the past. What I'd read to Colette wasn't even half of what I knew.

Rubbing my eyes tiredly, I waited for them to focus again on my roommate, who was sitting quietly across the room from me. When my vision finally cleared, I saw tears streaming down Colette's cheeks.

"What's wrong?" I asked, worried. I hadn't even heard her start sniffling. "Is it that bad?"

"It's just so . . . *sad*," she said, taking off her glasses and wiping at her face. "Sarah was just a woman who was different than her peers, and happened to fall on some bad luck. Then those people *destroyed* her for not looking or acting like them."

"Those *men* destroyed her because they wanted to control her, and she wouldn't do what they wanted," I answered, my hatred for Samuel Parris reigniting.

"The women weren't much better," Colette said, shaking her head. "People can be so cruel and hateful. It's been like that throughout history. We're punished for being unique."

I studied Colette and realized that my happy-go-lucky friend might have a dark side after all. It was true. People couldn't be happy all the time.

"Well, I guess we'll all have to be a little better at celebrating people's uniqueness then," I said, smiling at her.

She smiled back at me, before we both fell into silence. After nearly a minute, she spoke again. "What did you learn about the rest of her lineage? I mean, Dorothy ended up living, after all," she said.

"I guess she would've gone on to have her own kids," I said. "But if I were her, I'd be more than a little concerned that my own daughter might have me killed one day, too. You know, karma and all."

"You should find out what happened to her," Colette said, pulling a tissue out of her pocket and blowing her nose loudly.

I cocked my head to the side and looked at her curiously.

"Do you know something that I don't, Colette?" I asked. "If you do, you can just tell me."

"Do a little more research," Colette insisted. "Then I'll answer any questions you still have."

Chapter Twenty - Six

An hour and a half later, I stumbled upon what I assumed Colette had wanted me to find. Thirty minutes after that, I was positive I'd found it. And it changed everything.

"Moll Brenner was related to Sarah Good?" I asked, dropping the iPad onto my mattress and looking over at my roomie incredulously. Colette, who'd been practicing writing words in the air with colored magic residue, like a sparkler on the Fourth of July, paused and then began to write the word "Moll" in the air.

"Yep," Colette answered, continuing to connect the letters slowly. "Moll was Sarah's great-great-great-granddaughter."

I pulled my knees up to my chest and rested my chin on them as I studied her. Colette stopped casting as soon as she felt my eyes on her, and then relaxed back on her bed with a semi-sad look on her face.

"And Moll was your great-great-great-aunt," I said quietly.

Colette just nodded in response. Looking down at her lap, she studied the fabric of her skirt.

"That's why you're so protective of Moll's memory," I said, everything beginning to fit together like found puzzle pieces.

"Not *just* because we're related," Colette insisted, looking up at me again. "Moll was innocent and they still subjected her to a horrible fate. Just like Sarah, and even her own daughter, Dorothy. People are so quick to persecute. Nobody takes the time to get to know anyone before making a judgment."

"Is that why you don't tell anyone you're related to them? You're afraid of what people will do?" I asked. "Colette, I promise I won't let anyone hurt you. You can bet on that. You might not be in the Cleri, but you're one of us as far as I'm concerned."

"Thanks, Hadley. That means a lot," she said, giving me a small smile. "But that's not it. I don't actually think people will hurt me. It's more like . . . people assume things when they know where you come from."

"Believe me, I know. But so what? Who cares what people think of you?" I answered. It was true. I knew I was a good, kind, strong person destined for greatness. If others wanted to think differently, the last laugh would be mine when all my dreams were coming true and they were still trying to come up with theirs.

"That's easy to say when your relative is Bridget Bishop," Colette said, sarcastically. "Bridget is probably the most famous witch in history, not to mention one of the most powerful. *Of course* you don't worry what people think of you. Everyone treats you like the second coming."

"That's not true, Colette," I said, even though there was *some* truth to what she said. When people found out I was related to Bridget, they *did* look at me differently. With a newfound respect, almost. One that I hadn't earned, but was assigned. And though I never felt pressure to live up to her legacy, I couldn't help but feel like I was constantly in her shadow. My hope was that someday my name would stand on its own. Of course, my name wasn't holding much weight with my coven lately.

"People are far less impressed when they discover that your family is famous for being poor, adulterous, and crazy as a loony bin," she said. "Witches in our family have worked hard over the last century to change that perception, so we can at least try to get a fair shake."

"Colette, you're not your relatives," I said, forcefully.

"I know," she said. "And I actually don't mind who they were really. They were different and that should be okay. And that's all I want: for others to accept me for who I am. Crazy outfits and all."

I smiled. "Well, I think you've definitely succeeded in that," I said. As we both let Colette's confession sink in, my mind started to wander. "Hey, Colette? Can I ask you something about Moll?"

"Sure," she said. "I'd rather you learn about her from me rather than through the gossip mill. What do you want to know?"

"What do you think happened to her that night?" I asked.

"I've had dozens of theories over the years about what it must've been like for Moll after those kids ditched her in the woods . . . but I honestly don't know what happened," she answered.

"Theories?" I asked, curious to hear what they were.

"Well, one was that she ran away and started a new life. I like to think this was true, because in my version she finds a life where she fits in and is happy," Colette said. "But then there are the alternatives. Ones that aren't so . . . positive. I worry that some sort of wild animal got to her and she was hurt and alone.

Or that she was so upset over the kids' prank that she took her own life. The worst is thinking that she might've wandered the woods until she had no more strength and just lay down to die, her ghost doomed to be stuck there alone forever."

"So you think it's possible she's still out there? Like, her spirit's haunting the woods or something?" I said, carefully.

"Are you asking if she was the one who did all that stuff to the boys' theater?" Colette asked, a frown forming on her face.

"That, and maybe the whole vine in the woods and shower incidents? I've also been having these bizarre dreams . . . ," I said, trying my best not to sound too accusatory. "I mean, after hearing everything that Moll went through, I wouldn't blame her for being angry and lashing out. I'd want payback on all those little witches if they left me in the woods, too."

"I don't think it was her," Colette said adamantly.

"Not even for payback?" I asked, knowing I was riding the line of pushing Colette's good nature too far.

"It wasn't her style," she answered. "Trust me, our family has obsessed over this for more than a hundred years now. Moll's younger sister, Mary, who was also my great-great-great-grandmother, ended up returning to Brighton three years after Moll's disappearance to attend the intensive. As soon as she arrived, the rumors about the "Witch in the Woods" began. Mary never mentioned that Moll was her sister, and since she was Moll's polar opposite, she became quite popular among the other campers. Ultimately, she ended up having the experience Moll had *wished* she'd had.

"Despite the warnings of the campers and counselors, Mary would often wander off into the woods. Sometimes it was just for thirty minutes, while other days she was gone for hours. She'd come back with batches of flowers and distribute them to her friends, giving them enough of a reason for her to be gone for such long periods of time. But Mary was on a mission. She knew what had happened to Moll and didn't think it was the whole story. So, she started to do her own investigation."

"What did she find?" I asked.

"Weird things started to happen," Colette said, nodding. "But not in the ways you think. Or the ways that are told around here. For one, the flowers that Mary would come back with weren't picked by her. No matter where she'd wander off to in the woods, she would find a pile of perfectly plucked flowers sitting alone as if waiting for her. Sometimes when she walked around by herself, she'd think someone was whispering her name. Other times, Mary would swear someone was following her. In letters, she told her mom that she'd see shadows beside her own when no one else was around.

"But it wasn't just Mary who was experiencing stuff. Others at camp claimed they had, too. Things would go missing from the girls' rooms, diaries would be left out as if they'd been read— all stuff that could be attributed to silly pranks. Only, no one was ever caught doing them and it began to happen year after year. Mary attended Brighton until she turned eighteen and then returned for a decade as a counselor. She told others that it was because her time at camp was the best of her life, but our family knew that it was because she was certain that Moll was still there. Mary wasn't sure whether she was alive or if it was her ghost, but camp was the only time she felt close to her sister.

"So, see. Moll's tricks were always innocent. Taking trinkets, leaving flowers, reading diaries . . . she did these things because she just wanted to be a part of a world that had never accepted her. *Maybe* it's possible that she did the amphitheater thing. *Maybe*. But Moll wouldn't have *hurt* innocent people like with the shower and hanging stuff. I'm certain of that. You need to find someone else to pin those on, Had."

I could tell that she believed what she was saying and from what little I knew about Colette, I found this to be enough. She was a searcher of truth and she wouldn't insist on something if she wasn't totally sure about her facts. So, either she'd been misinformed by her ancestors, or she was right, and Moll wasn't the one who was out to get me.

But then, that left me back at the beginning, with no real suspects. Well, one, but I was the only one who thought Brooklyn was a viable option for evil.

"Now, can I ask *you* something, Hadley?" Colette asked.

"Of course," I said.

"You said that you were having weird dreams," she said, picking at the dried food stuck to her skirt. "What were they about?"

I'd been hesitant to tell Abby the full extent of my dream, both because she had turned out to be one of the hooded figures in it and because I didn't want to stress her out over something that might've been nothing. But Colette had just told me one of her biggest secrets, and I felt like I should reciprocate. Besides, it had begun to get pretty lonely keeping this stuff to myself. Asher had been spending more and more of his free time with the guys, and the girls had broomsticks up their butts about something and were ignoring me. Jinx was still recovering from her PTSD and I couldn't put that kind of stress on her again. And even if Fallon and I had been closer, I wouldn't have confided in him since it looked like he and Abby were sharing more than just a friendship.

Ew.

Colette was probably the only person close to me whom I could talk to without her either freaking out or scolding me for not trusting Brooklyn. So, I took a chance on a new friend.

"I dreamed that I saw someone outside, wearing a cloak

and walking into the woods. I followed them and they met up with two others. They were chanting, doing some sort of a spell that I didn't recognize. And then I noticed that they had my ring," I said, holding up my hand for Colette to see. Her eyes grew wide as I spoke, but I continued. "Just when I was about to leave, one of the people raised their heads and I saw that it was . . ."

Should I tell her? I didn't want to cast undue suspicion on Asher's sister based on a silly dream. But I also didn't want to lie to Colette. Not when she'd been so honest with me.

"I saw that it was—" I started.

"Abby," Colette said.

My mouth dropped open as she finished my sentence.

"Uh, how did you know that?" I asked, bewildered.

"I had the same dream," she answered, sighing loudly. "Only, I wasn't walking through the woods. I was watching *you* walk through the woods. And I saw when Abby revealed her face."

This was too unusual to chalk up to coincidence. "Does this happen to you a lot? Like, have you popped into other people's dreams before?" I asked her, trying to get a grip on what she was saying.

She shrugged and then looked at me shyly. "Define 'a lot.'"

Oh, boy.

"Well, it's not *every* night or anything," Colette said, wringing her hair around her finger nervously.

"But this isn't the first time?" I asked.

She shook her head.

"Colette, this is *insane*!" I exclaimed.

"I don't mean to do it. Sometimes when I share a room with people it just . . . happens. I'm really sorry, Hadley—" she stammered.

"Are you kidding?" I asked. "What an amazing gift!"

When she realized what I'd said, she blinked at me confused. "Wait, you're not mad at me?"

"Why would I be mad at you, Colette? I might be a little annoyed that I don't have that power, too, but *mad*? Not at all," I said. "Look, not every witch is given specialty powers. You're really lucky."

"Wow. Okay," Colette said, not sure how to react to that.

"What did *you* think of the dream? About it being Abby who was casting against me?" I asked.

"Well, dreams can mean a few things, depending on who you are and how your brain reacts to the world around it," Colette said, going into smarty-pants mode. "For some people, dreaming allows their brains to try to work through problems they're dealing with in their waking life. Oftentimes though, the issues become clumped together, to the point where the dreamer can't make sense of it while awake, although their subconscious is able to make sense of it in its dream state. Then there are those who utilize a larger percentage of their brains while asleep than the rest of us. These people can tap into past and future experiences, memories, and really focus on self-awareness. In this respect, the sleeping life acts as a sort of psychic experience for the dreamer. Then, there are those who don't remember their dreams at all. I know through experience that it's not that those people don't dream, it's that they don't have the awareness necessary to recall the information their dream life has provided for them.

"The thing about dreams is that they're really there to provide us with insight into the world around us. It's just a matter of how we use the information we're given. People are quick to dismiss the warnings in a dream, because it seems too outlandish or confusing. But often, if you learn to listen to yourself and trust your instincts, you can really utilize all the talents at your disposal. Does that make sense?" Colette asked, looking at me for confirmation.

"Um. Sort of?" I said, not absolutely sure I followed everything she'd said, but getting the gist.

"Let's look at it this way. When you dream, does it often come true in real life or help you to accomplish tasks when you're awake?" she asked me.

That was easy. I'd had dreams of things that had taken place in the past (Bridget's hanging, and more recently, the ones about Sarah Good, Tituba, and Sarah Osborne) as well as ones that had involved my mom in the present.

"Yes," I responded.

"Okay, well then, chances are, your dreams are more prophetic than problematic," Colette said. "This means that you can probably trust most of the contents of your dreams as they are, as opposed to trying to piece together the meaning like you would a puzzle."

I wasn't sure what to do with this info. "So, that would mean that Abby's my *enemy*?" I asked, hating the way it sounded out loud.

"Well, dream-reading isn't an exact science," Colette said, shrugging. "And this is my first time in one of *your* dreams. I'm not sure if we're looking at a perfect reflection of what's actually happening or if your dream is just a distorted version of reality. This is where you have to search yourself and find the truth within your own heart. What did *you* think the dream meant?"

I took a deep breath, because once I said it, it would be out there forever. And somehow that made it all the more real. Also, I wouldn't be able to ignore it anymore.

"I thought it actually *had* happened," I admitted quietly.

"The next morning, I even checked to see if my feet were dirty from running through the woods. But they weren't, and I still had on my ring."

"All that tells you is that you weren't actually in the woods," Colette said. "Not that the rest of it didn't happen."

"I hate to say it, but it would explain everyone's behavior toward me lately. I wanted to chalk it up to catty-girl syndrome, but it can't just be that," I said, rubbing my face with my hands. "Did you recognize the spell they were doing?"

Colette shook her head. "No. And I've been thinking about it ever since. But it doesn't even sound familiar."

"Do you think they're *really* casting against me?" I asked next.

"It's possible," Colette said, thinking. "Or it could just mean that you can't fully trust those around you right now."

"Ugh. Not again," I said, groaning out loud. "I've done this dance before . . . the whole 'there's a traitor amongst you' crap. What happened to being able to trust your coven members?"

"In a way, that's the beauty of being on your own like me," Colette said, partly joking. "No one to screw you over."

"I guess," I said. "But far fewer people to borrow clothes from."

"I think my personal style is an acquired taste anyway," Colette said, chuckling.

"True." After a few seconds, I grew quiet as I thought about what this all meant. "So if the others have turned against me, then who made them do it?"

"What do you mean?" Colette asked, not following.

"Well, I know my coven and after everything we've been through, we wouldn't betray each other if we could help it," I said. "Meaning, someone has to be making them do this. Someone who wants me out of the way."

"Are you saying—" Colette started.

"Yep," I said, cutting her off. I didn't need to mention Brooklyn's name for Colette to know that's where my head had already gone. "But even if she *is* behind it, what am I supposed to do? The others have made it pretty clear that they don't think Brooklyn's bad. They're not going to believe me."

Colette shrugged. "Then we get proof," Colette said. "If Brooklyn's forcing Abby and the others to sneak out at night to plot against you, then we wait until Abby thinks we're asleep . . . and we follow her."

Chapter Twenty-Seven

Except the next couple of nights were completely uneventful.

Directly following the discovery of Colette's dreaming abilities, the two of us had put a spell on the door so that we'd be alerted by a faint buzzing in our bodies if anyone tried to get in or out. That way if Abby left at any point in the night, we'd know about it. We tested the enchantment before going to bed to make sure it was in working order, and only when we were satisfied did we close our eyes. Every morning that we awoke after an uninterrupted night of sleep I became less convinced that I could trust my dreams as being anything more than just that.

If Abby had been acting like her regular self, I might've felt a little bad about doubting her at all. But she and the other Cleri girls were still shunning me, having now taken to eating their meals at a completely different table than the one I sat at. And being that Fallon and Abby were now a package deal, he'd migrated to their side of the dining hall, too. When I'd asked him about it, he'd just said that he'd given up under-standing women a long time ago.

As much as I prided myself in being independent and strong, the fact that everyone was deserting me . . . hurt. More than I expected it to. And if I was being honest, more than I *wanted* it to. And even though I knew in my bones that there was a spell behind it, and we weren't best friends to begin with, and that I didn't need *everyone* to like me to survive in this world, it felt awful to know that I was pretty much *alone* in this.

Asher may not have jumped on the "we hate Hadley" band-wagon, but things still weren't back to normal between us. Sure, he *said* he was over our tiff in the hallway, but I could tell he was still annoyed. He was spending more and more time with the guys, and since I wanted to keep the peace, I let him.

I set my whole focus on proving that Brooklyn was trying to ruin my life. I balled up all the feelings I was having about possibly losing my coven and my boyfriend and placed them in a locked box that I would open later. When it was safe. Otherwise I'd shut down completely and evil would win.

Luckily, on the third night, we finally got our big break.

My eyes shot open in the dark as I felt the buzzing begin in my fingers and toes and spread to the rest of my body. Staying still so that Abby wouldn't be alerted to the fact that I was awake, I waited for her to make her move. After a few sec-onds, light began to fill the darkness as our door was opened wider, and I was briefly able to see Colette lying in the bed across from me. Her face was sans glasses and her eyes were closed. I could see her chest rising and falling underneath the blankets, as if she were in the middle of a deep sleep.

Making almost no noise at all, Abby slipped out of our room, leaving us both alone again in the dark. I counted to ten before slowly sitting up in bed and looking over at the clock.

Three a.m.

The witching hour. So predictable.

As I threw back my covers, Colette did the same, nearly startling me right off of my mattress.

"I didn't think you were awake," I whispered as our beds lowered to the ground.

"That's good," she said, putting her glasses on. "That means that Abby believed it, too."

"So, I guess it's true," I said, surprisingly unhappy about the fact. Part of me had been hoping that I was wrong. That Asher's sister *wasn't* out to get me. Sometimes it sucked to be right.

"Now we just have to figure out exactly what she's up to," Colette said.

"Let's get out there then," I said. "I want to get this thing over with."

We threw on hoodies and stepped into flip-flops before moving quietly over to the door. Opening it slowly, I peeked out to see if Abby was still around. When I saw the hallway was empty, we hurried out and headed straight for the stairwell at the opposite side of the cabin.

Following the same path I'd taken to sneak out for our Cleri meeting, I gestured for Colette to stay close to me as we pushed open the door to the outside and stepped out into the cool night air. I placed my finger against my lips and pointed to where Abby was just disappearing into the woods. Colette's eyes grew, but she remained quiet and didn't move until I gave her the signal.

When I was sure we were far enough behind Abby to follow her without getting caught, we took off across the grass, staying off the dirt-and-rock pathway to keep from making noise. Just as we were about to enter into the cover of trees, we both heard the sound of a branch breaking and raced to hide.

Sliding behind a nearby tree, I watched Colette dive behind a bush to avoid being seen.

A few seconds later, a shadow appeared about three feet away from where I was standing. Only, it was walking *out* of the woods instead of into them, and the silhouette appeared to belong to a guy. I took a step away from my cover to try to get a closer look, but it didn't help. I needed him to turn around so I could see his face.

I wasn't looking to get caught, but I also wasn't convinced that the figure wasn't out here to meet Abby. Turning to Colette, I gestured for her to stay hidden while I made my next move. She looked worried, but remained behind the bush. Trying only to move every time the figure took a step, I made it about five feet before he realized he was being followed and turned to confront me.

"Hadley!" Asher said, his face registering surprise and then changing to confusion. "Hi."

"What are you doing out here, Asher?" I whispered, not wanting to blow my cover completely, if Abby was still in the area.

"I could ask you the same thing," he said, the smile dropping from his face.

"I asked first." It was childish, but I knew *I* had a good reason for being out of our room at night. I couldn't think of any excuse he could give that would make a nighttime jaunt without me okay.

Despite the blunt nature of my question, a smile danced its way across Asher's lips. "You are *so* adorable," Asher said.

This was the blanket response Asher gave me whenever he wanted to avoid having an *actual* conversation. He hid behind a compliment, hoping it would derail me from whatever information I wanted from him. Asher did it all the time when we first met—but that had been mostly to hide the fact that he was a witch. And working with Team Parrish. The tactic had annoyed me then and it hadn't gotten any cuter. "That might be true, but you're not answering my question," I said, not letting him get out of this one.

"Okay, Had," he said with a sigh. "But it's really not a big deal."

"I usually don't like your answers when you start off that way. . . . ," I warned.

He rolled his eyes at me. "I was just out here with the guys. You know, goofing around."

"Goofing around—in the middle of the night?" I asked, not believing his excuse one bit. "You couldn't wait until it was light outside? Or goof off with the guys in your room? What could you possibly be doing out here in the woods with a bunch of guys?"

Asher shoved his hands into his pockets and shrugged. "It's guy stuff, Had. I don't ask you what you do with your girlfriends when you hang out."

"That's because we don't go sneaking off at night, wandering creepily through the woods," I said. Although as soon as I'd said it, I realized that's exactly what Colette and I were doing. "Speaking of . . . where are the guys? You know, the ones that you're apparently out here with?"

"I don't want to have this argument again, Had," Asher responded, starting to lose his patience with our conversation. "What are *you* doing out here?"

Uh-oh. I hate it when the tables turn.

My eyes shifted over to the bush where Colette had been hiding.

"Out for a walk," I said finally. This was technically the truth. "I couldn't sleep. And then I thought I saw someone out here . . . so I came to investigate."

"Now who's being evasive?" Asher said, crossing his arms.

"I'm telling you the truth," I said.

"So am I," he answered.

We were at a standoff. For some reason, neither of us was willing to admit fully why we were there. For a moment, it made me sad to think that there were things we both wanted to keep from the other. But then I began to recall everything I'd ever heard about relationships and tried to remain calm. From what I knew, every relationship changed and morphed. It was just that Asher and I had been in the "honeymoon" phase for so long back home, that it was hard to think of us as transitioning into that place where it wasn't all roses and puppy dogs.

On the other hand, did Asher and I really have to be around each other 24/7 to feel complete? There'd been a time when I believed that a girl didn't need a man in her life to be happy. And even though I loved being with Asher, I knew I could survive without him if I had to. So maybe a little time apart wouldn't kill us.

This was just the natural ebb and flow of a relationship. Sometimes you were hot and heavy, and other times . . .

"Okay," I said finally, conceding. A girl had to pick her battles, and right now, I needed to get back to mine. "Sorry I freaked out. Go and have fun with the guys."

"We're finished for the night," Asher said, softening instantly and taking a step toward me. "Want me to walk you back to your room?"

"It's all right," I said, appreciating the gesture but needing to get moving. I had no idea where Colette had disappeared to, and Abby was probably long gone by now. I would have to hustle if I was going to find either of them. "I sort of want to finish my walk."

He nodded, staring at me for a few seconds before leaning

down and pulling my face to his. The kiss was sweet and over much too soon. And then he was backing away, his eyes still on mine. With a wink and a smile, Asher finally turned his back to me and headed toward the cabin alone.

As soon as Asher was through the side door, I took off running into the woods, far less careful than I'd been before. It was darker than in my dream and I fought to see more than a few feet in front of me. A couple of times I narrowly avoided running head on into a tree and had to push off the damp bark to keep from colliding with it. Sticks and rocks seemed to jump out in front of my feet, threatening to trip me and leave me sprawled across the tightly packed dirt. I somehow managed to stay upright, and after ten minutes, I slowed to a light jog, wondering how far into the woods I'd have to go to find another human being. Right now, all I could hear was my own breathing. Even the typical sounds that one would find in the forest seemed to be gone. There was just silence.

I turned around in circles, trying to figure out where Abby or Colette might've gone, looking for any sign that they'd even been this way. But there was nothing. Just darkness and stillness and silence.

Too much silence.

And then, it was like all the sound in the whole forest came rushing at me at once. There were screams and howls, bugs fluttering, birds squawking, the rattling of wind through the leaves. Before I even knew what was happening, I was on my back and was being dragged by my ankles through the woods. My brain was fighting to keep up and it took a few seconds to realize that the yells I'd heard were actually coming from me. Leaves and twigs embedded themselves into my hair, creating a rat's nest of serious proportions and partially obstructing my view of the forest as we blew by. I reached out blindly, hoping to catch ahold of something to stop my momentum, but my hands came up empty. Nobody was pulling me and from what I could see, there was no rope tied to my feet. Yet, I was definitely being dragged against my will somewhere into the woods.

I tried to pull myself up into a sitting position, but as soon as I'd gotten halfway there, I began to tumble and roll, hitting every part of my body before skidding to a complete stop. Breathing heavily and still trying to get my bearings, I stumbled to my feet and looked around, expecting to see the person who'd summoned me. But there was no one.

"Who's there?" I screamed, no longer worried about getting caught, because it was clear I already had been. A fact I was *not* happy about, I might add. I was still disoriented and although I couldn't feel the extent of my injuries, I knew I'd be hurting in the morning.

"I know you're out here!" I yelled, louder this time. I was growing more and more agitated with every passing second and wasn't sure what I was going to do when Abby *did* step out of the shadows.

What I heard next, though, wasn't a voice. It was more of a grunting. At first, I couldn't tell which direction it was coming from, but as I began to walk around, the sound got louder. I rushed down a path behind me, searching frantically for the source of the noises.

It was too dark to see at first, but as I ran closer, what loomed in front of me began to get clearer. In the beginning it was just a shape above me. I thought it was a part of a tree moving in the wind.

It wasn't.

As I crept up to it, I began to make out a pair of legs. They swayed in the air less than ten feet away from me, and were just about eye level. I made out a pair of arms next, resting limply against an equally limp body. Finally, my eyes made their way up to the head of the person. It was cocked grotesquely to the side, eyes wide and mouth open as if midscream. Only, there was no sound coming out. Just a look of sheer terror staring back at me.

The body hung from the tree, periodic gusts of wind giving it the appearance of a puppet being controlled by its master.

I took a few hesitant steps forward until I was able to make out the face of the victim. That's when I began to scream.

"Colette!" I shrieked, rushing toward my friend.

Chapter Twenty-Eight

I'd barely made it a few feet before someone stepped onto the path in front of me, blocking me from my intended destination. It was a figure, once again sporting a long cloaklike garment that covered the wearer from head to toe. Since it was practically pitch black underneath the forest trees, it was impossible for me to see the face of my assailant.

I knew it was most likely Abby, and that made me mad as hell, but I was going to have to deal with my feelings later. I needed to get Colette down from where she'd been strung. It was a sight I'd seen far too many times in my dreams, and only recently experienced myself. But Colette looked scary up there. Too still despite the swaying. I prayed that she was okay and that I'd be able to get to her in time. I *had* to get to her in time.

I started to rush toward Abby, planning on tossing her aside before continuing on to Colette, but as I moved, two more shrouded figures stepped onto the path, joining the body I'd earlier thought was Abby.

Now I had no idea who was in front of me.

"It would be in your best interest if you moved out of my way. Like, *now*," I said angrily.

I took a step to my right, and annoyingly, so did the three of them. They followed me again when I moved back the other way. I stopped and folded my arms over my chest, before cocking my head to the side.

"Okay, now you're seriously starting to piss me off," I said. "And when I get mad, I get all fight-y. People get hurt. It's a bad scene all around. Hell hath no fury like a witch scorned and all that. Now *move* or I'll move you."

Instead, they just stood there staring at me through the black spaces underneath their oversize hoods. It was eerie not knowing who was under them. Or what, considering no one had spoken yet. Was it possible they were something else entirely?

I guess we'll see soon enough.

"Your funeral," I said, shrugging before running straight at them.

My enemies weren't ready for my attack, which I quickly decided would be of a more physical nature, and as I threw my leg upward and flew through the air, they staggered backward slightly, trying to avoid the hit. But I was right on target and my flip-flopped feet made contact with the solar plexus of the center figure. A satisfying "ooof" escaped the mouth of the person and I watched as they fell to the ground and rolled a few times before coming to a stop under a nearby tree.

Barely slowing, I blocked a few punches the cloak to my right hurled my way, then made a few jabs of my own. Each connected with various places on the person's body and reverberated up my arm. I still may not have known exactly who was under the robes, but it was clear they were hurtable.

The second person fell to their knees just as I felt my hair being yanked backward. I was forced to follow the momentum of my assailant, or risk losing the locks I'd grown out for years, and found myself being turned in a circle before coming face-to-face with another of the goons. I tried to peer through my hair and into the person's face, but my view was totally obstructed.

Doing the next best thing, I grabbed the wrist of the hand that was still gripping me and pulled it toward me as I performed a high kick that would've made my old cheer coach cry, socking the person upside the head. Flexibility had always been a strength of mine and it looked like even though I'd been out of practice for a while, I still had it.

Another one bit the dust.

This finally freed me to head for Colette, my adrenaline pumping like crazy now. So much so, that when another robed shape came at me from the left I didn't think before acting. This one was new, joining in the fight midway through, but I didn't care. As number four dived straight for my legs to try to take me down, I jumped into the air, reaching for a sturdy branch above me. My fingers gripped the rough bark as I swung my body forward like an Olympic gymnast and pulled myself up and over the branch like it was a bar, and then watched as the figure slid across the dirt and hit the trunk below. I continued to circle the limb until I'd completed the rotation and jumped back down to the ground beside my attacker, who was no longer moving.

Closing the distance between Colette and me, I found myself hesitating. What if she was dead? Would she be cold already? How would I get her back to the cabin? Fear engulfed me as I was brought back to the moment that I'd realized my mom was no longer alive. I'd totally lost it then. It had taken me forever to even *begin* to deal with the loss.

Get her down now, Hadley! The words seemed to scream their way through my head, despite the morbid memories.

Lifting up onto my tiptoes, I grabbed Colette around the shins and tried to push her upward in an attempt to either get her down or make it so there was some slack on the rope. Neither worked and I strained to see what I was dealing with.

Only, when I looked up I nearly let go of Colette altogether. *There was no rope.*

In fact, there was *nothing* holding her up in the air at all. She was simply floating there above me. Like a ghost.

Still, just because there wasn't a noose around her neck didn't mean she was free from danger. Not from whatever magic had her in its grip at least. Taking a step back, I squared my shoulders and forced myself to breathe deeply. There wasn't enough time to calm myself, so after inhaling twice, I aimed and let loose the spell a half a foot above Colette's head.

"Exbiliby totalitum!" I yelled. The trunk behind Colette exploded into splinters.

Damn. Missed.

I could hear footsteps falling on the forest floor behind me. Without turning, I knew that more people had joined the previous four. Which meant this was going to get real ugly, real fast if I didn't get Colette down. Now. And even then, I wasn't sure I could defend us both.

Starting to panic, I tried again.

"Exbiliby totalitum!"

This time I could feel the magic being severed, and I rushed forward to catch Colette as she fell. Luckily, I was able to soften most of the blow . . . for her, at least. I, however, fell under her weight, my hip smacking the ground hard. I felt a burst of pain as something sharp ripped through my clothes and into my skin.

"Mother of magic!" I screamed out loud, but didn't let go of Colette.

I wanted to inspect my injury, but one look up showed that the figures were almost on us. So I struggled to a standing position, and forced the pain down.

No time. Toughen up. Think fast.

I tried to take a step with my bad leg and it nearly buckled underneath me.

This is not good.

"Colette!" I yelled, glancing back at my friend and seeing her wince slightly.

A wave of joy flowed through me at this slightest of movements. It meant that Colette was still alive. Now if I could just get her to become functional again, we might get out of this alive. . . .

I turned back to the robed gang running up behind me. There were seven of them now. Most of the ones that I'd previously left on the forest floor were up again, seeming none the worse for wear. I'd been able to handle four of them earlier, but that had been with my adrenaline running on full blast and no complications. Defending a passed-out Colette, while suffering from a bum hip, were both complications.

Groaning through the pain, I took a sturdier stance and then closed my eyes to concentrate. Feeling the power building up inside my body, I focused on what I was trying to do. It was only for a few seconds, but it was enough to channel my gifts toward my enemies. Opening my eyes again, I concentrated on the middle of the flock flying toward me.

"Immobius totarium!"

I yelled it with as much force as I could, my arms raised as if to physically stop them. All seven of them immediately froze mid-run. It was like hitting the pause button on the DVD player. They were immobile.

For now.

My hands fixed on the dark figures, I peeked back at Colette, who still hadn't moved. Taking a careful step backward, and then another, I made my way to where she lay. Her glasses were on the ground a few feet away and her clothes were just as dirty as mine.

"Colette!" I yelled, trying to get her attention.

Nothing.

"CO-LETTE!" My cheer voice somehow broke through and her eyes fluttered open and looked up at me groggily.

"What?" she asked. Her voice was hoarse and she immediately brought her hands to her throat, rubbing it gingerly. Then, realizing where we were, she started to panic. Colette rushed to her feet as she spotted the group of caped bad-guys behind me, and then tripped over a fallen branch, ending up back on the ground.

"Chill out. They're frozen," I assured her.

She squinted to try to see for herself that what I was saying was true. I used a spell to send her glasses through the air and back onto her face where they belonged.

Colette didn't seem any happier being able to see now that she could accurately count how many people were in front of us. But at least she was awake. That was certainly a plus.

"We *need* to get out of here," Colette said, inching toward me as she spoke.

"I'm right behind you," I answered.

We began to make our way around the motley crew of hooded shadows and at first I was just happy to be getting away from them. But then it hit me. I still had no idea who they were.

And I needed to know my enemy.

"I don't *feel* you right behind me," Colette said, reaching back for my hand and only getting air.

"Sorry, Cole. There's something I have to do first," I said, slowing down next to one of the shrouded figures. "You can go on ahead if you want. But I have to find out who these guys are."

When Colette didn't move from her spot, I lifted an eyebrow at her.

"You sure you don't want to go?" I asked.

She snorted. "Into the woods by myself? No thank you. You saw what happened the last time I did that . . . I think I'll just take my chances with Darth Vader and the Funky Bunch here."

I nodded and returned my focus to the silhouette in front of me. Taking a deep breath, I got myself ready for what I might find when I pulled back the hood. Reaching out my hand, I realized that it was shaking slightly. With nerves or adrenaline, I wasn't sure. Ignoring my better judgment, I grabbed ahold of the material and ripped it back.

And gasped.

My whole world began to implode as I recognized the eyes first. I'd never be able to forget those eyes. They'd stared straight into my soul and discovered all my secrets. The dark color swirled around like a stormy night, almost making me faint from the effect.

"Not again," I said, before collapsing to the ground.

Chapter Twenty-Nine

Colette caught me before I hit the ground and helped me back to my feet, gripping my arms until I was steady again. But I wasn't sure I'd ever feel steady again. Everything was wrong and so, so horrible.

I took a step forward and my breath caught as I spoke. "How could you *betray* me like this, Asher? Again." It came out as a whisper.

Asher stood in front of me, still frozen in his spot. The cute, dimpled face that I'd grown to not only love, but trust, was scrunched up in a feral snarl. His eyes, which usually looked at me with such care and affection, were hostile. It was like looking at a stranger.

I wasn't prepared for the flood of emotions that torpedoed through me during those next few seconds. The sorrow and intense pain that hit my gut was unlike anything I'd ever felt before. It was so much worse than when I'd found out he was in cahoots with Samuel. I'd barely known him then. Now we had time behind us—over six months of constant contact—and experiences, and memories, and a bond that made this betrayal so much more devastating.

Sadness parlayed into anger, and before I knew it was coming, my hand was whipping out and slapping Asher hard across his face. My hand stung as I pulled it away. Colette took a step back, as surprised as I was that I'd just attacked the guy I loved. But as far as I was concerned, he'd gotten off easy.

Because what I wanted to do was *kill* him.

I started to plot ways that I could hurt him as badly as he'd hurt me. Teach him that you don't mess with the Bishop women. I could curse him so that he'd grow disgusting hair all over his body like a human werewolf. Make him talk as if he'd been sucking on helium balloons for the rest of his life. Turn Abby against him.

As much as I wanted to get my revenge, none of these things seemed quite appropriate. And deep down, I knew that I didn't have it in me to dip into my inner darkness.

But that didn't mean I wasn't going to kick his ass for breaking my heart.

I reached out to smack him again, but Colette stopped me. "Uh, Had, I think you need to see this," she said. The seriousness in her voice made me turn to look at her.

"What?" I asked, slightly annoyed at being interrupted.

Colette didn't say anything, but reached out and threw off the hood of the figure closest to her. I gasped as Asher appeared next to her.

Whipping my head around to the figure beside me, I stared into Asher's beautiful face. Then, I looked at the person next to Colette and saw him again.

"Have I gone temporarily insane or are there *two* of him?" I asked Colette carefully.

"If you're crazy then so am I," she affirmed.

It didn't make sense.

"Wait a hot second," I said, an idea forming in my head. I walked over to another figure and ripped off his hood.

Asher.

Colette did the same, going around to two others and revealing who was underneath their cloaks.

Asher.

And Asher again.

When we'd finished unveiling them all, Colette and I found ourselves standing in the woods in the middle of a sea of people who all looked exactly like my boyfriend.

"What the hell . . . ," I said, confused and upset.

"Why do they all look like Asher?" Colette asked, turning to me for answers.

"Because Brooklyn wants to destroy me," I said, matter-of-factly. "And she knows this is the way to hurt me most."

"It doesn't make sense. . . . ," Colette said, shaking her head incredulously.

"Well, it's about to," I said, taking a deep breath, a new-found anger building inside of me. Only, this time, it wasn't geared toward Asher.

"Colette, you might want to step back," I said and then followed my own advice. Colette scurried to stand behind me as I fell into my casting stance. I could already feel the magic coursing through my body, like the universe knew what I was going to do next and it was welcoming the spell.

"Realto naturasa!" I called out. The words echoed into the night, loud enough to wake the dead. A breeze picked up around us, and the noise that the leaves and branches made as they swayed on the trees created a ghostly backdrop for the moment.

As we watched, the faces of all the Ashers began to melt like wax figures sitting in the hot sun. Their chins began to droop first and then eventually dripped off, making a sick slurping noise as clumps fell to the ground below. It was a horrifying sight and if I hadn't been ready for it, I might've run screaming for the cabin. But I knew the spell was working.

"What did you do?" Colette asked me, horrified.

"A spell to show their true selves," I said. "They're shedding the masks they're wearing. Not exactly pretty, is it?"

"It's like watching a horror movie," Colette said, turning her back so she wouldn't have to see anymore. I have to admit, I would've looked away, too, if I wasn't so hell-bent on finding out who was underneath it all.

Twenty seconds later, most of the Asher masks had disintegrated, revealing the truth. Seeing Abby's and Jasmine's faces hadn't been surprising, though I'd be lying if I said it didn't hurt. More shocking was finding Sascha and Jinx, as well as three other random girls who were attending the intensive with us. Two were giggly clones who followed Brooklyn around. One was practically a stranger.

What could they *possibly* have against me?

"Why are they doing this?" Colette asked as if reading my mind.

I just shook my head.

"That's what I want to know," I said finally. "We need to unfreeze them to find out who's pulling their strings."

"Are you sure we have to let them go? I mean, there's that whole pesky incident where they tried to *hang me* before. . . . ," Colette said, letting her words trail off. She was trying to make a joke of it, but I could tell by the sound of her voice that she was still shaken. And why wouldn't she be? I knew firsthand how it felt to be the target in the middle of a bull's-eye.

"You can go back if you want, Colette. I'm not gonna judge you if you do," I said, sincerely. "It's just that, I sort of have to figure this whole thing out. It's dangerous to have an enemy that you don't know, because it makes it almost impossible to fight them."

Colette stood there and thought about it for a moment before deciding to stand her ground. Alongside me. I appreciated the gesture more than she knew and turned back to the others.

"Okay. Here goes," I said, letting go of the freezing spell.

As the magic wore off and the others began to move again, I yelled out another spell and watched as big orbs of water appeared above each of their heads and then rained down on them like burst water balloons. The liquid soaked through their clothes within seconds, and some began to sputter, while others shrieked in response.

"O-M-freaking G!" Sascha screamed, her fists balled up by her sides angrily. "What the hell? This is *so* not funny!"

Jasmine wiped black eyeliner from underneath her eyes slowly as she searched for the person who'd just super soaked her. When her gaze fell on me, her eyes narrowed to slits.

"You nasty little witch—" she said and began to stalk toward me. But then she recognized where we were and hesitated, looking around for some sort of clue as to what was going on.

"Why are we in the woods?" she asked finally, her eyes moving across Abby, Sascha, and the others, who'd all stopped moving now and seemed to be thinking the same thing.

"That's what I was wondering," I said, placing my hands on my hips, "when I followed you all out here."

Technically we'd only followed Abby, but she'd led us to the others. It was pretty much the same thing.

"You followed us?" Jasmine asked with a snort. "You must

be cracked, because I was asleep in my bed up until a few seconds ago."

"Why would we come out here, anyway?" Abby asked, taking a daring step toward me.

"Apparently to cast against me," I answered.

Even in the dark, I could see Jasmine roll her eyes at me. "I swear, you have an ego the size of a monster truck," she said. "We don't *care* about you enough to cast against you. So, next theory . . ."

"Fine. Whatever," I said, already tired of her attitude. "Just because you don't seem to remember doing it doesn't mean it didn't happen. The bottom line is, you've all been meeting here in the woods at night, and doing spells meant for *me*." I didn't bother telling them I knew this because of a dream I'd had. "You did something to my ring, chanted like weirdo jungle-people, and danced around a fire. And now you're all hating on me like I've actually *done* something to you. So, either you're supremely jealous and plotting against me—in which case, I have no problem being your enemy—or someone's put the whammy on you so you'll do their bidding. I think it's the latter, but please, tell me if I'm wrong."

Jasmine looked over at Abby, who shrugged, and then at Sascha and Jinx, who were just standing there like sad, drowned cats. After a few moments of silence, Jasmine's body relaxed slightly and she folded her arms across her chest.

"You're not making this up?" Jasmine asked, eying me suspiciously.

I crossed my heart and then pointed at the sky. "You can ask Colette. She's the one you guys magically strung up over there."

Jasmine winced at the mention of this.

"Seriously? That really happened?" Sascha asked Colette. Colette nodded her head.

There was fear in their eyes now as they began to believe us. That they really were being controlled without their knowledge and had no idea what they'd been doing.

"Say we believe you," Abby said pointedly. "Who's pulling the strings and why are they targeting *you*?"

"Why else?" I said. "Power."

In this case, power over me and those that I loved.

Chapter Thirty

"Okay, I'm officially creeped out right now," Sascha said.

We were all back in my room, having headed there after successfully sneaking back into the cabin. I'd rounded up Asher and Fallon along the way. I called it an "emergency meeting," and as far as I was concerned, that's exactly what it was.

The second I'd seen Asher, I'd fallen into his arms, kissing him long and hard. Dane and Hudson had watched while lounging on their beds inside the room and whistled at us as we had our moment. When I finally pulled away, we were both breathless and Asher had a dreamy look on his face.

"What was that for?" he asked.

"I'm sorry I slapped imposter you—twice—and thought of all those awful ways to curse you when I thought you'd screwed me over," I said, the words pouring out like they were all stuck together.

Asher blinked at me, trying to process what I'd just said. Finally, he reached down and held my hand. "You're forgiven?" he said still confused, but guessing this was the right thing to say.

"Thank you," I said, and then gave his hand a tug. "Now we've gotta go. Emergency Cleri stuff."

Once we were all gathered inside the room, I called our meeting to order.

"Someone's out to get us. Again," I informed them, diving right in.

"You mean *you*. Someone's out to get *you* again," Jasmine said, sarcastically.

"Say it any way you want, but someone's been using you like a deranged puppet. The old Jasmine would've been furious to find out that she was being controlled by anyone. Maybe you've become more comfortable with blindly following others, but—"

"Nobody *controls* me," Jasmine said forcefully. She paused as she thought about what I'd said and then continued. "But if someone *has* been doing spells on us, I'm going to seriously kick their asses. It won't even be funny."

"Well, so far our mysterious enemy—or enemies—has gotten you to meet secretly in the woods at night to do spells. They almost made you all hate me, and they nearly got you to *kill* Colette tonight. And you don't remember *any* of it," I said. "I'd say something weird is going on here, wouldn't you?"

I waited for them to say something, but Jasmine was clearly annoyed that she'd been put under a spell and was too proud to say so out loud. Abby hadn't said a word since we'd gotten back, except to claim she was fine when Asher had asked her how she was. Besides that, her lips were, as usual, sealed.

"This is so *freaky*!" Sascha said suddenly. "It's like . . . I feel so annoyed by everything you're saying, Hadley, but I have no idea why. I know this is all because of a spell, but I still sort of just want to yell at you. I have to literally *force* myself not to say the mean things I'm thinking about you in my head. How weird is that?"

It was more mean than weird for me, but I didn't say so. Because I knew that they all must be restraining themselves. They were *trying* to fight the magic and that was no easy feat. I was going to have to cut them a little slack until we were able to do a counterspell, which I was already starting to formulate in my head.

"We need to figure out who's targeting the Cleri and why. And then we have to stop them," I said.

"No offense, but if this is a Cleri thing, why is *she* here?" Fallon asked, pointing at Colette. Blunt as always, Fallon once again hadn't thought about what he was saying before he'd put his foot in his mouth. I scowled at him, hoping it would be enough to make him apologize. But Colette jumped in before he could take anything back.

"Um, they nearly used me as a human piñata tonight. I think that earns me the right to find out why," Colette said. It was the first time I'd ever heard her even remotely forceful. Nearly dying could do that to a person. And I liked the new her.

"Fair enough," Fallon said with a nod and then let it go.

"Should we maybe tell the Cleri elders?" Sascha asked.

"I think we've already established that we're more powerful as a group than the elders are, Sascha. Besides, there aren't that many left that we could go to," I said, thinking about my dad. He'd sent me to camp, thinking it would be a safe place for us. I didn't have the heart to tell him that he'd sent us right into the belly of the beast. He'd never forgive himself. "We handled things on our own once, and we can do it again."

"Should we all go home? Just leave camp?" Colette chimed in.

I shook my head. "We tried that with Samuel, but he just followed us. Location doesn't matter. If someone wants us gone, they're coming at us wherever we are."

"How do we figure out who's doing this?" Jinx asked. She'd been quiet so far, and at first I'd worried that she was freaking out. But as I studied her face now, it wasn't fear she was feeling. It was something else. Resolve maybe? No, stronger than that. And then it clicked.

Jinx was *angry*.

And I was almost positive it wasn't directed at me. It was anger toward whoever was messing with us. I almost smiled as I realized that the perfume had worked its magic. Jinx was back.

"Every time I've seen you guys under the spell, there hasn't been anyone else around obviously controlling you," I said, slowly. "We need to do something that will catch the person in the act."

What I really meant was that we needed to catch Brooklyn in the act, but I knew by now that they'd have to see it to believe it. So, I left the blame out.

"How do we do that?" Asher asked.

I wondered if he was finally ready for the truth. That sometimes people just turn bad. Would it destroy him all over again? Would it make him less likely to trust another girl-friend? Or has he known, deep down, this whole time, but just didn't want to admit it?

"I'm gonna need to make another trip into the woods for more supplies, but by this time tomorrow you *will* be able to defend yourselves against this spell. No matter who's casting it," I said.

What came next would be much harder.

•••

I headed out just as the sun came up the next morning, set on getting all the ingredients I'd need for the protection perfumes before our classes began. Colette offered to go with me to help, which I appreciated. The more hands, the quicker we'd get back. We'd all agreed it would be best if the others stayed behind; no use in their trying to fight their feelings of hatred toward me while the spell was still working.

I gave Colette a crash course in herbs and plants, and then we spread out to find everything that was on my list. When we'd plucked the last flower, we both went back to the cabin, and I set out right away to make perfumes and colognes for all of us. I figured the sooner everyone was protected, the better. Once everyone was wearing their new concoctions, I'd be able to breathe again.

But that sense of ease didn't last, because as soon as I'd finished the potion portion of my morning, I was reminded that the Brighton Challenge was beginning. Today.

The universe couldn't have had worse timing.

"I'm *so* not ready for this," Sascha said as we waited for the counselors to show up at the amphitheater. "I'm horrible at tests."

The perfumes had started to work almost immediately after they'd been put on, but the girls said the urges to hate me hadn't disappeared completely yet. So they were all keeping a safe distance, despite the fact that they weren't shooting death stares my way anymore.

"I don't think this is the kind of test you can study for, Sascha," Colette said, popping from one foot to the other nervously. "It's all instincts and natural skills."

"Which you have experience with already, because of our battle with the Parrishables," I said. "You know how to handle yourself in a crisis."

"I guess," Sascha said, halfheartedly. "But there are so many more talented twitches here. There's no way I can compete."

I didn't want her going into the challenge thinking she was going to fail, though. I wanted all the Cleri to do well today. Even if I ended up winning the whole challenge.

"Please. You know you're awesome, Sash," I said encouragingly. "You're strong, talented, totally hot, and way powerful. You're a Cleri."

"Just go in and do the best that you can," Jinx added, giving her a supportive squeeze.

"Hello, twitches!" a voice rang out through the air, commanding all of our attention.

We turned to see the three counselors standing up onstage. They were each wearing red, but their outfits were as different as could be. Miss Peggy had traded in her usual vest for one in a candy-apple color. The pins had been transferred over though, which made it almost difficult to see the fabric underneath. Mrs. Jeanette was wearing jeans and a crimson blazer, buttoned up over a black shirt. And Mrs. B was flashy as always in a form-fitting, bloodred cocktail dress with ruching around the midsection and bodice. If she hadn't been standing in the middle of camp, you'd think she was going to a Hollywood party. But for Mrs. B, every day was a party.

"Is everyone ready for the Brighton Challenge!" she yelled out to us. About half the crowd screamed back like they were at a rock concert. The rest of us were just eager to get on with the festivities.

"Are you sure we shouldn't tell them what's going on?" Colette asked as we watched the three women attempt to pump up the audience.

"I thought about it," I admitted. "But at this point, we don't know who we can trust. And believe me, I've been on the wrong end of an angry adult before—so much worse than being grounded. Better to deal with this ourselves until we know who we're up against."

"Gotcha," Colette said, turning back to the stage.

"Okay, let's get started!" Miss Peggy yelled out, motioning for us all to take our seats. Once we'd quieted down, the three women summoned chairs for themselves and then relaxed as they explained what was about to happen. "As you know, this will mark the first annual Brighton Challenge! The obstacles you will compete in today are designed to test your power levels, casting ability, strength of character, reaction time, accuracy, intelligence, creativity, and execution of skills. We encourage you to use a mixture of your human instincts as well as your natural magical drives. It's a balance of the two that will propel you forward in this competition."

"Not only will you be graded on your ability to finish each obstacle and make it to the end, but we will be monitoring how well you execute each. If you fail to complete any challenge, you will automatically be disqualified," Mrs. Jeanette said with little feeling.

"Mrs. Jeanette sure knows how to suck the fun out of everything, doesn't she?" I said under my breath. Sascha and Jinx snickered, but Colette was too focused on what was being said to get my joke. She was probably the only other person who wanted the apprenticeship as badly as I did. Of course, our motives were totally different, but we both knew the opportunity would be life changing.

In fact, Colette might actually be my biggest competition here.

"Each of you will be equipped with special gear for the duration of the competition. A wristband will track your progress, as well as act as an alert to the movements of your fellow twitches," Mrs. B said. "If you are disqualified, either by cheating or failing a challenge, all the jewels on your wristband will glow red until it has been disarmed by one of us. That will be your sign that it is time to head back to home base.

"Of course, if you're a competitive person like me, you'll want to know how your competition is doing." She winked at us conspiratorially. "So, to keep you all up-to-date on the progress of your fellow campers, each time a competitor is sent back to camp, a jewel on your wristband will light up with a golden hue. It will stay lit until either you are disqualified or have returned to camp at the end of the competition. Also, if another camper completes the course, a jewel on your wristband will glow green."

"In the end, those who complete all the obstacles set in front of them will then be scored by the three of us, leaving only one girl and one boy at the top," Miss Peggy said. "Those will be the two to win an exclusive apprenticeship with the witch of their choice."

"How will you know how we're doing?" Eve blurted out.

I looked over in her direction, but my eyes fell on Brooklyn who was lounging in the chair next to her. She was wearing a pair of short shorts, which showed off her Amazonian legs. I had a great figure myself, but Brooklyn's stems extended all the way to her armpits.

When Brooklyn noticed my staring, she gave me a challenging look. I shot a confident smile back at her and then turned my attention over to the counselors, who were already answering Eve's question.

"We've enchanted the forest to make it so we can see what's happening to any of you at all times," Mrs. Jeanette said. "You won't be able to see us watching, but we *will* be."

"We can even do instant playback!" Mrs. B said excitedly,

raising her arms in the air like a cheerleader. "The NFL has nothing on us!"

"Yes. That's right," Miss Peggy said, trying to get back to the matter at hand. "Are there any more questions?"

The trio looked around until they spied someone with their hand up and pointed to a place just behind where I was sitting. We all turned to see that the hand was attached to Abby.

"Yes. You there," Miss Peggy said, pointing to her.

"What are the obstacles and how many are there?" Abby asked. I couldn't tell by the inflection in her voice whether she was excited about the competition or dreading it. Apparently, just because she was being more vocal didn't mean that she was turning into a whole new person.

"We can't tell you exactly what the obstacles are, as that would take away from the spontaneity of the challenge. But we *can* tell you what you might be able to expect while you're out there," Miss Peggy said.

"There will be a total of five obstacles you must pass in order to finish the course. Each one will grow in difficulty, and it is up to you to discover how to pass them all. Your wristband will glow purple for exactly five seconds once you have correctly finished the obstacle. That will be your sign to move on to the next challenge," said Mrs. Jeanette. "Though we will not tell you what each obstacle is, it will be clear when you come up against it. Move straight through the woods until you reach the end and your wristbands alert you that you've completed the course. If you veer into another camper's designated area, a force will block you from entering."

"You're all very talented witches—you wouldn't have been accepted into Brighton if you weren't—so, we're not going easy on you. We're trying to find the best of the best by celebrating the talents you possess as witches, and the challenges you're about to face will reflect that," Miss Peggy said ominously. I was so used to her constant bubbliness that hearing the dip in her voice was unnerving. "Please keep in mind that at no point will you ever be in *real* danger. Though your circumstances might feel dire, we have safeguards to ensure your safety at all times. We're taking this competition seriously, but not at the expense of your lives."

A hush fell over the group as we all took in this information. Given the weirdness at camp, I was beginning to get a bad feeling.

"But above all, remember to have fun, dolls!" Mrs. B said with a twinkle in her eye. "And let the best witch win!"

Chapter Thirty-One

"I know it's because of a spell, but it's super annoying that you look good in everything." Sascha pouted as she looked down at her own clothes. She had on plain black leggings and a blue tank, both of which flattered her figure but didn't exactly make her stand out. I tried to tell her to just zap herself another outfit, but she'd explained that she didn't have the same eye for fashion that I did.

This was true, but I worked hard on my looks. Most of my spare time was spent poring over high-end mags and fashionista blogs.

Right now was no different.

"Thanks?" I said, not sure if it was a compliment or a dig.

As I'd waited for everyone to get their wristbands hooked up, I'd snuck away to the bathroom to take a second to prepare my battle clothes. I performed a quick glamour spell, conjuring up an edgy little outfit I'd seen on one of my favorite kickass actresses in *Self*. The shorts were a cotton/spandex mix and fitted tightly over my muscular thighs, coming to a stop about three inches below my butt. The red shade of the shorts made sure I'd stand out when the judges were watching me kill it on the obstacle course.

The top was the same material, but covered the full length of my arms with thumb holes to keep the sleeves from riding up. It was black like the night, except for a stripe of red, which extended from my armpits to my wrists, giving off a flash of color if I lifted my arms. A hood gathered loosely behind my neck in case I needed the extra protection from the sun, which was a possibility considering I had no idea what to expect from the day.

My favorite part of the outfit was the back of the top, though. Directly below the hood was a hole in the material, leaving my back completely bare. The sports bra was built into the front, so all you could see was my perfectly porcelain skin where material would normally be. It was all business in the front, party in the back. And I was in *love* with it.

The whole outfit was completely unexpected, but I thought that fit me perfectly. The others had no idea what they were up against.

"Does everyone have a wristband?" Miss Peggy yelled out as she attached a band to the last girl in her line.

We all raised ours into the air in response. After letting my arm drop back down, I took a second to admire the piece of athletic jewelry. It was actually really cool, in a sporty kind of way. The band was made of a thick, hard rubber that connected side-by-side on one section of the bracelet, like a snake coming around to meet its own tail. It was bright white, so the jewels, which were placed equidistance apart along the length of the band, could stand out better when they were lit up. Despite its delicate appearance, the counselors had assured us they were pretty much indestructible.

I ran my finger across the length of the band, enjoying the rough-then-smooth-then-rough rhythm of the design. If it wasn't so much like wearing a lojack, I might've even added it to my weekly bling lineup.

"Okay, if everyone's geared up, please follow me," Miss Peggy said, leading the way alongside the other two adults. For a moment, they looked so serious that it seemed more like they were leading us to our execution rather than a fun magical obstacle course.

The thought made me shiver.

Once we were at the edge of the woods, the counselors slowed to a stop and then told us to spread out. Colette took her place on one side of me and Jinx on the other. Beyond Jinx was Sascha, Jasmine, and Abby. By some sick twist of fate, Eve was right next to Colette and beside her stood Brooklyn.

Keep your enemies close I guess.

I rubbed the soles of my feet into the ground, hoping to gain some traction in the dirt. I rotated my neck to the right and it cracked loudly, then I repeated the motion to my left, feeling satisfied as my body began to loosen up. Reaction time was all about keeping yourself open to everything that was happening around you. When it came to surprises, laserlike focus was not your friend.

I looked over in Colette's direction and saw that both Eve and Brooklyn were staring back at me. Not happily, I might add. I wondered if they knew I was onto them?

"Good luck, guys," I said sweetly, trying to throw them off with kindness.

The tactic didn't work.

"We'd say that to you, too," Eve said nastily, "but we hope you lose."

Eve sneered at me, but Brooklyn didn't say anything at all.

Instead, she just adjusted her bracelet before setting her eyes forward.

That was it. I was through with being the bigger witch in this situation. I didn't care if I owed them or not for cutting me loose in the woods. It was officially *on*.

"I'll put in a good word for you when I do my apprentice-ship," I said, confidently. "A powerful witch can always use a good janitor."

As Eve's face fell into a scowl, I turned to face Miss Peggy, Mrs. B, and Mrs. Jeanette as they lined up in front of us, signaling that the competition was about to begin.

"Will everyone please line up on the X in front of you," Mrs. Jeanette said, pointing at the place on the ground where the letter was etched clearly into the dirt. As I looked up, a large stoplight appeared out of nowhere and hovered a few feet in the air in front of me. A glance at the lanes next to me showed that the other competitors had them, too.

"When the light turns green, please proceed to the first challenge," Mrs. Jeanette continued. "And don't forget, you *will* be timed, you *will* be monitored, and if you don't complete an obstacle, you *will* be disqualified."

"Everybody stand ready!" Miss Peggy yelled, raising her hands in the air toward the floating stoplights. We all crouched down like we were about to start a race. Some of us looked more at home as we prepped than others. For instance, as clever as Colette was, she had decided to wear a frilly, lime-green skirt that had about a dozen layers to it with a loose-fitting tank top showcasing large, bright yellow bananas. The outfit itself was bananas, and I had no idea how she was going to manage running around in it, but I wouldn't have expected anything less.

"Off you fly," the counselors said in unison, and the count-down began.

The stoplight in front of the first girl in line glowed from red to yellow and then green, and we all watched as she took off running into the woods. Once she'd disappeared, the next girl was signaled to go, and so forth. By the time it was Jinx's turn to go, my heart was hammering in my chest and I had the same feeling I'd always gotten before performing with my cheer squad.

I so have this.

Jinx started off at a slower jog than I knew she was capable of, but I was happy to see that she appeared confident. At one point I'd wondered whether I'd ever see her this way again. And here she was, going off into the unknown and up for the challenge.

I was alerted back to my own stoplight, which had finally lit up red as Jinx sprinted for the trees.

Red.

Yellow.

Breathe.

And just when I thought it would never come, the bottom orb lit up in a vibrant green color and I began to run as quickly as my legs would take me.

I had no idea where I was going or when I would encounter the first obstacle, so I started by focusing on moving as fast as I could. Trying to stick to a straight path, I listened to the pounding of my sneakers against the ground, while straining to hear for the other competitors.

But all I heard was me.

We were all only about twenty feet away from each other in both directions, so the fact that I wasn't able to make out the others as their breathing labored and they lumbered through the trails was a little disconcerting. But then again, the counselors had said they'd enchanted the forest for the duration of the competition. It was entirely possible that they'd isolated us from one another, so we couldn't cheat or become distracted while moving through the course.

So, I pushed forward and tried to focus a hundred percent on what I was doing.

I'd been running for about seven minutes and was just beginning to feel the familiar burn in my legs and lungs that always came with an intense workout when I saw a monstrous thing start to grow right in front of me.

Here we go!

As I got closer, I could see that the wooden structure was flat and smooth and stood about twenty-five feet straight up in the air. It quickly became clear that I'd reached my first obstacle, since I'd hit a wall. Literally.

Knowing it was a long shot, I slowed my gait before going to the far right side of the wall and trying to move around it. But as I'd expected, as soon as I started to step into the open space on the side, my body was pushed lightly backward. Like an invisible rubber band pulling my body away from the easy way around.

No matter. It wouldn't have been a challenge if it were that simple.

So, I rushed back to the middle of the wall to study the surface again, this time for clues on how I was supposed to get up and over it. The counselors had said to use a combination of our human skills and our magical talents to pass the obstacles, so I tried to quickly figure out what I was supposed to do in this case.

I looked around for something big to prop up against the wall, which would put me closer to the top of the structure. But there was nothing. There were plenty of trees to climb, but none were near enough to the wall for me to get up and over. Knowing I was already wasting time, I took a step back.

Magic it is.

"Revosio immersa!" I shouted, aiming the spell at the construction in front of me.

As the words to the revealing spell left my mouth, there was a little shudder in the surface of the wall. I blinked my eyes, not sure what I was seeing at first, and was momentarily mesmerized by the swirling patterns of the wood. But after a few seconds, the exterior, which had been smooth before, suddenly became riddled with holes. Holes that didn't go all the way through to the other side, and were only about five inches in diameter. Without hesitating, I stepped forward and stuck one of my hands inside.

My fingers immediately closed around a groove in the gap of the wood and then my free hand found another hole and grabbed on. Taking a deep breath, I pulled up with my arms until my body was off the ground.

It was like rock-climbing—something I'd never done before, but had always wanted to try. And honestly, it wasn't all that hard. After you've lifted another girl into the air and held her there as she balanced on one foot, lifting your own body weight is easy.

Once again, cheerleading saves the day!

I started to move steadily along, finding one crevasse after another and slowly making progress. Until suddenly, there were no more holes above me. I searched around, but the surface remained smooth from that point on. I was about eighteen feet in the air by now and no matter how I worked it out, there was no possible way to reach the top from where I was.

Clinging to the wall, I could feel my muscles begin to twitch with fatigue. It had seemed easy when I'd been moving. But now that I was stuck, it was like my body weight had doubled.

I looked down at the ground. No way was I going back the way I'd come. Besides the fact that I didn't want to have to start over again, I knew that the holes in the wood had gotten me this far for a reason. There had to be another way over. Something that I wasn't seeing.

Tipping my head back, I squinted in the sun and tried to find a solution. I could blow holes in the wood and continue to climb my way up. But then I'd have to let go of one hand in order to cast accurately. And given how quickly I was starting to tire, I wasn't sure I'd be able to do it another four or five times before I collapsed. There was also the possibility that I would blow the whole damn thing up. Would Mrs. Jeanette have made it that easy to get through, though? Just remove the object by blowing it up? It was hard for me to see them going that route.

No, I was sure they wanted us to go *over* the wall. So, how was I going to do that? And before my arms fell off?

I studied what I had at my disposal: This flat wall? No help there. A tree? As I'd noted earlier, the branches weren't long enough and it's not like they could stretch . . .

My gaze slowed as it ran over a group of vines that drooped down from a nearby sapling. Would they be strong enough to withstand my weight? I shook my head and laughed, as I wondered why I hadn't noticed them before.

Taking a few deep breaths, I transferred all my weight to my left hand and pointed over to the creeper that was on the tree just over the other side of the wall.

"Elingua astonia!"

The vine began to move, farther and farther until it had snaked its way over the wall and down toward me. When it was close enough for me to grab, I carefully tested its strength, first pulling on it while holding onto the wall, and then finally by gripping it with both hands.

Mustering up what was left of my strength, I planted my feet against the flat side of the wall and began to climb the rest of the way up. Every step was agonizing and my arms burned like they were on fire, but I forced myself to keep going. When I finally reached the top, I dragged my butt up and over until I was lying on it. As one of my legs hit the other side of the wall and dangled there, twenty-five feet above the ground, my wristband glowed a brilliant shade of purple, signaling that I'd passed the first challenge.

Chapter Thirty-Two

Getting my feet back on the ground was actually much easier than climbing up had been. I channeled my inner Jungle Jane and swung down using the vine. And just like that, I was moving again.

As I jogged toward the next challenge, I wondered how quickly the others had managed to get over the wall. I may not have been as fast as I would've liked, but I also hadn't exactly been slow in figuring it out, either. I was confident that I was still in the lead or at least up there and that was good enough for now. I could always make up the time as the day went on.

The important thing right now was to keep moving.

So I did. I fell into a rhythm as I ran, synching the sounds of my feet with the inhalations and exhalations of my breath until they created a nice little beat. In my head, I began to compose a song that would fit in with the background noise, all about how I was going to win the Brighton Challenge and prove, once and for all, that I was better than Brooklyn and her cronies. That I was the head witch.

Just as I was perfecting the chorus, a sudden resistance came over my body and it became hard to move forward, until finally, I couldn't at all.

I'd found my next obstacle.

"What do you have for me now?" I asked out loud, pushing my hand forward and feeling it bounce back to me softly. I walked to the right and then over to the left and found that I couldn't move around it, either. Doubling back the way I came, I was perplexed to find that at some point the invisible force field had closed up behind me too, leaving me in a sort of locked box with nowhere to go. I'd never had problems with claustrophobia before, but knowing that I was stuck there, even momentarily, left me feeling nervous.

Nobody liked being caged, least of all, me.

Looking around, I searched for some kind of clue as to what the counselors wanted me to do here. I doubted I was supposed to go up and over the invisible wall. It was too much like the last challenge. And besides, what was I supposed to do? Fly? Standing a foot away from the back barrier, I studied everything around me.

Was I supposed to go *through* it?

Shrugging and feeling like I didn't have any other options, I lifted my arm and took aim at the path in front of me.

"Exbiliby totalitum!" I yelled, feeling the power surge through my body, down my arm and out through the tips of my fingers.

The air crackled in front of me as the explosion hit what looked like nothing. Electric currents shot out to the sides like they were following an unseen maze. And then they evaporated.

Did it work?

I said a silent prayer and then sprinted full speed into the direction of where I'd just sent the spell. For a second, I thought it had worked. I was just about to pump my fists in the air, when without warning I was thrown backward like a snapped rubber band. Only, there was nothing to cushion my fall, and I landed on my butt several feet away.

"Well, *that* was an epic failure," I muttered, frustration coursing through me. I got to my feet huffily.

With a determined look, I went back to the same spot I'd stood in before. I scuffed my feet in the dirt a few times and then concentrated before trying the spell again.

"Exbiliby totalitum!"

The same thing happened, and I watched the power of the spell spread across the air. I didn't have to humiliate myself to know it hadn't worked. Again.

But before I could try another tactic, I felt something hit my back. It wasn't hard. More like a pressure building up behind me. Confused, I turned around and brought my arm out, only to find it bounce back toward my body.

That can't be right.

I knew for a fact that a few minutes before, this wall had been several feet away from where I was standing now. Yet, here it was, at my back. I looked down at the dirt to make sure I hadn't gone back further than I'd thought. But the markings were there, same as before.

What the spell . . .

A lightbulb went off in my head and my heart began to race. I hadn't moved; it was the invisible wall that was pushing itself forward. Closing me in.

I took a step forward to test my theory and counted the seconds as they went by. Birds chirped nearby and the sun shone through the trees, warming my arms through the sleeves of my shirt. I was getting hot and uncomfortable and my head was screaming to move. But I stayed put and counted.

Twenty seconds passed by before I felt the wall at my back again.

Panic began to build inside me. The invisible box that I'd found myself in was getting smaller and smaller, and if I didn't find a way out of here fast, I was going to be stuck in here with nowhere to go.

And then I'd lose.

Fighting off the fear, I forced myself to focus on the matter at hand. I had to get out. And there *was* a way—that much I knew—I just had to solve the puzzle first. Looking ahead, I took in everything around me. Where was my clue? What could be used to get out of this? Where was the key to unlocking this challenge?

Searching the area as if it were one of those pictures where something just doesn't belong, I began to consider every object in front of me until I found the answer.

I almost didn't even notice it. In fact, my eyes had swept over the spot nearly a dozen times since I'd been standing there, and I'd never picked up on it. But now, while I was looking for things that didn't fit in with the surroundings, it made total sense.

I'd found my target.

It wasn't red and white like the targets we'd had during our practice sessions. The circular-shaped board actually blended in with the tree it was hanging from, but clearly showed a circle within a circle within a circle, just like a bull's-eye. And I was positive that I'd have to hit it in order to move on.

I felt a pressure at my back again and took another step forward.

I needed to work fast.

Lining up my hand with the target that hung in a tree about twenty feet away, I said the exploding spell again, this time as loudly and potently as I could. My aim was perfect, and with a deafening boom, the object blew to pieces. This time the air in front of me glowed purple before fading back to the clear path beyond. Hurrying to the spot where I knew the invisible force-field had just been, I paused before cautiously taking a step forward. Scrunching up my face, I waited for my body to hit resistance.

But there was nothing.

I took another step forward.

Nothing.

And another.

Still nothing.

Then, I started to run.

About thirty feet ahead, I began to feel the pressure grow in front of me again. So, I slowed down and tried to find the target. This time there were two. One hidden in the bushes of a nearby shrub and another just behind a tree branch. I'd have to destroy a limb before I could hit the target, but it wouldn't be too difficult.

As I started to take aim, I was pushed off balance. Only this time, the wall continued to move me forward. It was slow, but constant, with no counts between its movements. Which meant I didn't have time to waste. I had to find the targets and destroy them as quickly as I could.

I took aim and wasted the board in the bush and then switched over to the tree in front of the second target. Squaring up, I shattered the branch into a thousand little toothpicks and then did the same thing with the board that had been located directly behind it. The air glowed purple and I started to sprint again until I could tell I was supposed to stop.

This time I feverishly combed the woods, trying to find the next targets. Only, there weren't any that I could see. Yet. Alarms were going off in my head, telling me that I needed to keep moving otherwise I'd be trapped. The back wall was moving more quickly now, and it would catch up to me any second.

"Come on! Where are you?" I shouted to the empty forest.

Just as I said it, there was a flash of movement to my right. My head flew around and I saw it. The bull's-eye. It had popped up above a large rock. But as I watched, it dipped back down again and out of sight.

Curious.

Another flash had me turning in the opposite direction and I saw another board poke out from behind a small tree-trunk. This time, I was ready for it and sent the exploding spell its way before it could disappear like the other one had. The sound the wood made as it splintered was satisfying, but the air didn't glow purple like before, which meant the section hadn't been cleared yet.

Seconds later a third bull's-eye appeared more than thirty feet away and I had to squint just to get a good look at it. Taking aim, I said the spell, but missed. Blinking a few times to clear my sight, I set back up and this time hit the target.

Without seeing it, I could feel the force coming up behind me.

Gotta move!

But the air still hadn't turned purple yet, so I had no other choice but to wait impatiently for something to happen. Finally, the first target that I'd seen, popped back up from its place behind the rock and I sent a spell its way, hitting it dead-on.

"Boom!" I yelled as the invisible wall turned purple and allowed me to finally move forward.

After that, I alternated between running and shooting,

running and shooting, all the while knowing that at any moment the wall behind me could box me in. I was playing magical Whac-A-Mole, only the prize was power and bragging rights.

I kept on, blowing up targets left and right and then sprinting to the next. Until I came to the thirteenth set. I knew this was the grand finale even before it started. There was something in the air as I waited for the targets to appear. And when they did, I barely had time to think before I was sending exploding spells into the forest.

The third target that popped up was a life-size cutout of Abby. I was so shocked to see her face appear in the woods, that I froze at first. Once I'd regained composure, I raised my hand to do the spell, but hesitated.

Would they really want me to blow up my roommate?

Seconds ticked by as I considered this, and just as I was going to force myself to do something, a bull's-eye materialized just over cutout Abby's right shoulder. With a smile, I adjusted my aim and obliterated the target, leaving my boyfriend's sister intact. After that, there were more targets and more red herrings—in the form of Colette, Jasmine, Jinx, and even Brooklyn and Eve. Part of me wanted so badly to blow up the last two, but I knew it would've disqualified me. And a better revenge would be when I won the whole thing and then revealed to everyone what Brooklyn had been up to.

The moving wall began to push me forward before I'd finished, and I dug my heels into the dirt to try to buy myself more time. I hit the targets as quickly and accurately as I could, but I was getting flustered. How was a girl supposed to concentrate under this kind of pressure?

Using both my hands, I pointed at two targets at once, watching as they blew up ahead of me. And then there was silence.

The wall disappeared from my back and the air in front of me glowed purple, followed by my bracelet, which lit up in the same shade. Directly after this, jewels began to light up red. One after another they glowed deeply, showing me how many people had just been sent back to camp.

One.

Two.

Three.

Four.

Five.

It continued on until nine gems were lit. Nine twitches hadn't survived this round. They'd admitted defeat, but I was still here. I'd passed challenge number two.

"And they all fall down," I said, taking a deep breath before moving on.

Chapter Thirty-Three

My head was telling me to hurry up, but my whole body was screaming to give it a break. Slow down. Take a breather. My legs were on fire, I was struggling to catch my breath, and my mouth felt like I'd swallowed cotton balls. In other words, I was in sad shape.

"Do we get water breaks out here?" I asked the deserted forest, knowing full well no one was going to answer me.

Desperately thirsty, I forced myself to keep going, now at a pace much slower than before. A cross between a shuffle and a ramble, I propelled my feet forward despite my exhaustion.

What felt like an hour later, but might have only been five or ten minutes, I came upon something that made me stop and collapse to the ground with happiness. Like a mirage in the desert, it was exactly what I'd hoped for.

Leaning on the smooth surface of a tree stump, I grabbed the two notecards that had been propped up against a bottle of water. Sweat dripped down my brow, and I wiped it away with my sleeve. I couldn't remember a time when I'd been so thirsty, but I took a second to look at what the card said before knocking back the bottle.

Drink me.

Well, okie-dokie then. Why I'd needed instructions to do this, I wasn't sure. The direction and setup were very *Alice in Wonderland*, and I knew what happened after *she* drank the Kool-Aid. Still, the Brighton world was far less sinister than the one Lewis Carroll created, so I figured that here, water was probably just water.

At least I hoped, because I frantically twisted off the cap and drank over half of the contents in one long, continuous gulp. The feeling was glorious as the icy-cool liquid made its way down my throat and quenched the dried-out hollow in my chest and stomach. My need was so intense that I'd forgotten to breathe as I sucked down the water and had to fight to get air into my lungs when I pulled the bottle back from my mouth.

Deep breaths, I reminded myself as my gasps turned to pants and then eventually back to normal. Once I'd calmed, I flipped over the next card and continued to sip my supply.

Take your break, you've earned your stop,
You're on your way right to the top.
But you're not done, there's more in store,
A slither, some creeping, a moan, a roar.
Face your fears and let them pass,
Leave no reflection in the glass.
Don't try to fight, just let it go,
Better stay hidden than meet your foe.

I turned the card over, hoping there was an answer key somewhere that would let me know what the heck this riddle meant. As it was, I had no idea what I was supposed to do. "Take a break"—I could do that. In fact, I was rocking that part of the obstacle right now.

But the rest? The rest sounded ... ominous. Creepy, slithering? That can never be good.

My eyes darted around for something that might jump out at me, but everything was still. There wasn't even a breeze in the air—something I would've welcomed at the moment. The water hadn't done much to cool me down internally, and I felt like I was practically boiling in the sun.

Standing up again, I wandered over to the shade of a nearby tree. It couldn't have been more than ten degrees cooler over there, but it was enough to give me at least a modicum of relief. I read through the riddle a few more times, still unsure what it was telling me to do, and then leaned back against the trunk of the tree, taking a few seconds to close my eyes and just relax.

The truth was, I heard it before I saw it.

There was a rustling of leaves, the sound of footfall on the ground, twigs breaking softly. My eyes shot open and I searched the area. Someone or something was there—it just hadn't shown itself yet. This meant it was possible it didn't know that I was there, either.

Frozen in place, I waited for the thing to show itself. I was pretty sure that I was entering into the third Brighton obstacle.

And after some water and a brief rest, I was ready for it.

Or at least, that's what I thought, until the thing stepped out from behind the bushes not twenty feet away from me and I nearly fainted.

Seriously? A panther?! There wasn't a lion available? I wanted to yell it out for all the counselors to hear, but thought better of it, considering what was stalking my way.

Instead, my mind began to race as I took in the sight of the sleek creature in front of me. This was no overgrown house-cat. The black beauty slinking into the clearing was a powerful predator. Muscles bulged underneath smooth dark fur, and I followed the length of its legs down to its enormous paws. I almost gasped when I saw its razor-sharp claws; they were several inches in length and I knew from the Discovery Channel what they were used for.

Ripping girls like me into shreds.

Maybe that wasn't totally true, but at the moment it was the only thing I could picture.

Turning my thoughts back to the fact that this was most likely part of the challenge, I went back over what the card had said.

Take a break.

Did that.

Something scary will show up.

The panther definitely qualified.

Then there was the part about facing your fears, a mirror, and hiding? All of which, by the way, seemed to contradict themselves. Why were riddles so ... complicated?! People should just say *exactly* what they mean for once. At least that way they'd be guaranteed to get the desired result. All this "I'm saying this, when I really mean that," beating-around-the-bush bull—

Wait.

My ranting had managed to give me an idea. One that could possibly help in this very situation.

Pushing my back even harder against the tree, I slowly took my hands from their spot on my thighs and placed them behind me. I could manage to flee to a tree and climb high into it, but then how long before it followed me? Freezing him was another option, but the riddle hadn't said anything about running away. It had said to "stay hidden."

Taking the time to bring my hands back to the trunk of the

tree was an excruciatingly slow process, but as I moved, I knew it was what I was supposed to do. My heart gave a leap as I finally made contact and realized that I might not turn out to be kitty kibble after all. I concentrated on allowing the essence of the tree to take over my being. I thought about the roughness of its bark, the strength of its stature, the rings around its insides, and the deep green of its moss.

Then I whispered the words as quietly as the breeze. "Conselus disguisen camocon." It might not have been loud, but the intent screamed volumes.

The tingling began in my fingers and then a warmth spread over my body. It was slow at first, but then picked up speed until, finally, I looked down and saw that I'd disappeared.

Not disappeared. Blended into my surroundings.

Just like a chameleon.

It was perfect timing, too, because a few seconds later, the panther began to saunter in my direction. Right toward me, in fact. They say that animals can smell fear and mine was coming off in waves. I hadn't exactly been a cat person to begin with, so supersizing the animal and then adding a variety of instruments of torture had me sweating bullets. And I couldn't help but feel that the panther knew it.

He was less than a foot away now, and his eyes were trained right on me. Fighting off my rising panic, I shut my eyes as tightly as I could and thought about the feel of the tree beneath me. Mrs. B had said that we needed to have a strong connection to the object in order to duplicate it. And right now I was holding on for dear life.

Ten seconds went by. Fifteen. After twenty seconds had passed and I still hadn't felt the panther's teeth cut into my gut, I dared to open one of my eyes just a sliver. But it wasn't enough to see, so I opened it the rest of the way.

And came face-to-face with the panther, paws straddling both sides of me, its breath hot on my face. My worst nightmare came true as its mouth opened up, and it let out a deafening roar.

I was sure that I was dead. When the panther was done with me, there'd be nothing but shreds of flesh left. The cat would run away with my bones and lick them dry. The headline would read:

CAMP CRISIS
**Girl has face eaten off by panther
during camp obstacle course; it wasn't pretty.**

I used to think that the worst way to go would be via thousands of paper cuts, because it would be a slow and painful death. But at the moment, I wanted to amend my initial thoughts on dying. Being eaten alive by an oversize kitty would be worse. Much worse.

It took everything I had in me not to scream. In fact, the only thing keeping me from doing so was the thought that people would remember me for being a wimp. If I was going to be taken out, it wouldn't be while screaming.

At least *that* much I could control.

So I stood there, as still as I could, despite the fact that I was trembling slightly, and closed my eyes. I didn't need to see it coming. Deep down I knew that it was unlikely that the counselors would let us perish out here, but I also recognized that even the best-laid plans went horribly wrong sometimes.

Several seconds went by, the longest in my life. And still, no shredding. Minutes passed and I was still alive. Finally, I opened one eye and then the other, the suspense of it all nearly killing me.

The panther was gone. Not totally gone; I could see his butt wiggling as he walked away, passing through a set of bushes across from me before he disappeared completely.

I waited a few minutes after he'd left before I dared to move again. And even when I did, it was as quietly as I could. I pulled myself away from the tree, letting the spell fade as I moved. I stepped back into the sun even though I was sweating bullets, still stunned by what had just happened. As I turned in the direction that I thought was forward, my bracelet glowed purple before adding more red gems to the band. When the jewels stopped lighting up, I counted how many people had failed this round.

Seven other twitches hadn't been able to fight their biggest nightmares by blending in with their surroundings and had been disqualified, bringing the total number of people out of the race to sixteen. More than half the girls at camp were eliminated and I'd survived.

Barely.

With a single backward glance, I gathered my wits and headed toward the next obstacle.

Chapter Thirty-Four

I was moving more slowly now. Both because of the stress of the last challenge and because I knew the next one was going to be even harder. Better to take it slow than wear myself out completely before I got to the end.

As I walked, I began to wonder who might've been eliminated from the competition already. I liked to think that the rest of the Cleri were smart enough to get through each of the obstacles, but even I had to admit that they'd turned out to be more difficult than I'd expected. Still, fourteen girls were left in the game, which meant there was a chance everyone had survived so far.

Unless the others hadn't gotten to the third challenge yet.

I couldn't get the image of the panther's toothy mouth out of my head. Its hot breath on my skin, saliva dripping from its teeth . . . Was everyone going up against the same creature? Or was the challenge geared toward the individual? After all the trauma that Jinx had been through, I despised the thought of her having to face something like this.

Especially since she'd made so much progress in the healing department.

I shook my head to clear the obsessive thoughts and found that I felt a little fuzzy after. Stopping where I was, I tried to get a grip on what I was feeling. Slightly dizzy and a sudden difficulty in focusing.

I blinked my eyes to try to clear them, but it was like I was looking through fogged-up lenses. Something was . . . off.

Was this what post-traumatic shock was like? Had the panther thing traumatized me?

I couldn't think of another explanation. There was no reason I should feel this exhausted or out of it. This . . . tired.

My body started to get heavy and my head begged for me to lie down and rest. So I obliged. I plopped down onto the ground as gracefully as a hippo and let the palms of my hands graze the top of the grass beneath me.

I smiled lazily. I liked the feel of the blades between my fingers. Soft and silky. My head lolled on my shoulders as I looked down to see that it wasn't grass that I was touching at all. It was flowers. The scent infiltrated my nostrils and I inhaled deeply.

Ahhhhh, lavender.

"Lavendula," I said slowly. I was surprised to hear my words were slurred and I giggled at the sound. "Often called lavender . . . you can tell this plant . . . by its purple-blue color . . . and sweet floral scent. Helps aid in sleep and relaxation."

My head flopped to the right and I spotted another flower I recognized. This one was white with a yellow center. Rows of them lined the dirt trail, making it into a pretty sort of walkway.

"Chamomile . . . A daisylike plant . . . most widely used to help bring on . . . sleep and has antianxiety properties."

I cocked my head as I started to sense a pattern, but I was having trouble putting it all together. Spotting yet another nearby plant, I placed my hand to my head and rubbed it wearily. Everything around me was fading away.

"Valerian . . . Sweetly scented pink . . . or white flowers . . . that've been known to possess . . . sedative values . . ."

My words trailed off as it all seemed to click. I had to get out of there. Looking forward, I could see that I still had quite a ways to go before the flowers around me dispersed. I wouldn't have to go as far if I backtracked, but then I'd be moving farther away from my goal. If I stayed then I wouldn't be going anywhere. Except maybe to sleep.

In the end, I decided my only choice was to move backward and find some other way to get to where I needed to go. So I began to drag my tired body along the ground. It was all I could manage at that point. Every inch felt like a mile's worth of exertion and I had to ignore the voice inside of me that kept telling me to just give up and take a nap.

Winners never sleep.

The mantra randomly appeared in my head and I moved a bit with every word.

Winners.

(Drag.)

Never.

(Drag.)

Sleep.

(Drag.)

After a while of doing this, my head began to clear. It was slow at first, but then it was like I was waking up, little by little. In fact, when I was able to finally stand again, I realized what had just happened. The flowers I'd just stood in were better than an Ambien. All we needed was a herd of sheep and even the biggest insomniac would've been down for the count.

"You sneaky little witches," I said under my breath, still retreating from the fragrant bouquet behind me.

When I was finally at a safe distance, I studied the woods around me for something that could help get me through the Garden of Sleepville without passing out. The answer ended up being much easier than I thought. In fact, it was almost as if this particular obstacle had been created *just* for me.

Catching my second wind, I rushed around the forest, looking for all the flowers and plants I could find that could help me.

I ripped flowers from their roots and pulled petals from the stems, mentioning what each thing was used for, for the benefit of the counselors who were watching. When I'd gathered everything I needed, I sat down and began to make my serum. Stuffing the broken and mashed-up petals, stems, and flowers that I'd collected into the bottle of what was left of my water, I shook the contents vigorously. As I let the oils mix together, I performed my mom's infusion spell.

When I was finished, I opened the cap and studied the contents carefully, then looked at the flower patch ahead. Wearing the perfume wasn't going to be enough to get me through this challenge. It was going to take more than that for it to work.

With a deep breath, I tipped back my head and swallowed the remaining water.

"Ugh!" I said, shuddering.

It was like drinking potpourri. Pleasant to smell, but not meant for drinking. Without pausing, I shook the rest of the contents out into my hand and smashed it up into a gross-looking mixture. Then, using it as a paste, I rubbed it underneath my nostrils until I couldn't smell anything else.

A boost of energy and alertness burst through my body,

better than a shot of espresso. My head started to buzz excitedly, and my legs wanted to move, and I knew that the concoction was doing its job.

I was going to fight flower with flower.

Taking a running start, I tore through the field of lavender, chamomile, and valerian. At first I felt nothing. Just my surge of vigor and eagerness to go, go, GO! But eventually, the paste began to fall away and the other flowers began to break through my force field, leaving me feeling woozy again.

I willed myself forward, even though my legs had begun to slow, because as tired as I was, I could see the end of the path now. The foliage started to disperse around me, and pretty soon, there were just a few sprigs scattered about.

Finally lumbering to an area free of blooms, I fell to my knees dramatically. Taking in one more whiff of what was left of the paste, I wiped my face clean and then sat there just breathing the normal air.

Talk about flower power.

My bracelet glowed purple and I stood up to meet the last challenge.

As I walked away from the flower patch, six more jewels lit up red, signifying those who hadn't made it to the last round. That meant, out of the thirty of us who'd begun the challenge, only eight were left, including me.

I wished I knew who was still in the competition. Not that it would help anything. There could still only be one winner in the end—and I was determined that it would be me. But, if for some bizarro reason it wasn't, I at least hoped it would be another member of the Cleri or even Colette.

Actually, pretty much anyone except for Brooklyn and her sidekick would be fine with me.

THE WITCH IS BACK

I trudged forward. It had been a long day and I was running out of patience and steam fast. All I wanted to do was wrap this challenge up.

"One to go," I reminded myself as I speed-walked along the path.

If the obstacles were meant to get harder each time, the last was sure to be a doozy. Would we be dodging firestorms? Swimming through rivers of hungry piranhas? My mind couldn't begin to guess what they had in store for us as a finale.

I just hoped I was ready for it.

Even before I arrived at the top of a hill, I knew this was it. I'd reached the end of the road. What I'd do next would determine whether I won this whole thing or went home a failure. One thing was for sure: if I was going down, I was doing it in a blaze of glory.

The butterflies had been building up in my stomach as I approached the peak, but I pushed them deep down and forced a look of resolve onto my face instead—which immediately fell again once I saw what lay below.

"Well, *that* can't be good," I said.

Before I could psych myself out, I sprinted down the hill toward the only thing that stood between me and winning the competition.

A giant black hole.

What I'd thought was just a hole in the ground actually turned out to be more like a hollowed-out crater. It extended from one force-field wall to another and was at least forty feet in length. Maybe longer. The point was, it was too far to jump over. Even with Michael Jordan–type skills, no one was getting across.

Also, it was *pitch black*.

For some reason I couldn't see past about two feet below my

shoes. It was as if light just couldn't penetrate the area. Like I wasn't meant to see what was down below. And *that* was scary.

Stepping into the unknown with no idea what you could be up against? Not my idea of a good time.

I took several steps back and placed my hands on my hips as I thought about my options. Looking around, I tried to find something I could use to cross the open space. But there was nothing. I tried casting a spell to close up the hole, but that was a waste of time. I'd even done a spell to pump water into the area, thinking I could swim across it. But the water just kept coming, while the hole never filled. I sent an orb of light over the edge, but it fell until it disappeared, swallowed up by the blackness like a smothered flame. I placed my hands on top of my head and looked up at the sky in frustration.

Because I'd known all along what I was going to have to do.

"You're *really* gonna make me go in there?" I asked. My hands dropped to my sides dramatically. "*Fine!* Suit yourself. But FYI: bad things tend to happen when I'm in the dark, and I can't be held responsible for what happens next."

Then, with a flourish, I jumped into the abyss below.

On principle, jumping into a black hole is usually never a good idea, but for some reason it was what the counselors wanted us to do. So I obliged, because . . . well, what other choice did I have?

If I wanted to win, that is.

I have no idea how long I fell, or how far down I went. It was an unusual experience. Like I was entering a place where time didn't exist. I kept waiting for the ground, wondering if not knowing would make landing less awful. Was it better *not* to see the terrible things coming at you? Or did knowing help you to prepare yourself for the inevitable?

THE WITCH IS BACK

The last thing I'd anticipated was water.

I'd expected the hard ground. Or maybe a bed of snakes. Or even goo. But my body slipped through the icy surface of the water, shocking me back to reality. I didn't have time to think, to close my mouth, or take one last breath of air. I disappeared into another kind of darkness, hoping it wasn't forever.

Fighting my way to the surface, I pumped my arms as hard as they would go, knowing that there wouldn't be much time before my air ran out. I counted the seconds that I was under, until finally I broke through and gulped at the air hungrily. Gasping and sputtering, I frantically treaded water as I waited for my eyes to adjust to where I was.

When they didn't, I pushed hard with my left hand and lifted my right one into the air above me.

"Ignatious radiulma!" The words echoed in my ears.

A faint glow began to fill the space around me and within moments, I could see what I was dealing with. It appeared to be an underground cavern. Dark and dank. The kind of place you hoped to never end up. Yet here I was.

The place was so big that my magiclight wasn't quite able to spread to every corner, but it illuminated enough for me to see a shoreline to my left, so I headed for it. When my feet finally touched the ground again, I silently rejoiced and did a sort of runny-jumpy-hop thing until I was back on dry land again.

Shivering in the low light, I started to miss the burning rays of the sun. It was cold down here and being soaking wet didn't help.

"One homemade dryer coming right up," I said in the dark. I'd never realized how much I enjoyed talking until there was nobody around to listen.

I wonder what that says about me?

I shrugged and said, "Aeromus une cyclenae!"

Immediately, a burst of air whipped around me, pulling the droplets from my skin and clothes and tossing them every which way. Ten seconds later, I was dry again. Not exactly *warm*, but I figured if I got moving, that would change, too.

So I headed in the direction of the only opening I'd seen in the room, pulling the light along with me with magic. The tunnel I walked into was small and it was hard to see where it led. The directions kept changing and every few minutes I'd come to an *L* in the passageway and have to turn another way. But I kept going.

Because I was being led somewhere. Toward who or what, I wasn't sure. Thankfully, I didn't have to wait long for my answer, because as I rounded one last corner, I saw a faint light up ahead and walked toward it until I entered a room smaller than the one I'd been in with the mini-lake.

And there, waiting for me, was someone I recognized.

"You," I said.

"You," the voice hissed back at me across the darkness. "*Please* tell me I get to kill you now."

Chapter Thirty-Five

"I highly doubt that's what the counselors had in mind, Brooklyn," I said, starting to circle the room slowly. "Unless you know something that I don't."

True, it sort of made sense that the final obstacle would have us competing against each other, but something about this didn't feel right. Call it witch's intuition, but this challenge felt different than the others.

"Scared to have a spell-off with me, Hadley?" Brooklyn asked, raising a perfectly plucked eyebrow.

She was calling me out.

"Is that what we're doing here?" I asked, trying to get her to show her cards.

The truth was, as soon as I'd seen it was Brooklyn, I'd wondered if we were still in the challenge at all or if she'd just lured me down here as some sort of a plan. And if it was the latter, I was actually kind of impressed. It would've taken some crafty magic to get me away from the others, when we were supposedly being watched by most of the camp. But I'd learned through Samuel that if a person wanted something bad enough, they would find a way to make the impossible happen.

Well, they'd try to, at least.

But just like with the Parrishables, I wouldn't go down without a fight.

"Finally sick of coming in second, so you brought me down here to duke it out?" I asked, baiting her. We might've been on her turf, but we were going to play by my rules. "Big mistake."

"You're the one with *my* sloppy seconds, Hadley," Brooklyn spat. Her words were filled with venom and the air in the cave seemed to get even colder. "Then again, I suppose it was bound to come to this. Me against you. Fight to the finish. This world's not big enough for the both of us."

"Omigod, enough with the clichés already!" I said, popping a hip and sounding annoyed. And I sort of was. How could this skinny little thing think she was any match for me? Did she not know who I was? What I could do? "I still have no idea what Asher saw in you."

I knew it was a low blow, but she'd started this and I was going to do whatever it took to take her down first.

Brooklyn narrowed her eyes at me. "Why don't we end this now?"

"I thought you'd never ask," I said, falling into a fighting stance.

My adrenaline began to pump as I easily dodged her first spell and it zinged past me. Following it with my eyes, I watched the magic hit the wall and then disintegrate. This was interesting. Her spell hadn't ended in an explosion, which meant she wasn't casting to kill. Was she just trying to play me? Make me underestimate her so she could slip something past me? Whatever the case, I adjusted the spell I was about to cast so that it was less . . . lethal.

"Why so angry, Brooklyn?" I asked, shooting a shocking incantation her way. It barely hit its target, but she flailed a bit before regaining her balance.

One, nothing.

"I mean, besides the fact that Asher's into brunettes now. Well, actually, just *this* brunette," I said, pointing at myself. "Forget to take your Lexapro this morning?"

Shaking off the shock I'd given her, Brooklyn smiled back. "Me? Angry? Not at all," she said. And for some reason, I believed her. This caught me by surprise. "It's not like it's *my* friends who are ditching *me*. Talking about *me* behind *my* back. Doing everything they can to get away from *me*. And what about that boyfriend, Hadley? Seen much of Asher lately? I've heard he's been MIA. Now why do you think that is?"

This time, I was distracted by what Brooklyn was saying and didn't get out of the way of her counterspell. As a burst of light hit me, I was enveloped in a sort of bubble that began to fill up immediately with water.

Again with the water!

Just as it reached the space near my neck, I busted through it with a particularly powerful explosion spell, spraying droplets of water everywhere. Including on Brooklyn, who didn't seem to notice *or* care. This made me even more annoyed.

"What is it with you trying to drown me?" I asked angrily.

Instead of drying off, I instantly sent an orb of magic her way, which forced her backward through the air. She hit the opposite wall with a thud and then struggled to get air back into her lungs.

How's that for a witch fit?

I rushed over to her and placed my foot on her chest, pinning her up against the wall.

"Hey! Watch it. You're getting dirt all over my Siriano," Brooklyn said and then sent me flying with her own spell.

I landed with a thud nearly ten feet away. We both sat there on the ground, studying each other and breathing heavily from the fight, waiting for the other to make the next move.

"You really *are* out of your mind, aren't you?" Brooklyn asked, trying to get to her feet.

"What are you talking about?" I asked annoyed.

Brooklyn gave me a look. "Witch, please. I haven't even *tried* to kill you yet. You're the one who's been messing with me."

This time it was my turn to be confused. "I haven't done *anything* to you," I said, relaxing a little. "Except come to Brighton. You're the one who's trying to steal my boyfriend, brainwashing my friends, and setting all these traps to try to get me killed."

"You're cracked. I haven't done *any* of those things," Brooklyn said. Then she paused. "Okay, so I'm not exactly thrilled about you and Asher, but he's a loyal guy. If he's chosen to be with you, nothing's gonna change his mind. I get that. And I'm moving on."

"Then why did you trick me into coming down here?" I asked.

Silence. "This wasn't me," Brooklyn said, shaking her head emphatically. "I thought this was part of the challenge."

I was beginning to wonder if she could be right. Had I so totally misread the situation in assuming Brooklyn was here to fight me? But if this was a challenge, then what was the obstacle? All the rest of them had been pretty clear on what we were supposed to do. This one, however . . . there were no clues. Just two enemies wandering around a hole in the earth where it was unlikely that people would find them.

Brooklyn must have come to the same conclusion that I did, because her eyes grew big before turning to meet mine. "This *is* an obstacle, right?" she asked.

I shook my head. "Wow. You're smarter than you look."

Brooklyn scowled and stepped toward me. "That smackdown can still be arranged," she said walking toward me, trying to look as menacing as she could.

"Hold on there, Beach Barbie," I said, placing my hand in the air as I tried to work things out in my head. We'd both been brought here, because someone had secretly hoped we'd destroy each other, or at least be injured trying. So, either someone was after Brooklyn or they were after me. . . .

"We've been set up," I said finally, looking over at Brooklyn.

"What are you talking about?" she asked.

"We were tricked into coming down here."

"By whom? And why? What do they want with *us*?" she asked. All good questions and ones I was eager to find the answers to as well.

"When I learn how to read minds, I'll be sure to let you know," I said, looking around the room we were in with a fresh set of eyes. It was round and had multiple passageways coming and going from where we stood. It made me wonder what the other corridors held.

"Why don't you leave that kind of magic up to the pros?" another voice said sinisterly. As someone else stepped out from one of the doorways and into the light, Brooklyn and I took a step forward before turning to face our attacker together.

Chapter Thirty-Six

"For the love of everything witchy, can't you two do anything right?" Eve asked, slowly sauntering forward as she looked us over critically. "I give you two the *perfect* opportunity to destroy each other and this is what you do? Have a catfight? Call each other names? Talk about a *major* disappointment."

She looked like Eve, even talked like her, but this person in front of us was a different girl entirely. The feisty brunette had always been a drag, but before, she'd been Brooklyn's backup. Her sidekick. Her no-mind-of-her-own drone. Now, here she was exuding a confidence I'd never seen. She stood taller, made uninterrupted eye contact, and walked with purpose. And as she got closer to us, I began to notice something else that was different about her.

Her eyes.

They were *black*.

I'd only seen eyes like that one other time, and death and destruction had followed.

It can't be. . . .

I looked over to see if Brooklyn had been expecting Eve's grand entrance, but she looked just as shocked as I was to see her there. Maybe even more so. Which meant that Brooklyn had been played, too. Betrayed by her friend.

Looks like we had something else in common, besides Asher.

Eve continued to walk around us. "I mean, *come on*! Aren't you supposed to be some überwitch or something, Hadley? You walk around camp all cocky about having 'gotten rid of Samuel Parris' and how you eliminated his loyal followers, but you can't even kill a bratty wannabe who's trying to go after your boyfriend? It's just pitiful," Eve said, pacing in front of us. She was getting worked up and I watched as her fists opened and closed threateningly.

"And Brooklyn. Jesus. You are an awful excuse for a witch. You screwed over everyone who cared about you last year just so you could be popular—and then you *didn't even use it*. Who does that? Who gets everything they want and then squanders it? You must've gotten lucky when you destroyed The Elite, because let me tell you . . . you are *so* not fit to be a leader." Eve was seething now.

I could see Brooklyn stiffen beside me as her former lackey verbally bashed her. She may not have been reacting on the outside, but no doubt that anger was building on the inside. I prayed she'd hang on to it until we needed it. Because from the looks of it, we would.

"When I caught you using magic at school, and watched you obliterate Gigi and her crew, I thought I'd found my *soul mate*. That we were kindred spirits. That maybe we were meant to rule this world *together*."

"I don't think she swings that way, Eve," I said, trying

to alleviate some of the tension that was being directed at Brooklyn. Not that I liked the blonde now or anything, but it would be easier to get away if both of us were still conscious. But this did nothing to stop the runaway train Eve was on. Not one bit.

"After selling out your so-called 'friends' that day in Ms. Zia's office, I held on to that tape of you doing magic at school, thinking that maybe I could use it to blackmail you into handing over your throne," Eve said. When Brooklyn heard this, she gasped, her eyes growing big. It was the first real reaction I'd seen her give since Eve had shown up and I had no idea what they were talking about. "But then I saw how you were planning to use your popularity and I figured you'd hang yourself eventually. And you pretty much have."

By now, Brooklyn was back to wearing a stony expression, her arms folded over her chest and giving Eve a calculated look. This didn't derail Eve though. "You didn't even use your status at school to your *advantage*, Brooklyn! You treat everyone like they're equal, when they aren't. *We* are better than them. It's called a *hierarchy* for a reason, you idiot," she said, her chest heaving with exertion. She closed her eyes then and took in a few deep breaths. I considered ducking into the closest passageway, but felt bad about leaving Brooklyn behind with Eve. "So, when I found out that Hadley was heading to camp—the same camp you went to last summer—I figured I'd let you two extinguish each other. Kill two birds with one stone, so to speak. Because, let's be honest. The most powerful witches don't actually have to do the dirty work themselves. They have people do it for them. But then you just *watched* this bitch make out with your man all summer and didn't even want any of us to go after her. You're pathetic."

"Did you really think I'd *kill* her just for dating my

ex-boyfriend?" Brooklyn cut in. Her voice was steady and strong. "I mean, yeah, I may have *daydreamed* about it, but actually doing it? Just because he found someone new? And after I hurt him like that? No way. That's crazy, Eve."

"Crazy?" Eve asked, taking a few more steps toward Brooklyn. I took a small step in between them without thinking. "I'll tell you what's crazy. That people think they won't get what's coming to them."

"What happened to you to make you so angry, Eve?" Brooklyn asked, sounding sad for the girl. At first I didn't understand why she felt anything for her, but then remembered that at one point the two had been friends. Well, Brooklyn had thought so.

"Why am I so angry? Maybe it's because people like you don't stand up for yourselves and those around you suffer because of it."

Brooklyn winced at the words as if she'd been hit.

"You let people like *her*"—Eve nodded at me—"step all over you. You put people like *her* up on pedestals instead of tearing them down where they belong. You don't even try to stop her when *she* destroys other people's lives."

The focus had somehow changed to me with no warning and we all knew it. I watched as Eve turned to advance on me now. Her eyes were like two black onyx bullets aimed right at me and the sight was terrifying.

"You let people like her get away with *murder*, instead of helping to avenge the deaths of your best friend's *parents*, who were just following the commands of their coven leader, and trying to do what they thought was right!" Eve shouted, a tear slipping down her cheek.

Whoa, what was Eve talking about? I'd *never* killed anyone. Well, except for maybe Samuel, but I wasn't even sure of that . . .

"You should get your stories straight, Eve because—" I tried to get the rest of my sentence out, but she was already moving on.

"Nobody seems to have the balls to punish you for the lives you've destroyed, Hadley. I'm here to change that," Eve said, her face just inches from mine now.

I could see Brooklyn standing just beyond her, not sure what to do. She began to take a step forward like she was going to do something to try to stop Eve, but I gave my head a tiny shake that I hoped would make her stay. Brooklyn wasn't ready for this fight and if she got involved, she'd just get hurt. Or get in the way. At least at this stage, anyway.

"Well, payback's a witch, Hadley," Eve said menacingly. "And so am I."

And with that, she threw a spell at me that ripped into my skin.

"Why is everyone always trying to kill me?!" I shouted as I clamped my hand down tightly on the fresh wound. Blood poured out of my left shoulder where Eve's spell had made contact and seeped through the spaces between my fingers. It felt like a chunk of flesh was gone, but I was too busy—and admittedly, freaked out—to check the damage. I'd seen what a spell like this had done to Jinx and didn't need to witness it up close and personal on myself. Besides, I had a more immediate crisis to worry about.

Like a really pissed-off, trigger-happy, overly-emotional twitch.

"Maybe you should take the hint," Eve spat, her hand raised and ready for another round.

"Listen, Eve. I get that you're upset," I started, trying to hold her off until I could figure out a way to get us out of there. "But I'm telling you—I didn't kill your parents. I don't even know who your parents are."

THE WITCH IS BACK

Behind Eve, I could see Brooklyn turning and looking down one of the entrances of the tunnels. Turning her attention back to me, she made a face that I couldn't quite read, before glancing again at the exit behind her.

Was she seriously considering leaving me here? If she did, I swear I'd hunt her down and . . .

"Of course you don't remember them, Hadley. Why would anyone expect Little Miss Popular to remember something like that? Someone as self-absorbed as you? No, you probably had more important things to occupy your time with. Like makeup and prancing around in front of your dimple-faced boyfriend," Eve said.

"Hey!" I cut in. "I do *not* prance."

"Whatever! You've proven my point anyway. You're so involved with your own charmed life that you don't recognize when you've ruined another," Eve said.

Now, Brooklyn was moving toward Eve again, sneaking up on her from behind. I pursed my lips, wanting to warn her back, but also not wanting to draw attention to her.

"My parents were there that night at your cabin. They came after you in your stupid shed and they both died at *your* hands," Eve said.

"They were trying to *kill* me, Eve," I said, getting annoyed now. How could she blame me for this? "I was just defending myself. I didn't want to hurt anyone, but like you said . . . they attacked *me*."

"Because *you* were messing with our futures," she said. "You wanted to stand in the way of witches coming into our birthrights. Of becoming the rulers of this world."

"No. They attacked me because some wackadoodle who fancied himself a reverend told them to," I countered.

My eyes darted over at Brooklyn who was just seconds away from closing in on Eve.

321

"He's *not* crazy," Eve said, her eyes wild. "He's our leader and he's teaching us the way—"

It was at that moment that Brooklyn chose to cast her spell. Only, somehow Eve knew she was there and spun around just in time to deflect her spell. Then, with a flick of the wrist, she tossed Brooklyn up into the air before sending her soaring through one of the tunnels and into the darkness.

There was something about the action that felt scarily familiar. I'd seen that exact move done before. To someone else.

To me.

I yelled out Brooklyn's name, but there was no response from the dark passageway. Despite my mixed feelings for Brooklyn, I didn't want her hurt. Trying to save my life from a deranged witch was enough to earn a little concern from me.

"Parris taught you to be an *assassin*," I shouted, seething.

Eve nodded as she started pacing again in front of me. "I suppose you could put it that way. I like to look at it as teaching me how to survive and thrive. But potato, po*tah*to."

Now I was getting mad. This was like talking to a crazy person. We were going around and around in circles and accomplishing nothing. It was all a waste of time. And I wanted to get out of there, find my friends, and put the whole sucky day behind me. Stop the cycle of insanity once and for all.

"There's one thing you're forgetting, Eve," I said, letting go of my shoulder and taking a bold step toward her. "Your mentor? The one who's *really* responsible for your parents' deaths?"

I paused for dramatic effect as I got right up in her face.

"I *beat* him."

Eve growled in response, the sound coming from deep down in her gut. As if from her soul—or the place where her soul used to be. Before she could react, I swung my good arm around and made contact with the side of her face. She hadn't been expecting it, so the hit was clean, and clipped her so hard that my hand vibrated with pain.

Not a smart move considering that now both my arms stung.

Luckily, I still had my legs and I began to use them, too. I placed my foot against her stomach, which was unobstructed now that her face was in her hands. Pushing her back as hard as I could, I watched her tumble backward and hit the ground hard. Then I sent a stunning spell her way, but she'd already scrambled back to her feet.

"Enough!" Eve screamed at me.

The force of her voice stopped me before I could get off another round. Was it possible I'd underestimated just how powerful Eve was? After all, she'd managed to get us here and had already busted a hole in my shoulder.

"You think you have all the answers, but here's where you're wrong," Eve said. "Reverend Parris isn't dead."

My blood ran cold and for a moment I thought I might pass out.

"You're lying," I said, mostly trying to convince myself of the fact.

"Who do you think gave me the powers I needed to fight you? Think about it. I've nearly killed you, what, three times now? I'm the vessel that evil flows through."

Eve laughed maniacally. The sound bounced off the walls around us and echoed down the individual tunnels. But once the cackle faded, there was something else I could hear, too. It was faint, but there. A scratching. Footsteps. Dragging.

I had no idea what it was or where it was coming from, but it was getting closer. And now Eve had noticed it, too.

"Ahhhh, yes," she said, still smiling at me. "Right on time."

The sounds were coming from one of the tunnels behind Eve and we both turned toward the noise.

"I have to admit, I was sort of annoyed when you realized what we'd been up to in the forest," Eve said, back to pacing around. "And I'd hoped that seeing Asher as your betrayer would send you over the edge. But then that know-it-all Colette had to stick her nose where it didn't belong. I didn't think you'd be able to come up with a protection spell so quickly, but somehow you managed. You were *lucky*. Again."

"I was *good*," I responded, even though at this point I knew arguing was useless.

"Never mind though. Because as strong as your spells were . . . mine are stronger," Eve said. This time we both looked back at one of the cave entrances and watched as all the girls from camp, including my entire coven, appeared. They were clearly bewitched, with eyes that were glazed over and a sort of stomp-walk-slide you'd expect from a sleepwalker. Or a zombie. A few girls dragged an unconscious Brooklyn between them, while someone else struggled to get away from the grabby hands of a few others.

"Hadley!" Colette shouted, trying to fight her captors, but failing.

"Colette," I answered, but forced myself to stay put, so as not to start a war prematurely. "Are you okay?"

"Yeah. I think so," she answered uneasily. "They just won't let me go and I don't know what's going on and . . ."

"Quiet, Teletubby," Eve snapped, sending a spell at Colette that immediately zipped up her lips. Literally. "You've done enough talking."

"Why are they here?" I asked her, nervous now that I was up against over two dozen jacked-up twitches instead of just one deranged one.

"Oh, well, this is sort of my gift to you," she said, faking sincerity. "I know you're close to your coven, so I thought I'd bring them here to help share in your last moments. At least until they tear you apart."

A lightbulb came on in my head. She was going to manipulate them into killing me. I was going to die at the hands of my own coven members. Just like Bridget had.

History has an effed-up way of repeating itself.

"Unless you want to fight them off, which works for me, too," Eve said. "A little collateral damage never hurt anyone. Oh, wait . . ."

She let the sentence trickle off as she made it clear that no one would be free from pain today. We would all be punished in one way or another. Either by being attacked ourselves or by having to live with what we'd done to stay alive.

"I'm not going to hurt my friends just because you've messed with their programming," I said, refusing to play into her game. "Deep down, they're still good people and they care about me. I can't hurt them."

"Well, we'll just see about that," Eve said and then stepped aside. "Go get her, girls."

And without hesitation, they all came at me at once.

I turned around to survey my options. I could leave. Take off down one of the many tunnels, but where would it lead? If the others were anything like the one I'd come from, my back would be against water pretty quickly. That's if there wasn't something else waiting for me in the dark.

And besides, I couldn't leave Brooklyn or Colette behind. Not in the state they were in. Helpless and captured, because of me.

But I wasn't going to hurt my friends or the other twitches, either. They were just innocent bystanders caught in the middle of a centuries-old feud. It wasn't their fault. They couldn't help themselves.

My options were limited and I had no idea what to do. The others had just about reached me now and I contemplated letting them have me. Do their worst and hope I survived. But deep down, I knew that wasn't my thing.

I was a fighter.

And I was going to go down fighting. Just as I raised my hand to cast my first spell, a bright white light filled the cavern, causing everyone to stop in their place. It was so blinding I had to put my arms up in front of my face to shield my eyes. It was like looking directly into the sun.

And then everything went black.

Chapter Thirty-Seven

I came to, still inside the dark and dirty cavern, only to find I was now propped up on my feet with my back against the wall. Invisible straps held me in place; I could feel the pressure of them across my chest, hips, thighs, and shins. They were so tight that I could barely move, and my arms were strapped down firmly by my sides, making escape impossible.

My chin had been resting on my chest while I slept, but now I forced my head up until I could see what was going on.

"Finally," a voice said from my left. "You drool when you sleep, you know?"

"Do not," I answered, bending my head to one side so my neck would crack and then doing the same on the other. I was sore all over, but nothing seemed to be broken. The blood had even begun to dry around the gash in my shoulder.

Turning to Brooklyn, I saw that she was in the same situation that I was. Suspended in the air by unseen chains, unable to move.

"How's it hanging?" I asked, cracking a joke, because we both could use it.

She rolled her eyes at me and then laughed. Then her face grew more serious. "I've tried casting to break free, but I can't even move my fingers. And my magic won't work without it."

I nodded, knowing what she meant. I'd already tried moving my hands to no avail, too. Twisting my head to the right, I noticed for the first time that we weren't the only ones shackled to the wall. Eve was there, too. So were the rest of the Cleri and the other campers. Everyone was lined up in a row, like human-size decorations hanging on the wall. Most were still out cold, but a few had begun to stir and appeared to be just as confused as we were to be held in place.

So who, then, had put us there? Things were getting weirder, and weirder, and panic was beginning to grow in my chest.

The time had come to take drastic measures.

"Look, Brooklyn, I know we're not really friends . . . ," I started.

"That's the understatement of the century," she responded.

"But . . . ," I said, continuing. "I think we're gonna have to work together to get out of this."

I tipped my head toward the invisible chains.

Brooklyn sighed and let the back of her head rest against the wall as she took in what I was proposing. "Fine. But it doesn't mean we're friends now."

"Of course not," I said.

"And I still don't really like you," she said.

"The feeling's mutual."

"And I reserve the right to go back to ignoring you after we get out of this."

"Okay, I get it. We're *frenemies*. Can we move on now please? Maybe get the hell out of here?"

She gave me a tiny nod.

"Okay, any chance you saw who did this?" I asked Brooklyn, hopefully.

"Nope. Woke up a few minutes before you did," she answered. Her hair was a bit messed up and there was a goose egg growing on her forehead, but for someone who'd just been knocked around by her former best-friend-turned-psycho-witch after nearly completing a full obstacle course, she looked pretty darn good.

Bitch.

"In fact, I don't remember anything after trying to get Eve away from you—you're welcome by the way," she continued. Then her forehead wrinkled up in confusion. "What are they doing here?"

I looked over at the others, who, for the most part, were all awake by now, murmuring and groaning and probably wondering the same thing.

"Eve brought them here hoping they'd turn all angry mob on us," I said, trying not to hold it against any of them.

"Well, it looks like it sort of worked," Brooklyn said, sounding calm, but her face giving her away. She was just as freaked to be here as I was. She was also just as *proud*, and her ego wouldn't allow her to reveal just how scared she was. To me or to anybody else.

"Not totally," I said. "Whoever did this got Eve, too. So, at least there's that."

"Does that mean we're looking for someone even crazier then her?" Colette chimed in.

I hadn't even noticed her on the other side of Brooklyn, but there she was, awake and alert, her lips zipper-free. Considering the circumstances, I was really happy to see her.

"I don't think I can take any more surprises," Colette added.

"Surprises, surprises. Oh what fun!" a high-pitched voice said from somewhere in the room. "Let's look in my purse and find us one."

To our horror, a girl bound out from the shadows and scurried over to us unnaturally.

Almost right away, I knew she wasn't one of the girls at camp. First off, she was wearing a white nightgown that just skimmed her ankles. The style was plain and the fabric cheap and scratchy, resembling a burlap sack. There were stains along the bottom and muddy prints on the front of her frock, like she'd wiped her hands off on it dozens of times.

Her voice sounded incredibly young, but when she finally got close enough, I could see that she was actually around our age. Her hair rose up like a wild rosebush around her face, leaving shadows in places so it was difficult to make out her features.

What I *could* tell was that she was skittish. Even when she peered up at me, her eyes flitted from side to side like at any moment she expected to be attacked. She moved around erratically, talking mostly to herself and not making much sense.

Great. So we'd traded in one crazy for another.

"Who are you?" I asked her as she grabbed at my clothes and studied me from different angles.

"Oh yes, yes. I had a name once long ago," she said, rushing down the line of girls along the wall. "But they took it away and now nobody knows."

"Who's *this* crackpot?" Eve asked, apparently awake.

"Well isn't that the teapot calling the kettle crazy," I said, watching the stranger make her way back to us. Once she'd ended up in front of me again, I asked gently, "What do you *want* us to call you?"

"Call me the forest or a pretty set of pearls. Call me the

justice for all forgotten girls." Then she giggled uncontrollably.

"So her name's Pearl? Or maybe Justice?" Brooklyn asked me.

"Let me out of here!" Eve screamed then, startling all of us, including our captor, who began to run around the cavern, looking for a place to hide. She finally settled for the shadows of one of the entranceways.

"Shut it, Eve!" I yelled at her. "You're not in charge anymore."

"We'll always be in charge," she challenged back.

"Says the girl who's currently strapped to a wall," I said under my breath.

Then I turned back to Brooklyn and Colette.

"Is it just me or is there something really familiar about her?" I said to them.

"A cousin of yours, perhaps?" Brooklyn said with a chuckle. I didn't laugh but tried to place her instead.

"She's familiar because we *know* her," Colette said finally. Her eyes had grown wide and her face had paled.

It was almost like she'd just seen a . . .

Oh, shit.

"Moll?" I called out in the direction of where the girl had disappeared. "Is that your name? Moll Brenner?"

A few seconds later, the girl stuck her head back out into the light and looked at me curiously. She took a hesitant step forward and then another. And then she ran over to me, until we were almost nose-to-nose.

"Moll," she said. But that was it. No rhymes, no incoherent sentences. For the first time, she was clear.

"Omigod," Colette said breathlessly. "It's really her."

"Who is she?" Brooklyn asked, not following.

"She's the Witch in the Woods," I said sadly as I watched

Moll scoot backward a few feet and then sit down on the ground in front of us and hug her knees to her chest. She rocked back and forth, creating a rhythm with her motions.

She'd been so young and so lost back then. And it appeared she still was.

"No shit? The Witch in the Woods really exists?" Eve asked with a snort. "Well, that makes this easier. Hey, Moll. Let me go and we can wreak havoc together. Get rid of these *bitches* once and for all."

Moll looked over at her, a frown on her face.

"Why are you keeping us here, Moll?" I asked her.

She shifted her gaze back onto me.

"You're cruel, and you hurt, and you bring so much pain," Moll said in a sing-song voice as she rocked. "The bad must get punished and it will come down like rain."

"That. Is. Awesome," Eve said with an evil smile. "Because those girls over there? They're the bad people. They've hurt so many . . ."

"No, no, no, no, NO!" Moll yelled, shutting Eve up immediately. She ran over to Eve and covered her mouth with both hands. "You hurt the innocent and will reap what you sow."

Eve's face fell. For the first time since I'd met her, she seemed scared.

"You've all hurt and deserve to disappear," Moll said, quieter now. "I will take you with me and no one will shed a tear."

I wondered where she planned to take us. To the place where the other campers had left her? Wherever she'd ended up when she'd died?

I looked over at the others tied to the walls. They didn't deserve this. Then again, neither did I, but maybe if she just took me, then I could find a way out eventually. . . .

"Moll," I pleaded, terrified now. "I know we haven't exactly been the best examples of good twitches, but that doesn't mean everyone's bad. Please, let the others go. You can take me. And Eve—because let's face it, she's just an evil person. But let the others go. They're the good guys."

Moll squinted at me. I could feel her weighing what she thought was true with what I was saying. Still, she didn't seem convinced.

"See Jinx over there? She saved my life once." I motioned with my head in Jinx's direction. She seemed dazed from the spell Eve had cast on her and the others, but otherwise she appeared to be fine. "Jinx took a spell for me, right in her gut, trying to keep me safe from a really bad guy."

I continued.

"And next to her? That's Jasmine. She's superprotective of the other members of our coven and looks out for them when she thinks nobody's looking. She's the most honest person I know," I said. I flipped my head to the other side. "That's Colette. And she's actually related to you. You're her great-great-aunt. She stuck up for you when everyone else was saying you were hurting people here at camp. And she's really smart and brave and talented—she's everything your lineage wanted to be but couldn't because of crappy circumstances you couldn't help."

Colette smiled at me, a tear running down her cheek.

"And Brooklyn, well she's really . . . fit," I said grasping at straws. When she gave me a look that said, "are you kidding me?" I forced myself to try harder. "Brooklyn helps people fall in love. She just wants everyone to be happy."

It killed me to say it, but I had a feeling it was true. There had to be a reason that Asher still thought so highly of her and I don't think it was because of a love spell.

As much as I wanted her to be the villain of this story, she wasn't.

Moll considered all of this and after a few silent moments she nodded her head.

"So be it."

And then, Moll raised her hand and the others disappeared. Everyone except for Colette, Eve, and me. The three of us remained pressed against the wall, unable to move.

Still, I breathed a sigh of relief to see that Moll had let the others go. I didn't like that Colette was still here, but Moll had at least given me *something*. She wasn't the ghost everyone had made her out to be.

"Thank you, Moll," I said gratefully, as I began to devise a new plan to get Colette and me out of there, too.

The disheveled girl tiptoed over to Colette, who, shockingly, seemed to look happy despite the fact that she was still here.

"Hello," Moll said.

"Hi, Moll," Colette answered, still strapped to the wall. "My great-grandmother used to tell me stories about you, that her mother had told her. You know they never stopped looking for you. Where have you been this whole time?"

Moll looked down at the ground and then back up at her great-great-niece. When the two of them were next to each other, it was easy to see the family resemblance. Even with the dirt that marked both their faces, they still looked alike.

"I went away," Moll said quietly. "Life was too hard. I couldn't brave the day."

"But you did come back every so often, right? To prove that you were still here?" Colette asked.

Moll nodded.

"You're the one who left the message at the theater, didn't you? 'I'm watching'?" Colette said, watching her face. "You wanted us to know that you were watching us. Making sure people treated each other right."

Moll nodded again.

"But the whole world's not like the kids who hurt you back then," Colette said. "There are some great people out there. People who care about you and invite you into their lives and treat you like a friend. You just had a *really* bad experience. Life can be magical—if you let it."

After a pause, Moll smiled. "Then you let it," she said. "Let it be magical."

And, suddenly, Colette dropped down from her place on the wall, freed from what had bound her. Colette steadied herself and then reached her hand out slowly until it hung in the air next to Moll's.

"I will. Promise," Colette said "But one more thing. Hadley is *not* a bad person. She is as good as they come. The world needs heroes like her in it. Someone to make the hard decisions and be brave when the rest of us can't. If she'd been around when you were here, things wouldn't have turned out like they did. Please. Don't take her from us. We still need her."

Moll remained silent and stared at the girl who had her own blood running through her veins. It was nice to hear what Colette thought of me, but I knew it was a desperate plea. After all, I *had* made some questionable decisions in my life. I'd been selfish, unthinking, and often argumentative. I'd been jealous and plotted against others. Who knows, maybe that qualified me as a bad person. Or a good person doing bad things. Either way, what was about to happen was out of my hands.

"Stop with the vomit-inducing family reunion!" Eve shouted, breaking up the moment. "All of you are just sheep who should've been slaughtered a long time ago. You're an embarrassment to our kind and I'm going to wipe you out the first chance I get. And if I don't, then the reverend will, because he knows that people like you don't deserve to walk this—"

"Good-bye," Moll said and just like that, Eve was gone. Her last words echoing through the passageways as if she was drifting away from us.

"What did you do with her?" I asked, shocked at what had happened.

Moll looked at me with a childlike smile on her face. "I will take care of her," she answered and then gestured to Colette, "if you will take care of *her*."

"Okay," I said, scared to ask Moll to elaborate on just what was to become of Eve.

"Make your lives magical," Moll said again and then Colette and I disappeared too.

Epilogue

In a blink, we were back at the beginning of the Brighton Challenge, amidst a now frantic crowd of counselors and stunned campers. Brooklyn was busy trying to explain to everyone what had happened in the caves, which wasn't very easy considering the other girls couldn't recall a thing after starting the competition. There was just a huge chunk of time missing and they each had roaring headaches, like they'd been magically roofied. The counselors had impatiently listened to Brooklyn give her version of the story, but as soon as she'd mentioned the Witch in the Woods, they'd pretty much shut down.

An evil witch they'd believe. But a *ghost* witch? Yeah, that was out of the question. Maybe the adults had never experienced a visit from an ancestor before or possibly they just didn't want to believe that ghosts could exist too. Whatever their reason, our counselors dismissed our explanation.

Beyond that, they were also having a tough time believing

that it was Eve who'd created most of the chaos. They'd never suspected a twitch was actually behind the girls' going missing from the counselors' radar. They'd just assumed it was a glitch. Eventually they'd noticed that those who'd been disqualified weren't making it back to camp, and knew something was wrong.

So, they'd gone looking for us, but we were nowhere to be found. Even the boys' side had gotten involved in the search, but all it accomplished was getting both Asher and Fallon so worked up over our disappearances that the male counselors then had to focus on keeping them from starting a riot.

By the time Colette and I finally *did* show back up at the cabin, Asher practically tackled me. He was so happy to see me that he smashed my face into his chest and held me there until I forced him to let go.

"I don't ever want to be away from you again," he said.

It was what I'd wanted to hear from him all summer, but it wasn't enough. Not anymore. After nearly getting killed, calling a truce with the girl I'd thought was my sworn enemy, and facing a tragically angry ghost-girl, my patience was gone. No more tiptoeing around the subject of us. I was too tired to worry about how I sounded. It was time to be a hundred percent real with the love of my life. And if he couldn't handle it, then tough.

"I'm all yours, but you're going to have to start being honest . . . beginning with what you've been doing every night," I said. "And speaking of . . . I need to be a priority in your life again. I'm glad you have friends, but I miss my boyfriend."

Asher looked at me totally confused. "I told you, I've just been hanging out with the guys. . . ."

"Doing what?" I responded, feeling like we were heading into yet another fight.

THE WITCH IS BACK

Asher looked like he was trying to work something out in his head and finally he sighed and gave in. "Fine. There *is* something I haven't told you," he said, looking down at the ground.

"Just say it, Asher," I said, my stomach tightening.

He was nervous, I could tell. "The guys and I sneak out at night to . . ."

Here it comes

". . . we play Witches and Warlocks, okay?"

I blinked at him, completely stunned.

"That Dungeons and Dragons for witches game?" I asked, raising my eyebrows.

"It's not nerdy like D&D. It's sort of more like a fantasy football game, but for witches. There's casting and role-play and I just made Witch-Master, and completely destroyed Hudson's coven and . . ."

"Please stop," I said, closing my eyes and pinching the bridge of my nose like I was fighting off a headache. This was what I'd been stressing over? "How did I not know that my boyfriend is secretly a . . . big-ass nerd?!"

Asher's face went from concerned to annoyed to playful in about five seconds.

"Yep. That's me. I'm a closet nerd and you're stuck with me," he said, leaning forward and kissing me deeply on the lips.

"Well, at least now I won't have to worry about you attracting other girls," I said, walking away. "What with the possibility of your secret getting out and all."

His eyes got real big. "You wouldn't dare!" he yelled, running after me.

"After the day I've had, I think I'm capable of just about anything," I said, looking back and giving him a wink.

• • •

By the time I'd answered all of the elders' questions, eaten dinner, and returned to the cabin, it was well after midnight. I was exhausted and felt like I could collapse at any minute. All I wanted to do was sleep off this whole day.

But when I stepped inside my room, Abby was there. Sitting on the back of the couch, staring in the direction of the door like she'd been waiting for me. She didn't even wait for the door to close before she started to talk.

"Hadley?" she asked, her voice soft.

"Hey, Ab," I said, walking over to my bed and sitting down gracelessly.

"Can I talk to you?" she asked, joining me on my side of the room, but sitting down more carefully.

I raised an eyebrow at her curiously before saying, "Sure. What's up?"

I bent down and untied my shoes, using one foot to kick off the other, until both were free to move around. I let out a contented sigh and sat back up to look at my boyfriend's sister. I didn't know what this was about, but I hoped it was quick. I was going to pass out any minute now.

"Um, well, I just wanted to say, you know . . . I'm sorry. For everything before with the . . . hating you and all," she said.

I could tell this was hard for her. Not only because she wasn't a big talker, but because she'd once again been used as a pawn in someone else's game. It had to be frustrating.

"It's okay, Abby," I said, before she could continue. "I get it. You were under Eve's spell. There's nothing you could've done to fight it."

Abby looked down at her lap. "Well, thanks for that," she said, "but I also haven't been exactly welcoming to you. The last time a girl dated my brother, she broke his heart. And in a way, mine, too. I didn't want that to happen again, so I guess I didn't allow myself to get close."

I nodded because I totally understood. She was just looking out for the people she loved. I would've done the same thing. And I respected her for that.

"But I'm going to start trying," she said, raising her eyes to mine. "I won't be braiding your hair anytime soon, but I'm gonna try."

"That means a lot, Abby," I said. "Because the truth is: I really love your brother. And I think we could be friends if you just let us."

"I think so, too," she said. Then, taking a big breath, she got up from my bed and started to walk back over to hers.

"Abby?" I asked, causing her to look back at me. "In the interest of our new budding friendship, I think there's something I have to tell you."

"What's wrong?"

I hated telling her this, but she deserved to know what was happening.

"Well, when I was down there with Eve, she said something that could be really bad if she was telling the truth," I said, slowly. "She said we didn't actually kill Samuel that night."

It was almost as if Abby had been waiting for this news for months and she just stood there waiting for the rest.

"And she said that he was coming back," I finished.

Abby grew pale and stiffened as I said this last part. She never had told any of us what had happened when the reverend took her, but it would be naive to think it wasn't horrible. This was probably the worst news I could have given her.

Way to ruin a beautiful moment, Hadley.

"What are we going to do?" Abby asked, almost in a whisper.

"Same thing we always do," I answered. "If he comes back, we plan, we train, we fight."

Colette bounced into the room then, walking past both of us and collapsing onto her bed. "Why's the vibe so wonky in here? I thought Eve's spell had worn off by now."

"It's nothing. Just a long day, that's all," I answered, giving Abby a look that said not to repeat the news about Samuel. Then, I turned to our other roommate. "Why are you so happy?"

"Hudson just asked me out," she said, squealing happily.

"Wait. Asher's roommate, Hudson?" I asked, in disbelief. "Isn't he a jock or something?"

"Yep. A jock who digs smart girls," Colette said, pushing her glasses up on her nose with a flourish. "We're going to hang out tomorrow night. Now what should I wear . . . Oooh, there was this supercute jumper thing that Aunt Betsey had in one of her shows once that could be superiffic!"

My head was spinning with how quickly she was moving around the room. "One of her shows?" I asked. "Colette, who is this aunt of yours, anyway?"

Colette stopped moving and found her phone. Flipping through a few pictures, she finally came to the one she was looking for and passed it to me.

"Your aunt is *Betsey Johnson*?!" I exclaimed, flipping through dozens of pictures of Colette with the famous fashion icon. It all made sense now. The incredible outfits. Colette's wacky personality. Her insistence on being an individual.

"Yeah," Colette said, plainly. "Who did you think she was?"

"Betsey-freaking-Johnson," I muttered to myself as I shook my head in disbelief. "Incredible."

Colette continued to flutter around the room, picking out tops and pairing them with skirts and then throwing them in a pile and moving on to the next outfit. I turned back to Abby who just shrugged in response.

"I think we need to tell the others," Abby said, going back to the conversation we'd been having when Colette had walked in.

I nodded. "But not tonight," I said, yawning and falling back on my mattress. Immediately, I felt it lifting into the air. "Let's give everyone one last night of uninterrupted, night-mareless sleep. It may be the last one we have for a while."

And then I was out before the bed had even stopped moving.

OCTOPUS

The Key to Becoming a Good Thinker, Think on the Other Hand

Presented to

Kingwood Branch Library

By

**FOLK – Friends of the Library
Kingwood**

**Harris County
Public Library**

your pathway to knowledge

WALLACE ROARK

Wasteland Press
Shelbyville, KY USA
www.wastelandpress.net

Think Like An Octopus:
The Key to Becoming a Good Thinker,
Think on the Other Hand
by Wallace Roark

First Printing – August 2010
ISBN: 978-1-60047-475-0

Printed in the U.S.A.

To
Carol
Partner in Dialectic

"For every woman who makes a fool out of a man,
there is a woman who makes a man out of a fool."

Acknowledgments

I want to thank the countless students who for thirty years helped me grow these ideas. Without their encouragement, this book would not be. Special thanks to Lucas King who insisted that I write. Bill and Betty Farmer read the first few chapters; Jerry Fleming read an early draft; my wife, Carol, who has always believed in me and who listened to me read the entire manuscript—all made useful and needed suggestions. I am particularly grateful to Mary Ann Radmacher for extended encouragement. I was blessed with a sensitive and wise editor, Jill Ronsley, who cleared up and cleaned up many of my shortcomings; and with a n accessible publisher whom it was a joy to work with, Timothy Renfrow. I also want to acknowledge Jenny, Susan, and Sarah for their support all across the years.

CONTENTS

Author's Note

This book is the outgrowth of thirty years teaching university students—and myself—how to think (Not *what* to think—that is a completely different matter. It is unlike any other book on thinking you will find in that it is neither a textbook nor an essay in philosophical theory. It is not written in abstract scholarly language, nor does it involve complex logical formulas and techniques to be practiced and memorized. Most books on thinking are more academic, are written in technical language, and emphasize scholarship or they go off in many directions. Nearly all of them are intended as textbooks. In contrast, I address the ordinary person, in plain and simple language. But don't misunderstand, this is not *Thinking for Dummies*.

These skills and patterns of thinking have been developed and tested inside and outside the classroom. And for decades now, not a day has gone by that I haven't used and confirmed the principle of this book, the Dialectic.

Outstanding and weak students alike have told me that learning to think has transformed their lives. It has helped graduate school students reach the top of their class, and they have carried its benefits over into their professional practices. I have seen it change the experience of young people from every corner of the earth. That's why I know it will work for you.

Students are always encouraging me to share my understanding and use of the Dialectic more widely. So, to address the "larger classroom," I have brought together and simplified material that was scattered through a variety of university courses, teaching situations, and informal conversations. The result is *Think Like An Octopus*.

Any stories I tell about myself are true. Others, for the most part, are fictionalized from actual situations

Who Is This Book For?

- Ambitious young people on their way up in the business world
- Students, in particular those preparing to enter graduate school
- Young women awakening to ideas of liberation
- Engaged couples and newlyweds
- Those considering divorce
- Smart and aspiring young adults who missed the chance to go to college
- Those who feel they don't measure up intellectually
- And, ultimately, all who read books and care to improve their lives

PART ONE

Consider Other Perspectives and Possibilities: Think Dialectically

CHAPTER ONE

"Be Ye Not Mentally Lazy"

Most of us grow up convinced that the authority figures in our world are telling the truth—at least, largely. I certainly did. But while I sensed a core of truth in their dogmatic statements, I knew in my gut that on some points they were wrong. I recognized there was more to it than they let on, and, often, that "more to it" was what mattered most. I also knew that some of the people and views they so strongly condemned were not as bad as they were made out to be. Many of the wrongs they attacked were not always totally wrong. Although, at the time, I could not have articulated it, I was developing skepticism.

However, since I was well socialized, I never considered questioning these authority figures. They were bigger, older, smarter, richer, and they held the power to reward or punish; there was no future in challenging them.

Meanwhile, my classmates made better grades, were better athletes, better looking, and more popular. I was not a leader—no one ever followed or looked up to me, and I was painfully aware of my own inadequacies. Yet, I was also vaguely aware of the limitations of these more popular and more gifted classmates, as well as those in authority.

I was nearly fifty years old before I realized the full implications of those childhood perceptions. Gradually, I came to see that my tacit disagreement with society comprised the elements of a more honest and complete approach to truth and life. The seeds of a new way of thinking had been planted. That way I later came to call the Dialectic, the theme of this book.

After floundering through life for long years, I finally learned that it is easy to become a good thinker. Good thinking, however, is in short supply because many of us are mentally lazy and because it requires something more than mere critical thinking, keen intellect, and formal education.

On the Other Hand

What it takes to become a good thinker is to make "on the other hand" your habitual response to ideas, whether your own or others', spoken or written, formally or informally expressed. No matter what is presented, always consider what might be "on the other hand." No human statement is ever complete, something is always left out, there is always more to be said, and it is always possible that what has been presented might be wrong. Develop a deep sense and appreciation of human limitations, determine to make "on the other hand" thinking second nature, and you are on the road to becoming a good thinker. Results will appear almost immediately. You will become a voice to be reckoned with.

Is that all there is to it? No, but if "on the other hand" thinking becomes a regular practice, you will quickly become a respected thinker. I remember from my youth that the Sears, Roebuck and Co. catalog offered a choice of merchandise at varying levels of quality: *good, better, and best*. You already have read enough to reach the genuinely *good* level of thinker.

When you come to understand the larger dimensions of the Dialectic —the proper name for "on the other hand" thinking—and add an elementary understanding of how logical thinking works, you will become a *better* thinker.

And if you are still with me when we come to the last pages of the book, we will consider how you can—using your unique personality and place in the world—become the *best* thinker.

Becoming a Thinker

Daddy was a workaholic and always gone, Mother was an old-fashioned housewife—a good one, busy doing all the work that entails. So I was pretty well left alone, and, by default, became a lonely, lazy dreamer. I roamed the rivers, creeks, and hills, knowing I had been born fifty years too late to be the cowboy or mountain man that I read and dreamed of. I drifted mindlessly through the years until one day I found myself a high school graduate. I remember three graduation gifts, one of them in particular. Neither the creamy-yellow sport jacket nor the fancy corduroy shirt of many colors ever looked right on me, but somehow I have remembered them. The third was Mother's gift of a book of inspirational poetry and prose, *Quests and Conquests*. For years, I enjoyed reading the book but was never inspired to do anything. The book didn't change me, but Mother's inscription written in the front of the book, "Be ye not mentally lazy," haunted me.

Mother's admonition was based on accurate observation. I don't remember having ever thought much about anything for the first twenty years of my life, but when I read her inscription I knew immediately that I needed to do whatever it was that she was calling for. However, I neither knew what to do nor how to go about it. The problem was that I had no thinking equipment, skills, or coaching, nor any prior encouragement to think (few schools or homes teach us how to think). It would be long years before I made any progress in that direction, but Mother's words were never far from my consciousness. I felt their challenge continually.

Several years later, I was in a theological seminary studying to become a minister. There I heard Professor Gordon Clinard declare that the greatest weakness of Southern Baptist preaching was shallowness. Immediately, I vowed that my sermons would have depth. During seminary years, I worked—still without adequate tools for thinking—at exploring the depths of God's word and of human experience. I depended on others—teachers and books—to do my thinking for me. But although I trusted them, but I knew they were missing something.

Only when I was given my first teaching position and found that I had to teach—and, thus, learn—logic, did I finally discover a method of systematic thinking. Logic, I came to realize, should be required of all high school graduates—not symbolic logic, but traditional, elementary logic.

Now I was a beginning philosophy teacher and confident of my ability as a thinker. But I had a lot to learn. It took a half-dozen years of teaching philosophy before my approach to thinking crystallized as the Dialectic. I completely rewrote my philosophy courses, making the Dialectic central, and have taught it now for more than thirty years. Mother would be proud of her easygoing son because, among faculty and students alike, I have gained a reputation for making people think. They tell me they now think about things they never reflected on before, and from perspectives they would have never considered. Let's talk about how you can improve your thinking ability and practice.

But on the Other Hand

Some years ago, Don Schlitz and Paul Overstreet wrote a song about a young man who found himself tempted to spend the night with a willing young woman. At the moment it seemed like the thing to do, but as he was debating it within himself, he noticed the ring on his left hand. The logic and reality of marital love sent him home to his wife.

This song was called, "On the Other Hand," and was made popular by Randy Travis. It indicates the importance of dialectical thinking for even the most careless of us. On one hand—every day, throughout the day—we see things we believe to be right and that feel right at the time, but on the other hand, there is always more to be considered. On one hand, we are ready to act; on the other hand, it is always possible that we might be wrong and regret what we did.

In life, too much is at stake for our conduct to be decided by "one-handed" thinking. President Harry Truman once told his cabinet members that he wished they would find him a one-handed economist. He said that every economist that briefed him presented a good analysis of the economic situation, and advised an appropriate course of action. However, Truman complained, once they laid all this out, they would say, "But on the other hand …" and proceed to build the case for a different analysis and course of action. He wanted someone who had *the* answer.

The truth is that no single way of looking at anything ever sees the whole picture. There is always more. The philosopher, Mortimer Adler, made the strange claim that the greatest contribution Greek civilization ever made to our culture was the idea of *men* and *de*.

These odd little words are particles in the Greek language, commonly translated into English as *on the one hand/but on the other hand*. When we think of all of Greek culture, sculpture, philosophy, and drama, we might wonder what Adler was thinking when he made such an audacious claim. Why would he say *on the one hand/but on the other hand* is the greatest contribution of the Greeks? Because it is a concise expression of the most powerful thinking tool known to man, and the subject--the Dialectic--this book is about.

The Dialectic

The Dialectic will not make you a better person—that is a whole different issue—but it will make you a better thinker. It will keep you out of a lot of trouble. You will not be surprised easily or often. It will make it easier for you to understand and get along with other people. Others will begin to respect you and your ideas more than they have in the past. If you are a student, you will become a better learner, perform better in the classroom, make better grades, and gain broader understanding and deeper insight. If you are married, you will become a better and more appreciated spouse. If you are part of a team at work, you will become a better and more valuable team member.

If all this sounds as though the Dialectic is some kind of a magic pill or silver bullet, you are hearing it right. No matter who you are, what you are interested in, or what you do, it will fit you. It will apply directly to what you are about. *And* it is easy to learn and put to use.

Think like an Octopus

"On the other hand." That's the silver bullet. That's all it takes to become a good thinker. It's that simple. But on the other hand, it helps to notice still another hand, for there are indeed other hands. I was sitting at the breakfast table, reviewing plans for my first philosophy class of the day and thinking specifically about the Dialectic. Then I remembered that I had a problem student in that class. In thirty-some years of teaching I had only had three problem students; this was one of them. He was one of those back-row, disruptive whisperers. I had spoken to him about it a couple of times, to no avail. He seemed to have a lack of respect for me. So I shifted my mind from preparation for class to preparation for dealing with this aggravation.

I spent two years in the army as a basic training officer. I had experience in sounding tough, and I could make the appropriate face to go along with the speech. I'd never used that style in teaching. However, that morning, I was considering it. But, on the other hand, that is not a good style for teaching. On the other hand, I could quietly inform him that if the whispers did not cease, he would receive an "F." On the other hand, I wasn't sure that would be a fair course of action. In fact, he might dare me to try it (he was the kind to do that). On the other hand, I had to do something because he was disrupting the class. So, on the other hand … Wait a minute, how many other hands do I have?

On the other hand is the dialectical formula. It is *the* way. But on which other hand? Mentally, we have more than two hands. Our left hand has its own right and left hands, and they have theirs. We need to think on as many hands as possible. An octopus could think "on the other hand" several times before it ran out of perspectives to examine. We need to learn to think like an octopus.

In most situations, there are many "hands" to consider. Don't forget any of them. And, like a construction supervisor, hire other hands if they are needed. Don't settle on an answer, conclusion, or idea until you have to, there are always other hands to turn to. Consider others—even your enemies, maybe especially your enemies—and think like an octopus with all eight hands.

However, you will ask, if we seek to examine all "hands," how can we ever make a decision? True, we will never have time to check them all out, but don't quit early, especially, if there is a lot at stake. And when we have to stop considering and act, we then use the best judgment we can make at the time based on better thinking—always realizing that what we do may turn out wrong.

And what about that recalcitrant student, the one I was trying to decide how to deal with when I began to think about all those other hands, about an octopus? After considering several other hands, I quietly warned him that he would fail the course if he continued to be disruptive. And it worked with him.

CHAPTER TWO

Thinking Made Easy

It is common to hear someone say, "Thinking is hard work," but that is not so. Thinking is not that hard, if you know how to do it. Many things are hard work if you have no training and experience at the job, but not unusually hard once you learn the relevant skills, tricks of the trade, and have the right tools. For most of us, digging ditches would be grueling labor but the experienced ditch digger knows to sharpen the shovel before he begins work and to wear boots that have sturdy construction, particularly a heavy sole and good arch support.

Supposedly, the "work" that more people fear than any other is public speaking. However, almost anyone who has earned the right to speak on his topic, and is enthusiastic about letting others hear his ideas, can make a good speech. His passion will help override his stage fright, and his earned right to speak on the subject will supply the needed confidence.

Knowledge of a simple outline such as the following, can organize most speeches: Ho Hum, Point, Explanation, Example, So What? Assume your audience is half-asleep or disinterested (*Ho Hum*) and begin with something that will wake them up. Then state your *Point* clearly, *Explain* what it means, how it works, and so on, give a concrete *Example* or two, then let them know how you would like them to respond (*So What?*). With only a little experience of this approach, anyone can do a satisfactory job of speaking in public. And feel good about it.

No, thinking, like any other work, is not as hard as the untutored expect it to be. The hard thing about thinking is overcoming our inertia. To the lazy, any work is hard. Most of us follow the thinking of the herd. We live largely by habit, letting others do our thinking for us. We live by slogans and commonplace beliefs.

Mental Habits

It is not easy to stop living by an unthinking, unconsidered acceptance of conventional wisdom, or by decisions we have made merely because, in the moment, they felt right. On the other hand, for some—antisocial mavericks—it is hard to break loose from their rebellious, reactive pattern of always thinking contrary to the established order. Thinking is not hard, but the will and determination to think, and to persist in it, this is hard, until it becomes a habitual, characteristic trait. Then, it is easy.

It is easy to coast along, living by habit and the socially acceptable, without ever actively engaging the mind, just leaving it in neutral most of the time. The simple argument of this book is that once we understand the Dialectic, a smidgen of logic (in Part Two), and identify our own basic beliefs and ultimate goals (Part Three), thinking will become easy. But it becomes easy only as we engage the gears of the mind and put it to work.

Thinking Invites Trouble

Be aware, however, that the Dialectic will bring new troubles into your life as you begin to recognize problems that dialectical thinking has made you aware of but that you had rather not deal with. Moreover, you will find that you have to be careful—in school, with your spouse, at work—because others will not always appreciate the changes that clear thinking often calls for. So, on one hand, we want to do our own thinking and act on the basis of that thinking, but we need to be careful how we negotiate our relations with other people.

Therefore, before you read further, be warned: Thinking is dangerous; this is a dangerous book.

When, in 1937, Lyndon Johnson first went to the House of Representatives, his fellow Texan Sam Rayburn, House Majority Leader, counseled him: "Lyndon, the way to get along is to go along." The truth is that any time we begin thinking, we are apt to make enemies. And, in our one chance at life between the cradle and the casket, we need to make as few enemies as possible. One of the most dependable ways to avoid making enemies is to go along with whatever the majority thinks.

But, at the heart of good thinking is the realization that much we have been taught is not true. Once we accept the idea that authorities, even experts and professionals, *could* be wrong, we begin trying to figure why their views are accepted. If we believe we have discovered something nearer the truth, we may begin to question socially accepted truths and conventional wisdom.

There is another danger that accompanies thinking. If we think on anything long enough, we are likely to tell others what we have been thinking, or put our thoughts into action. Any time we put our thinking on public display, we have chosen a quick and easy way to lose friends and alienate people. Societies cannot operate without consensus. Those who do not go along commonly are ostracized or ignored. They find they have become social misfits.

But on the other hand, what are we to do if our mind or conscience will not let us "go along?" What are we to do if our mind will not walk away and find other things to think about? What if we insist on what we see as the truth? What if our mind will give us no rest until we do our own thinking?

What happens is we decide that although thinking is dangerous, not thinking might be more dangerous. Maybe socially accepted wisdom is a lie, even if it is a lie that works well. However, we find that this is one sleeping dog that we cannot let lie. Error or ignorance may appear to work better than the discovery and revelation of truth, but we suspect truth has never been given a fair trial. No matter what the cost, some of us are going to think. But if we are to challenge accepted wisdom with any degree of confidence, it is important our thinking be clear, comprehensive, and cogent.

OTOH, BOTOH

In one sense, all there is to becoming a better thinker is to pause and think, *on the other hand*. But on the other hand, there is much more to it than this. After we have considered the Dialectic more completely, *on the other hand* will still be the bottom line but it will mean a great deal more to you.

None of this requires that you become an intellectual or a philosopher. Dialectical thinking is for life's everyday, moment-by-moment decisions, dilemmas, and working relationships. It requires nothing more than the standard God-given equipment that comes with being human. Therefore, we all are included.

The basic pattern of good thinking can be remembered with the acronym, *OTOH, BOTOH*, "On The One Hand, But On The Other Hand." Ever since Plato, philosophers have called this OTOH, BOTOH way of thinking the Dialectic. No other approach to understanding can match it. No idea can be of more practical value—at any hour of the day, in any situation. The Dialectic is a necessary part of our approach to life if we would be wise in our judgments and conduct. By itself, it is not sufficient to make us wise, but it is an indispensable element in our mental toolkit.

Again, you don't have to become a scholar or a genius. You don't have to be "a brain," at least no more of a brain than God makes every normal human. All you need is a desire to improve your thinking, to make fewer mistakes of judgment, and to develop a more useful understanding of other people, thus, improving your relationship with them.

What this book presents is a method of thinking that many people use naturally; it is one part of our common sense. Don't let the term Dialectic throw you. Some people use the term in very sophisticated ways, but we will be using it in the broadest sense—a sense that comprehends the simplest and the most sophisticated and technical usages.

You may be plain mentally lazy, as I was, or think of yourself as mentally ordinary, but with the Dialectic, you can improve your life by becoming—rather quickly and easily—a better thinker than most of the people you deal with daily. It is almost effortless. And it is guaranteed. You may prefer to be a doer rather than a thinker, but remember that thinking *is* doing. Thought is required in deciding what to do, how best to do it, and how to evaluate the work when it is completed. You can improve your performance simply by using the dialectical method as accompaniment to everything you do.

Not Thinking Is Dangerous

If you are not a dialectical thinker, you will continually have problems that could easily have been prevented, problems that are the result of misunderstandings on your part. Without the Dialectic, you are more likely to be blind-sided because you haven't looked at the other viewpoint. You are more likely to have difficulty getting along with people who are important to you, because you haven't taken seriously their unique perspective. You are likely to regret the attendant results.

Some people believe that logic is the pathway to good thinking. Logic is very important and will make you a much better thinker, but logic alone is not adequate. Good simple logic makes our thought clear and precise, but that alone is not enough. As we will see in Part Two, logic is a component of the Dialectic. It is immeasurably useful, but has serious limitations.

In universities and in business, critical thinking is often pushed as the way to good thinking, but it also is inadequate. Thinking in the critical mode is, in the strict sense, an analytic process. Analysis, by definition and nature, leads to disintegration; by itself it cannot integrate. Again, the Dialectic is a corrective to critical thinking.

Logic and critical thinking are both important. They are essential considerations if one is to become an exceptionally good thinker. But on the other hand …

Nor will it be enough to have a lot of good common sense because, for one thing, "common sense" is a vague idea. It might even include the Dialectic, but everything depends on what we mean by "common" sense, and on who shares this sense in common with us.

The only way to become a good thinker is to think dialectically, to make the Dialectic as natural as breathing. Isn't it presumptuous of me to say it is the *only* way? The dialectical answer to this says yes and no. It is the only way, but by its very nature, the Dialectic challenges the idea that the Dialectic is the only way. It tells us "there is always something more," and that "we always might be wrong," as well as, "no human statement is complete by itself." The Dialectic says there is more to good thinking than the Dialectic includes.

However, if there is more, that more is merely the other hand of the Dialectic.

CHAPTER THREE

The "How" of Thinking

General George Patton's Advice

General George Patton said: "Never tell people how to do things. Tell them what to do and they will surprise you with their ingenuity."

That depends on the people and the task. I am certain that General Patton always made sure before taking his troops into battle that they had been taught *how* to aim and fire their weapons, how to disassemble and clean them, and how to operate and maintain their tanks and other vehicles. He wanted, as a minimum, for his men to have been through basic training in military "hows."

Patton did not take raw recruits straight from the streets, schools, factories, and farms, put them on the battlefield, and then order them to defeat the enemy. He did not win his great victories simply by telling his soldiers what to do and leaving it up to their ingenuity to figure out how to do it.

We often follow Patton's advice. We tell people to "Think about it," or "Think it over," and we ask, "Why didn't you *think*?" But we cannot assume that, left to their own ingenuity, people will know how to think. They may not. But they can learn. And, after you have read this book, you will know how to think.

Needed: a Method

We don't require much instruction before we can use a computer effectively, but we do need to be taught how to perform a few simple procedures. We don't need much instruction before we can drive an automobile, but we do need some instruction and practice before we can *safely* drive a car. And we do not need much instruction before becoming able to think better than most people. Although some of us might be good thinkers by nature, most of us require—and all of us can benefit from—some special instruction and practice.

After reading and practicing chapter four, you will have completed basic training as a thinker. That will be enough to satisfy some of you. That may be all of the book you read. Learning how to read easy music and play the piano was enough for me. That was all the music I had serious interest in learning. No advanced musical training for me, no long hours of practice, just occasional playing for my own ears, usually with one finger on the right hand, is good enough for my own entertainment.

If, however, you want to become good as a thinker, you will find benefit in every chapter. And, of course, I hope you read the rest of the book. Reading it will help you understand what you are working with, and it will show you how to use the Dialectic in all areas of life. You may find yourself living on higher ground than you would ever have imagined possible. What makes me suggest that?

I assume you are not like dim-witted Harry Robarts in Patrick White's novel *Voss*. Harry was "glad to offer his services to someone who might think for him." On the contrary, you are already a thinker of some sort or you would not have picked up this book. If you are already a good thinker, you will rapidly improve all your thought processes. Whatever your situation, you can do it.

This is not a gimmick, not a "limited time only" offer, not a trick of some kind. I am not a writer looking for an idea to sell; I am a teacher. I don't deal in gimmicks and commercial ideas. For the past thirty years, I have dealt with ideas and thought; I am a philosophy teacher. My students have dug into Plato and Aristotle, Kant, Kierkegaard, Comte, and Nietzsche. They have investigated epistemology, existentialism, ontology, and axiology (terms you won't find used in this book). The clue to good thinking isn't a passing fad. It has been tested rigorously for centuries. Now I make it available to you, without big words and without any need on your part to know and understand philosophy.

My entire reputation—limited as it is to a small area of central Texas where I have chosen to quietly enjoy life—has been built on my ability to teach people to think. When students leave my classes, they often say I am the first teacher in all their schooling who has made them think, and who has helped them learn how to think. When I speak in public, the most common responses are, "I'd never thought about that before," "You make us think," and, "You gave us something to think about." The other common response is, "You make it so easy to understand," and "You make it so simple." That is what I can do for you. I have written this book because, after spending my whole career in the classroom at a remote little university, my students have insisted that I need to write so I can teach the process of good thinking to a larger classroom. One that includes you.

I know you can do it because I have been teaching dialectical thinking for more than thirty years and have seen all sorts of people become good thinkers. Many of them became better people in the process. Some didn't. Their thought processes were improved, but their character was untouched. Jesus, in his story about a sower who lost three quarters of the seed he planted, seemed to tell his followers to expect only limited success. But he said that where there was appropriate response, success would be astounding. I hope for something like that for my readers.

It Is Not Too Late

As I said, I was almost fifty years old before I learned how to think. You are not too old. It is not too late. You *can* learn to think. And again, it is easy.

I have heard that if you can walk, you can dance, if you can talk, you can sing, and if you can write, you can draw. To my amazement I learned, in middle age, that all this is true. I am not a good dancer, but I can dance; only a fair singer, but I sing; and I've learned to draw quite well. I had never thought I could. I have also learned that if you think at all, you can become a good thinker—probably not an Einstein, but a respected thinker nonetheless.

What You Will Gain from this Book

- Skill in developing, correcting, and expanding your own ideas and insights.
- Skill at critiquing what you hear and read from others.
- Skill in functioning as an effective team or committee member.
- You will become a more convincing and respected speaker and writer.
- You will begin to persuade your critics to seriously consider your position.
- You will become more logical in all you think and do.
- You will easily spot the illogical and inconsistent in all you hear and read.
- You will learn to see more clearly where others are coming from.
- You will easily distinguish mere probabilities from inescapable necessities.
- Your use of language will become increasingly clearer.
- You will come to think before you speak.
- You will come to know yourself better.
- You will come to see more clearly where your thought is coming from.
- You will come to see more clearly where your own thinking is headed.
- You will learn much about the dialectic of life itself.
- You will develop a greater appreciation of other people.
- You will become a wiser and more considerate person.
- Your life will become richer, more productive, and more wonder filled.

You Will Become

A person whose ideas must be reckoned with.
A person of greater integrity.
A person who is rarely blind-sided.
A better conversationalist.

A better learner.
More honest, moderate, and modest.
More confident.
More respected and more respectful.
More patient and appreciative.
More open to change.
More courteous, considerate, and sympathetic.
More patient and less arrogant.
More aware, and less apt to go off half-cocked.

We think in order to clarify, comprehend, and create. Ultimately, we think in order to decide, to appreciate, and, thus, to act and become. If we don't think, we live muddled, uncomprehending lives, stuck in the habitual and overwhelmed by a complicated world. We make wrong decisions, appreciate little, do things we regret and that harm us, and never become persons of character and wisdom.

Looking Ahead

Good thinking, at its best, includes three different but interconnected considerations. First, we must consider perspectives other than our own—we must think dialectically. Further, we must consider the implications of our ideas—we must think logically. Finally, we must consider our own mind, heart, and aim in life—we must think purposively. In keeping with these three essential considerations, the book comprises three parts.

Part One lays out the basics of the Dialectic and explores its fundamental nature, which is consideration of others and other ways of thinking and living. It expands dialectical thought and shows how it is involved in all aspects of our daily lives and what it can contribute to those lives. It also introduces the concept of bipolar understanding. When we become aware of the bipolarity that pervades our world, many of our disturbing dilemmas and contradictions evaporate. Our lives adjust to a more rhythmic and harmonic resolution of common tensions.

Part Two offers a user-friendly survey of the most helpful elements of logical thinking. Much of Part Two we already know as common sense, but it will help to bring that common sense into sharper focus. It describes the fundamental nature of logic: a method of assuring consistency in what we say, how we think, and, ultimately, how we live. It distinguishes, in clear and simple language, the difference between deductive and inductive reasoning.

Part Three addresses the content and purpose of our thinking. As I said earlier, the Dialectic is the key to good thinking; it is the heart of the book. Logic sharpens the abilities of the dialectical thinker. It makes you more than a *good* thinker; you become a *better* thinker. But neither of these tells you *what* to think, nor even *why* you think, any more than a pencil or a computer tells you what to write or for what purpose. Neither the Dialectic nor logic has any content. They can be used effectively by the scoundrel and the saint—as well as the rest of us.

If we are to become the best thinker possible, we have to consider who we are and what we are about in life. Part Three helps us clarify what we believe to be the truth about life, what we are personally convinced of—our basic convictions. In Part Three, we will become more aware of our personal values—not only what we believe to be true, but what we believe to be important and worth giving ourselves to. It challenges us to determine and decide what we want out of life, and, more importantly, what we want to become. Finally, it shows that all our thinking, dialectical and logical, is rooted in and aimed toward the ideas emphasized in Part Three. In the end, it pulls the entire book together, correlating the elements that go into making us the best thinker we can possibly become.

We Have a Responsibility to Think

Thinking is not what life is all about, but it is a vital part of it. Thinking shapes our decisions, and our decisions shape our actions. Thought seeks truth in order to make decisions as a basis for action, as an aspect of living and understanding the meaning of our lives. Our study will enhance the various elements of thought: analysis, synthesis, comparison, contrast, implication, evaluation, imagination, arrangement, and review.

Better thinking leads to better living. As certainly as every normal person can walk and talk, so everyone can think—and, you can, without question, learn to be a much better thinker.

Not only is it in our own best interest to become better thinkers, but we also have a moral obligation to think more clearly in order to make better moral decisions. The reason behind many bad things that happen in the lives of individuals and society can be expressed in the words of a blundering friend of mine, "I just didn't think about *that*." We have a moral and social, as well as prudential, obligation to think about *that*.

A dominant reason for the prevalence of divorce is that there are many important things people don't think about before marriage. I am sure that Garth Brooks' song "Unanswered Prayers" resonated for a lot of people. The song tells of a fellow who, in high school, wanted a particular girl so much that he prayed God would let him have her. But he didn't get her. Years later, with his wife, he saw her at a football game, and, seeing the changes in both her and in himself, wound up extremely grateful that God had not answered his prayer.

(God was good to me. I got the one I prayed for, and have been grateful for almost sixty years.)

Whether our concern is marriage and family or other social issues, one of the major ways to develop a better society filled with good people is to learn and determine to think more clearly, completely, and creatively. I hope you share that conviction and dream.

CHAPTER FOUR

The Dialectic

Exactly what is the Dialectic? It can be most easily understood by contrast, the contrast between dialogue and monologue. A monologue is an extended uninterrupted speech by a character in a drama, often a one-person monologue spoken to an audience. In a monologue, only one person speaks. No response from others is allowed. You are probably familiar with the dramatic monologue as a form of popular entertainment featuring someone such as Bill Cosby, Jerry Seinfeld, David Letterman, or Tevye in *Fiddler on the Roof.*

In contrast, a dialogue includes at least two speakers responding to each other. What each says is influenced by what the other has said. One speaker may have to say something other than he had first intended because what the other person has said requires a new response.

However, simply because two people are in a conversation with each other doesn't necessarily mean they are having a dialogue. Often our interchanges are merely reciprocal monologues; we each are attempting a fundamentally uninterrupted and extended speech. We have something we want to get said. When someone interrupts us, we pay little attention to what he has to say. We are only waiting for a break in the other's monologue so we can resume our own monologue. Although more than one speaker is involved, there is no interactive dialogue taking place.

Dialectic

The Dialectic is rooted in the idea of dialogue. The core idea is that other perspectives, positions, and possibilities must always be taken into account. The Dialectic is rooted in a principle that can be expressed in three ways.

- No human statement is ever complete by itself. By the word *statement* we should understand this is not necessarily a single sentence. Sometimes a paragraph makes a single statement. A speech may do that, as may a book, a law, or a television program. Whether a statement is simple or elaborate, it remains true that no human statement is ever complete by itself, and, therefore, is never the whole truth.
- There is always more that can be said. Always there is something else, no matter what we are talking about. Some aspects have been left out. The world, and our life in it, is too complex to be reduced to a single statement.
- It is always possible that we might be wrong. In whatever we think or say, we could, on occasion, be wrong. To believe otherwise is to claim that we are infallible, that we are never mistaken. But humans are not infallible. We do make mistakes—and often.

So the Dialectic grows out of the realization that there is always another side, another perspective that must be taken into consideration if we are to approach the full truth. To think dialectically is to always consider the possibility of our own error and then to examine our thought to see where the flaw might be. We can never take it for granted that what we think is the truth, and certainly not that it is the whole truth. (At one point, I considered using "Considerate Thinking" as the title of this book. Consideration is what it is all about.)

Several months after an automobile accident with a driver in a stolen car, an accident that totaled our Buick, the police finally found the offender and a date was set for his trial. I was called to court as a witness. Judge Ellis's docket was full, so I sat through two afternoons of trials before they got to our case, and began to realize that being sworn in was going to present me with a problem. As a philosopher, I knew that I could not tell the truth about the accident because it all happened so fast and so much was involved that I had the truth only as I remembered it. Moreover, I was not in position to know the whole truth. And again, I knew that it was always possible that I, as a human being, could be wrong. How could I swear "to tell the truth, the whole truth, and nothing but the truth" (whether with God's help or not)?

In a court of law, we may "swear to tell the truth, the whole truth, and nothing but the truth," but the truth is we cannot do what we swear to do. We can never know the whole, and often, unintentionally, some of what we say may be in error. The Dialectic automatically searches for other ways of looking at the same thing. The dialectical thinker seeks out those who hold different views and asks for their response to his own ideas, with the expectation that these voices will lead to some modification of his own thought.

One task of a courtroom is the effort to determine, as best is possible, what the truth is. It should not be assumed that any one witness could establish the irrefutable truth. Fortunately, I never had to face the issue because the case was settled out of court and thus I was saved from confrontation with the traditional oath.

More of the Story

As noted earlier, Mortimer Adler said that the words *men* and *de* are the greatest contribution the Greeks made to civilization. Quite a claim. A dialectical claim. These words are commonly translated, "on the one hand," "but on the other hand." In a Greek text, the little particle *men* may show up in an unexpected place. It is sometimes not even translated, but it always indicates that a particular aspect of an issue is being presented. When, somewhere later in the text, *de* shows up, it indicates that we are now looking from a different perspective.

Whatever is being presented, the good thinker's characteristic response is, "But on the other hand." (Make it your screensaver.) The Dialectic warns us to never forget there are other perspectives; it reminds us to remain constantly aware of the other side.

Paul Harvey's *The Rest of the Story* was an instance of the Dialectic. For more than sixty years on the radio, he told us stories, true stories, but saved a surprising twist to end with. Having given this last piece of information, he ended saying, "And now you know … the *rest* of the story." On one hand was the story; on the other hand we learned the rest of the story.

There is always more to be said. In a sense, the scholar's footnotes are similar. There are many kinds of footnotes. Sometimes they tell us the source of the noted material, sometimes they refer us to other pages or other books that will tell us more about what has been noted in the text, and at other times they add explanation, definition, or asides.

The Dialectic is the language of relationship. It keeps us from forgetting others and our relationship to them. It strikes out against individualism, isolationism, absolutism, and all self-centeredness. The dialectical ear is always listening. The dialectical eye is constantly searching. The dialectical voice is always considerate of the listener. Whether we think of family or workplace relationships, love or any other of life's relationships, they are bound to disappoint, disintegrate, diminish, or fail without the Dialectic.

Dialectical thought is always in process, never complete. "What have I left out, what have I not considered?" These questions become routine. "What if my presuppositions are wrong?" Part of the processive character of the Dialectic is that it is always developing, alternately expanding, then focusing. It grows and is enriched. It sharpens and clarifies.

Among the Philosophers

I first discovered the Dialectic deep within the pages of the book *General Philosophy* by Elton Trueblood. Trueblood gives it only a half-dozen pages, but for me, it resonated immediately. My way of thinking, understanding, analyzing–and my way of living–were transformed and have never been the same. The Dialectic became a major part of who I am, but none of the ideas in this book (well, almost none) are original to me. The Dialectic is not something new. It has been around at least since the dialectical relationship of Adam and Eva, whoever they were. It is ancient. I am merely attempting to present, in a way that is simple, clear, fairly complete, and useful, what others before me have practiced and taught.

Historically, three major philosophers—Heraclitus, Socrates, and Hegel—developed the Dialectic, each somewhat differently.

The Unity of Opposites

Heraclitus stressed the unity of opposites. He believed that contradiction is the source of everything. Only as both sides struggle with and against each other is development possible. Thus, opposites effect a unity. They become parts of a new order that has resulted from their conflict. In traditional logic, contradictories cannot both be true, but in actuality the tension between them is the driving force of life, expanding and enriching even as they are constantly changing: male and female, night and day, work and play, nature and technology, emotion and reason ...

Heraclitus is most famously known as the ancient who claimed we can't step twice into the same river. The river flows constantly. The river we step into the second time is not the same as it was when we took that first step. The current changes continually. The chemical makeup of the water varies slightly each time we dip into it. Everything about it is in flux. That is a core idea of Heraclitus: everything is in flux, everything flows, nothing remains the same. The only thing permanent is change.

Moreover, when we step into the river the second time, we are no longer the same person who took that first step. We now have experienced the river as we had not before our first step. We, like the river, are constantly in flux. When I was a boy setting trotlines in the Chikaskia River in northern Oklahoma, it seemed to me that it was always the same river, the Chikaskia. Much in life does seem to be constant. Much appears unchanging, but Heraclitus is the apostle of change. Everything changes constantly, even if infinitesimally.

Thus, we must always take into account that things might differ from what experience tells us. We must learn to look for what the eye of habit does not see, the mind of habit does not think. Heraclitus bids us, like the highway sign at the railroad tracks, to Stop, Look, and Listen. We must look both directions–and also up and down–before proceeding with life. We must make dialectical thinking our new eye and mind of habit.

Everything Can Be Questioned

We don't know much about Heraclitus himself. In the ancient world, he was called "Heraclitus the Obscure." We don't know what drove his thinking. With Socrates, however, we have a good idea of what he was about. He wanted people to think about and think through whatever they had to say—particularly, if they were dealing with life issues. He found that most people he talked with did not understand what they were talking about. Their mental laziness amazed him.

The word got out in Athens that the Delphic Oracle had declared Socrates to be the wisest man in the entire city. Socrates knew that could not be true because there was so much he did not understand. Thus, he began a search to find those who were wiser, those who were not as ignorant as Socrates knew himself to be. He went to the most respected, the most successful, the most powerful citizens and questioned them about their knowledge and understanding. Repeatedly, he found that they knew and understood even less than he did. He realized that much of the time they did not know what they were talking about.

So, after seeking out all those who might be wiser, he decided that the oracle was right. He, after all, was the wisest, in the sense that he was at least aware of his ignorance; at least he did not pretend to understand things. The Socratic wisdom and the Socratic ignorance were synonymous. He came to believe that "the god" (he was a Greek monotheist) had called him to help his fellow citizens become good people by becoming good thinkers.

The Socratic dialectic takes the form of intense, purposive conversation. Socrates never allows the dialogue to degenerate into a mere bull session or a bantering of the conventional wisdom. He kept the conversation directed toward clarification of the problem at hand. His method was to ask if his fellow participants meant what they said. Usually, just like us, they claimed that they meant what they said, they knew what they were talking about.

Socrates would then ask them to explain what they meant by some key word or phrase, particularly when they used heavy words such as justice, love, courage, good, excellence, integrity, or beauty. When they had explained how they were using words or sentences, he then suggested that if this were what they meant, then something else, something they could not accept, would also have to be true. By continual questioning, he showed their definitions to be inadequate, incomplete, or even self-contradictory.

Let's suppose one of us commented on the beauty of a rich red rose on a bush and the other asked what she had meant by *beauty*. Further suppose the answer was, "Just look at the rich red color, have you ever seen anything more beautiful?"

"Oh, so you mean that the beauty of the rose lies in its redness."

"Yes, that's what makes it beautiful."

"So, if we see a pure yellow rose, we cannot say it is beautiful, because it is not red."

"No, that's not what I mean. A yellow rose can be beautiful, as can a pink or a white one."

"Ah, so do you mean that beauty lies in pure, rich color?"

"Yes, that is exactly what I mean."

"Look across the street at the young lady on the sidewalk. Don't you think she is beautiful?"

"She is very beautiful. That is Jessica Taylor, everyone knows how beautiful she is."

"Does her beauty reside in the color of her skin, or of her hair, her eyes, or her clothing?"

"No, there is more to beauty than color."

"So, what is this 'more' you speak of?"

In such manner, Socrates led others to rethink their ideas. His goal was to expose ignorance so that the search for truth could begin. All of this was done through guided, persistent, and purposive conversation. The resolution of the issue at hand always depended on the interaction between the two participants. Socrates never told others his own ideas, but rather led them to think through their own. Teachers, lawyers, parents, and others have picked up this "Socratic method" and continue to use it to this day. This is Socrates' use of the Dialectic.

"The Dialectic Is Logical, Ontological, and Historical"

Before we leave the philosophers and go back to the world the rest of us live in, we need to look at one more of them, Georg W. F.

Hegel. (With Hegel, we must slow our reading down, study carefully, and think about what he has to say.) Hegel believed that the Dialectic is what everything is all about. Specifically, he said, "The dialectic is logical, ontological, and historical." In other words, it is how our minds work (logical), what is fundamentally and ultimately real (ontological), and how all history moves (historical). Everything is dialectical (thus, the Dialectic is the only way to understand anything).

Not only did Hegel believe that all reality is dialectical, he also systematized it, reduced it to a logical order, an order that always involved three processive elements.

I suggest you now find a blank sheet of paper and draw a triangle—one line across the base with two lines converging at the top. Hegel thought in such triangular patterns, or, as he called them, *triads*. Think of the bottom left corner as the starting point of your thinking, action, or understanding. It's the place you hold to, where you take your stand. It is what you believe or plan or hope for.

This position, Hegel called the *thesis*. It might be anything from your income to your job or hobby. Spiritualism, surgery, snack food, or the school board, all could be the starting point—the thesis—for your thought.

Now look to the bottom right corner of the triangle. This represents what Hegel called the *antithesis*. By this, he meant anything that stands apart from your basic thesis. It could be its enemy, its opposite, or merely something left out or ignored by the thesis. It is something to be considered over and against your thesis.

Suppose, for instance, your thesis is an illness for which the doctor has recommended surgery. The surgery is scheduled and seems to be the best course of action. On the other hand, you are uneasy about going under the knife, and there are medicines that sometimes take care of the problem without resort to surgery. These medicines would be an antithesis to surgery.

Ordinarily, there are many antitheses, although only one or two may be significant. In this example, acupuncture might be a promising option—a further antithesis to consider. Another would be foregoing the operation and taking your chances without any medical treatment.

Remember Heraclitus and the unity of opposites (thesis and antithesis)? Remember he said that conflict is the source of everything? Now look at your triangle, at the bottom corners—your thesis and antithesis—and give your attention to the line between them. This line carries their differences, puts them into active conflict, puts our mind into tension. Thought is the business of recognizing both ends of the line—thesis and antithesis—and seeking the best way to resolve the tension between.

The answer may come quickly or it may take hours, months, or years. Meanwhile, the thesis and antithesis (antitheses) are in dialogue with each other in a growing dialectical tension. In our medical example, this is when you feel the tension and go to a specialist for a second opinion. The new physician sees no need for surgery. Now the tension increases between two medical opinions. What should you do? You trust your family doctor, but the specialist is the best in the state. Weeks pass, weeks of indecision and anxiety. Subconscious tension builds. You lose sleep, become irritable, eat all the time, and your condition worsens.

You decide to go ahead with surgery, but, meanwhile, you have begun Googling for help. Repeatedly, you find reference to a new medicine for your problem. You ask your doctor about it. He tells you that surgery and the new medication together would work the best.

After surgery, you are given a prescription for the new drug, and within a few months everything has cleared up and you feel like your old self again. You are now at the peak of the Hegelian triangle/triad. You have reached a *synthesis* of the thesis and antithesis.

Thesis, antithesis, and synthesis—this is the recurrent pattern of the Dialectic, according to Georg Hegel. The synthesis does not come about as a gradual progression from a foundational beginning. Rather, it is through the opposition between a thesis with which you take your stand and an antithesis that stands in challenging opposition to it. It is struggle, tension, and uncertainty that rule until a synthesis finally emerges. Rather than a smooth and gradual movement up the sides of the triangle, it is more as if the synthesis pops directly up out of the tension between surgery and the nonsurgical options.

It is a rule of the Hegelian dialectic that every thesis has an antithesis. Moreover, every synthesis comes to be seen as a more satisfying place to take our stand. Thus, it becomes our new thesis. It doesn't take long to realize that there are new antitheses, and the process starts all over again.

In this book, I will not limit the Dialectic to the Hegelian version of it, but his systematic logic is very useful. We will refer to it often.

We must remember that the antithesis is not always the opposite of the thesis. For instance, if paper is the thesis, what would we understand as its opposite? Canvas, pencil, fire? Depending on the context, many things might be understood as the antithesis of paper, although not necessarily its opposite.

The synthesis may be only a slight modification of the original thesis, it may be the midpoint between thesis and antithesis, or anywhere between. It might even be much closer to the original antithesis than to the original thesis. Nonetheless, because the synthesis is a more satisfactory position than either of the earlier options, it becomes the new thesis.

The process is ongoing. Man marries woman, they have a child. The child grows up, marries, has a child, and the process moves along. One nation wars with another until some resolution is accomplished, then after a period of calm, the resolution is challenged. This, Hegel believed, is the pattern of all reality.

The root reason for this is that all is related, everything is connected, and we cannot escape all the others—personal and impersonal—in our relational world. We are not absolute; we cannot isolate ourselves. We are linked inextricably with each other, with the entire ecosystem.

Conversational Dialectic

Although some would distinguish conversation from the Dialectic, in the broad sense, conversation is an aspect of the Dialectic. The Socratic dialogues, although conversational in appearance, are more focused than an ordinary conversation. Whereas it is normal for a conversation to make many shifts of subject matter and operate on varying levels of intensity, the Socratic dialogue sticks to the subject, pursues an objective, and excludes discussion of trivia. In this sense, the Dialectic and conversation can be distinguished. Nonetheless, there is value in recognizing the dialectical character of free conversation.

In a conversation, varying points of view emerge, which are often challenged. Even the common shifts of topic make the important contribution of bringing up perspectives that have not been considered before by some of the participants. The Dialectic is involved wherever differing positions are recognized and dealt with.

CHAPTER FIVE

The Dialectic at Home

Home is where life gets itself together (or pulls itself apart). Home is our first school. Rebel against it as we may, the Dialectic of home life cannot be shaken. It shapes our thought, habit, and action more than we are aware. We are much more like our parents than we suppose. On the other hand, to the degree that we rebel against parental example, it is that example calling the shots, telling us what we do *not* want to become. As with most of us, I was a parent, perhaps even a grandparent, before my dialectical relationship with home came into focus.

Are You Listening?

Deep into his sermon, he would lean over the pulpit and ask, "Dear hearts tonight, are you listening?" That was a long time ago, but I can still hear him addressing his congregation with these old-timey words of endearment. Daddy used the rhetoric of a bygone era, but everyone in the church knew that they were dear to him, and we knew he wanted us to pay attention because his sermons were punctuated repeatedly with, "Are you listening?" After all, what is the point of preaching if nobody is listening?

And what about us? What can we accomplish in our conversations if no one is listening? If we are going to live with each other, we will have to listen, hear, and acknowledge each other. If I don't listen, or at least look, I may not realize when you are hurting and that you are about to go under unless someone comes to your rescue. If I don't listen, I may not realize how much you care, or even that you care, about me. If we don't listen to each other, we each merely speak our own respective and reciprocal monologues and except when presented by professional entertainers, most monologues quickly become boring. We need dialogue. We need to hear each other.

Daddy's "Dear hearts tonight, (he didn't often use this term with the Sunday morning crowd) are you listening?" was not a strictly rhetorical question. He wanted to see it in their eyes, their posture, and even in the expression of their faces. He wanted to know that they were engaged with him.

Yet the sermons were monologues, as most sermons are. He would not have appreciated it if someone had spoken out with an answer. His question was more a device to maintain or recover attention. On the other hand, I might be wrong, as I have been so many times about Daddy. It is too late now for me to ask him, but although he didn't expect a spoken response he might have welcomed it; he might have welcomed the opportunity to engage in true dialogue about the Christian gospel. The more I think about it, the more I suspect that he might have welcomed it. But neither he nor the congregation of six or eight hundred people expected it because that is not part of the accepted pattern of public worship. I wonder what might happen if immediate spoken feedback became an expected part in the sermon?

On the other hand, if the preacher is to expect his congregation to listen, he had better have been listening to them during the week. If he doesn't know their problems, hopes, fears, dreams, doubts, excitements, moral dilemmas, existential crises, laughter and tears, his sermon may miss the people completely. They may continue to come, thinking it is somehow important that they be in church Sunday morning, but it will not be long before they stop listening with any sense of expectation and hope. Preaching will be boring—an accurate description of altogether too many Sunday mornings. Again, what about all the rest of us and all the talking we do? If you don't listen to me, why should I listen to you?

Daddy listened to his church members—to everyone in the community—better than he did to his three sons. Many of you might say the same thing about your fathers. Fathers often engage in more genuine dialogue on the job than they do at home. One reason is that, like my father, there are many dads who spend precious little of their time at home, and when they do get home, they are already talked out and tired. Maybe that is the reason. I don't know. I do know that Daddy rarely seemed to hear me, and that there was so much I wanted to say. But, before I got started trying to make some sort of connection, Daddy would stop me. Instead, he gave clear dogmatic instructions guaranteed to get my life moving on the right track—before he even knew what I was attempting to say. He was good at discouraging dialogue.

For the first thirty years of my life, I felt that he never heard much I was trying to say. Across the next thirty-three, we had a few times when we heard each other and responded to what we heard. Sometimes we argued late into the night, long after others had gone to bed, closing their doors to shut out our fierce, loud efforts to understand and to reconcile. And there were times—rare times—of confession. Daddy listened as I confessed fears, weaknesses, disappointment, and anger. To my amazement, on two or three occasions, Daddy confessed the same to me. On those occasions I was thrilled that he treated me as a real person, as a confidant, as someone he loved and trusted.

Daddy died in 1997. The night before the funeral—at which I was to be the speaker—I stood beside his open casket looking into that face I had known for sixty-three years and cried in lonely anger for the years of opportunity lost to both of us. So few were the hours we ever listened to each other. Precious as those times were, they never began to fill the void that I felt in my relationship to a man who, for nearly forty years, was one of the most loved and respected humans ever known in Blackwell, Oklahoma and Gainesville, Texas. He was a truly great man and, in my confusion and anger, I still was able to speak appreciatively of him to the hundreds who came to the funeral. But I miss him, and not just now; I always did.

Was he afraid? Was he afraid of what he might hear if he listened? Was he afraid that if he revealed much of himself I would lose some degree of respect? There were a few times late at night, after I was an adult, when he hinted at a self-image that he dared not acknowledge. He told me, once, that he wore the stern face and used the no-nonsense voice to ward off any attempt to penetrate his defenses.

Isn't that the all-too-common human story, at least in the United States? We are afraid to let conversation move much deeper than a recitation of socially accepted pattern of speech. There is a certain reciprocity, but not much, in our exchanges about how we feel, what we think of the weather, the economy, our favorite TV show, or our favorite ball team. I suspect that sports and gossip bring us closest to anything that resembles true dialogue. Beyond that we guard ourselves, and continue to inhabit a silent loneliness.

Mother Listened, But ...

Mother was different. She was a patient listener—usually. I could talk with Mother about anything—and at length—and did so for over three-quarters of a century. In her presence I could express myself knowing that I was not likely to be squelched. I could dream dreams that had no possibility of being realized in the real world. So I felt much closer to Mother than to Daddy. On the other hand, Mother mostly listened. She never said much, told me little of what she thought about my words, and gave little advice and few instructions. Except on one or two subjects—bird-watching was one—she rarely revealed many of her own thoughts, feelings, or dreams (I've often wondered what they were). She listened to my monologues, knowing that listening, all by itself, is good for the human soul and some of the best therapy possible.

So I was raised in a home that knew little dialogue. It was a family with three brothers, who each went his own way, only occasionally acknowledging the existence of the others. I doubt that we were an unusual American family. And other societies would doubtless recognize this experience.

I don't know how well this describes the homes in which Mother and Daddy themselves grew up, but I have heard enough from cousins and other family members to believe my parents' homes were much like mine, and that the pattern could be traced back for at least a generation or two. Moreover, I fear that my own daughters might see this as a description of their father and their own experience. (My wife was a different kind of mother to our children. She and our daughters dialogued; they connected, not always in the best way, but they got involved in trying to know and be known. This remains true, and continues with our grandchildren. Because of her, we are a close-knit family. Her family was much the same, and I'm sure other such families exist.)

Somehow we don't take time for each other; we don't listen to those nearest to us. We are family, that is, we are *familiar* with each other, but don't *know* each other. And, thus, we don't know ourselves. Without the opportunity to learn what others feel and think, we don't understand clearly our own inner life. Without sharing our thoughts and feelings with someone else, our own self-perception remains out of focus. We can know ourselves only in dialogue with others.

Getting married made me a better thinker. I am a man and men need to hear from women if we are to complete our thoughts, and if we are to clarify what we think. That is one reason I married. That way I always have a woman handy to serve as my antithesis, my complement—the yin to my yang.

Without dialogue I cannot become a whole person. If in the home we don't share our inner lives, we remain family, but are *familiar* with each other only in a limited sense. Without the exchange of ideas, plans, hopes, and fears, we never live in community on this earth. Our pain, our emptiness, and our horrors are, in large measure, rooted in our lack of dialogue. It is a historical commonplace that the declaration of war is immediately preceded by the announcement that "talks have broken off." They usually have broken down because the negotiation between diplomats is, too often, an exchange of reciprocal monologues. Each tries to convince the other side, but neither seeks to hear and understand the other's heritage, position, predicament, or philosophy.

However, we are stuck with each other. Our radical individualism and egoism cannot eliminate all the others—people, nature, and God—linked with our lives. The twentieth-century French thinker Jean-Paul Sartre argued that "hell is other people," but he also tells us there is *NO EXIT* from this world of others. We are inescapably social, made for relationship, and directly linked with the natural order. If we fail to take *others* into account, we risk denying our humanity and destroying hope for a human and global future. Because everything is ultimately connected and interrelated in one great ecosystem, we must acknowledge otherness, listen and respond to it, and work toward a more satisfying harmony of all its parts, including the part that is our self. Apart from dialogue, we are doomed.

On the other hand, we have available a method of thinking and living that can clear the way to a more promising, satisfying, and humane future. That method is the Dialectic.

Marriage

Her family had lived on the border of poverty all her nineteen years. Frequently, they crossed that border. One day, frustrated from being told again there was no money for a movie, she said, "When I get married, I'm going to marry a rich man."

Her father's immediate response, "You'd better marry someone you love."

"Well, it's as easy to love a rich man as to love a poor man."

We marry because we believe there is something to be gained: wealth, prestige, acceptance, stability, power, or whatever else we feel is lacking in our life. We believe marriage can fill that need. Most of us, however, unthinkingly hope to marry the handsome fellow or the beautiful girl with an attractive figure.

My wife once said she married me for my beautiful hair, my beautiful eyes, and my intelligent mind. My hair has long since been gone, and we were married less than four years before she had to see my eyes through the lenses of glasses. I hope I don't lose my mind. We had our first date sixty years ago, and I would hate to lose her after all this time.

Ideally, we marry for that vague thing called love. Often this indefinable experience, falling in love, overrides all other intentions, hopes, and dreams.

Where does thought come into the picture? Is choosing a marital partner to be given deliberate consideration, or would that remove the romance and reduce the relationship to careful calculation? The philosopher Immanuel Kant, one of the handful of greatest thinkers in history, was once in love, but he realized there were many considerations to be reflected upon. Choosing the idea of marriage as the thesis of his deliberations, he realized the enormity of antitheses, the tensions they raised, and the possible syntheses they might lead to.

On one hand, we should use all the time we have available to think things through before making serious decisions. On the other hand, there are occasions when our time is limited. Sometimes we must decide now or never. Sometimes it is dangerous to wait. Kant did not realize that a prospective bride might grow impatient. Before he had time to consider all that is—or might be—involved in marriage, he learned that she had given up and married someone else. He never married.

Anyone contemplating marriage in the twenty-first century should give some thought to the odds against successful marriage, at least in the United States. When marriage is on your mind, divorce is the most obvious antithesis. Any clear-thinking person must realize the enormous tensions that can develop between the idea of marriage and the potential for divorce, or between the fact of marriage and the possibility of divorce. Being "in love," while it might be an essential element of a good marriage, provides little assurance of enduring marital stability. Something to think about.

I've said that the Hegelian dialectic can be understood simply as the movement from thesis and antithesis to synthesis. I also said that we would need to look beyond this simple pattern into the complexities Hegel had in mind. According to Hegel, we could take our stance anywhere, thus, even an antithesis could be taken as a thesis of its own. The synthesis always becomes a new thesis. Whatever our original thesis, we will find that it is the antithesis to other theses. Each thesis has multiple antitheses and each thesis/antithesis may lead to any number of potential syntheses.

How might this work out when marriage is being considered? Marriage is going to be the synthesis of a male and a female. Ordinarily, however, little thought is given to the obvious: he will think like a man, she like a woman. And men and women are different. This tension will increase across time, being reconciled only as a succession of syntheses are reached.

Let's look at a particular case. Lisa has lived all her life in Grass Valley, California, a small town in the heart of the Gold Rush country. Her father is a carpenter, her mother a clerk in Lew

Howard's Drugstore. Lisa is the youngest of eight children. Her eldest sister has children Lisa's age. She is the only one in the family to have attended college. She is the most devoutly religious. She is twenty years old.

Tim had lived in eight towns all over Kansas, Oklahoma, and Texas, before going to college. He got his entire high school education from Andy Dekaney High School in Houston, where his father was a petroleum engineer and his mother was a traditional, stay-at-home mom. He has two younger brothers that he has little in common with, except they share the same parents. The family is Presbyterian. Tim lived with Sharly for two years before she left him for another guy. He dated very little for the next year, then began seeing Lisa. He is twenty-five. They met at Oklahoma State University where both were enrolled: she as a sophomore music major, he as a second-year senior marketing major. They have been engaged for a little over a year.

How many different thesis-antithesis-synthesis triads could you make of this? I hope they have spent a good bit of their time together this past year thinking about it, talking about it. For instance, take only one small tension they must deal with. She has two brothers and five sisters, all older and with less education. If she is the thesis, they have been the antitheses, and she now brings to marriage whatever synthesis has been made of that. He is the eldest of three brothers. He has never paid them much attention, while, unbeknownst to him, they have looked on him as their hero. He the thesis, they the antitheses, and he brings to marriage whatever family synthesis this has led to.

The Hegelian dialectic says that all reality exists in this triadic relationship; all history develops dialectically, and, therefore, if we are to be in touch with reality, we must think dialectically—thesis, its antitheses, and the multifarious syntheses possible. Life is complex.

The easiest way to simplify it is to embed "but on the other hand" in our minds. Then be alert and attentive to how much lead time we have before decision must be reached.

Donna was a cut above everyone else in my high school graduating class. We were always a bit in awe of her. She was the smartest and most sophisticated, wealthy and good-looking. Art was the playboy of our class, highly sophisticated, wealthy, handsome, and suave. They married within a year after graduation.

I knew the lady who was their housekeeper. She knew what their marriage was like. And she told me. Donna was often out of the public eye for months at a time, recovering from beatings, waiting for bruises to disappear, and afraid to talk with anyone. She had learned that Art was a heavy-drinking, very abusive man. She took it for three years before putting a bullet through her head.

How did this come about? She was the smartest in our class. Always prepared, always knew the answers, intensely involved, she was loved by all our teachers. Where were her smarts when she said yes to Art Hall? Always thoroughly prepared for classes, why did she not know what she was getting into in this marriage?

My best guess is that, perhaps like most of us, once she "fell in love," her mind took a vacation. Ordinarily, we give little thought to what marriage involves and what marriage to this particular person entails. We are sure that love will work it all out. Not many take the route of killing either themselves or their spouse, but we are well aware of the numbers who find themselves in miserable and failed marriages.

Herbert and Margaret were the classic high school marriage: a big football hero and the smartest girl in the class. She was committed "until death do us part," so she stayed with him through all his shady and crooked business dealings. She stayed while he spent a year in prison. Never a happy marriage, but she stayed with him.

When they were in their middle-sixties, they bought an elegant new home. The next year, they celebrated their golden wedding anniversary. Less than a year later, he moved out and rented an apartment across town. Margaret learned of it when she came home from work to an empty house.

Then came the divorce.

(Not long afterward, to the surprise of all of us, she went on a date to Las Vegas with an old man she had just met, and soon they were married.)

After dating Bobby Lee for her first three years of college, Charlene took a philosophy course where I taught the main ideas that I'm presenting in this book. By the middle of November, she had reconsidered a lot of things about marriage, herself, and Bobby Lee. They had been engaged for six months when she came and told me that the course had taught her how to think, and that it led her to realize marriage to Bobby Lee would be a horrible mistake. I didn't probe, and she didn't tell me the particulars.

She had put the academic idea of the Dialectic to work, and thought better of the status of her love life. When you learn how to think, and, rather than following others, think for yourself, your life will begin changing, sometimes dramatically.

(Seven years ago, she married a medical student. They now have a handful with three boys, and a new medical practice; the marriage looks good, and they seem happy.)

Don't get serious about dating anyone without stopping for a dialectical checkup. Don't even think about marrying, until you have given it a dialectical test. Sex, as prominent, important, and fun as it is, cannot be the main consideration. Trust and reliability should be the foremost considerations. Run as soon as you discover a hot temper—it won't change, it will only get worse. Finances and in-laws are ignored at great cost. Think like an octopus. There are, always, many other hands to consider.

Philosopher Alfred Whitehead called it "the fallacy of misplaced concreteness." He was talking about the difference between our ideas and the world of concrete reality.

Concrete reality is the world as it is apart from our understanding of it, our idea of it. It is the world as it actually is—actual individuals, communities, love affairs, wars, businesses, grass, automobiles, clouds, and trombones. It is actual, specific instances of events and things, not our *idea* of family, of children dying of starvation, or of hurricanes. It is *your* family, *this* child named Ndondo that is dying, Hurricane "Katrina."

The mistake—the fallacy, as Whitehead called it—is mistaking our ideas for actualities. Ideas exist only in our minds. Ideas are mental actualities. They do exist, but only in the world of our thought. The *idea* of marriage has no concrete reality, there are only actual marriages. The fallacy of misplaced concreteness is to believe we will find our actual marriage to be just like our idea of it. It is to misplace the concrete with the mental.

Barry and Rachel fell in love with each other, so it seemed to them, but more likely than not, they have fallen in love with their idea of each other. "Love is blind" to many concrete realities that the rest of us see. They, however, have composed an idea-lized image of their beloved, based on their dreams and their experience. In the illusory world of courtship, they see in each other only the idea-l.

Then they marry. The honeymoon ends when they find their marriage partner fails to conform to the idea. Marriage—this actual marriage of Rachel and Barry—is, at many points, not like they supposed it would be. Marital problems, at heart, arise from a refusal to accept and adjust to the concrete character of life together.

"You are not the man I married. You have changed." These words are common in the early years of marriage. But no, neither the husband nor the wife has changed. What has happened is that they have become dis-illusioned. Quite often, our ideas of each other, and of the nature of marriage, are illusions. Yet we allow ourselves to believe the reality will match the illusion. We have made the mistake of misplacing the concrete with a dreamy idea.

Ideas are necessary guides, suggestive of life's road, of its speed limit, its potholes, curves … but the ideas are not the road any more than a map is the territory it symbolizes.

No matter how good we become as thinkers, we must always remember the distinction between what we think and what actually is, was, or will come to be. This applies to the teacher's idea of what she will do in the classroom today, the painter's idea of the picture she is about to paint, our idea of what a church or minister is, or how the boss will respond to any one of our requests.

On the one hand, think, but on the other, remember there are always more "other hands" than we can wrap our minds around. Expect the unexpected.

Consider other perspectives. For some of us, that means we first must realize there are perspectives other than our own. Bill Hendricks, a theologian, was one of the finest men I have known, one of the most brilliant and learned—some believed he even thought in Latin. Some would also say he was rather arrogant. Everyone looked up to him. No one challenged him.

One fall, there came on the faculty a scroungy-looking little Dutchman, also a theologian, named Jan Kiwiet. He was, as someone who knew him said, "a Dutchman in whom there is no guile." A modest man, he was a published scholar. At a faculty get-together before school started in the fall, Hendricks was pontificating about some doctrinal issue when, to the shock of everyone, Kiwiet, our new man, innocently, but without hesitation, said, "Bill, that's just what you think. Other theologians, they think different." Yes, Doctor Hendricks, there are perspectives other than your own, many of which are worthy of consideration.

I have written about considerate thinking and its part in the making of my long, rich, and satisfying marriage. Carol and I entered marriage after thinking, romantically, that we had talked through everything that could be considered. We had done this for more than four years before marriage. We thought we agreed on everything. But, we brought two widely divergent family perspectives to the actual marriage. I was not a considerate thinker at the time of our wedding.

It took years of obstinate and persistent challenges before I, rather than coming down to her level, realized that in reality I was not up to her level. She had a hard time convincing me, against my heritage, that she was a person as much as I was, with the same rights, with a mind of her own. And a sharp mind it was, sometimes coupled with a sharp tongue. I was a slow and highly resistant learner. She was not about to leave me, nor was she about to leave me with my obsolete mindset. I loved her and she persisted. She prevailed. And I became a better man.

She changed my views on sex, money, raising children, television, in-laws, and who knows what all else. I moderated her views on money, religion, housekeeping, and perhaps another thing or two. For long years now, we have thought through almost everything together and arrived at comfortable, practical consensus. Our minds complement each other. We have found that neither of us thinks clearly nor productively unless we depend on mutual input, checks and balances.

Compromise

Compromise, for all its dangers, risks, and the warnings against it, makes human society possible. Marriage, the home, economics, and politics—whether local, state, national, or international— all live by compromise. It is the glue that holds social structures in place. It is not optional. It is a necessity, a daily necessity. Few things are as risky as compromise, but few are as essential.

One day, my wife and I were filling in and signing some legal forms. One question asked how long we had been married. The answer was fifty-eight years. The notary public who was assisting said, "Wow. That's impressive. You don't hear that much anymore. What is your secret?"

"Compromise," I answered. "Daily compromise. A marriage cannot last, in fact, I don't think it can exist, without compromise." Those who study the causes of divorce commonly list—and link—a lack of communication, compromise, and commitment. Marriage is a daily OTOH, BOTOH. It is a complex of countless theses and antitheses, with a constant commitment to finding some degree of synthesis or compromise.

Yes, there are situations where we cannot compromise. When dealing with a state of affairs where the other entity is committed to upholding a single principle, we cannot compromise unless we are willing to subjugate everything else to their one principle. Abraham Lincoln said he was afraid of a "man of principle." He found them very dangerous. He noted that although we could work with men of principles, with the man of a single principle, we waste our time offering any concessions. They would be taken as signs of weakness, and would change the other side not in the least.

Compromise is the law of life together. It is so necessary and so potentially dangerous, we need to be always prepared to make some concessions, except in those cases where compromise would be disastrous. There is one basic criterion for making a decision in these cases: our values. We need to know what we value, that is, what would we be willing to give up in order to hold on to the things we value. For Patrick Henry, liberty was the highest value. He would not compromise with anything that might cost him his freedom: "Give me liberty or give me death." We should always be ready to consider making concessions unless we find ourselves in the place where we are unwilling to give at all, where we are prepared to say, "You can kill me, but on this point I will not change. I am prepared to die on this hill."

CHAPTER SIX

The Medical Dialectic

In the summer of 2009, our daughter had four major surgeries to correct almost unbearable physical problems. It was a medically dialectical summer. The medical dialectic comprises three things: doctor/patient relationship; the doctor's thought pattern, particularly in diagnosis and choice of treatment; and the nature of medications.

Doctors Are Not Gods

The Dialectic dictates that we live by dialogue with each other. In a medical situation, this means that: we should be prepared to tell the doctor clearly and concisely what we understand our problem to be; the doctor should be a good listener; and she should be prepared to engage her patient in question and answer dialogue. Too often we give our physician an incomplete and somewhat vague account of our symptoms and their history. If our problem is at all serious, we might be wise to take written notes with us lest we forget something important.

In Neil Ravin's novel, M.D., he tells of a woman who after months of being treated for asthma, told her doctor that she only wheezed when she was in his waiting room, a room furnished with wool-upholstered chairs. And she was allergic to wool. When asked why she had never before mentioned this, she responded that he had never asked. Needless to say, her physician cancelled all her medicines and suggested she stay away from his waiting room. Who was at fault in this situation? Was it the doctor, or the patient? He had not asked, she had not told. No Dialectic at work.

We need to give our doctors the clearest and fullest information we can, and we need doctors who will listen and be willing to deal with our questions. Otherwise, the Dialectic will not work. If we find ourselves with a doctor who has a god complex, one who dictates without listening, a doctor who makes us uncomfortable, nervous, or angry, we should find another physician. If, for some reason, we question the doctor's decisions, the Dialectic strongly suggests we get a second opinion before proceeding. The doctor-patient relationship is one of the most important elements in our ongoing health.

Earlier, I said that our daughter Cynthia had a medically dialectical summer. She dismissed her family physician and a prominent specialist because of, among other things, unsatisfactory doctor-patient relationships. Moreover, Googling led her to seriously question the procedure the specialist had scheduled. She searched for another specialist from whom she could get second opinion. When she did find the one specialist in the state who was qualified to deal with her specific condition, she found that, even there, she had to separate herself from one of his arrogant nurses.

Cynthia took the initiative for her life and health and did extensive research on her problem. On the World Wide Web, she found that the procedure recommended by the first specialist was dangerous and had many enduring side effects. But, she he was able to track down, via the Internet, the Houston specialist who, by way of three surgeries, ended her problems and restored her to a normal life.

Forty-some years ago, I had a troubling medical problem myself, so I went to one of the most respected doctors in Fort Worth. After examination, he said, "As soon as you can take off work for two weeks, you need surgery." The problem was that, at the time, I was dealing with the scholarly demands of doctoral studies, working a forty-hour job, and was married, with three teenage daughters at home. There was no way I would ever be able to take off two weeks without serious consequences at home, work, and school.

A friend suggested I see the school physician. He was an elderly gentleman who devoted one day a week, pro bono, to the school. The rest of the time he was a member of the faculty at Baylor Medical in

Dallas. After he examined me, he scoffed at the other doctor's opinion and told me there was no need of surgery at all. He had a few suggestions for self-help and dismissed me. The first doctor's call for surgery could be seen as the thesis—the starting point—and the school doctor's opinion as the antithesis. My problem was real. It was aggravating. I wanted help, but I could see no way to take two weeks off. I felt the tension between the two opinions.

I could not trust expert medical opinion to make the decision. The experts disagreed. Which was right? Or was there, perhaps a third option? Two doctors and I were involved in this dilemma. Ultimately, I was in the driver's seat. I was the controlling agent in this Dialectic. The road signs pointed in opposite directions. I decided to trust the old physician and at least postpone the idea of the operating table. I learned to live with the problem and now, more than forty years later, although I still sometimes wonder about surgery, I am glad I went for a second opinion.

How Doctors Think

Doctors think like the rest of us. Some of us are better thinkers than others. Most of us, as adults, think within the parameters of our training. Once we are well trained, we tend to fall into habitual patterns of thought. The farmer sows his wheat in September, the teacher continues to think that grades above ninety are to be graded "A," the merchant begins in September, if not earlier, thinking about Christmas sales. And the physician tends to use tests and follow procedures that have worked well in the past.

After I began writing this chapter, Dr. Jerome Groopman published a book, *How Doctors Think*. I revised this section and it is now greatly indebted to Groopman's book. He addresses two fundamental issues: poor thinking on the part of many doctors; and the pathway to good medical thinking. Although he does not mention the word, the book's thesis echoes the Dialectic. Doctors, he says, need to recognize the fact that it is always possible they could be wrong in their initial diagnosis, to realize there is always more to be considered, and, thus, to ask what else it could be, even, what the worst might be.

Groopman introduces his book with the story of a woman who over a fifteen-year period had seen almost thirty doctors, had been examined and tested from seemingly all angles, but had grown steadily worse. A consensus had formed that her problems comprised an eating disorder, irritable bowel syndrome, and some sort of mental illness. As she went from one doctor to another, her records followed her, thus, the previous diagnoses followed her. Each new diagnosis was some variation of what the doctors read on the records they received. This is a typical pattern in human thinking. If everyone else thinks a certain idea is true, we are apt to think the same way. It is easier than thinking for ourselves.

Grudgingly, Groopman relates, the lady went to one more specialist, a doctor who recognized the symptoms for the earlier diagnoses, recognized that the correct measures had been taken to treat these problems, but felt something more was involved. Do you remember that at the foundation of the Dialectic is the idea that "no human statement (medical or otherwise) is ever complete by itself; there is always something more?" So, one more unpleasant test was run and it was discovered that she had a condition that, at the time, was relatively unknown: gluten allergy. It explained everything, and with proper treatment, she improved rapidly.

One of the most satisfying comments ever made to me by a student was when Oma came in after class one day and commented: "I notice something different about you from other teachers. No matter what question anyone asks you, you always begin thinking about it from scratch. Unlike other teachers, you don't seem to reach into your mental cabinet and pull out the well-prepared answer." Often doctors make the mistake of giving a standard diagnosis when faced with what seems to be a set of standard symptoms. If flu is "going around," and you come in with the same symptoms, you are apt to be treated for flu with no thought given to it. Like all the rest of us, Groopman argues, doctors tend to go with the quick and easy answers. They have other patients waiting.

There are several reasons for this tendency among physicians. They are human. In medical school—as in other schooling—they are not trained in thinking skills. Rather, they are trained in scientific method. They locate the medical field in the domain of science and understand themselves as scientists. They are also trained to recognize certain patterns of symptoms, tests, and treatment. But the problem is that we don't all fit the same pattern.

Another problem that militates against good thinking is the patient load that limits the doctor's time to think things through. Good thinking takes time, and doctors simply don't have time. This problem explodes, Groopman notes, in the emergency room with its crises, bed shortages, and overload of anxious patients in the waiting room.

If the situation is to improve, we must take the initiative and ask questions such as: "Doctor, what is the worst this might be?" "What else might it be?" and "Why did you say that?" We must tell our story and the doctor must listen. It is our responsibility to help our doctors think. The Dialectic must work if we are to get good medical attention. If your doctor won't enter in dialogue, change doctors. Your health, and sometimes your life, is at stake.

Side Effects

The Dialectic of medications tells us that we must always consider side effects, or, as it might be called, "the law of unintended or unforeseen consequences." This law states that often there are unexpected but logical consequences to our decisions and actions. We could say that we should always expect the unexpected, never be surprised by surprises.

All medications have side effects. Some of these are positive, some are negative—although, usually when we speak of side effects we are thinking of the negative. For some drugs, whether the side effects are beneficial or not depends on other factors. Aspirin, for instance, is taken for relief of minor aches and pains, but it also thins the blood—in some people, dangerously so. However, it is commonly prescribed, not for aches and pains, but specifically to thin the blood as a precaution against stroke.

Cancer is a particularly tricky illness to deal with. Radiation and chemotherapy (treatment with "poison") have saved or prolonged many lives, but there is no guarantee. Side effects are almost guaranteed (although I have had two friends who took chemo with no apparent side effects at all). With cancer treatment, the side effects can be so serious that some prefer to risk or accept death rather than endure the misery of radiation or chemo. This is so with many medications. On the one hand, they can be salutary, but on the other hand they may have unintended consequences that cause some of us to forego the medicine, preferring to live with our problems, however severe they may be.

The Dialectic of Good Health

When it comes to our health, the Dialectic dictates that we consider more than going on a diet. Nutrition is a necessary, but not sufficient element of good health. Other considerations are essential, such as exercise, sleep and rest, sanitation, work, regular checkups, and attitude. We also must avoid certain abusive habits: drugs, including alcohol and tobacco; overeating and eating junk foods; becoming a couch potato; promiscuous sex; unsafe driving practices; and we all know most of the rest. The maintenance and restoration of good health is many-handed. Each item listed above has other hands of its own, and some of those hands have still other hands. Think like an octopus.

CHAPTER SEVEN

Magnetic Thinking

We seek stability. All our lives, we seek the security, comfort, and peace of stability. We don't like uncertainty. We want things to be settled, to be definite, to stay in place. The Dialectic, however, is dynamic and is the only appropriate response to a dynamic world of uncertainty. There is a special class of relationships where we tend to claim certainty: things that we see as opposites, where we stand on one side or the other, where there is a distinct right and wrong, true and false, black and white, with no space between, no gray areas. We feel we must choose one pole or the other. I call this a bipolar tension. It's a special form of the Dialectic: the Dialectic of bipolarity.

Definition

I use Dialectic in a broader and more inclusive sense than many others, but I use *bipolarity* in a narrower, more particular sense. In this chapter, I give it specific definition: It is a relationship between two seemingly incompatible opposites, a relationship in which neither pole is true by itself. It is not, as many say, a relationship of opposites in which both poles are paradoxically true. The poles are true only in the dialectical tension between them. Truth always lies somewhere between the poles, never at the pole. Sometimes, it is almost indistinguishable from a polar position, but still unpolarized, still in tension with the other pole.

Both or Neither?

So much for an attempt at definition. What am I talking about? The simplest approach to understanding bipolarity is to picture a magnet. We know that each pole of the magnet is charged—one positive, the other negative. Neither of the poles is the more important, neither the more necessary. If both poles were to be made positive, the magnetism would be lost. So if both were negative. The opposite poles set up a magnetic tension between. The magnetism is dependant on the tension rooted in this opposition of the poles.

Many of the most basic features of our world exist in bipolar tension with each other. Take, for instance, the classic tension between of the sovereignty of God and human freedom. These seem to be complete opposites, incompatible with each other. In its strongest statement, if God is the sovereign ruler of the universe, everything that happens is as he directly ordains. Everything is done precisely as God desires, with no option for variation. Humans are left with no freedom of choice. On the other hand, if humans are genuinely free, they may contradict God's desires, in which case, God is not sovereign in the strongest sense. Similar bipolarities characterize many of the basic realities of life and our understanding of it.

Quite commonly, these contradictions are accepted as *paradoxical*. The reference to paradox is intended to make contradictories acceptable while leaving them inexplicable. We need to note that the idea of contradiction, in the strict logical sense, means that one element—pole—must be true and the other must be false. When two things contradict, they cannot both be true. In a paradox we have that which seems to be contradictory, yet in which both elements seem to be true.

An understanding of bipolarity enables us to make sense of this and present a reasoned resolution to these difficulties. In contrast to many understandings of bipolarity, the concept I present affirms not that both poles seem to be true, although contradictory. Rather, I affirm that in a bipolarity neither pole is true—not by itself. Just as a magnet's positive or negative pole is magnetically useless if it exists by itself, so in bipolarity either pole is untrue, *if taken alone*. Both poles are true, but only in tension with the other pole.

In the example of God's power and mankind's free will, you might notice that the Bible doesn't merely state that God is sovereign. It also emphasizes human freedom. But it doesn't just emphasize human choice and responsibility, it also claims God's control. We want to affirm that both are true, independently of the other— objectively true. But we live in a world where everything exists in relation to other things. Nothing exists independently of anything else. Thus, truth always exists in some relational context. Bipolar kinds of truths are true only in relation to each other. I reiterate, neither is true *by itself.*

Our common response to bipolarities is to either accept the copout notion that they are a paradox, or else we polarize. We agree they are contradictory—that the truth of one implies the falsity of the other and *vice versa*—so we feel compelled to defend one and attack the other. This is the root of many of our problems: we cannot accept the tensions inherent in bipolarity. If we affirm the truth of one and reject the other, the tension is eliminated. But we fail to consider the necessity of tension in the real world.

Everything exists and is held together in tensions of all sorts. If all tension—muscular, cellular—were eliminated from our bodies, they would collapse into a protoplasmic heap. Tension is a necessary part of reality. Only inappropriate tension is a problem.

General Bipolarities

The following relationships seem to be bipolar in character: freedom and determinism; objectivity and subjectivity; personal and social; fact and value; singular and universal; feeling and thinking; theoretical and practical; being and becoming; ideal and actual; material and spiritual.

And there are many other common bipolarities of life:

Community	Character
Tension	Release
Solitude	Company
Work	Sabbath
Worship	Service

Being	Doing
Doubt	Belief
Decision	Habit
Environment	Genetics
Is	Ought
Situation	Rules
Act	Wait
Yin	Yang
Serious	Lighthearted
Individual	Community

Again, truth exists in the tension *between* the poles. Note that it does not rest in the center between them—it does not rest at all. Truth—and life and reality—move all along the spectrum between. Today, in this situation, relative to this moment, it may lie in the center, but later in the day, when the situation has changed, it may be closer to one pole and further from the other, still feeling the tension from both directions.

Living the Tension

At times truth may lie so close to one pole that it seems to be polarized. The difference is that, no matter how close to one pole, it still feels the pull of the other. Once polarized, however, we feel no tension at all. And then, we are out of touch with the real world, the world of tensions. Today, talking with you, I may sound like a flaming liberal, a dogmatic liberal. The difference between me and the liberal is that I am still aware of the conservative pole and the values and challenges it holds. Thus, next week, talking with a liberal, I may sound like a hidebound conservative. Again, however, I have not allowed myself to choose a pole, I am still in the tension, the living, moving tension. Truth, reality, and life exist along a fine line that continually moves between the poles.

Too many of us are uncomfortable with tension, change, and the relativity of living this spectrum. In our desire for stability, we want to be solidly anchored like a great oak tree. We are called, rather, to the stability of the eagle soaring high in the air, apparently with no support. The eagle, however, as it rides the wind currents and thermal air columns, is as secure as the oak. But it is a dynamic security, not a fixed and static one. Life has to be engaged moment by moment. We can never lock in to safety.

So learn, when confronted by an either/or situation, to stop and consider the possibility that a bipolarity is involved. If it is the case, we should not accept the either/or that we are presented with. If the occasion is bipolar, we recognize that it is both/and, and must make a judgment about where across the spectrum we should take our stand. Always make it your habit, in the face of either/or, to consider and be prepared to deal with the bipolar.

We polarize for seemingly good reasons. When we take a polar position on anything, it gives us a sense of security. Polar positions are absolute. They leave us with no questions. We polarize because at the polar position we do not have to think. And, as always, it is easier to follow our comfortable crowd—security, with no need to do the work of thinking, and plenty of company.

But the power of a magnet lies in neither its positive nor its negative pole. Rather, the power resides in the tension between them. Were we to decide against negatives and make it all positive, or vice versa, we would be left with a piece of mere metal.

We are called on, regularly, to pick a pole: conservative or liberal, pro-life or pro-choice, freedom or determinism, capitalism or communism, socialism or individualism. "Which are you?" we are asked. Every time we adopt a polar position, something is destroyed, something vital. Reality, life, and truth exist in those polar tensions.

If we insist on the supremacy of individual rights and reject the claims of society, our thinking is invalid. If we claim that individual rights must be subordinated to the needs of society, our thinking is invalid. Neither pole, taken alone, is ever right. Only with the support of a healthy society can an individual attain her full potential. Only when composed of a diverse body of well-developed individuals can a society maintain its health. The bipolarities of life are true. They are right, but only in relation to each other, only when the tension is acknowledged.

Nor should we look for truth in a middle-of-the-road balance. Reality, life, and truth exist along an unceasingly shifting, fine line somewhere between the poles. Think of the tightrope walker with her balancing pole. It is rarely held perfectly horizontal. Sometimes it is tipped a little to the left or right, and sometimes it is tipped rather deeply one direction or the other, whatever is needed for the walker to maintain her balance. At times we see the pole tilted rapidly back and forth, from one side to the other.

Activity and Rest

A fundamental dialectic is the bipolar movement between activity and rest. We have day and night, six work days and a Sabbath, break time during the work day, the growing seasons and winter, two hours of driving on the road followed by a rest stop. (Federal law allows truckers thirteen hours on the road and mandates at least ten hours off duty before driving again, although many studies show this to be an inadequate rest period.) If we stay only at the pole of activity, we eventually burn out; if we stay too long at the pole of rest, we accomplish little or nothing. We need both.

So it is with thinking. Think too long and your mind gives out. On the other hand, don't quit too soon. I remember when our university bestowed an honorary doctorate on a wealthy south Texas farmer and businessman. In his acceptance speech he said he often was asked the secret of his success. He told us it was just three words: "A little more."

Thinking is work. In the early stages of becoming a considerate thinker, it can be hard work. The mind balks and says, "Leave me alone." When this occurs, see if you can give it "a little more." Try to think of one more "other hand" possibility, one more aspect of the antithesis, or another facet of either thesis or antithesis. One more try, then give it a rest.

The oak tree and the grape vine need winter's dormant period so they can digest, stabilize, and incorporate the gains of the growing season. They need winter also for rest, restoration, and recovery. The birds of the air, the beasts of the field, the reader and writer—people like you and me—all need daily sleep. Some of us get by on a little less, others of us seem to require a bit more, but we slight our sleep only at great risk.

When the mind tires of working, it calls us to move, for a while, toward the other pole: mindlessness. Myself, I check CNN online for a news update, get a snack from the kitchen, play a card game with my wife, go outside and enjoy the wide diversity of my native plant yarden, or watch my little flock of bantam chickens. It might be a good time to go shopping, visiting, or to bed and sleep. Do just about anything, but give thinking a rest.

I spoke of thinking as hard work, particularly as we begin deliberately to think according to the dictates of the Dialectic. The "a little more" stretches the mind, even as a little more stretches our physical muscles. Just as we grow stronger lifting weights, gradually increasing the weight, so our minds grow stronger as we gradually demand more of them.

Think, think a little more, retreat, rest, allow time and space for re-creation. Cognitive ability will grow. Some of us will require more, some less, mental rest and restoration. Give yourself whatever time is required to enable you to come back with readiness and enthusiasm. The time will come when thinking is no more tiring than walking or talking. The Dialectic calls for some kind of rhythmic movement between activity and rest. Think about it.

Aging

The morning I turned forty-five, before I even got out of bed, I decided that I was now "old enough." All my life I had heard, "You're not old enough ..." to remember ... to do that, to wear that, to understand ... to enjoy.... On that day, February 15, 1979, I decreed that I was old enough for whatever.

But that notion begat another: I may be old enough, but I was not yet "old." So, at forty-five, I began to prepare for old age. I began studying gerontology. In succeeding years, I began carefully observing elderly people. I soon concluded that most people, if they live long enough, flunk old age. At least most that I have observed did not have a happy ending to their story.

Those who had accumulated wealth, had risen to prestigious positions of leadership, or had the sophistication that accompanies world travel and education from elite universities, people such as these I have watched. And, in large measure, I've seen them end their years in the misery of emptiness. As a result, I began in earnest to study individuals who had earned good grades in aging. I knew my time would come, and I wanted to know the joy of a life fulfilled.

Now I am an old man in my seventies. What have I learned across the past thirty years? I've learned that the secret of successful aging lies in the bipolar dialectic of continuity and change, the every-changing, but necessary tension between thinking—and, thus, living—like a conservative and like a progressive. Tradition and novelty.

Somewhere along the way I read and bought into the idea that the secret of successful aging was the ability to adapt. Those who can't—or don't, or won't—adapt are shunted off the road of life into the ditch of bitterness. Yes, adaptability is essential. It is a necessary, but not sufficient condition for a good old age. The ability to adapt is one of those poles that is invalid when taken by itself. It makes its contribution to life, to old age, only as it lives in tension with the other pole: the commitment to hold on to those things that we have staked our lives on, believe in, and have integrated into our character.

On the other hand, necessary as it is to hold on to the best of the past, conservativism is insufficient to lead us to what the poet Robert Browning called the "best [that] is yet to be, the last of life for which the first was made." To adopt a purely conservative stance toward life is to become stagnant, then sour, then morose; it is a guarantor of misery.

It takes both. Some of us will need to maintain more continuity with the past, and keep more traditions, while others will need to venture more into the new cultures that continually emerge. But all of us must conserve that which we most value and believe in. All of us must adapt to some of the unavoidable novelty that seems so foreign to the world in which we spent most of our lives.

Myself, I hold to the matchless personal and social value of traditional marriage with its associated lifetime vows. In a world that increasingly distances itself from the natural, favoring rather the man-made modifications and replacements of nature, I am a determined conservative of the natural, the wild, and that which is essentially untouched, left in its apparently chaotic biodiversity. The blue bib overalls and western-style hats that are part of my rural Oklahoma heritage and that I still wear much of the time help give continuity to who I am.

On the other hand, I am on good terms with Gmail, blogging, Twitter, Facebook, cell phones, and solar panels. I relate easily and comfortably with the generation of body piercings, tattoos, iPods, and MTV. They speak a different language, dress differently, and represent a culture completely foreign to what feels natural to me. But I made the choice back when I was forty-five that I would gradually become a naturalized citizen of this new nation, the nation of the younger, because, as is commonly said, I know that we are more alike than we are different.

It has not been easy to live feeling the strong pull from both poles. I have often lost my balance, often allowed myself to be pulled down, often failed to live the tension. Often I think I could relax and feel more comfortable if I allowed myself to completely polarize, but that would be to choose to lose so much that is vital.

Reason and Emotion

Another fundamental—essential—element of good thinking is the dialectical bipolar tension between reason and emotion. As in all true bipolar relations, neither of these, taken by itself, is valid. Good thinking exists only in the tension between the two. And there is no magic balance. Sometimes it is primarily emotion that powers good thinking, on other occasions reason rides in the driver's seat. In either case, the other is consulted and taken seriously. Considerate thinking finds its place all along the spectrum between the two poles.

The movie *Guess Who's Coming for Dinner* draws its power from the tension of racism in conflict with love. Matt Drayton (Spencer Tracy) and Mr. Prentice (Roy Glenn) are convinced that their beloved children, "Joey" Drayton (Katharine Houghton) and Dr. John Prentice (Sidney Poitier) have lost their minds. The fathers are totally convinced that this interracial marriage would be a horrible mistake. They can think only of all the potential problems that would accrue were the marriage to take place. The situation remains at an impasse, until, finally, Mrs. Prentice (Beah Richards) confronts the two "old" men.

She speaks to their feelings, which she says have dried up long ago. She rebukes them for having forgotten what it is like to be young and deeply committed, as this young couple is. Her pain-laden challenge wakens Drayton's heart and mind. Now he understands the situation as a whole, and in an impassioned speech, pours out the love and commitment to his wife that has not diminished across long years of marriage. The issue is resolved. The marriage receives the blessing of both parents.

Only as love's emotion arises in antithesis to racism's reason can any of them think clearly and thus see beyond their preconceived ways of thinking.

Freedom and Determinism

Freedom and determinism? We need to understand this dialectic if we are to think clearly.

We are free to make choices. The range of our choices, however, is limited. Heredity and socio-cultural heritage limit our options. Every free choice we make determines a wide range of future options. Many decisions we make are irreversible, while others can be reversed. So the development and character of life is determined by heritage, circumstances beyond our control, and personal decisions made within these limits.

We are and are becoming the embodiment of the dialectical interaction of these three factors. These are the elements that comprise the bipolar tension between determinism and freedom.

We are free to choose neither our genetic makeup nor our social heritage. My immediate heritage involves the Great Depression and World War II, rural southern Oklahoma, and small Baptist churches. My more distant heritage includes poverty-stricken, uneducated, Scots-Irish farmers who fled the Irish Potato Famine and became Appalachian hillbillies. I had no more choice in any of this than I did of the genes that gave me a tall, slender frame, blue eyes, and an introverted personality.

If you were born in Vietnam in the 1960s, the daughter of a United States Marine and a Vietnamese mother who, before the war, had lived in a well-to-do home, your heritage would be quite different from mine. Perhaps now you live in Caldwell, Kansas where your husband has become a successful realtor, and you are an active member of the PTA. In your mind and heart, you are still Buddhist.

Your thinking and mine will come from widely differing starting points. Although it is unlikely, it is possible that we might find common ground and come to similar conclusions for similar reasons. This could happen only after many dialectical considerations.

None of us chooses our heritage, yet it is an inescapable element of our body, soul, and mindset. It provides the fundamental framework within which we find our personal options for making decisions.

Heritage precedes and predetermines our present situation. Like heritage, we have no control over circumstance. Circumstance includes all the factors that surround our present life. Heritage is past, circumstance is present. It continually is forming and re-forming our character. Whether we live in Zimbabwe, western Pakistan, New Zealand, Japan, Haiti, or Canada, place and society affect our being.

Our circumstance may be war or wonderful peace, dire poverty or worry-free comfort, loving parents or a dysfunctional family. We may have in-laws in prison and others who should be, or we may have married into the most loved and respected family in town. It matters not what our circumstances might be, they are involved in the dialectical process that defines who we are.

Heritage and circumstance cannot be changed, but we have some degree of freedom in choosing how we respond to these external factors, factors that establish the boundaries enclosing our options. Will we accept or reject the guidance of parents, school, and religion? Will we marry, divorce, or remain single? Who will we marry? (She or he also will have a choice in the matter.) How much schooling? Will we take care of our health, abuse it, or take it for granted? Do we choose and pursue life goals or, like driftwood, go wherever the current takes us or drops us? Do we live for the moment or do we take the longer view of life?

Heredity and circumstance limit our field of options—they may even limit our mental capacity for choice—but within these limitations, we are free to decide the course of our own lives.

Heredity and circumstance are external forces. They are among the "facts of life." But, as with all facts, we are free to interpret and frame them as we choose: "Two men looked out from prison bars; one saw mud and one saw stars." To a degree, the facts of our lives are what we make of them, how we see them. You and I alone ultimately are responsible.

Now, one last consideration about our freedom to decide ourselves: every choice has rejections riding along piggyback. If you choose to marry Fumie, you have determined that neither Linda, Ming Ling, Dorta, nor anyone else can ever be your first wife. If you marry Fumie, you have rejected the option of being a lifelong bachelor. Every yes is a no to something else. Each decision we freely make determines many of our future options, some of which—for better or worse—are irreversible.

Moreover, remember, it is always you who are doing the thinking, the particular you that, in the light of all the above, you have become at this point. Too often, that is a hand we fail to consider. You and I alone ultimately are responsible.

PART TWO

Consider Foreseeable Consequences: Think Logically

CHAPTER EIGHT

Let's Be Reasonable About It

Without logic, our thought is always at risk—the risk of inconsistency, the risk that our ideas will not fit together but rather will contradict each other, the risk of becoming a mere hobgoblin of ideas like a cluttered garage. Logic is about consistency, about how things do or do not fit together. Above all, it is about what can or cannot follow from any given starting point.

Contrary to popular belief, everything is logical. Later, I will have more to say about this claim. Meanwhile, since everything follows from something else, anything is open to logical clarification.

Logic is not different from the Dialectic. It is a particular and rigorous instance of dialectical thinking. (Interestingly, math is a particular and extremely rigorous instance of logic.)

If we are going to talk about good thinking, that means that we will of necessity deal with logical thinking. Conventional wisdom says that good thinking is either logical or critical thinking. Yes, but it is more than this. We have seen that good thinking is dialectical thinking, considerate thinking. Good thinking is OTOH, BOTOH. On the other hand, logic, like bipolar thinking, is a particular form of the Dialectic. Although critical thinking—a ubiquitous but ambiguous concept, however you define it—is not what good thinking is *all* about, it is one part, one that we shall ignore because it is already implicit in all this book says.

The Dialectic is the only way to become a good thinker, but, on the other hand, logic is a valuable assistant. As noted earlier, in the Sears, Roebuck and Co. catalogs of the 1930s and '40s, many items were available in three different qualities and priced accordingly:

good, better, and best. For instance, we could buy a "good" shirt, or a "better one," or their "best." The Dialectic will make us good thinkers. If we add logic, we can become better thinkers. Part Three of the book will explore how we can become the best thinkers possible.

A mere smattering of logic will make a good thinker better. The better we understand logic, the better thinkers we will become. The path we have traveled getting acquainted with the Dialectic has been an easy road, the curves gentle, and although we have been climbing slowly uphill, we've scarcely noticed it. As we turn to a consideration of some of the most useful elements of logic, the road will rise sharply and be a bit bumpy in places. We may have to negotiate a muddy spot or two, but this is a road I've been traveling for many years and I will guide you the entire way.

I should acknowledge something that you may have recognized many pages earlier, that is, that many people by nature are considerate thinkers. The ideas discussed thus far have not been new. So it will be with logic. Some of us are naturally logical. Therefore, some of us are naturally good thinkers (I am not one of those). Some of us are even better than good, just as some are naturally good listeners and thus, good counselors, and some have natural agility, coordination, and vigor, and, thus, are good athletes.

But these all benefit from training. Although a person might be by nature a considerate thinker, one who always considers other possibilities and perspectives, once they understand the nature of the Dialectic, they can think more quickly, easily, and profoundly. So it is with logic. With a little training, they can move to a new level of confidence in their reasoning.

The development of a logical attitude and a little logical skill can go a long way. Both are needed. We will try to establish both, logical attitude and skills. Logic is primarily a guide to consistency in our thinking. It can validate our ideas. It is a way to check whether these ideas can be trusted. Thus, it is an invaluable antithesis to the basic Dialectic.

We are going to explore only the most useful points of logic's landscape. We will be bypassing many of the more popular stops where serious students of logic spend a good bit of time. If your interest is stimulated, there are good books that cover what we will miss. On the other hand, most logic textbooks devote their attention primarily to symbolic logics that are highly sophisticated, but for ordinary people such as you and me, are fairly useless. We don't need that. We have enough on our minds without adding unneeded clutter.

What Is Logic?

So we turn to logic. Logic is about the consequences of our thinking. It demonstrates and/or validates the progression of our thought. On one hand, it calls on us to consider the foundations of our thought and, on the other hand, it examines the validity of their relation to each other and to the conclusions drawn from them.

Logic is simple. Or, it can be as complex as you want to get. We will keep it at its simplest without becoming simplistic.

All logic begins with an "if." Logic, like math, has no content. One plus one equals two, but math (one form of logic) cannot answer the question, "one plus one what?" Are we talking about ducks, trucks, spoons, or senators? Math neither knows nor cares. All it can tell us is that "if" you have one truck and buy another, you then have two trucks, but math knows nothing about trucks, gardens, boyfriends, or mopeds. Logic, like math, has no content.

Logic is about "if" and its possibilities. It is about what follows "if." If such and such is true, then logic tells us the consequences: what follows, must follow, cannot follow, might follow, probably will or will not follow. In some cases, it tells us there is no way to know what will follow. So the fundamental form of all logic is "if, then." If this, then that: for sure, impossible, maybe or maybe not.

(If, at this point, you are not prepared to do some serious learning, this chapter and chapter nine can be skipped without noticing the loss. But there will be loss.)

Conditional Reasoning

If Sybil's dress is black, then it is a dark dress—necessarily so.

If Sybil's dress is dark, then it probably is black or navy—a good probability, but not necessarily so.

If Sybil is thirty-five and drives to Anne's wedding in a Mercedes, then we can assume she has a driver's license—very likely, but not necessarily so.

If she drives up in a late model Mercedes, then we know she is rich—could be, but it could belong to her rich uncle who let her borrow it.

If our Sybil owns a new Mercedes, then, for breakfast, she had yogurt, figs, fresh turnip slices, and a demitasse of Café Cubano. Huh? What does a Mercedes have to do with an exotic breakfast? No relationship at all that I can think of.

Logic is about the relationship between the if and the then. As above, the car we own has no connection with a breakfast. Logicians call such a statement about an automobile and breakfast, a *non sequitur*—it "does not follow."

I've taught logic for thirty-some years and finally have come to realize that it can be defined most comprehensively and cogently as "the way of studying *what follows*." Logic is ordinarily—and appropriately—defined as the study of argument, of reasoning, of inference, and/or of proof. It is all of these, but they are merely variant ways of saying it is the study of what follows.

The value of logic is that it has precise ways of determining whether our thinking is valid. For now, one example of its precision will do. What follows is a standard logical form. It can be trusted to tell us what follows.

If Rosalinda and George are living together, then they are married.

As a matter of fact, they have been living together for six years.

Therefore, they are married.

How do we test this argument? (In logic, an argument is a series of statements, one of which is a conclusion drawn from the others.) If the first statement—the "if, then" statement—is true, and if the second statement is true, the "therefore" statement must be true. There is no possibility for the conclusion to be false *if* the previous two statements are true. For the present purpose, it is irrelevant that, in the twenty-first century, the first statement in our example about Rosalinda and George is not necessarily true. Logic simply tells us what would follow if it were true.

Any line of reasoning that takes the form illustrated above leads to a necessarily true conclusion if (in logic, remember, there is always the "if") the first statement (the major premise) is true and if the second statement (minor premise) affirms the truth of the if clause (the antecedent), then a conclusion that affirms the then clause (the consequent) is necessarily true. It does not matter what content our "if, then" statement includes. If we follow the *form*, the *pattern* of the previous paragraph, and if the "if, then" statement (major premise) is true, the conclusion must be true.

Logic, however, can tell us nothing about the truth of our premises. We have to establish that by some means other than logic: accepting an authoritative source, common sense, experience, or by consensus. All logic knows is that if certain things are true, and if they are stated in a standard logical form, then it has the tools and techniques to test the truth of what follows. (There are many standard forms of logic, most of which we will ignore in this book.)

For now, let's look at three other arrangements of the previous relations.

If Rosalinda and George are living together, then they are married.

They are not married.

Therefore, they are not living together.

Again, this conclusion is necessarily true, *if* the major premise is true (even though in the twenty-first century, it is not true, but remember, logic works with "ifs.") Now we have seen two valid forms of conditional reasoning. When the minor premise affirms the "if" clause (the antecedent), then a conclusion which states the "then" statement is necessarily—no way out of it—true. On the other hand, as we have seen, if the minor premise denies the truth of the "then" clause (the consequent), then a conclusion that denies the "if" statement is necessarily true.

These are the two forms of the argument that, if supplied with a true major premise, can render a conclusion that must be true. We might call these two forms: 1) Affirming the Antecedent; and 2) Denying the Consequent. That simple language might be worth the effort taken to memorize it and how it works.

Conditional reasoning has two forms that are invalid. Invalid simply means that any argument set in these forms cannot be depended upon to give us truth in the conclusion. Here is one form. We can call it, Denying the Antecedent. It would look like this:

If Rosalinda and George are living together, then they are married.

They are not living together.

Therefore they are not married.

I hope you can see that this conclusion might be either true or false, and the argument given is of no help in knowing which. It is an invalid form. It does not lead to a dependable conclusion.

A second invalid form is Affirming the Consequent. It looks like this:

If Rosalinda and George are living together, then they are married.

They are married.

Therefore, they are living together.

Who knows? If we want to know whether they are living together, we would have to check it out for ourselves because this invalid argument tells us nothing dependable.

I will not attempt to take us further into logic at this time. If you want to understand what you've just read, it will be necessary for you to stop reading, review, and make up ten conditional arguments of your own and try them in all four forms. Write them down. Here is one to start you off.

If those kids are still up watching television, then they are in trouble.

(Are they still up?)

Therefore, (Are they in trouble?)

You may think you already understand, but logic is like learning to play a musical instrument or learning a foreign language. We cannot fully understand, nor will the mere intellectual understanding be useful unless it is put into repeated practice. Ultimately, we want it to become a habitual pattern.

The Dilemma

Sondra Miller owed $8,700 on her Visa card—credit limit $10,000. Some months she could not even pay the interest. Her Ford Excel—torn upholstery, sagging headliner, and slick tires—was overheating, and she still owed Arredondo's Automotive $273.41 from three months ago. Yesterday, she got a cutoff notice from the water department. Dr. Sondra Miller, Dean of Social Sciences at Martin Luling College, had gotten herself into a bit of a bind.

Her twenty-two-year-old daughter, Mercy, divorced, had moved in with her three months ago. Eighteen-month-old Cerise came along as part of the homecoming package.

At Martin Luling, however, things were going well for Sondra. Besides administrative responsibilities, deans were required to teach three courses each semester. The classroom was her living room. As soon as she stepped into the room with thirty-seven students of experimental psychology, all her troubles evaporated. Nothing in the world existed except Sondra, psychology, and her students.

Moreover, as a dean, administration had come easy for her. This was her thirteenth year at the college, the past four as dean. No one on campus understood the school—big picture and detail—as well as Dr. Miller. She was the most respected and most loved person on campus. Three years ago, she was named, "faculty member of the year." Although she was a good administrator, and somewhat enjoyed it, the only reason she had accepted the deanship was financial.

Her money problems had begun four years ago when Jeff left her to marry a girl he had met at the workout center. Divorce left her with only a small remainder of the long division—a common condition of divorced women.

One morning, Dr. Pulaski, the president, had asked her to step into the vacancy left recently by the departure of Dr. Eichenbury. "Ike" had been Academic Vice-President for eleven years. A $12,500 raise would accompany the promotion if she accepted. Sondra asked for a couple of days to consider it.

Sondra Miller was a good thinker, except she had never had much interest in financial matters. Now she had to think about money.

She had no choice but to accept the raise and run with it. Or, so it seemed. However, she reminded herself, we *always* have choices.

If she accepted, there were strong negatives to take account of. As a full-time administrator she would not be teaching, and teaching, she believed, was what supplied oxygen to her soul. And, as a vice-president, she would be committed to all the policies of the administration, whether or not she agreed with them.

But, she thought, she would have a voice in the policies and procedures of the college. She knew what changes needed to be made, and how to make them come about. Surely, she could negotiate some of them into policy. The $12,500 was shedding its light over all her considerations. Two years at that salary and she could be solvent. Almost.

As she felt the strong pulls from the yes and the no, she realized that she was facing a standard-form logical dilemma. The dilemma is a deductive argument—a valid form—therefore, if the premises are true, the conclusion must be true.

The dilemma is a set form, useful when we are faced with two alternatives. Ordinarily a dilemma refers to two alternatives, both of which are unpleasant.

The dilemma has the following logical form:

Either one thing *or another*.
If one thing, *then* consequent A would occur.
If another thing, *then* consequent B would occur.
Therefore, either A or B.

As she had done so often in the past, Sondra pushed the supper dishes to the side, picked up pen and paper from the nearby telephone table, and wrote this:

Either, Or
If … , Then
If … , Then
Therefore, Either Or

Either I say yes or no to the president's offer.

If I say yes, then I will have money, can make an impact on the entire school, and acquire greater prestige, but also, I would lose the classroom and freedom of speech.

If I say no, then financial disaster looms. But on the other hand, I *am* a teacher. That is not a role I fill, that is who I am. (There are other considerations, but these dominate.)

Therefore, I either take the money I so desperately need, and lose my soul or I enjoy a life of deep satisfaction and live like a pauper—dumpster-diving and all—sell my house and get a cheap apartment.

One of the good things about writing out a dilemma is that it shows that you have choices, and clarifies what they are. The dilemma is a valid logical form. That means that *if* the premises are true, the conclusion reveals your only options. But at least you have two to choose between.

Sondra felt better now that her dilemma was laid out in writing because she knew that dilemmas could be challenged. When faced with a dilemma, we have three options available.

Faced with the threat from the dilemma bull's two horns—either/or—we can grab one horn, hoping it is weak, and break it. If we can prove one side of the dilemma is false, or less than the whole truth, or partly truth and partly fiction, we may not be as badly off as we think. We may have been able to break one horn and escape its threat.

Potentially, either horn can be broken. In Sondra's case, she thought, "Whether the dilemma bull attempts to hook me with the left horn or the right, I can grab it, because now I see that if I say yes, I don't have to give up teaching. I would lose the classroom, but for years I have made notes for a book on the psychology of the World Wide Web. I can write and teach more people with a book than would ever enroll in my class.

"On the other hand, if I say no, I can persuade Mercy that if she and Cerise are going to live with me, Mercy must get a job. She would have no problem finding work, and if she could contribute at least a thousand dollars a month, that would almost match the raise Dr. Pulaski has offered me."

A second option, when dealing with a dilemma, is to go between the horns—jump over the bull's head and not be gored at all. Is there a way between the horns? Is this an either/or situation, or are there other options? If we can show that it is not a simple "on the one hand or on the other hand" circumstance, we can think like an octopus and come up with at least a third *hand*, a third option, maybe more.

Sondra considers telling President Pulaski that she would be happy to take a year or two off from the classroom and serve as an interim or temporary vice-president, then go back to the classroom. The break might be good for her. Besides, with a couple of years of that big money, she might be able to become solvent and find ways to lower her standard of living without too much sacrifice. This would take her between the horns: neither "yes" nor "no," but, "for a while."

A third option, perhaps the default option, is the knowledge that if the dilemma can't be compromised, she is still left with a choice. There are alternatives. She can decide which is the lesser of the two evils and comfort herself with the realization that she will not have to cope with the frustrations and pain of the greater evil.

Maybe most of us could settle this easily in our gut, without reducing it to a formal dilemma for analysis. I, however, do this rather often—several times in writing this book—and have found it quite helpful in clearing my mind. I settle my quandaries with a relatively cool head and find myself at peace with a decision that has been given deliberate consideration.

Either P or Q
If P, then R
If Q, then S
Therefore, either R or S

Three approaches to dealing with a true dilemma: break a horn, go between the horns, or take your choice of the conclusions. Quite simple and clear. Think of three or four dilemmas of your own, write them down, and try it.

Deduction's Major Flaw

All the arguments we have dealt with are *deductive*. In a deductive argument, whether conditional, categorical [see Appendix], or dilemma, if the premises are true and the form valid, the conclusion *must* be true. We call such an argument a *sound* argument. A sound argument is a deductive argument with true premises and a valid form.

We now know how to test for validity. But what do we do about the premises? Where do they come from? Can we prove them to be true? The only way to offer public proof that any statement is necessarily true is to demonstrate that it is the conclusion of a sound argument. But if our premises are the result of prior deductive arguments, we could go back infinitely without finding certainty.

All our common sense of truth and all scientific proof of truth are rooted in a different kind of logic: induction. Induction cannot give certainty, it can only provide probabilities. Probability, however, proves to be the law of life, the source of all our truth claims.

Psychologically, it would seem that we must have at least a few certainties as the foundation for our thinking, but logic fails us in this quest for certainty. It may be that we have to build our lives on something other than unshakable, absolute truths. We build our lives on what we believe to be true—our convictions.

We turn now to investigate inductive reasoning.

CHAPTER NINE

Probable Truth

Induction

The philosopher Bertrand Russell told a story to introduce inductive logic. I have adapted Russell's story for that same purpose. My version, however, is more elaborate than his.

In early May, Hoot Shoemake bought fifty two-day-old Rhode Island Red chicks, as he did every spring. When they outgrew the brooder, he moved them into a coop out in the barnyard. Every day about sundown, he would lock them in the coop so they would be secure from raccoons, coyotes, foxes, owls, and other nighttime predators. In the morning, a little before sunup, he would let them out, give them fresh water and feed, and let them run and play, scratch for bugs, and chase grasshoppers. In the evening, he would shut them back into their nighttime security. This was the daily pattern.

June came and then July. Life was wonderful, especially for the little chick that Hoot's daughter, Kaycee, had named "Rhoda." When it was dark, she was always securely locked in and huddled up close to the rest of the little flock. When it was light, she was always free to run, play, scratch, chase grasshoppers, and enjoy fresh water and all she wanted to eat. As far as she could remember, this had been the pattern for every day of her life. Therefore, inductively, when daylight came one morning and Rhoda heard Hoot's footsteps coming, she knew what the day would bring. Except ...

Except that all days are not created equal. Some days are exceptional. What little chicken Rhoda didn't know was that this was

Sunday, July 11, and the Shoemake family had invited the preacher to eat lunch with them. So she was surprised, no, shocked, when, as she stepped out the door of the coop, she felt a wire hook around her leg. Her world turned upside down, then went black as Hoot's huge hand enclosed her head, then everything went awhirl as Hoot began to wring her neck. The next thing you knew, Rhoda had entered the ministry.

(Kaycee cried and would not come to the table. Hoot hadn't realized that, out of all the young chickens, he had caught, and then his wife, Connie, had fried and served up, Kaycee's Rhoda.)

Chicken Rhoda had extremely good reason—at least for the information she had available—to believe that today would be no different from all the other days of her life. It is the same with us. When we go to bed tonight, we are certain that, if we live through the night, we will see daylight again tomorrow and dark tomorrow night.

Yet, the only reason we have to believe this is inductive. This has happened every day of our lives, and so far as we can determine, it has been so throughout history. We have very good reason to believe in the twenty-four-hour cycling of daylight and dark. But we do not have deductive certainty, because tomorrow is not included in any of our premises.

Sound deductive arguments must have conclusions that are totally dependable because, and only because, they have a valid form and the conclusion is already implicit, is already contained, in its true premises. Inductive conclusions always go beyond their premises— sometimes they make a large leap, but on the other hand, sometimes it is only a very small step. I live in central Texas. When in August we have eight days straight with the temperature over 100°, it is a very small step to the conclusion that tomorrow will be hot.

What about the following argument? "Traffic can be dangerous, especially for pedestrians, therefore, the next time my neighbor Gordon Smith walks across the street, he will be hit by a car." This is a very weak argument. Gordon is a man in his fifties and has walked across streets all his life. On the other hand, the next time he crosses the street is, at present, only a possibility in our mind. We have no way of knowing with certainty what will happen.

"The next time Gordon crosses the street, he will be hit and killed by a drunk driver." This is a much weaker argument. Again, although inductive arguments may be strengthened or weakened, they lead only to probabilities. And that may be good enough. It may be all we can ever have. Strong inductive arguments give us probabilities that may provide sufficient foundations for thinking and living.

Unfortunately, in induction, there are few ways to test the form of an argument.

One last note. In the argument, "The next time my neighbor Gordon Smith walks across the street, he will be hit by a car," do we have any *reason* to believe this? Although it is highly improbable, it is a possibility. It is completely reasonable to believe that a person crossing a street might be hit by a car. It does happen.

I wrote this page two weeks before the 2008 United States presidential election. In the Electoral College, 270 votes are needed to elect a president. At that time, Barack Obama appeared to have 277 electoral votes committed.

Inductive reasoning, from these premises, would conclude that Obama would win the presidency. This conclusion was probable, but, unlike with deductive thinking, there could be no certainty that Obama would be elected. Unlike deduction, an inductive argument can be strengthened or weakened by additional premises. So, for example, if Obama were to have become involved in a major scandal, or a psychotic breakdown, or if all undecided voters were to have decided to vote for John McCain, then these added premises would make the conclusion that Obama would win the presidency less probable. But, if all states leaning toward McCain had turned to Obama, this would have made the conclusion highly probable, but as long as there was even a slight chance for failure, there could be no certainty. (As a matter of fact, I wrote this page on the night of the third presidential debate. Just moments before, national polls indicated that Obama had won the debate. He was judged to have won all three debates. If this had been added to the argument it would have been immediately stronger, more probable.)

If you have read all of the book up to this page, inductively I can know some things about you: I can conclude that you probably will read the rest of the book; you probably read several books a year; and the life of the mind is probably important to you. Induction may not give us certainty, but it does give us knowledge.

"That's All There Is to It?"

"No, I don't want a cat or a dog. I don't want a pet of any kind. You have to feed and water them every day. They've got you trapped almost like you were in jail. You can't just up and leave for a few days without making arrangements for someone to care for them. Vacations are out. Those are the facts and that's all there is to it. Stop trying to talk me into getting a pet."

"No, Rita, that's not all there is to it. Besides those are not facts."

By now, we have learned that no matter what is said about anything, we can never say, "That's all there is to it." No, the Dialectic has told us that there is always more that can be said, more to be considered.

"Rita, think about this. You are sixty-seven years old and living alone. You're always talking about how depressed you get. Well, let me tell you … No, just let me tell you a few things about pets. You talk about facts. It's a fact that people with pets live longer and suffer much less from depression. You spend a lot of time watching television, so I know you have time to feed and water a cat. A lot of people with pets talk to them and they say it does almost as much good as an expensive counselor.

"Here's another thing. Many people take their pets with them when they travel. There are motels these days that have accommodations for pets.

"Maybe those excuses you made are facts, maybe not. We need to talk some other time about what facts are. Sometimes, I think they merely represent a strong consensus about something. They may be nothing more than agreed upon stories. However, that's another issue for another time. But you can't shut off discussion by simply saying, 'That's all there is to it.'" There are always other things to be considered."

"Look, Lou, my dear butinsky friend, I'm not going to argue with you about it. When I said, 'That's all there is to it,' what I meant was, I don't want a pet, and I'm not going to get a pet. That's a true fact, and that's all I'm going to say about it. I'm not going to listen to any more. End of subject."

Now Rita has revealed her real reason. It has nothing to do with the meaning of "that's all there is to it," nor is there any point in debating facts. She simply doesn't want a pet any more than she wants to go on a diet of cabbage and black beans. Rita has the right to her choices.

But, "that's all there is to it?" Never. I am writing this on Friday night, September 12, 2008. For two days now, with the approach of the huge Hurricane "Ike," people on the Texas and Louisiana coasts have been told by the National Weather Service to evacuate certain low-lying areas. Now they are being told that if they stay, it will mean certain death. Implicitly, they are saying, "If you remain in your homes, you face certain death, and that's all there is to it." Says who? In all probability, that warning tells it like it is. It remains, however, only probability.

A regular feature of the news media is the story of someone who has survived the impossible. I hope there will be survivors of this hurricane who can tell their story, indicating that there was more to it than common sense could imagine. (There were such survivors.)

Induction/Deduction Complementary

I thought I was having a heart attack. I had just gotten out of an eleven o'clock class and was in my office talking with a student when I began noticing a slight, but definite pain in the center of my chest. It continued. I tried deep breathing, but it only got worse. I was no longer giving the student my full attention.

The pain became so severe that, in an attempt to find relief, I lay down on the floor, flat on my back. By then, I had told the student what was going on. Lying down, still breathing deeply, the pain only worsened. My student suggested I go either to see my doctor or to the emergency room.

I drove straight to the doctor, and was lucky enough to catch him in his office during the noon hour. First, the stethoscope, then other tests, but in the end he concluded that my heart was perfectly okay. My problem, he said, was "acid reflux." From a shelf, he took a bottle of Maalox and told me to take three or four swallows. I did, and in a few minutes felt fine. He gave me a sample bottle, told me to buy some—liquid or tablet—and take it whenever I felt the earliest symptoms.

A year or two later, the same thing occurred after I had gone to bed late one night. The pain got so serious and scary that I was certain it was a heart attack. Time had passed and I had forgotten about the Maalox. I drove to the emergency room, only to have them tell me the same thing Dr. Cutbirth had told me on the earlier occasion. Across the past thirty-some years, I have had this same experience at least two or three times a year. Maalox, always, has brought immediate relief.

Since my mid-thirties, I have had numerous physical examinations—the most recent being last month. Without exception, I have been told that I have the heart and circulatory system of an eighteen year old.

Based on these premises, I have drawn the conclusion that whenever I have chest pain, it is not my heart, but rather, acid reflux. If the chest pain is not accompanied by pain going down my left arm and perhaps nausea and upset stomach, I know that acid reflux is causing the problem. How do I know? Inductive reasoning has proven it so highly probable that, as far as I'm concerned, it is the truth.

Therefore, I know, deductively, that when I experience chest pains, even in the earliest stages, Maalox will relieve the pain. Let's look at this in two valid standard deductive forms.

If I have chest pains, then the cause is acid reflux.

On occasion, I have chest pains.

Therefore, on those occasions, the cause is acid reflux.

In this conditional argument, the minor premise affirms the antecedent of the major premise, yielding a true conclusion. The premises were arrived at by inductive reasoning that yielded such high probability that I treated them as true statements. I reasoned deductively from them to the solution to my problem. This is an instance of a common logical procedure: induction and deduction working together.

The chain of conditional deduction continues:

If I experience the pain of acid reflux, then Maalox will bring relief.

Occasionally, I experience the pain of acid reflux.

Therefore, I occasionally take Maalox and find quick relief.

This interplay between induction and deduction is the norm of our thinking. They are not competing alternatives; rather, they are complementary.

Now we can clarify the core distinction between deductive and inductive reasoning. Deductive arguments, if their premises are true and their form valid, always yield a true conclusion, but give us essentially no new knowledge. They merely make explicit what is already implicit in the premises. On the other hand, the conclusion of an inductive argument always goes beyond the truth of the premises. It gives us new, although only probabilistic, knowledge.

Gerald lives in a high-class house on Gray Fox Lane, and maintains a beautifully groomed lawn of St. Augustine grass.

Tyson and Teresa live two doors down, in a comparable house and with comparable lawn.

Tony and Lou live next door to Tyson and Teresa and have the finest and most traditional house and lawn on the street.

The same general pattern applies to all the houses across the street and down the next block.

Therefore, inductively, we conclude that Jess and Mary Beth, who live next door to Gerald and in a similar house, have a well-cared-for St. Augustine lawn.

This is highly probable, but not necessarily true. It goes beyond the premises. It may only be a short step beyond, but it may jump to the wrong conclusion. Actually, Jess and Mary Beth's lawn looks like a field of prairie grass.

Thus, induction cannot give us conclusions that are necessarily true or false. Induction yields only probability—degrees of probability from highly probable to highly improbable. Induction cannot produce certainty.

Deduction cannot deliver certainty unless we already have certainty about our premises. But where did we get that certainty? Most of the time, our "true" premises have been established by inductive reasoning—which of course has not established "truth," but only strong enough probability to convince us of its truth.

Few things seem as important to us as certainty, the belief that there are some things we can be sure of. It would seem that we must have some certainties to serve as the foundation for all our thinking, but logic fails us in this quest for certainty. It may be that we have to build our lives on something other than unshakable, absolute truths.

Much like inhalation and exhalation, deduction and induction are complementary. We can't inhale fresh air until we first exhale the carbon dioxide from our lungs. We can't exhale if we have not first filled our lungs with fresh air.

We cannot think deductively unless we have premises to reason from. Most of our premises are the result of inductive thinking. When, inductively, we have reached conclusions that are highly probable, we treat them as though they were obvious truths. We know, for instance, that if we turn the water faucet on, water will come out from the spigot. We commonly treat this as a certainty.

I am writing now on our granddaughter's computer in Arlington, Texas. We drove up here a couple of days ago, and intend to leave for home soon after lunch today. I know how long it will take to drive home. How do I know? Since 1974, we've made this drive more than two hundred times. When nothing goes wrong, we drive it in two and a half hours. If we have to make a brief stop or two along the way, it sometimes takes as much as three hours. When we came up this past Thursday, we drove it in two hours and forty-five minutes.

Using the past trips as premises, and assuming them to be true, deductive logic concludes that our trip this afternoon must necessarily take between two and a half and three hours (unless we make some unusual stops). So I can plan today's trip, knowing how much time to schedule.

What we've seen is that we commonly combine deduction and induction in a single reasoning process. Each plays a necessary part.

Logic Revisited

Remember that all logic begins with an "if." Therefore, it all begins with "on the other hand." If, in deductive reasoning, our premises are true and the form valid, the conclusion must be true. But only "if" the premises are true and "if" the form is valid. On the other hand, if they are not, our reasoning is flawed. If we are reasoning inductively and our argument leads to a highly probably conclusion, it is always possible that, on the other hand, we have ignored one or more factors that, when added, destroy or greatly weaken the probability of our conclusion. On the other hand, we might add one premise that would make our argument even stronger.

Logic can only judge the trustworthiness of the *way* we reason. It knows nothing about the content of our arguments. It is extremely difficult, if not impossible, to prove anything as true-without-question. Our truths are drawn from whatever or whoever we trust, from what we have chosen to believe is true. Always there is the possibility that we are wrong. *Trooth* is what we decide to *troost*. All logical reasoning starts with pre-logical beliefs and assumptions.

It remains true that all human statements are incomplete, there is always more to be said, and, it is always possible that we might be wrong. The purpose of the Dialectic, including the logical dialectic, is to help us do a better job of approximating truth, of coming ever closer to positions we can depend on. We become considerate thinkers in order to arrive at positions that we all—at least most of us—are willing to accept as truth, a consensus of belief. Ultimately, considerate thinking is about developing a common-unity; it is social in nature. In one sense, it is only in community, only as a social process, that good thinking can take place.

In Aimee and David Thurlos' novel, *White Thunder*, a strange attack has been made on Navajo Police Special Investigator, Ella Clah's life. The authors note that for Clah, so much of the bad side of human being and action made no sense, seemed illogical.

It often looks like that, doesn't it? Things simply don't make sense. Often there appears to be no logical explanation for things that happen or the way people are, but as we all know, things are not always what they seem to be. Appearance can be deceptive; reality can remain hidden from our eyes and our minds.

When our family moved to Texas thirty-five years ago, I began noticing an unusual, but apparently very popular, bumper sticker: "There Must Be a Reason." This both interested and confused me. It interested me because I am a teacher of logic. Logic is the study of reasoning so I readily agreed that "there must be a reason." No matter how enigmatic anything may seem to be, there is a reason for everything. Nothing happens without a cause. But the bumper sticker confused me because that was all it had to say. There was no fine print. There were no images. Just the philosophical statement: "There Must Be a Reason."

I doubted that this was a particularly philosophical town we had moved to, so why would cars by the dozen have a bumper sticker that was merely philosophical? That didn't make sense to me. The day finally came when, in a parking lot, I saw a lady getting out of a car with the ubiquitous bumper statement. I stepped over and asked her for an explanation.

She said it was to arouse curiosity and cause people like to me to ask for the meaning. The answer was that this was an incomplete statement. It required a living person to complete it, so she completed it for me: "There must be a reason why everyone banks at First National Bank." I guess that was good enough for me because I have banked there for more than thirty years and the institution has gone through five different names. At present, it is Bank of America. There must be reasons for these changes.

No, Ella Clah, the bad side of human being does make sense. And is logical. I've said there are reasons for everything. Everything can be understood logically. Remember, logic is both simply and comprehensively understood as: "The study of what follows."

The attempt on Clah's life followed someone's intentional decision. It could be anything from revenge to part of a rite of initiation into a violent gang. If it was not preceded by some intentional decision, then it was an accident. Accidents, however, follow some kind of failure: carelessness; a break in the steering linkage of a vehicle; or a hunter mistaking a person for a deer. Something lay behind the threat to Investigator Clah's life. Some perverse or accidental premise led to the conclusion that almost caused her death. She understood none of this at the time, but when Clah had done enough investigation, she would understand that someone had a logical reason, based on *their* premises, to want her dead.

The main reason we fail to see the logic in things is that we have our own beliefs and ways of seeing the world, ways that cause us to prejudge what can and cannot make sense. Therefore, we find it difficult to realize how different the experience of reality can be if people have different beliefs and ways of seeing the world than we do. If we can't see where they are coming from, many things do seem to defy logic.

Everything is logical, but it always depends on where things are coming from, on what premises we are prepared to accept. For instance, some of the mentally ill commonly think more logically that most of us. The problem is not with their logic, but with their beliefs and the way in which they see the world. If we accepted their premises, we would see how all their behavior makes good sense. The rocket scientist has a different worldview from the safecracker; their actions follow from their worldviews.

If you were to ask me what might be the major premise from which malice and evil arise, I must confess that I am left with ultimate mystery. I am prepared to consider the entire dialectic of explanations that have been given. Nonetheless, none of our words of explanation will be the last word. There is more to be said than we can understand; the major premise of all reality, the whole shebang, lies hidden in mystery.

People often speak of "cold, hard logic," they speak as if good logic is the final arbiter, the last word on everything. But is logic cold and hard? Should it have the final say? Most of us, I suspect, would answer, "No." Logic has its place and value, but there are times you have to go with your heart, your gut feelings, go with what you intuitively know is right. Go, sometimes, with whimsy, and be open to recognize and accept the serendipitous. Life, people, and relationships are more important than facts, pure reason, and logical validity.

This would be true if we followed logic as it ordinarily is understood. Let's consider math, a symbolic branch of logic. Yes, one plus one equals two. If we have one 1 and add another 1, we have 11. If we add 11 to 11, then we have 1111. So, 1 + 1 can equal 11 and 11+11 could be understood to equal 1111. These are cold, hard facts that cannot be challenged. But what is 1? It is either part of the language of pure mathematics or it is unrelated to any specific thing in existence except as a symbol. It is unidimensional. It has no content. It is simple.

Reality, on the other hand, is polydimensional. It is complex. If, in the home, you have one woman—wife, mother, homemaker—and you bring into the house another woman—grandmother, mother-in-law, or an adult daughter moved back home—you now have two women in the house. One plus one equals two. That is a bare fact.

Unidimensional. But, particularly if the second woman is going to stay—for a few weeks, or months, or indefinitely—the addition of number two goes far beyond the mathematical logic of addition.

Let's put it in a standard logical form:

If one woman lives here and another moves in, then two women live here.

One woman lives here and another does move in.

Therefore, two women live here.

This is a conditional argument in which the minor premise affirms the antecedent of the major premise, thus, it is a valid argument. In fact, it is a sound argument so the conclusion is necessarily true. One plus one equals two, and that's all there is to it. It is a cold, hard fact.

But, as you have already recognized, there is much more to it than this unidimensional presentation takes into account. Common sense knows that, as a general rule, two women living under one roof equals conflict. If logic is the study of "what follows," then we should logically conclude that this is a formula for trouble.

Each woman is a polydimensional reality, their relationships are polydimensional, each day is polydimensional, and the physical makeup of the house, its design and decoration are polydimensional. If we take these statements as premises and draw from them a conclusion, we know that it is highly probable that this arrangement cannot work harmoniously across any extended period of time.

Except in a logic or math class, we never deal with purely unidimensional terms and statements. We live with the psycho-logical, socio-logical, anthropo-logical, theo-logical, bio-logical, and eco-logical patterns of life and thought. Since these all deal not with symbols, but with actualities, they deal with polydimensionality, and, thus, certainty is never available to us. If we pick out from these realities some single dimension, and from this reason our way to certainty, the Dialectic will remind us to consider on the other hand, the multitude of the other interrelated and interactive dimensions.

Although certainty always eludes our grasp, we can come to understand and predict enough to help us deal successfully with this entire mystery in which we live, and which we ourselves are. In Part Three we will now look into who we ourselves are.

PART THREE

Consider Who You Are and Who Want to Become: Think Purposively

CHAPTER TEN

You Are The Thinker

Anyone can become a good thinker; anyone can become a better thinker, but if we are to be the best thinker possible, we must be people of good character. Our character precedes all our thought processes. We may develop the Dialectic as our habitual way of thinking; we might even do the necessary work and practice to learn some basic logic and use it when it is appropriate. More important, however, than the Dialectic and logic is the person doing the thinking. I hope this book doesn't get into the hands of an embezzler or a burglar, a terrorist or a drug dealer, an unethical politician or businessman because I do not want them to become better thinkers at what they do. On the other hand, I suspect that if they became truly good thinkers, some of them would realize they needed to change their ways.

All our thought is ultimately determined by who we are. Have you ever taken time to think about who you are, about what has shaped your life thus far, and what you hope to become and accomplish. or have you gone with the flow, drifting through life? Do you know what things are most important to you? Among those things, do you know what is your ultimate concern? Do you know what you believe to be true? Do you have goals you are working toward? These things form your character, and your character determines the value of your thinking. This last part of the book concentrates not on how to think but on who the thinker is—who we are.

Who Are You?

Are you a person of character, or are you a "character," or are you without character? Do you have good character or bad? Are you a character that people admire, or an obnoxious character? What is character anyway, and doesn't everyone have it? Are there people without character? Yes, there are some, because character takes deliberate effort and time.

The root meaning of the word "character" comes from a verb that means to cut, or to carve; it was a originally sculptural term. A sculptor takes a formless piece of marble and patiently carves it into a definite shape. When the formless has been given deliberate design, distinctive new form, it is now a "character."

In the characters of Chinese calligraphy or the characters of the English alphabet—A, B, C, D, … X, Y, and Z—each has been given a carefully considered shape. We have no trouble distinguishing an E from a P or a 7. Characters are not accidental; they are formed intentionally. If we stay with the idea of sculpture—not in the sense of carving, but in the sense of giving form—we see that the sculptor can take a shapeless mound of clay and mold it into distinctive form.

When we speak of human character, then, we are not referring to any innate qualities. We are not born with character, nor do years automatically bestow it upon us. A human life is the material from which human character may be formed. But this character will result only from the conscious commitment and effort of the individual.

When we speak of someone as a person of character, we are referring to someone who has a distinctive and reliable personality, style, and set of values. Thus, we can speak of a person with good character, or speak of someone as a bad character.

Occasionally, we say of someone, "She's a real character." We are not saying they are good or bad, only that they are distinctive. A "character" will often come across as eccentric or maverick—apt to burst into song in the elevator or on the airplane, for example. She is someone who, in a noticeable way, differs from the ordinary. Characters get our attention. They may be repulsive, comical, challenging, disturbing, frightening, admirable, or enjoyable. They glow with audacity. They inspire our envy.

Some of them become great leaders: Churchill was a character, as, on the other hand, was Hitler; Harry Truman was a character, as was Mohandas Gandhi; country music star Grandpa Jones, of *Hee Haw* and *Grand Ole Opry* fame, was as much a character as Madonna is now. And Dennis Rodman is a character. Few would question that, but few would call him a man of character. And the best thinking is done by people with good character. So, how is character formed? Where does it begin, what are the processes, and how long does it take?

"Character" development takes effort and time. Maybe when you were young you went, as I did, to a summertime Vacation Bible School (VBS). One VBS activity I remember is that we were given a large bar of Ivory laundry soap and a knife, and we were told to carve something out of the soap—a dog, house, person, or whatever we might imagine. I remember that Ivory soap was easy to cut; it offered no resistance to the knife.

Later, in elementary school, we were given balsa wood to carve. Balsa is the softest wood there is. It is soft all the way through, easy to cut. Years later, there was a period in my life when I made several pieces of sculpture. I worked with soapstone, mesquite wood, sandstone, and clay. I was never serious enough to tackle marble, ebony, or limestone.

Soap and balsa are easy. Soapstone, closely akin to talc, is one of the softest minerals. It can be scratched by the fingernail, and on the Mohs scale of mineral hardness (which goes from 1–10, with diamonds being a 10) soapstone is a 1. Soapstone carves almost as easily as a bar of soap or balsa, but is much more beautiful and varied in color. Unlike these, however, it is not uniform in its softness. Flaws in the stone commonly threaten the development of the carving. It may split or crack, ruining the shape that was being formed, thus, destroying its character.

The materials that a sculptor gives character to are resistant, in varying degrees, to the carving tool. Soap is barely resistant. Mesquite is very resistant. It forces the sculptor to cooperate with the nature of this specific piece of wood. And granite is a hard material, recalcitrant to work with.

With patience and skill, all materials can be made to yield to the will of the artist, at least to a degree. The sculptor must come to know her material and cooperate with its dictates; the artist and the material contribute to the final character of the piece.

When we set about the work of human character formation, we must realize that we are working with a very recalcitrant material, the human soul. This is the reason it takes time. This is the reason it cannot be rushed. It is well known that talent and skills can be developed at very early ages, but character development is another matter entirely.

We may force the personality into a particular form, but when the force is removed, the soul springs back to its original loose, indeterminate condition. Only commitment, repetition, and time will make the necessary changes.

Conscience

Our conscience sets some of the boundaries of our thinking and actions. It tells us when we are in danger of going out of bounds, and shouts when we *are* out of bounds. Our conscience is that thing inside of us that makes us hurt when we violate our accepted—personally accepted—inner standard of thought or conduct. It threatens to hurt us if we near the margins of our standard. John Stuart Mill called it a feeling in our mind, a pain, more or less severe, that arises when we violate what we believe to be our duty. A well-developed conscience is such a strong deterrent as to make it almost impossible to violate it.

It seems to me that the conscience is similar to the "adult" of transactional analysis and the "super ego" of Freudian thought, the voice that sets limits for us and threatens us with pain if we ignore those limits. For a lot of us, society—that is, family, community, and/or society at large—functions as our conscience. We have learned that if we go off limits from the accepted standards of society, we suffer. Society has many kinds of sanctions to keep us within bounds, so we accept those standards because life is much more comfortable if we do.

Most people seem to believe that we are all born with a conscience that tells us right from wrong. Some think the conscience is innate, just as sight and hearing are inborn standard equipment that humans are issued by nature. Others believe that God has placed the conscience within us. While it may be true that we are born with the awareness that there is such a thing as the distinction between right and wrong, we cannot depend on an inborn conscience to tell us what to do in particular situations and circumstances.

It is not wise to advise, "Let your conscience be your guide." It depends on whom we are talking to. It is unwise because a little observation of humans in action demonstrates that the conscience is not inborn. Rather, it is acquired. Ordinarily, it is acquired by the process of socialization., as we take on and accept the standards that society imposes on us. We are unaware of most of this imposition. As with all socialization, it seems perfectly natural to unquestioningly accept these standards, whatever they might be.

The capacity to develop a conscience may be innate just as the capacity to speak is innate, but language does not come naturally. We acquire the language of our native community, and do the same with the conscience. However, we can learn other languages. In situations where we move and make our lifetime home within the culture of another language group, it is possible that a second language will displace our native language. Even within a given language, we can change our grammar, vocabulary, dialect, or accent. The point is that, like language, the conscience is plastic—it can be molded, formed, reshaped.

Most of what we do in our daily life is not obviously controlled by laws. We eat, sleep, shower, go shopping, and go to work, all with little need to be aware of any laws. When, however, we get in our motor vehicle and drive on public roads, we are immediately subject to traffic laws. These laws regulate traffic in order to make the roads as safe as possible and to facilitate the flow of traffic, but once we get out of the vehicle, we live apart from traffic laws.

Most of what we think and do in our daily lives is not controlled or regulated by conscience. For the most part, conscience ignores the way we comb our hair, what we eat for breakfast, or how many hours we sleep at night. When we are thinking about how to pay our bills, which college to attend, what message to leave on our answering machine, or whether to play scrabble or watch a video, our conscience stays in neutral. It is only when we think about moral and ethical matters that the flashing red and blue light of our conscience illuminates and the alarm goes off. Like the sight of the highway patrolman parked beside the road, the flashing conscience warns us that our thinking and its potential practice is regulated by a set of shoulds or should nots.

If we are thinking logically about whether our actions would be right or wrong, our conscience is an auxiliary premise that must always be reckoned with. We can go against our conscience the way we can ignore the traffic laws, but thinking about or doing either is always risky. If we ignore the law, we risk an automobile accident or a costly traffic ticket. If we override our conscience, we will be haunted by guilt, depressed by the violation of our own self-image, and possibly be subjected to the disapproval of our closest associates.

The conscience—like the traffic laws, or the rules of a game—can be set aside, but this cannot be done painlessly. Yet once we violate our conscience—or any other regulatory agency—it is easier to do it the second time. The conscience is malleable and can be given new shape. With time enough, it can even be erased. Of course, the person with *no* conscience at all—the sociopath, the person with an antisocial personality—can never be a trustworthy, socially responsible, or wise thinker.

If we are to be the best thinkers, we must guard our consciences.

Models

Usually, the sculptor works from a model that he uses as a guide for his own creation. Almost without exception, whether conscious of it or not, the person of character has seen or otherwise come to know of someone he admires and respects, then decided to pattern his own life after the chosen model. We are talking about more than a "role" model. We are talking about choosing a model for life.

Our model could be anyone from John Wayne to a favorite aunt, a teacher, an entertainer, a neighbor, or Jesus of Nazareth. The development of character begins with a chosen model. I repeat, we sometimes are unconscious of having chosen this model. At other times, we deliberately set out to form our lives from a consciously chosen model.

Personal character begins with our admiration of certain people. Our character starts its development when we are attracted to models, people we hope to become like. Often we find our models first at home. (I was twenty-four before I learned that I had always been my youngest brother's model.) We find our models on film, television, in books, and in a wide diversity of sometimes quite unexpected places. We don't all feel drawn to the same people. Some of us are attracted to a chess player, others to a teacher, or a fiddler, a dancer, or a deacon.

Before proceeding with the discussion of life models, I need to distinguish life models from role models, terms that are often, incorrectly, used interchangeably. French existentialist philosopher Jean-Paul Sartre said that most of us don't live authentic human lives. Rather, we live roles. We live roles we have chosen or had imposed on us.

Wanting to become lawyers, doctors, teachers, welders, hairdressers, or cooks, we go to school or apprentice ourselves to someone in order to learn how to fulfill our chosen role in life. We learn how welders dress, how they talk, what skills they have with acetylene torches and electric arcs, and how to avoid the dangers of the occupation. We *become* welders. "Who are you?" "I am a welder." The role is our identity.

Some years ago, I was the supervisor of a crew of four young ladies, recent college graduates. One day, Julie showed up for work wearing a three-hundred-watt smile and carrying her left hand at an unusual angle away from her body. She had our attention. As she kept gently moving that left hand, someone finally noticed the diamond on her third finger. Congratulations began.

Chris asked, "Who are you marrying?"

"An engineer."

"When I get married," Chris bluntly replied, "I am going to marry a man, not an occupation."

I know a lady in South Carolina. I have known her since she was a teenager back in the early 1960s. She has a good voice and loves to sing—as a child she and her sister sang regularly on a local radio station. Her name is Frankie.

A few years ago, a friend told her she looked like Reba McIntire. So she went to her hairdresser and had her hair styled just like Reba's—it already was the same color. Add the right makeup, put her in front of the right studio photographer, and you'd wind up with a portrait of Frankie that could pass as a portrait of Reba.

Frankie learned all of McIntire's songs, worked on the phrasing and tonality, and wound up becoming pretty good replica of Reba. She would sing in local karaoke bars, several area clubs, in fact, anywhere she had opportunity to sing in public. The last I heard is that she had moved to Nashville, made a demo record, and was trying to find a label that would pick her up. She does not know herself. She has replicated Reba McIntire. But what more could anyone want? Maybe to become the best Elvis impersonator?

We all live in danger of conforming thoughtlessly to stereotypes of our chosen role. Our discussion here, however, is about life models, not role models. It is about becoming ourselves, developing our own lives, and learning how to do our own thinking of how any particular role should be carried out.

Human character is not produced by imitating the surface manner or appearance of a chosen model. Rather, it comes from recognizing the basic character traits that have gotten our attention, and blending them into our essential uniqueness; it is adopting core features of the model and adapting them to who we are.

Character development deals with basic traits such as the honesty of Abraham Lincoln, the selflessness of Mother Teresa, the well-rounded knowledge and interests of Oprah Winfrey, or the specialization of the ophthalmologist who does nothing but cataract surgery. We seek not surface externality but deeper traits like those of the administrator who operates strictly by the rules, or on the other hand, like the supervisor who is free from the letter of the law, who knows that to keep the spirit of the law we must at times recognize that, at times, the law should be bent. We may want to emulate the well-organized Julie Morgenstern, or we may be drawn to the character of someone like my great art teacher, Maurine Stewart, whose desktop made a junkyard look well organized.

So far, we have seen that two of the key elements involved in becoming a person of character are an attraction to a model and the commitment to develop some of her characteristic traits in our own lives. The next elements are time and habit. Only with a strong commitment to living, for instance, a Christlike or Christ-ian life will we be patient with the time it takes if we are ever to truly love our neighbor as ourselves, or love and pray for our enemies. Patience, kindness, forgiveness, courage to confront evil, even the willingness to interrupt our schedule to help someone in need, these become our character traits only when we can maintain a long-term commitment. We must repeatedly will ourselves to be what we want to become, until these traits come under the unconscious control of habit.

Habit

Plutarch said, "*Character* is long-standing habit." If Plutarch is understood to be saying, "All there is to character is long-standing habit," he is wrong. As we have seen, much more is involved in character formation. But if we understand Plutarch as saying, "Intention, conviction, commitment, and discipline lead us to form habits that remain stable across the long term, resulting in authentic character," then he is right.

We all know that our lives are products of genetics and environment. We grow within the limits they impose. For instance, a young man born in Bangladeshi poverty, condemned from childhood to labor thirteen-hour days, and reaching a mature height of five feet, two inches will never under any circumstances become a professional basketball player in the United States. This is merely an extreme example of how heredity and environment set the boundaries of our choices.

Within these limits, our lives are determined by how we choose to interact with what life brings our way. In large measure, character, stated positively, is long-standing habit; stated negatively, it is the result of conscience limiting our choices to our deepest convictions of truth and value.

Habit requires conviction, commitment, and time if it is to be determinative of whom we become. With bad habits, we are likely to develop bad character. With good habits, we are likely to develop good character. On the other hand, if we drift, leaving habit to chance and external forces, we are likely to become a cipher—a person of no significance and a drag on society. Genetics and circumstance set the range of our possibilities. Within that range, our choices set further, self-imposed, boundaries on our developing character.

All our thinking is rooted in who we are. The Dialectic will serve the Mafia or the government, the hacker, the hooker, or the saint. Logic works the same for the good as for the bad. The consequences of our thinking will be good only if we are good people.

At first, it takes continued effort to adopt and adapt to the shape of someone else. We may have to tackle it one trait at a time. Repeatedly, we forget and have to remind ourselves. This is the way habits are formed. Not until the newly acquired actions become habit, does character begin to form. This cannot come about without commitment.

It takes only a moment's thought to realize that it will take time, probably a lot of time, to develop a cluster of new habits. Character cannot be bought and put on like a new coat. There is no instant gratification. There is no shortcut. There is no fast track. Thus, there is no character formation without a lot of patience.

Going back to the word's sculptural origins, we find one reason character does not come about easily: the raw material we work with.

Some material is quite uncooperative and challenging. Often the challenge is the unpredictability, the surprises to be found when we are deep into the shaping process. We find an unexpected knot in the wood or an incipient crack shows up in the stone. When we study it, then, perhaps, we can work it into the enrichment of our sculpture.

The formation of our character works with one of the most resistant, unpredictable, and challenging of materials: the human person. This is a highly challenging material. It persistently refuses to take on new shape. Only with patience do we become a person of character.

Implicit here is the idea that the chosen character traits must fit together fairly well, or they will disintegrate. A person of character is a person of integrity. They are a unified whole.

To develop all the elements of character, we must have assistance—guides, teachers, supporters. It does "take an entire village to raise" a person of character. Good characters ordinarily emerge out of good communities. On the other hand, good communities are possible only if they are made up of people of good character.

Only when the appropriate pattern of habits become our characteristic way of being and doing, can it be said that we are people of character. Then, in large measure, our lives will become fairly predictable--even if one of our character traits happens to be that we are, in many ways, an unpredictable person.

Character development does not necessarily produce good people. The wrong model may have been chosen. We are surrounded by bad characters. It takes little investigation to see the bad characters on the scene that some have chosen to pattern their lives after.

If we want a life of lasting satisfaction and value, we must leave our chameleon-like ways behind and develop our own enduring "color." But it is not only for our own good that we need to become persons of character, the larger community needs a higher ratio than we now have of good versus bad models. We have a social obligation.

We are attracted to a model, commit ourselves to develop traits we admire and respect, and deliberately persist in choosing to follow this pattern until it becomes habit, until these have become the characteristic traits and virtues of our own lives. This will take time—and remember that time takes time—thus, patience is necessary. Gradually, it will all come together and we will be people of integrity, whole persons. These are all necessary conditions of character development.

It is one thing to read this, another to understand; one thing to understand, another to do; one thing to do, another to build things into a distinctive and unified life.

Habit is the pathway to character. Our characteristic traits and virtues, our distinctives, are established habits.

CHAPTER ELEVEN

Truth, Treasures, and Dreams

You will use the Dialectic differently from other readers because you are different. Your background, beliefs, values, and goals are unique. We each have distinct personalities, perspectives, and possibilities. Our best thought must be consistent with who we are. There is a logic of life. We are the basis of our own thinking—the thesis, the major premise—therefore, we must each determine what that is to be. If we are to think with integrity, we must clarify our basic beliefs, values, and goals. We must know who we are.

Ideally, to do the best thinking, we must be or become good persons, persons of good character. So we must know ourselves, our personal and communal convictions and values. We must determine and give shape to our own unique character. We cannot do our best thinking until we know who we are and why, not until we can clearly and concisely state our starting position in life. If we don't realize where we're coming from, there is no telling what will follow. We must know ourselves, decide who we are, and who we intend to become, then live the life of that person. We must live what we believe, else life disintegrates.

All our thought is rooted in what we accept as truth. What do you believe? What do you believe to be true? What do you feel certain about? What do you accept without question? What are your convictions, that is, those things you are convinced of? These core beliefs form the basic theses of our lives. They are, consciously or unconsciously, the starting point of all our thinking.

What Is True?

Personally, I am a Christian. I believe that Jesus is "the way, the truth, and the life." This I intend as the major premise in all my thinking. Thus, if I am to maintain my integrity, all my thought must be consistent with this fundamental thesis; it must somehow cohere with the life and teachings of Jesus of Nazareth as found in the New Testament.

On the other hand, I know a woman who rejects all religion. She believes in nothing that cannot be proved scientifically. She lives and thinks by what her senses can verify. I have a few other friends who have said that the only thing that matters in life is money. Without it nothing will work in the long run. It is the only security. As I have watched two or three of them, I find that this is the major premise of their lives. Everything I hear them say or see them do is consistent with this basic belief—a belief that is foundational in the thought of Ayn Rand. And there are others whose thought seems never to stray from how things will affect their personal appearance. They seem to believe that nothing will work out right, or that nothing matters if their appearance is not right.

The question is, do you know what you believe? Do you know why you believe it? Did you inherit it, receive it from some respected and authoritative source, or did you think about life and deliberately choose what seems true to you? If you don't know what you believe, it is time to find out. Some people believe that nothing is true. They believe in nothing, and believe there is nothing to believe. If this is what they believe, it will color all their thinking, all their use of the dialectic, all their logic. Whatever we believe becomes a major premise of our thinking.

Personally, although I could state many things I believe, there are only a handful of things I believe without question. As I said earlier, I believe that Jesus of Nazareth is "the way, the truth, and the life." I believe I married the right woman. I believe that, as a teacher, I have chosen the right vocation. I believe that, in this world, something is wrong, that things are not as they should be, as they could be. And, I believe that everything is related to everything. Thus, everything is affected by other things, and everything affects other things. Together, these form the foundation of my own thought.

Once we have clarified our core beliefs, we are prepared to become the best thinker that we, as an individual, can. Closely related to our beliefs is the importance of our personal values.

What Would You Trade For?

The turn of this century has been a time, in the United States, of great emphasis on "values." Most often, the word is misunderstood and misused. A value is anything that we would give up something for. It is for our values we give up the best years of our lives, our money, and energy. All of us have values. There is no separate group of people who are "values voters." We merely differ in what we value.

We all value the necessities of life. Among other things, we value rest, food, and pleasure. We differ about whether we value traditional morality or gay rights, the right to bear arms or extensive governmental regulation. But we almost all value our reputation and our home. We will give up time, energy, money, reputation, and sometimes friends in order to achieve and hold on to what we truly value. In most societies, money is involved in our other values, thus, we have to value money. And, as a consequence, we give up forty hours of the week in order to have the cash to exchange for other things. We all have values, but if we are to be good thinkers, we need a clear understanding of those that are important to us.

What values define your life? Pizza and beer, friends and family, a million dollars before you are thirty, personal integrity, time alone, social settings, silence, laughter? What would you give other things up for in order to have? I value my wife, writing, outdoor life, time alone and space, and the arts—music in particular, especially hymns and blues (contradictory as that may sound).

If you were to paint your personality, what commitments would be on your palette? At my age, I am committed to: loving and enjoying God and my wife, and writing. I have two subsidiary commitments: taking care of my health; and taking care of the quotidian in order that I can properly love my wife. I may do many other things of value, but these commitments have priority. Anything else can be neglected, ignored, or deleted without much pain or guilt.

What Do You Want?

What do you want to become and accomplish? What are your goals—short-term, intermediate, and long-term? When it is all over, who do you want to have been, and what do you want to have accomplished? Our goals give meaning to our present action, just as a lack of goals renders the present meaningless. Everything is done for some end. Our goals define us. *They* are the criteria for success, not the opinions of others. If we meet our own goals, we are a success. If we have no goals, we have no valid way to measure success, no actual way to succeed. We drift on the winds of the days.

If you've given no conscious thought to personal goals, start by setting goals for each day or week. My goal for today is to finish this chapter of the book, to write a blog, write on Twitter, take care of some family business, complete a project in the yard, and, as always, to be a good husband.

On New Year's Day, we tend to set certain goals for the year. Most of us wind up not taking these very seriously. Nonetheless, we need one-year, five-year, ten-year, and lifetime goals.

I am in my mid-seventies. My major goals for the remainder of my life are to be a good husband, and to write books, blogs, and micro-blogs. An instrumental life goal is to take care of myself, so I will be able to accomplish these goals. It is my goal to publish this book by the end of 2010, and to publish a second book, a book about God, by 2014. Then to continue writing as long as possible.

When we have clarified our beliefs, values, and goals, we have established the major premises from which and the purpose toward which all our thinking is directed.

EPILOGUE

I considered ending the book with a twist: "On the other hand, we think too much. Sometimes we need to act on impulse."

But then I remembered a story told me by the chaplain of a small Oklahoma prison. Back in the mid-1990s, a young convict and his cell-mate were talking. They were in a minimum security prison in the remote and heavily wooded mountains of southeastern Oklahoma. One prisoner was explaining that he planned to run for the woods and escape. When the time came and he carried out his escape plan, his cell-mate, on a spur of the moment whim, without giving it any thought, ran with him.

They were caught a few days later and given an added two years for felony escape. One fellow had carefully thought through his plan; the other ran on a sudden, unforeseen impulse. The impulsive convict had been due to be released within the following week. His impulsive action kept him locked away from his wife and children for two more years.

Yes, thinking all the time is not the way to live. Some of us think too much, plan too much, consider too many sides, and in the process miss life. Be whimsical, act impulsively, but don't forget the Oklahoma prisoner. Give your impulses at least a moment's consideration before acting.

APPENDIX

The Categorical Syllogism

If you had rather not get into abstract depths, you may want to ignore this appendix. But, if you do the work, it will be worth it. Do the exercises—paper is cheap.

Some years ago, I was summoned for jury duty. During the voir dire questioning, the prosecuting attorney asked my occupation. I replied, "philosophy professor." Whereupon, he asked, "If you are selected to sit on the jury, will you decide the case using syllogistic logic?" My answer was, "No, I will not reduce everything to syllogisms, but I will use good logic in making any decisions." (I wound up on the jury.)

What, you may ask, was the lawyer talking about? What is syllogistic logic, and what are syllogisms? This appendix is written to explain the nature and value of syllogistic logic.

First, we must locate the syllogism as one form of the Dialectic, specifically a form of deductive logic. As outlined in Part Two, deduction is that logic in which if the *form* is correct and the *premises* are true, the conclusion must necessarily be true with no possibility at all of being false. Notice that, like all logic, this rests completely on the "if." *If* the form is correct, and *if* the premises are true, *then*, and only then, is the conclusion of the argument necessarily true.

Before explaining the syllogism, A list of definitions may be helpful. You are not expected to remember all these when it comes to put them into practice, so I will review them at the appropriate time. These definitions serve as an introduction, and will help clarify the following discussion.

- **Argument:** a series of statements, one of which is the conclusion of the others.

Logic is often defined as the study of argument, and this is how the term is used. It does not refer to a heated discussion.

- **Premise:** those statements in an argument that lead to the conclusion, and upon which the conclusion is based.

- **Statement:** a series of words making an assertion that is either true or false.

Not all sentences are statements. Not all statements are expressed in a single sentence, although they could be. An entire paragraph, chapter, book, or speech may make one basic statement.

- **Term**: either the subject or the predicate of a statement. The term expresses some class or category. It may be one or several words, for example, boy, square, incisor teeth, Methodist theologians. Each of these is a category.

A statement tells us whether a particular term (category) is included or excluded from another, for example:

All chocolate cake is a dessert (all chocolate cakes are included in the category of desserts);

Some chocolate cakes are not iced cakes (some chocolate cakes are not included in, rather, they are excluded from, the category of iced cakes).

- **Standard Form** (for statements): all statements must include a subject term and a predicate term, linked by a copula (is or are).

There are four standard forms:

A: All [subject term] are/is [predicate term].
E: No [subject term] are/is [predicate term].
I: Some [subject term] are/is [predicate term].
O: Some [subject term] are/is not [predicate term].

Notice that the A and E forms are universal in nature, while the I and O forms are particular in nature. This refers to the *quantity* of the statement.

On the other hand, note that the A and I forms make positive statements, while the E and O statements are negative. This refers to the *quality* of the statement.

All standard-form statements must include one of the specific qualifiers and quantifiers shown above.

Note: In syllogistic logic, the quantifier, "some" means, "at least one" and can include "all but one."

A standard form syllogism must comprise one or a combination of these exact four forms.

- **Standard Form** (for syllogisms): a standard-form syllogism has two premise statements and one conclusion statement. These three statements have exactly three terms. If they are other than standard form statements or if they present more (or less) than three terms, they cannot be proven valid or invalid. They are not a syllogism.

Here is the classic syllogism, first presented by Aristotle. Note that it demonstrates what I have said.

[All] Socrates is a man.
All men are mortal.
Therefore, [All] Socrates is mortal.

Three terms: Socrates, man (men) and mortal. All three statements are standard A-form statements.

- **Validity:** only arguments can be valid or invalid. (Statements, by definition, are either true or false, arguments are not.) Validity is a matter of the *form* of the argument. A valid form is one in which, if the premises are true, the conclusion is necessarily true. A valid argument is one that can be trusted. An invalid argument, on the other hand, is a form that cannot be trusted to yield a true conclusion. It may or may not.

- **Distribution:** a term that very few clearly understand, but, fortunately, understanding is not necessary. However, when we learn to test syllogisms for validity, it will be necessary to know the distribution of the four standard-form statements.

Meanwhile, here is the basic pattern. The subject term of universal statements (A and E) is distributed and the predicate term of negative statements (E and O) is distributed. The subject term of particular statements (I and O) and the predicate term of positive statements (A and I) are undistributed.

Again, if this is too much, don't worry about it. There is no need to remember all of this at one time. This appendix is meant to be read slowly and reviewed often. You must do the exercises if you want to get it. Mark these definitions as a reference to use as needed in the following pages. Most of these definitions will be repeated in one form or another.

For now, look over the following examples of the categorical syllogism (argument dealing with the relation of three terms). Look these over a few times before continuing to their explanations. It might be good to wait until tomorrow to read more. For now, try to get some sort of picture in your mind. See if these examples clarify the form of the categorical syllogism. (These may be valid or invalid. We will check this later.)

All Starbucks coffee is superior to the coffee at the Red Wagon.
Some Starbucks coffee is not good.
Therefore, no coffee at the Red Wagon is good.

Some chickens are distinguished by the green eggs they lay.
No White Leghorns are distinguished by the green eggs they lay.
Therefore, some chickens are not White Leghorns.

All hunters are willing to kill game animals.
Some hunters are hunters in order to maintain their sense of manhood.
Therefore, no one willing to kill game animals is a wimp.

All artists are unusually sensitive to the world around them.
Some painters are not unusually sensitive to the world around them.
Therefore, some painters are not artists.

No vegetarian is a beef eater.
Some farmers are not beef eaters.
Therefore, some farmers are vegetarians.

No wise person is secretive with their doctor or lawyer.
Some frightened people are secretive with their doctor or lawyer.
Therefore, some frightened people are not wise.

All that is real is related.
Some ideas are absolute [not related].
Therefore, some ideas are not in sync with reality.

Remember that in the categorical syllogism, a "term" indicates a category or class. A "term" may be a single word, or a complex description. Here are some examples of categorical terms: tooth, front tooth, upper incisor, central incisor, upper left central incisor, the incisor with a filling on the face of the tooth, the tooth Jack Donovan filled in 1950, the teeth in my mouth that have fillings, the left upper wisdom tooth in Ndondo Mutizwa's mouth. Each of these is a term that names a class or category. (I wrote this section in the dentist's chair during the process of having one of my teeth—upper left bicuspid—crowned.)

In a categorical syllogism, the subject and predicate terms are joined by a copula: either "is" or "are." Most statements in ordinary language are not stated in standard form. Thus, they must be translated before they can be used.

"Jennifer does not like Miles," is a statement (in logic, a statement is a sentence or series of sentences that make a single point that is either true or false), but it is not a standard-form statement. "Jennifer is a person who does not like Miles" is a fair translation of the former statement, and, is *almost* in standard form. It lacks a quantifier.

Translations from ordinary language to standard-form statements often sound very awkward, but to be useful, all elements of standard form must be there. Thus, we simply have to consider whether we are speaking of "all" of Jennifer or "some" part of her. "All Jennifer is a person who does not like Miles" is a standard A-form statement. "Jennifer" is a category or class with only one member. "A person who does not like Miles" is a class that could have numerous members.

Again, before proceeding, it would be wise to review the set of sample arguments on page 117 in the light of this explanation of standard form categorical statements.

Take a deep breath. We are going a bit deeper into the explanation of the structure of the categorical argument. A categorical argument comprises three categorical statements: a major premise, a minor premise, and a conclusion. The conclusion is indicated by the word, "therefore."

Within the three statements that make up the categorical syllogism, there must be only three terms: two "end terms" and one "middle term." The middle term is the one that occurs once in the major premise and once in the minor premise. It is the mediating link that enables us to understand how the end terms relate to each other. End terms are found on either end of the conclusion and one in each of the premises.

Once more, I suggest that you stop and review the earlier categorical arguments. Review is most important. Take it slow and easy. Take your time. In each of them locate and identify the end terms and the middle term. If any contain more than three terms, they are useless, unless they can, by translation, be reduced to three.

Our explanation of categorical argument continues by introducing a concept that I do not clearly understand. Fortunately, we don't have to understand it, but, like so many things we don't understand, we do need to know it. I've taught logic for more than thirty-five years and still don't clearly understand the notion of "distribution," but we must know how it works in these arguments.

All universal terms and all negative terms are considered distributed. Others are undistributed. It looks like this:

A=Subject is distributed; predicate is undistributed.
E=Both terms are distributed.
I=Both terms are undistributed.
O=Subject term is undistributed; predicate is distributed.

These patterns of distribution, ideally, should be memorized if you plan to use this form of reasoning to test your thinking for validity.

Now, let's turn back to some of the prior arguments and see how all this comes together.

The two key words in testing a categorical argument are *validity* and *truth*. Statements are, by definition, true or false. Only statements can be true, an argument, in its entirety, cannot. A good statement is true. A good argument is valid. A valid argument is one in which the form of the argument can be trusted. This means that if the premises are true and the form is valid, the conclusion must be true. Validity is about the dependability of the argument's form. Far more forms are invalid than are valid.

Let's look at a useful way to test for validity. First, however, we need to determine that the argument is in standard form.

All Starbucks coffee is superior to the coffee at the Red Wagon.
Some Starbucks coffee is not good.
Therefore, no coffee at the Red Wagon is good.

Note that there are—as there should be— three standard categorical statements: A, O, E.

Note that there are—as needed—three, and only three, terms: Starbucks, Red Wagon, good.

Note the distribution: in the major premise, Starbucks is distributed, and Red Wagon is undistributed; in the minor premise, Starbucks is undistributed and good is distributed; in the conclusion, both terms are distributed.

Three rules determine whether a categorical argument is valid.

1. The middle term must be distributed once.
2. The end terms must each have the same distribution in the premises and the conclusion.
3. There must be the same number of negative terms in the conclusion as there are in the premises.

Let's apply these rules to the coffee argument.

Rule 1. Starbucks is the middle term, that is, it is the term that occurs in both premises. It is the term that mediates the relationship between Red Wagon and good. It is distributed in the major premise, undistributed in the minor premise. It meets the test of Rule 1.

Rule 2. Good is distributed in both instances, but Red Wagon, however, is undistributed in the major premise, but distributed in the conclusion. The argument is ruled invalid because it fails the test of Rule 2.

Rule 3. There is one negative term in the premises and one in the conclusion. Rule 3 is met.

If an argument fails on any of the rules, it is invalid. Thus, the coffee argument is invalid.

It is possible for the premises to be true, for the argument to be invalid, and yet for the conclusion also to be true, but its truth is not proven by the argument.

Let's look at some of these other arguments, because the more we practice, the more we begin to get it.

Some chickens are distinguished by the green eggs they lay.
No White Leghorns are distinguished by the green eggs they lay.

Therefore, some chickens are not White Leghorns.

I, E, O statements.

> Three terms: chickens, green eggs, Leghorns.
> Middle term=green eggs.
> End terms: chickens, Leghorns.

1. Middle term is distributed once—good.
2. Chickens undistributed both times, Leghorns distributed both times—good.
3. One negative premise, one negative conclusion—good.

This argument is valid; it passes all three tests.

Remember, validity relates to form. It says nothing about content. Thus, it means that any standard categorical argument with this form—IEO, and with the terms located as in the green egg argument—will yield a conclusion that is necessarily true, *if* both premises are true.

Here is the bare form, one of the several valid forms.
Some — are ...
No ___ are ...
Therefore, some — are not ___

Let's try it with premises we know are untrue, but, for practice, let's assume their truth.
Some rain is dry.
No deserts are dry.
Therefore, some rain is not a desert.

If, these dry premises were true, the conclusion would be true.

We've learned what a valid argument is. We know what a true statement is. Now to define a sound argument. A "sound argument" is one with true premises and a valid form.

A quick look at the hunter argument reveals that it is not in standard form, therefore, we can know nothing about its validity.

All hunters are willing to kill game animals.
Some hunters are hunters in order to maintain their sense of manhood.
Therefore, no one willing to kill game animals is a wimp.

This commits what we call the "four-term fallacy." If we were to call "hunters" the middle term and "willing to kill game animals" an end term, what is our other end term? There is not one, there are two. So we would either ignore this argument, or see if we could re-form it into a standard three-term argument. Since we don't have the space for a full study of logical techniques, we will ignore it and pass on to the artist argument.

All artists are unusually sensitive to the world around them.
Some painters are not unusually sensitive to the world around them.
Therefore, some painters are not artists.

AOO statements.
Three terms: artists, sensitive to the world around them, and painters.
The middle term is "sensitive to ..."
The end terms are artists and painters.

1. Middle term is distributed once—good.
2. Painters is undistributed both times; artists is distributed both times—good.
3. There is one negative premise and one negative conclusion—good.

This is a valid argument:

What about this one?
No vegetarian is a beef eater.
Some farmers are not beef eaters.
Therefore, some farmers are vegetarians.

EOI statements.

Three terms: vegetarian, beef eater, farmer.

Beef eater is the middle term.

1. Middle term is distributed once.
2. Vegetarian is distributed in the major premise and undistributed in the conclusion—this invalidates the argument.
3. There are two negative premises and no negative conclusions—invalid.

Any argument in this form would be completely undependable. The conclusion might be true or it might be false.

Do you remember that we saw there can be categories with only one member? Look at this one last argument:

All Wallace is a septuagenarian.
All septuagenarians are old.
Therefore, all Wallace is old.

Septuagenarian is the middle term.
Wallace and old are the end terms.

1. Middle term is distributed once—good.
2. Wallace is distributed both times; old is undistributed both times—good.
3. There are no negatives at all.

This argument is valid.

At its core, categorical argument is about inclusion in or exclusion from categories. The argument above, in its major premise, asserts that all of the category "Wallace" is included within the category "septuagenarians." The minor premise includes all septuagenarians in the category "old." The conclusion, therefore, includes Wallace in the category "old" because he has already been included in the category "septuagenarians," which is included in the category "old," thus, Wallace *must* be included in the category "old."

Let's go back to one of the arguments that deals with exclusion.
No vegetarian is a beef eater.

Some farmers are not beef eaters.
Therefore, some farmers are vegetarians.

The major premise excludes all vegetarians from the category of beef eaters. The two categories have no connection. The minor premise excludes some (at least one) farmer from the beef eaters, although it leaves open the possibility that some farmers might be included among the beef eaters. It says nothing about whether farmers and vegetarians include or exclude each other.

I hope the idea of inclusion and exclusion helps you better understand what is going on in this pattern of thinking.

I suggest you make up at least ten categorical arguments of your own and test them for validity.

As you are now well aware, no human statement is ever complete by itself, thus this book is not a complete statement of the dialectic. There is always more to be said—more than this book covers.

LaVergne, TN USA
04 April 2011
222822LV00007B/19/P

9 781600 474750